PASTOR
NEEDS
a Boo

PASTOR NEEDS
a Boo

MICHELE ANDREA BOWEN

ST. MARTIN'S GRIFFIN

NEW YORK

This is a work of fiction. All of the characters, organizations, and events portrayed in this novel are either products of the author's imagination or are used fictitiously.

PASTOR NEEDS A BOO. Copyright © 2014 by Michele Andrea Bowen. All rights reserved. Printed in the United States of America. For information, address St. Martin's Press, 175 Fifth Avenue, New York, N.Y. 10010.

www.stmartins.com

Library of Congress Cataloging-in-Publication Data

Bowen, Michele Andrea.
   Pastor needs a Boo / Michele Andrea Bowen.—First Edition.
       p. cm.
   ISBN 978-0-312-64337-9 (trade paperback)
   ISBN 978-1-4668-5083-5 (e-book)
   1. African American women—Fiction.   2. African American clergy—
Counseling of—Fiction.   3. Single mothers—Fiction.   4. African American
clergy—Appointment, call, and election—Fiction.   5. Church membership—
Fiction.   I. Title.
   PS3552.O8645P37 2014
   813'.54—dc23

                                                                2014000138

St. Martin's Griffin books may be purchased for educational, business, or promotional use. For information on bulk purchases, please contact Macmillan Corporate and Premium Sales Department at 1-800-221-7945, extension 5442, or write specialmarkets@macmillan.com.

First Edition: July 2014

10 9 8 7 6 5 4 3 2 1

This book is dedicated to my grandson, Malachi Elliott Price
(MiMi loves herself some "Mali").

Acknowledgments

The first thing I want to do is thank the Lord for blessing me with the opportunity to write and have this book published by St. Martin's Press. Then, I want to thank my editor, Monique Patterson; her editorial assistant, Alexandra Sehulster; and the wonderful copy editor assigned to work with me on this manuscript, Rachel Burd. Last, but definitely not least, thank you, Pamela Harty. You are a super agent.

My mom—thank you. My daughters—thank you. My family and my friends—thank you.

And to my readers—thank you!

"Then Naomi said to her, 'Just be patient, my daughter, until we hear what happens. The man won't rest until he has followed through on this. He will settle it today.'"
Ruth 3:18

This scripture was the inspiration for this novel because there are times when a good man simply needs himself a "Ruth."

Prologue

Marsha Metcalf sat at her desk with her chin pressed in the palms of both hands. She picked up a stack of folders on her desk and dropped them back down on it. How in the world was she supposed to get all of this work done in two and a half weeks? Even if she worked a seventy-five-hour week, didn't get sick, didn't eat, didn't bathe, and maybe didn't even brush her teeth, this could not be done in that amount of time.

Who was she trying to fool by putting on a brave face and acting like she could "make it happen"? No one person could do all of this work in this time, and her supervisor, Yolanda Richardson, knew it when she dumped all of it on Marsha's desk.

Marsha was one of five buyer-stylists at the exclusive Sebastian-Fleur Department Store in Durham, North Carolina. Her team looked high and low for the best merchandise at great prices, and they always made sure everything was always placed in the "just right spot" in the store. Marsha, one of two lead buyer-stylists, was so good at what she did that her coworkers were always telling her that she needed her own TV show.

Being the best had its drawbacks, however. The harder Marsha worked, the harder Yolanda rode her. There was nothing Marsha could do to make the grade with Yolanda Richardson. Yolanda criticized Marsha's every move. She checked and double-checked everything Marsha did, and sent her e-mails on everything, down to the way Marsha placed items on her desk and positioned her car between the parking space lines.

No one at Sebastian-Fleur understood why Yolanda had such an intense dislike of Marsha. As far as the people who worked at the store were concerned, Yolanda Richardson had it all—a deceased husband who had left her plenty of money, a custom-built five-thousand-square-foot house in the swanky section of Brier Creek, a sleek black Mercedes, a closet full of expensive clothes, and a cushy job.

Marsha Metcalf, on the other hand, was a single parent with sole responsibility of putting her only child, Marcus, through college on a ridiculously tight budget. She drove a 2006 Ford Escape that needed new tires and repairs, struggled to pay the rent on a modest town house, wore very economically priced clothes, and hadn't been on a date in four years.

If you put the two women side by side, one would think that Marsha had cause to envy Yolanda. But nothing could be further from the truth. While Marsha didn't like Yolanda Richardson, she didn't begrudge Yolanda's having what she had. Marsha did not understand how Yolanda could have so much and still be so mean, selfish, and just downright hateful.

What *was* it with women who acted like they had "the mean girl gene"? And why were they always so dagblasted mean to other girls or women who had so much less than them? One would think that as they matured, they would soften up, act right, and stop being so mean. But that didn't seem to be the case. Mean girls actually grew up to become extremely hateful women.

Marsha, who had suffered at Yolanda's hands back in college, was beginning to think this kind of thing would never end. She graduated from Evangeline T. Marshall University confident that she didn't have to see that particular mean girl again, only to walk in to church and then her new job and find, Whoop, there was Yolanda, in all of her pricey clothes, four-figure-designer-purse mean girl glory.

Yolanda and Marsha were both members of New Jerusalem

Gospel United Church in Raleigh, North Carolina. Marsha had joined the church many years ago, when it was still one of the smaller, homier congregations under the direction of Reverend Wendell Boudreaux, who was the quintessential pastor. Reverend Boudreaux was such a good minister that folk started thinking he'd make an even better bishop. It was a sad day when the pastor, now a newly elected bishop, got up in the pulpit wearing his same black robe with the red brocade crosses emblazoned down the front to preach his last sermon as the shepherd of New Jerusalem Gospel United Church.

It was rare that a brand-new bishop didn't show up to preach decked out in the purple regalia that signified that he was an official member of the episcopacy. It was even rarer for the bishop to break down in tears and ask the new pastor, Reverend Denzelle Flowers, to lay hands on him in prayer. As much as Marsha hated to see her beloved Reverend Boudreaux leave to join the ranks of the men who ran their denomination, she found herself intrigued by the idea of the younger, fly, and good-looking Reverend Flowers coming to take over the reins of their church.

Marsha shook her head at herself, thinking, "Why am I sitting here with all of this work to do and thinking about Bishop Boudreaux, Reverend Flowers, and that skanky Yolanda Richardson?"

She flipped through the folder of her favored project and let out a sigh of relief.

"It's about time Yolanda did something decent and give me the official green light on this project."

Marsha had been waiting for Yolanda to get approval from the store's regional manager to continue working with her friend, Takara Anderson, and a team of chemists and botanists over at Evangeline T. Marshall University on a new line of skin care and cosmetic products for the store. Takara was a whiz at coming up with natural products that were good for the skin and made you look good. Marsha had the eye for colors and textures and had helped them create some beautiful palates for eye shadows, blushes, and lipsticks.

She read the memo approving the project more carefully and frowned. Yolanda had done a loop-da-loop on her with this project.

"She is so rachet-acting and cheap!" Marsha exclaimed through clenched teeth. "I cannot believe this heifer allocated a budget that doesn't even cover a month's worth of gas for my car. I can't do anything with this chicken feed mess."

Marsha took in a deep breath and practically spit it out of her mouth. She didn't need to let Yolanda upset her like this. Plus, getting all anxious always gave her hot flashes.

She reached for a water bottle. It wasn't cold. Marsha couldn't stop this hot flash from popping up on her with room-temperature water. She needed something icy cold. Her body felt like an oven from the inside out.

"Whew. Calm down. It's gonna be okay. God said He'd supply your every need in accordance to His riches in glory by Christ Jesus. It's gonna be okay."

The scripture helped. Marsha calmed down, drank a few sips of the water, and flipped open her red laptop. She started pulling up a list of names of folk who might want to add funds to help this project's coffers.

The first name she saw was Charles Robinson, the owner and proprietor of Rumpshakers Hip-Hop Gentlemen's Club. She knew Charles wouldn't hesitate to help her. But Marsha wasn't so sure about being partnered up with strip club money. Every time she passed the counter with his makeup on it, she would always wonder how many times a stripper had clapped her behind to make it rain hard enough for Charles to put all of that money in the pot.

"Nahh . . . not old boy."

Marsha sat back in her chair and tried to think of someone else.

"Lamont Green would be perfect."

She pulled out her phone and was about to call Lamont's

wife, Theresa, when she heard some shuffling and whispering outside of her door.

"Do you think she's in there?"

"Of course she is in there, stupid," Marsha heard Yolanda whisper so loudly, she couldn't help but wonder if the girl wanted her to know she was standing on the other side of her office door.

"So, how are you going to tell her?"

"Tell her what?" another voice whispered.

"This," was all Marsha heard Yolanda say, right before she saw a sheet of Yolanda's trademark baby blue linen paper being slid up under the door. All of sudden the whispering stopped, as if the folk on the other side of the door were practically holding their breath in anticipation of what would happen next.

Marsha picked up the paper and read "YOU'RE FIRED," written in cursive with a bold, black marker. She stared at the paper, wondering if this was some kind of mean girl joke, when she noticed that there were more words.

"p.s., Yes, you read this note right" was written in Yolanda's handwriting.

"We have to cut back and **WHOOPS**, you lose. Clean out your desk and be out of the building before five today.

"Security is on the way over to your office. A guard will escort you to your car. We'll mail your last check to you next week, Yolanda Richardson, MBA."

Marsha stared at the note and blinked hard, as if that would make the words on that paper pop up and go away. This was unbelievable—not to mention terrifying. What was she supposed to do without a job? Pay the rent?

It had been quiet on the other side of the door, as if they were practically breaking their eardrums to hear what she was doing with that note. She heard somebody whisper, "Do you think she read the note?"

Hot and heavy tears formed in Marsha's eyes, ready to drop and stream down her face, all up under her nose, and into her mouth. What kind of people stood outside someone's office door waiting to hear what they would do after being fired?

Marsha held her head back and whispered, "Lord, please don't let me break down and cry like some little wuss who can't fight."

Her heart ached in the most horrible way and pulled down in her chest like it was too heavy for her body. How in the world was she going to get through this? There was her son's college tuition. There was the rent. There were bills. There was her health insurance. There was her hair!

There was too much to think about and worry about and take care of without the security of a job. She didn't know what to do. And she definitely didn't know how in the world she was going to get up out of this chair, open that office door, and walk out past all of those people—especially Yolanda Richardson.

Marsha picked up her phone to call her friend Veronica Washington but stopped when she remembered Veronica was starting her new job today.

She went down the contact list on her phone, and stopped again when she heard the loud mall security cop golf cart outside of the office window. "Let me get my black behind up out of here and quick," Marsha whispered to herself, while staring out of the window like she was a fugitive running from the real police. There was no way she was going to be escorted out of Sebastian-Fleur like she was the mall thief. And in front of Yolanda and those people? No way . . . nada.

She hurried and looked in her desk drawers and found two of those reusable Sam's grocery bags and filled them up with her things—fancy pens, calculator, folders, stationery, designer paper clips, and staplers. She saw a box of her business cards with the Sebastian-Fleur logo all over them.

"No way in hell I'm taking those with me."

Marsha threw the box of fancy business cards in the trash and took one more fast look around her tiny office.

"Oh, snap," she whispered. "The plans for the skin care line. Yolanda will never get her nasty, monkey-fool paws on this information—not on my watch."

She scooped up those folders, with all of that information in them, stood up, and placed the big, heavy bags on each shoulder. She tossed the remaining folders with the information for her newest work assignments in the trash can with the business cards, snatched up her purse, and grabbed the laptop.

Marsha sighed in relief that she had everything she needed. The only thing left to do was to call her folks at Eva T. Marshall and tell them to pull the plug on their project with stuck-up Sebastian-Fleur. Marsha looked at her watch. She had about ten minutes tops to get out of the store with her dignity intact.

She took in a real deep breath, balanced all of the stuff she was carrying, and opened the door.

Yolanda had been all on the door trying to hear what Marsha was doing and hoping she was in the office crying herself silly. She fell right into the office as soon as the door swung open because Marsha jumped aside to make sure she didn't block the fall. Yolanda grabbed the inside of the doorframe to stop from tumbling on her face, and winced when it squeezed in on her fingers.

"Maybe Cato Fashions will want to hire you," Yolanda snarled through a pained smirk. She was trying to regain her balance by attempting to stand back up on the outsides of her boots. Yolanda's ankles were twisted down toward the floor. It was a very awkward and painful position. It was also an opportunity to give Marsha a peek at the red soles of her boots. The price tags on Christian Louboutin boots was not for the faint of heart. And Yolanda knew that Marsha couldn't even afford a pair of these bad boys at the consignment shop.

Marsha didn't know why people like Yolanda didn't know when to leave folk alone. She'd already messed with her livelihood. She was trying to humiliate her by calling security to escort

Marsha to her car. And now, Yolanda thought she was adding an additional insult to this injury by practically standing on her ankles to reveal the red soles of those fancy boots.

But Marsha was now so beyond responding to the antics of her brand-new former boss. And she certainly wasn't paying heed to Yolanda's attempts to profile those shoes—the newest status symbols for working folk with high salaries. Marsha didn't even dignify that gesture over the boots with a passing glance.

"Yolanda, why do you care where I work, since I no longer work for your stank butt? And for the record, there's nothing wrong with Cato Fashions."

"You *would* say that," Yolanda said, and scanned Marsha's white denim capris and the white denim jacked trimmed with ruffles, her black-and-lavender tank, and her black-and-lavender, patent-leather, T-strap–styled pumps.

The irony in all of this was that Marsha's suit really had come from Cato Fashions even though her shoes had been pulled from the clearance-clearance rack bin at this very store. Marsha always found the best and cheapest shoes, because the brother in charge of pulling shoes and putting them on clearance was her buddy. He always kept as many pairs of shoes for her in the back room as he could.

She glanced down at her stylish shoes, which were accentuating her shapely legs, and then let her eyes focus on those super-expensive boots gaping out from Yolanda's stick-figure legs. Unfortunately there was not a pair of boots expensive enough to compensate for that.

"You know something, Yolanda," Marsha said quietly and evenly. "You spend all of that money on all of those clothes and high-end designer shoes, and you still look like an untrained zoo monkey."

"At least I have a man," Yolanda spat out. She knew she was not all that cute and always hoped she could hide it with her clothes.

"Yes, you do," Marsha replied evenly. "And you treat him

like he is supposed to stand on his head and bark because the ugliest and most ill-mannered woman in Durham gave him some after her husband died."

"Daaannnng," somebody whispered in the crowd of onlookers. Nobody had ever talked to Yolanda Richardson like that. And nobody had ever told her the truth about her looks.

"You are just jealous because nobody wants you, Marsha Metcalf. You can't keep a man or get a man. Why, for all of your so-called talents and smarts, you can't even keep a job," Yolanda spat out.

Yolanda started to walk away, and then paused, "Just so you know, Miss Marsha Metcalf/used-to-be Mrs. Bluefield, your late ex, Rodney, had you waiting on him many an evening while he was finishing up with me."

Marsha had always suspected Rodney went creeping with Yolanda while they were still married but could never prove it. Rodney was dead. But it still hurt to have it confirmed that he had cheated on her with this woman.

Yolanda was laughing. There was nothing better than reveling in the pained look on the face of a woman who discovered you had slept with her husband.

"Yeaaahhhhh . . . that's it, gurl!" Yolanda yelled out, and laughed some more. The horrified expression on Marsha's face confirmed that she knew the only way Yolanda heard that phrase was when Rodney had yelled it at her during the most explosive heat of the moment.

Marsha had started walking away. She stopped and said, "Go to hell, Yolanda. Oh, my bad. From the looks of your face, you've already been there."

"Yeaaahhhhh . . . that's it, gurl!" Yolanda yelled out again, hoping to get another pained look from Marsha. That zoo monkey comment hurt a lot. When Marsha didn't react a second time, Yolanda said, "You know your man told me that because I was rocking his world real good."

Marsha made sure she repented in advance, gave Yolanda the

finger, and then repented again. She walked off and out of the store as soon as she spied the security guard making his way in her direction. She hurried to her car, threw her things in the backseat, and hopped in and locked the door. The guard tapped on the window and raised the clipboard with the dismissal slip employees had to sign when escorted to their cars.

She acted as though she didn't see that man, started her car, and drove off, not caring that he had to jump out of the way to avoid getting hurt. Marsha remained calm until she pulled out of the store's parking lot and turned onto the street. Tears were streaming down her cheeks. By the time Marsha was on 40 East, headed to Raleigh, she was sobbing uncontrollably.

Chapter One

"New Jerusalem Gospel United Church. This is Dayeesha Mitchell. How may I help you?"

"Put me through to Reverend Flowers."

"Excuse you," Dayeesha said, frowning. She blew air out of her mouth loud enough to be heard by the caller. She couldn't stand Mr. Rico.

"What part of, let me speak to the pastor, don't you understand?" Rico Sneed spat out into the phone.

"Oh, no, you didn't," Dayeesha shot back. She looked over at the door leading to the pastor's private study, or the "inner sanctum," as her husband, Metro Mitchell, always called it.

"Look," Mr. Rico began, "I know your daddy is the big, bad, Big Dotsy Hamilton. And, you need to know for the record that I'm not scared of him."

Dayeesha started laughing. She'd always thought Mr. Rico Sneed was a big, bellowing poof of punk-time hot air. Now she knew he was that, and a big liar, too. Her daddy pimp-slapped Rico Sneed back in the early 1990s, before Big Dotsy Hamilton got saved and started working for the Lord. The word on the street was that Mr. Rico got slapped so hard, a man asked, "So, tell me, player. What does next week look like, since you just got slapped there?"

Mr. Rico had wanted to haul off and slap that man. But he managed to hold on to a remnant of his already ragged and deficient swag. Plus, Rico knew the man was Big Dotsy Hamilton's friend. He was also the person who told Big Dotsy that Rico was trying to steal one of his women away from him. Rico Sneed told the woman that he'd seen Big Dotsy down at the courthouse getting a marriage license to marry Dayeesha's mama. It was a bold, brazen, and outrageous lie. That day Big Dotsy had been dragged down to the courthouse at gunpoint by Dayeesha's mama's big brother to sign over one of his houses to her mother.

Unfortunately for Rico Sneed, Big Dotsy got wind of Rico's ploy, found him at the Sock It to Me strip club in Warren, North Carolina, and beat him like he stole something. According to Dayeesha's daddy's fans, Big Dotsy kicked Rico's butt and then made him run in front of his brand-new Buick LeSabre. When Rico got tired and bumped into the LeSabre, Big Dotsy put the car in park and pistol-whipped Rico for getting sweat on his new ride.

"You oughta be scared of my daddy, butt hole," Dayeesha said, laughing, and hung up the telephone. She stared at the phone a few minutes, hoping she had a good comeback line when Mr. Rico called back. Because a loudmouth like Rico Sneed always had to call back and have the last word.

The telephone rang, causing Dayeesha to jump. She hadn't had enough time to come up with good comeback lines.

"New Jerusalem Gospel United Church. This is Dayeesha Mitchell. How may I help you?"

"Dayeeeeesshhhhaaa," Marsha sobbed into the telephone. "IIIIII got fiiiirrrrreddd. What am I going to dooooooooo?"

Dayeesha Hamilton Mitchell stared at the phone. She'd been the church's administrative assistant for three years and had never heard Marsha Metcalf sound like this.

"Let me put you on hold," Dayeesha said quickly, and pushed the button before Marsha had a chance to whine some more into the telephone. She didn't want to hang up on the girl. But that whining was getting on her nerves real fast.

Dayeesha started to buzz the pastor's line but remembered

that he had gone to get them both something to eat. She was about to hit him up on the cell when she thought it best to try and get to the bottom of this before calling Reverend Flowers. Sometimes the pastor needed a buffer when folk called the church hollering and crying on the telephone. He had enough on his plate and didn't do well when he was forced to try and understand what somebody was saying in the middle of a crying and sobbing and calling on the name of the Lord fit.

"What to do? What to do?" Dayeesha said out loud, taking a moment to admire her manicure. She loved the new manicurist at the Raleigh store for her husband's Triangle-based chain of hip-hop stores, Yeah Yeah. Shontaye Reed was the only nail specialist in the area who could silk screen pictures onto your nails and make it look like she had painted the pictures with nail polish. The three Mitchell children's pictures were screened onto the second, third, and fourth fingers of each of Dayeesha's hands.

She looked at the image of her younger son, Jeremiah Crentwan, on her right ring finger and frowned. She needed to call his teacher and talk to him about Jeremiah's science project. Dayeesha flipped the phone off of hold, hoping Marsha had calmed down enough to be understood when she started to speak. She wasn't in the mood to listen to somebody talking like one of her kids when they were crying all over the place.

Dayeesha could hear Marsha sniffling and blowing her nose.

"Girl, calm the heck down and stop all of that sniveling. You are getting on my nerves," she said.

The phone was quiet on Marsha's end. But Dayeesha could hear that her breathing was calming down to a lower "drama index" rhythm. Sometimes folk who breezed through college in four years, and were all smart and good acting like Marsha Metcalf, had trouble handling the inevitable storms that could rage in your life no matter how good and perfect you tried to be.

Dayeesha's daddy, now the saved and redeemed Elder Dotsy Hamilton, always said, "People who pride themselves on doing everything just right can get the misguided notion that those

degrees, and following all of the rules, will stop them from having to deal with the hard times life will lay at your feet. Sometimes the storms of life make you stop trying to control everything
in your life. They make you stop being so prideful in yourself
and all of your *accomplishments*, and throw in the towel and say,
'God, I need you because I can't do this all by myself.'"

Dayeesha Mitchell definitely wasn't one of those folk who
had been real good and did everything the right way. She didn't
always have a degree from Evangeline T. Marshall University or
a job running the entire administrative division of a large church.
And she hadn't always been a married woman who went to church
regularly, either.

Years ago she had babies by Metro, but they weren't trying
to get married. They just liked going together. In fact, Dayeesha
used to be proud when Metro told people that she was his favorite Baby Mama. But that was before they got saved and got some
sense. Neither Dayeesha nor Metro could believe they used to
roll like that.

"It's really bad, Daye," Marsha whispered in the phone.

"Why is your crazy butt whispering into your own phone,
and you're in your car all alone? Who do you think is listening
to you?"

Marsha laughed for the first time that morning. Dayeesha
Hamilton Mitchell was a trip. Marsha said, "Girl, it's bad. I just
got fired and will get my last check at the end of the month.
Daye, I don't know what I'm going to do. I'm just getting back on
my feet from all that divorce stuff I went through with Marcus's
dad before he died."

Dayeesha nodded at the phone. Marsha had a point. She had
been through the wringer. Lost half of her income when Rodney
walked out, leaving her with a high mortgage, the IRS tax debt,
and credit card bills up to the wazoo.

Marsha had been a real trouper through all that. She bravely
filed Chapter Seven bankruptcy, gave up her beautiful home,
and moved to a smaller, cheaper place with such flair and style

you would have thought she'd planned it that way. The town house was half the size of the old house, but Dayeesha secretly liked it and the new neighborhood a whole lot better.

"Dayeesha," Marsha sniffled, "are you even listening to me? I got fired. Yolanda Richardson . . ."

"That monkey-faced Yolanda Richardson is behind this?"

Marsha nodded, and then remembered that Dayeesha couldn't see her. She said, "Yeah."

Dayeesha flipped on the speaker phone so that she could get up from her desk and walk around while talking. This was not a conversation you had with somebody sitting down.

"So what did that skank-ho-heifer say?"

"At first she just slipped a note up under the door," Marsha told her, wondering if Dayeesha had forgotten that she was at work, and *at work at church*.

"She is such a chump," Dayeesha spat out. "Marsha, if I wasn't trying to work out my salvation with fear and trembling, I would go over to that old stuck-up store and beat that Botox right off of that heifer's face."

"You think Yolanda has had some Botox shots?"

"Think? THINK? I *know* she has. Her face looks just like my daddy's face did when he thought he liked some new woman at his church. I know you saw Daddy when he was walking around always looking like he was scared the police was after him."

Marsha busted out laughing. She remembered seeing Dayeesha's daddy walking around looking like he was running from the po po. She had wondered what was wrong with him but never thought that it could be because of Botox shots.

"I hate you lost your job, Marsha. But you know all things really do work out for the good of them that love the Lord. And everybody at this church knows that you love the Lord so much, a lot of folk think He is your first cousin."

"Dayeesha, you are just as crazy," Marsha said with a warm chuckle.

"You feeling better, aren't you?"

"Yeah. A lot better than I did when I first called."

"Well, thank goodness you are calmer than you were when I answered the phone. I thought I was going to have to hang up on your butt for a moment there."

"You know that's wrong, Dayeesha."

"All I know is that it works. The number of irate, hysterical phone calls to our church has dropped considerably since I've been in charge of basic operations. So, do you want me to set you up with an appointment with Reverend Flowers?"

"Oh . . . I don't know," Marsha answered.

"But you called the church in crisis mode. So that means you need to talk to Reverend Flowers, right?"

"I don't want to worry the pastor, Dayeesha. He has a lot on his plate."

But you obviously don't mind worrying me, Dayeesha thought, and then said, "Miss Thang, this is kinda like his job, you know. You really need to talk to the pastor about this. Do you want to come in on the same day as Veronica Washington?"

"Why would I want to come and see the pastor with Roni, Dayeesha?"

"Because she just lost her job, too?"

"Veronica Washington is no longer worker for SNAC? I thought she just signed the contract as their marketing guru or something like that."

"She did," Dayeesha said. "But something happened and they reneged on her. No explanation. Just gave her a, Girl, bye, and her last paycheck, which was actually her first paycheck."

"That's messed up," was all Marsha could say. Of all of the people she expected to avoid losing a job, it was her friend Veronica Washington.

"Yeah, that it is," Dayeesha told her, and then said, "So, you want to come in to meet with Reverend Flowers this coming Tuesday at ten in the morning? Rev doesn't have a full plate on that day, and it's when Veronica is coming in."

"Yeah, I guess I can do that."

"Okay, I have you down for ten a.m. on Tuesday. Do you want to meet with the pastor alone before your meeting with him and Veronica?"

"Uhh, I don't think that'll be necessary, Dayeesha. I'm sure the meeting with Reverend Flowers and Veronica will be good enough."

Dayeesha started smiling at the telephone. Marsha was always finding a way to avoid being alone with the pastor. She didn't know why Marsha wanted to act like she didn't have a crush on Reverend Flowers—as if there was something wrong with that.

Reverend Flowers was supersingle. He didn't have a girlfriend. He didn't have a woman in his life he claimed to "care about." He didn't even have a good "friend-girl" he spent more time with than he did other women. As far as Dayeesha was concerned, the pastor's life was pretty dismal in the girlfriend department. It was like what she always said to Metro when Reverend Flowers started getting her on nerves, being all extra.

"Ain't nothin' wrong with Reverend Flowers, except pastor needs a boo. If he had a woman in his life, maybe he'd calm the heck down and quit worrying the poop out of me."

Marsha Metcalf fit the boo bill perfectly as far as Dayeesha was concerned, because the pastor was about as sweet on her as she was on him. He talked about Marsha a lot when she wasn't around. And Reverend Flowers always broke out into a big smile when he saw Marsha at church. Sometimes Dayeesha would make it her business to get right behind Marsha in the receiving line at the end of service, just so she could watch the pastor try and act like he wasn't happy to see her.

Only a trained eye like her own could decipher through all of that "I'm so into being a preacher, I don't need a woman right now" baloney Rev was always trying sell to folk. The only reason he was running from Marsha Metcalf like he was doing was because he was scared of falling in love—as if he weren't already there. No need to run from loving someone unless you loved them and was too dumb, stupid, stubborn, and ignorant to admit it. Dayeesha would have added "horse's ass" to the list, but she was thinking about this while working at church and did not want to have offensive thoughts in God's house.

Plus, Dayeesha had met Reverend Flowers's ex-wife, Tatiana Flowers Townsend, and could understand why he was afraid of love and commitment. She'd be scared of love and commitment if she had to deal with Tatiana, too. The woman was drop-dead gorgeous, and a stone-cold playah. Metro told her that Tatiana could trump any man who ran his game at full throttle in her sleep.

Maybe she needed to introduce Tatiana to Rico Sneed, so they could game each other to death. But then, that wouldn't work. Mr. Rico didn't have enough money for a gold digger like Tatiana. And she probably had the most game and would put her foot up Rico Sneed's butt in a playah play-on matchup.

Despite his troubles with Tatiana, Rev still had game. In fact, he used to be a skillful player who functioned at the top of the game. He was a retired FBI agent who had no qualms about shooting criminals; he was one of the "Baller, Shot-Caller" preachers in the Gospel United Church, had some deep pockets, and was so sharply dressed it bordered on the ridiculous. Reverend Flowers was also the player who didn't have sense enough to stop playing until several errant female church members clowned him during a church service. But he still had not been able to do a thing with Tatiana Flowers Townsend.

Dayeesha could understand why Marsha was uncomfortable around Reverend Flowers. Denzelle Flowers was fine—just over six feet, muscular build, caramel complexion, close-cropped hair with the perfect amount of silver sprinkled through it, full and round mouth, and those round, dark-brown eyes that got even rounder when he was excited, upset, or mad. But the pastor's best assets were his outstanding wardrobe and that high, round behind that seemed tailor-made for a pair of dress pants to hang off of.

Reverend Flowers had a lot of swagger and knew how to talk the kind of junk that would make a sister blush and say something like "Boy, you so crazy." Even though he had long since turned in his player's card, Denzelle's high-level game capacity was still apparent to most folk. And that could prove to be unnerving to a woman like Marsha Metcalf, who had spent very little time out in the world collecting cool points.

Now to be fair to Marsha, Dayeesha had noticed that she was someone you needed to be careful about trying to run game on. And that was probably the main reason Reverend Flowers was so uncomfortable with Marsha Metcalf. He knew he couldn't deal out any mess her way. He also knew that if he rolled up on Marsha as the "big dawg," he risked yelping away like a pup with a newspaper popped on his nose.

There was one pastor of a sizable Gospel United Church in Winston-Salem, North Carolina, who practically ran when he crossed paths with Marsha Metcalf. Metro once overheard him talking to Reverend Obadiah Quincey about Marsha, when she walked past them at an annual conference. That joker had said, "That is one scary woman. She knows too much and can see straight through you. And get this: She don't even know she can do all of that."

Dayeesha couldn't figure out what Marsha had said or done to make that preacher so scared of her, so she asked her what happened.

Marsha said, "Girl, I don't know what I did to that boy. All I did was have coffee with him at the Caribou Coffee place on Franklin Street in Chapel Hill. We talked and laughed for hours about a bunch of crazy church stuff. After that, he never contacted me again. At first, I thought I'd done something to him. I even asked Reverend Quincey's wife, Lena, about him. She told me the only thing he said was something crazy about me being 'scary.' Imagine that, Dayeesha? He thought I was scary. Me, scary. Girl, can you believe that?"

Dayeesha didn't say anything. She thought Marsha was quite scary to a seasoned player like that preacher. And that thought was confirmed when she talked to her husband, Metro, about Marsha and that preacher.

Metro suprised Dayeesha when he said, "Baby, a woman like

Marsha scares the hell out of a playah—especially one who is trying to operate undercover. He didn't know what to do with Marsha. She didn't chase him. She treated him well. He couldn't make a subtle suggestion about a secret rendezvous, because the baby doesn't have enough playah points to pick up on that. And she didn't get her butt on her shoulders when he didn't call or ask her out again.

"That scared the pee out of him. Brother like that don't know how to react to the very thing he is always preaching about—a Proverbs 31 woman."

Even though Metro was laying it all out in such a reasonable manner, it still sounded like the thinking of an imbecile to Dayeesha. She said, "Metro, that may be all well and good about old boy. But how do you explain why our Rev is so careful and guarded with Marsha? Sometimes he acts like he gets mad at her for just walking around and being on earth."

"You'd get mad at Marsha, too, if you were a man and you knew she was the kind of woman you could and should fall head-over-heels in love with. Rev just ain't trying to go out like that right now."

"Metro Mitchell, whoever heard of trying not to be bothered with someone you know will be a blessing to you?"

"It may be crazy, but it is true. Why do you think I acted the way I did with you for all of those years? Dayeesha, you had me all in love with you and I was Metro Mitchell. I wasn't having that at the time."

Dayeesha didn't say another word. She kissed her husband on the forehead and went to make sure their kids were doing their homework. She'd always suspected Metro of being guilty of something dumb like he had just shared. But to hear it out loud made it seem even more like the talk of a lunatic.

"Men are some complicated creatures, Lord," she whispered, shaking her head and answering the telephone. Dayeesha had a ton of work to do today, and she was wasting precious time sitting around thinking about men and their craziness.

She couldn't believe this day. First Veronica Washington lost her job and called the church all upset. Then Marsha Metcalf lost her job and called the church, crying and carrying on. And now it was her best friend, Keisha Jackson, on the other end, upset about being fired for going off on the athletic director's other woman over some "school supplies," cussing everybody out, driving her red-and-white Mini Cooper all over the landscaped lawn in front of the Athletic Department's building, and then escaping from the campus police when she saw their blue lights bearing down on her.

Dayeesha reminded Keisha that this was a church line and not the club line, and to stop cussing. She put her on the schedule for that same ten o'clock meeting with the pastor the other two recent firees were scheduled for. That was going to be some kind of meeting. She made a list of pastries, teas, and some fancy coffee she'd need to get, so that she would have a legitimate reason to keep going in and out of Reverend Flowers's office during the appointment. Dayeesha was not going to miss one word of that meeting if she could help it.

She was going over her "spy list" of goodies for the pastor's meeting with Keisha, Veronica, and Marsha when a big, thick brother with close-cropped hair and a silver mustache and goatee stormed into the church office and slammed the door behind him. Dayeesha got up and walked right past the man without opening her mouth, looking for the security guard.

"I'm telling the pastor to fire that joker," she mumbled under her breath, and then went back to her desk to finish working on her list.

"Am I invisible?" Rico Sneed snapped.

"I don't know. Are you?" was all Dayeesha said, without even looking up from her work.

The man reached over and knocked Dayeesha's bottle of Fiji water off of her desk and onto the floor.

"Is something wrong with you, Mr. Rico?"

"I told you to put Reverend Flowers on the phone. But no.

You had to get all smart and beside yourself. So I'm here, in your face. How you like that?"

Dayeesha didn't blink. She didn't frown. All she did was open a drawer on her desk, reach in it, and pull out the custom-made Glock Metro and the kids had given her for Mother's Day.

She took the safety off the gun and pointed the barrel at the man, using both hands like she'd seen Agent Prentiss do in her favorite TV show, *Criminal Minds.*

"Pick that water up, put it back on my desk, leave my office, and close my door softly. You are not talking to Reverend Flowers today or any day in the near future. And I'm telling my daddy on you."

Rico Sneed bristled and started cussing like he was out in the streets and not up in church.

Dayeesha stood up and held her head to the side with the gun aimed at Rico Sneed's hip. She hoped this fool would not do something to force her to shoot him. He already had his toes shot off by Reverend Flowers back in the day, when both of them were still young men.

Plus, shooting people was some real messy business—especially when they started bleeding all over the place, hollering, and getting on your nerves. Dayeesha did not feel like going through a police report because Mr. Rico pissed her off. And she especially didn't feel like having to order some new carpet for a second time in three months. They hadn't even had this new carpet long enough to clean it.

"You have exactly no seconds left before I start shooting."

Dayeesha's gun clicked, and Rico Sneed hightailed it out of New Jerusalem Gospel United Church. She saw him run to his car, hop in, and peel off the church parking lot, burning up all of the rubber on those new tires.

She put the safety back on the gun and put it back in her desk drawer.

"Served him right—coming up in *my* church bothering people like he don't have good sense."

Chapter Two

Reverend Denzelle Flowers sat at his desk gazing out of the huge picture window in his office. New Jerusalem Gospel United Church sat nestled in the middle of eighteen acres of land. It was a sweet patch of property in Raleigh that wasn't too far from the North Hills Mall section of the city.

The original church building was a quaint, white, wooden structure that looked like the prototypical Southern church—black or white. But the old building had been remodeled to house New Jerusalem's outreach ministries—Prison Ministry, Benevolence Fund Program, Scholarship Fund, and the New Jerusalem Job Bank.

People would walk up the redbrick path leading to the outreach ministries building, take a moment to admire the lovely garden, walk in, and end up detouring to the area that used to be the sanctuary. The staff members had now grown used to folk being late for their appointments because they wandered into the old sanctuary and stayed there a while to have a heart-to-heart conversation with the Lord.

While the old church building was warm and inviting, the new church facility was amazing. Using Turner Cathedral AME Church in Marietta, Georgia, as a template, the new New Jerusalem Gospel United Church was a magnificent brick structure that could seat five thousand members comfortably. There was an IMAX-quality sound system, big screens, and a comfortable pulpit designed to make you want to preach yourself happy. The choir loft would make you want to sing for hours, and the orchestra pit begged to be loaded down with the best instrumentalists in the area.

The most notable feature in the sanctuary was the stained-glass window/wall behind the choir loft that had several scenes depicting Jesus' three-year ministry on Earth. And since Denzelle was a stone-cold brother, he made sure the folk making the glass windows for his church stained Jesus a rich dark chocolate, with an Afro that looked like he had gotten an edge-up from the ancestor of the barber who cut and shaped Denzelle's hair.

The interior was a pale golden color with darker gold accents, and ruby velvet pew cushions were set in golden wood pews. Whenever one of Denzelle's fraternity brothers walked up into his church and saw colors that hinted at a leaning toward the crimson and cream, they added a little extra to their offering amount. New Jerusalem members often joked about how many programs the Kappa Alpha Psi fraternity had supported at the church because of their deep affinity toward the church's decor.

The church had everything Denzelle could think of putting in a church—a large banquet hall to host large events and receptions, educational and conference rooms, music rooms, three choir rooms, a movie theater, a roller-skating rink, a state-of-the-art gymnasium, and a modest-size theater for church plays. There were playrooms for the younger children, game rooms for the teens, hangout rooms for the young adults, two libraries with two full-time librarians on staff, a softball field, a playground, indoor and outdoor pools, and the lovely, award-winning garden.

Yet in spite of all of this fabulous stuff, it was the pastor's suite that made Reverend Denzelle Flowers the envy of his ministerial colleagues around the state of North Carolina. His office was painted crimson, with deep cream coloring on the wood trim and wainscotting. There were golden hardwood floors that matched the desk, credenza, and coffee table. A dark-gold suede sofa sat in front of the coffee table, surrounded by crimson suede chairs the looked like they belonged in the lobby of the most ex-pensive five-star hotel.

One wall was full of photographs of the church, the pastor, the members, and events. Another wall showcased a rich array of original artwork by local black artists. And the last free wall was dedicated to books from floor to ceiling, with a fancy rolling ladder that could be used to sail across the room in search of the perfect text. But it was the rich, crimson Italian leather chair be-hind the pastor's desk that made some folk want to fight Denzelle for this office. That chair had a custom-built massage system, along with an electric heater to warm and sooth a brother's tired and sore joints on a cold day.

Denzelle had a pile of stuff on his desk—invitations to preach, diversity training for new FBI recruits, a schedule to go to the gun range for target practice, and a training session for the new preachers in the denomination. And this was all outside of his normal duties as the pastor of New Jerusalem.

Folk just didn't know how much was involved in running a large church. A good pastor had to serve as CEO, COO, spiri-tual leader, visionary, teacher, investment banker, development officer, and social worker. Maybe that's why few folk just woke up one day and decided, "Hey, I think I'd like to become a pastor." The best pastors were called, and a few of them were dragged into the ranks kicking and screaming.

Denzelle would be the first to admit that the last thing he had wanted was to become an ordained minister, and especially a pastor of a church. He had been ecstatic when the FBI recruiter came to Eva T. Marshall while he was still a college student and made it clear he was exactly what the bureau was looking for at that time. Denzelle was so excited about this opportunity that he doubled up on his course work and was on his way to graduating from college early. He even gave up his starting position as a point guard on the basketball team to make sure he didn't lose that cov-eted spot up in northern Virginia.

But while Denzelle was working overtime to become Agent

Flowers, the Lord added to that calling and compelled the crime fighter to also go out on the battlefield for Him as an ordained minister. The night this calling was put into action, Denzelle had been drinking and talking trash on the landing of the apartment he shared with his line brothers in the fraternity.

His uncle, Reverend Russell Flowers, was exhausted that night. But he had felt the Lord tugging at his heart all week about his wayward nephew. Russell knew Denzelle had been called into the ministry. He wished it had been Denzelle's older brother, Yarborough, the Lord had called, instead of his brother's spoiled youngest son. Yarborough would have been so easy to give this "thus sayeth the Lord" speech—but not that Denzelle. Russell only hoped he didn't roll up on that boy all laid up with some fast-tailed coed, trying to *convince* him to make her his Kappa Kitten.

Russell wasn't sure about the exact building or number of Denzelle's apartment when he reached the complex. He drove around for a few minutes, looking for an overabundance of crimson-and-cream K-A-Ψ T-shirts, along with laughing and shrieks from the young women invited to party with the fraternity brothers.

It didn't take long to find Denzelle and his boys. "Humpin" by the Gap Band was blasting out of the speakers they had set on either side of the apartment door. Two young women were dancing with three of the chapter's most prized and sought-after frat brothers with paper cups in their hands. From the looks of their moves in those little tight shorts, Uncle Russell could safely assume they were not drinking Tang.

He wished there was a way to just grab those little girls by the collar and drive them back to their dorms. It was clear they thought this was the way to the hearts and favor of these young men. Unfortunately, nothing could be further from the truth. This was basically a frat house party, and the ball was definitely in the young men's court. But these little girls probably thought they could handle themselves and the situation, because they were partying with a bunch of Kappas and not with a bunch of Qs.

Uncle Russell sighed, thinking, "These babies think those smooth and suave, always striving to say the right thing in public exteriors mean these young brothers are going to work hard to behave themselves."

He watched one of the young men grab his date around the waist from the back and mumbled, "He is going to behave himself with that little girl whenever hell freezes over."

And Russell figured correctly that Denzelle was as slick as a can of slick oil when it came to his dealings with women. That was not a good way for any man to be—and especially one who would soon find himself as an official man of the cloth. Russell had had many conversations with the Lord about the way men ran game on women. He detested that kind of behavior in a man— even if the man was his own flesh and blood. Men, both young and old, simply didn't understand how much they trampled all over their own blessings and joy playing ugly games with women and igniting the anger of the Lord.

Denzelle's line brother saw Uncle Russell first. He took his arms from around his date's waist and got up off of being all up on her butt. He nodded and said, "Sir," clearly impressed by Uncle Russell's expensive diamond-and-ruby tie pin that identified him as a lifelong member of the fraternity. He wondered why Denzelle hadn't told them that Uncle Russell rolled like that. No wonder he was so cool and GQ.

Denzelle was standing with his back to Uncle Russell, twirling his candy-cane–colored Kappa Kane and drinking out of a bottle of Johnny Walker Red. He drained his whiskey bottle and tapped his cane on the concrete of the landing like he was getting ready to break off into a step. A young woman walked up the steps grinning right at Denzelle. She was a fine thing in those tight jeans and snug red halter top.

"Lawd, ha mercy," Denzelle said, and tapped the cane on the

ground again. He was about to smack on his lips like he was hungry when he saw those breasts on the girl. They made him feel like dropping down on his knees, praying, and thanking God for making them thangs right when He made this girl.

Denzelle smacked on his lips again, and then stopped cold when he saw the horrified expression on his frat brother's face and the subtle nod for him to turn around. Denzelle turned to meet the steel glint in his uncle Russell's eyes.

He tried to straighten up and pull it together, but he was drunk and not able to pull it off too well.

Uncle Russell closed his eyes and prayed, "Help me, Jesus."

Denzelle knew deep down in his heart that Uncle Russell had come here to give him the word that he was called to serve in the ministry. He had been dreading this moment for months. Why him? He was the bad and spoiled little brother. He was the lady's man. He was the brother who liked to get drunk and get high. He was the one who needed a whole lot of work to make him right for the ministry.

Uncle Russell wanted to snatch that cane out of his fraternity brother/nephew's hand and beat him with it. Denzelle was a piece of work. And Russell knew that was precisely why the Lord had called his nephew into the ministry.

The Lord loved to call the Denzelles to straighten up and go to work for Him. Years from now his nephew would win many souls to Christ because he "got it." Denzelle would know exactly what his parishioners were talking about when they shared their struggles with coming out of the world to serve the Lord.

Uncle Russell knew that the boy did not want to give up drinking, cussing, and hitting every piece of tail that wasn't nailed down just to put on a collar and preach. He knew Denzelle had his heart set on going up for FBI training as soon as he graduated and moving to the DC area, where he thought all of the action was. And he also knew Denzelle wouldn't get past go if he got stupid and tried to act like he didn't know what time it was.

His nephew could try and play games with the Lord if he wanted to. But Russell would not advise such a foolish move. All one had to do was scan the Book of Jonah to figure out that running from the Lord was really a waste of time. The Lord threw Jonah's scary behind down in the belly of a whale. But there was a chance that God might choose a different way of getting Denzelle's undivided attention—like, say, throwing Denzelle down in a locked basement with a bunch of really ugly women who would do anything to get with him.

Russell looked Denzelle square in the eye and said, "Boy, I'm tired, and I have had to deal with nonsense all week during the annual conference. So I'm going to give it to you straight. You're called into the ministry, son. And judging from the way you've been trying to live it up, you've felt the Lord laying something on your heart. You won't be the first preacher to try and run from being a preacher. But I can tell you that it won't work."

"Then can I have this last night to get myself one good booty call, Uncle?"

Russell popped Denzelle upside the head.

"Boy, you are going to divinity school and to train with the Board of Examiners for the Gospel United Church. You are talking crazy, like you only have a week to live."

Denzelle didn't say anything, because it felt like he only had a week to live. He knew what being called into the ministry meant. He would have to walk the straight and narrow. He wouldn't be able to hang out with his frat brothers and have a good time.

And that was a shame, because his line brother and friend, Charles Robinson, was working on getting them into the newest and hottest strip club in the area. Denzelle knew that once he started training to become a minister, throwing two fat handfuls of bills at a hot stripper would definitely become a "gone are the things of the past."

The full-breasted coed sashayed by again and sneaked a smile over at Denzelle. He looked like he was talking to his father. The last thing she wanted was for that fine Nupe's dad to tell him to stay clear of her. Because that old dude definitely looked like a preacher who didn't take mess off of anybody.

Denzelle sighed heavily and said, "So Uncle, what am I going to do about sex?"

"Get married?" Uncle Russell answered, and then closed his eyes and said, "Father, Lord, Jesus—give me strength."

"*Damn*, that's messed up," Denzelle swore under his breath, praying Uncle Russell hadn't picked up on his knee-jerk response. He desperately hoped the FBI would call him quick and hopefully get him away from all of this preacher stuff.

Training for the FBI, even as one of the few black recruits in his class, had been a walk in the park compared to what Denzelle went through to become a pastor. It wasn't because they didn't treat him well—they did. He was, after all, Reverend Russell Flowers's nephew. But it was hard to walk the straight and narrow when all he could hear calling his name was the newest favored liquor, a joint, a jumping party at the Kappa frat house, and a fine, hot woman.

Denzelle tried everything to get off the preacher track but to no avail. Nothing he did worked. He tried to avoid reading his Bible but could barely sleep for scriptures he didn't even know he knew popping up in his head. Had he really been in church so much that scriptures were practically second nature to him?

He even went so far as to write a tacky sermon on a note card in pencil after drinking all night when assigned to preach during one of the chapel services for the divinity school program he was enrolled in. Denzelle knew he had this one in the bag: He figured that when he walked in there looking like crap from his hangover, and then they heard that messed-up sermon, they would run him to his car and beg him to leave the program and never come back. No such luck—two divinity school students came down and got saved after hearing his sermon, "Getting Saved Ain't for No Punks."

Actually, Denzelle had the best time preaching that sermon. It was hilarious, and he whooped and hollered and wiped his face with a handkerchief until he accidently preached himself happy. He intentionally murdered the king's English and used slang and jokes and carried on until he preached those two brothers down to the altar. All of that next week folk were walking up to him, saying, "I ain't no punk man, I know the Lord."

About the only good thing that happened to Denzelle as a result of being asked to preach that sermon was the number he had gotten from the sister who had been assigned to put flowers in the chapel that week. But that was short-lived. After he preached that sermon, and her brother was one of the two men to get saved, she told him, "Give me back my telephone number. You are a real preacher. I ain't going to hell over you. I don't care how fine you are, and how good your booty looks in those pants you wearing."

Nothing helped, not even when he decided to go to a frat party with the sole intent of getting drunk, getting high, and getting laid. As soon as he stepped up in the frat house and placed an order for a shot of tequila, the chapter president came over to the bar where he was standing. The president frowned and said, "Brother Flowers, may I speak to you on the porch."

Denzelle nodded and followed him out of the house.

"Brother Flowers, have any of your frat brothers done anything to offend you or do you any harm?"

"Huh?" Denzelle answered. He got along with all of his chapter brothers.

"Have we done anything to offend you?"

"Naw, Brother Kincaid. You know it's nothing like that. I mean, why would you think that?"

"Frat, Frat," Charles Robinson walked up and said. Charles patted the sister hanging on his arm on her big, round behind and sent her back into the frat house, where the music was getting funkier and hotter by the second. He looked at that booty wistfully, twirled a red toothpick around in his mouth, and chimed in: "Look, Denzelle. What Brother Kincaid is trying to tell you is that you are up in here trying to get a shot of tequila, trying to smoke some good weed, trying to get some tail, when what you need to be doing is reading your Bible so you can bring us sinners a word the next time we come to chapel to hear you preach.

"You are a man of the cloth, and now a member of an even more important fraternity—as hard as it is for me to admit that. We can't let you come up in here putting us in danger of getting into some real trouble with the Lord simply because we were stupid enough to let one of His protégés come up in here and act like he don't know Him like you really do."

Denzelle opened his mouth to protest. But Charles raised his hand to silence him.

"I don't want to hear it from you, frat," Charles said. "You have been walking around this campus trying to act like you are not as tight with Jesus as you really are. And you can't do that. It's dangerous, and we ain't having it. I know you know the scripture in Revelation about what the Lord will do to folk who think they are all saved and stuff, and what they really are is lukewarm."

Both Brother Kincaid and Denzelle tilted their heads to get a good long look at Charles Robinson. Charles was one of the bad boys in the chapter. He was the last person who was supposed to know what was in that Bible. And Revelation, too? This was getting way too scary.

"What?" Charles snapped at them. "Y'all both know that my auntee is an evangelist, and so saved Jesus probably calls her on the telephone just to chitchat about what's going on in Durham, North Carolina. You think she hasn't hit me up with some Revelation, trying to scare me to Jesus?"

Brother Kincaid and Denzelle kind of nodded. Charles's aunt Margarita was one of the savedest people they knew.

"Charleeeeee," Charles's woman said from the screen door. "I'm getting cold."

Brother Kincaid paused, and then started laughing. It was seriously hot up in that house. He said, "Frat, you better get in there and take care of that fast. And you," he told Denzelle, with a stern expression spreading across his face, "you need to leave and go do what the Lord bids you to do. And you bet not come back unless it is for a chapter meeting and you are serving as our chaplain. These parties are now off-limits to you."

Denzelle was too through, even if he was secretly touched by the love and concern of his fraternity brothers. That was the way folk were supposed to act with preachers—hold their feet to the fire to do right. He went back to his car and drove over to Honey's Restaurant off of 85, because it was one of the few places open at this time of night in Durham. He had never been real fond of their coffee, but the pecan waffles were pretty decent in the wee hours of the morning.

As soon as he walked in he spotted his best friend and fellow divinity school student, Obadiah Quincey, sitting in a booth looking like his dog had just died.

"Obie man? What you doing out here at this time of night?"

"I was thinking the exact thing when I saw your red Camaro slide into that parking space, D," Obadiah said.

"Frat house put me out," Denzelle answered, sounding a little on the pitiful side.

"Mine did, too," Obadiah commiserated. "Man, all I wanted to do was drink one beer and play one hand of poker. Was that so bad?"

"I don't think that was too bad," Denzelle answered, thinking that Obie's frat brothers were even stricter than his about these things. At least he was trying to cut up. But Denzelle knew that Obie wasn't trying to doing anything like what he'd been planning for the evening.

"Dang, man," Obadiah said, and put syrup on his waffle. "I guess we are officially preachers, huh."

Denzelle reached out for some skin and just nodded. They had somehow officially crossed over into being men of the cloth.

"Precious memories," Denzelle whispered to himself. He and Obadiah had stayed up all night eating waffles, drinking Honey's watery coffee, and talking about what it would be like to be full-fledged men of the cloth. He picked up a picture of him and Obadiah, taken the day they received their final papers and preacher's licenses, and were approved for full ordination. They were so young back then. Obadiah's solemn face stared back at him, looking almost the same, with the exception of the silver streaks in his hair.

They had been through a lot in the more than thirty years of being best friends and fellow preachers. Thirty years was a long time to be charged with trying to get a bunch of black folk in Durham and Raleigh on the King's High Way. Denzelle loved the black church. But church folk were something else. And he couldn't wait to get to Heaven to ask the Lord about His decision to call him to such a great commission. Well, actually, Denzelle could wait to get to Heaven. As much as he wanted to hear the answer to that question, he was content to wait on the opportunity to present it "face to face."

Chapter Three

It didn't seem like he'd been in this business that long, even though Denzelle could see the decades of time passed in the silver sprayed across his head and in his mustache. Where had the time gone? He should have felt like a seasoned warrior on the battlefield of the Lord. But there were times when he still felt like a rookie.

To most folk Denzelle was not only a seasoned preacher, he was a man held in high esteem, and one who was to be feared—especially if you found yourself on the wrong side of the law. Anybody staring down the barrel of one of his guns needed to be scared. They also needed to start praying and making one last attempt to get right with the Lord.

Denzelle made quite a name for himself back in the mid-1980s as both a preacher to watch and the FBI agent to fear, when he served as a major player in one of the most successful drug busts in Durham County while simultaneously helping his denomination do serious damage to some crooked and corrupt preachers in the Gospel United Church.

He helped dismantle a powerful southeastern drug cartel run by the notorious Dinkle Brothers of western North Carolina. By the time Denzelle got through with Harold and Horace Dinkle they were relieved to go to jail, at an undisclosed federal facility, away from everybody interested in what they were compelled to tell the feds. Agent/Reverend Flowers had received many

awards, along with a key to the city of Durham, for his work on
that case. He also moved up in the Gospel United Church, and for
a young pastor was given one of the better church assignments at
that time.

Tabernacle Gospel United Church, in Greensboro, North
Carolina, was a midsized congregation with a strong operating
budget and a dedicated group of members. Tabernacle knew it
was the training stop for preachers on their way up to the more
prestigious and wealthier congregations. And the church considered it something akin to a calling to be able to provide the kind
of foundation and training needed by ministers on the fast track,
like Reverend Denzelle Flowers.

The good folk at Tabernacle Gospel United Church fell in
love with their new pastor, with his bad self, almost the moment
they met him. Several ladies took note of how pastor always
dressed, and they were especially impressed on the Sunday he
showed up at church in a tailored, Carolina blue suit that fit his
body better than they imagined his gun fit in its holster.

As one woman put it, "Normally, I ain't for a man in a pastel-
colored outfit. But daggone it, if pastor has given a whole new
meaning to the term Easter suit. And those baby blue gators?
Lawd, ha mercy."

The church's resident hoochie secretly agreed with that assessment. That Tar Heel suit fit Reverend Flowers so well it gave
her cause to ponder on what was up in that suit to make it hug all
of the right spots on her new pastor's body.

Sharlena Maxwell licked her lips when going through the receiving line after service and said, "Pastor Denzelle, you served up
this morning's sermon so hot and good, you made me hungry."

Denzelle, who knew he was looking good in that suit, with
the silk, blue, and cream paisley–printed lining in the suit coat
and the silk tie matching the print in the lining, smiled back at
his fine parishioner, took her hand, and said, "Sister . . ."

"Sharlena. My name is Sharlena Maxwell, Pastor."

Denzelle gave her the smile that got him in so much trouble

while an undergrad. He knew he was looking at nothing but one hundred and twenty-five pounds of pure trouble, with a name like Sharlena and matching from head to toe in an electric blue silk suit, electric blue silk hat, electric blue pumps and matching purse. Denzelle figured with all of that blue, baby had to be wearing a bright blue bra and bikini panties. There was nothing better than getting an eyewitness full of a big brown rump stretching the strings on some itsy-bitsy blue panties.

He said in his best preacher voice, "It is a pleasure to meet you on this great and blessed Sunday that the Lord has given us."

Sharlena sucked on her tooth and looked the pastor right in the eye. She grinned, pleased that her grin made him squirm. Sharlena had maneuvered quite a few secret rendezvous with preachers and knew when she had managed to get under a minister's skin. A brother out there in the world would have been licking his chops and working hard on a good comeback line. But a preacher? And a pastor at that? That brother would retreat into preacher minutia and try and play it off that she was getting next to him.

She thought, "This is going to be fun, 'cause this preacher is good. He smooth, too." And then, Sharlena said, "The pleasure is all mine, and hopefully will be yours," in the sexiest voice she dared use in the receiving line at church.

Later that afternoon, while eating at K & W Cafeteria with her best friend, Sharlena said, "Girl, it is just a matter of time before I find out what those blue pants are covering up."

Her friend dipped her fork into a delectable piece of chocolate cream pie and said, "I heard that."

Denzelle was a great preacher. He was also a very personable pastor who had a genuine appreciation of all of his parishioners— young and old. As much as those ladies were busy discussing everything about their pastor they didn't have any business discussing about the pastor, the other members of the church were busy discussing how much life and pizzazz and fire he brought to their church.

Practically all of Tabernacle Gospel United Church was impressed with Denzelle being both a pastor and former field agent with the FBI. They, and especially some of the women, didn't know what to do with a man who could handle the Bible and a gun with such proficiency.

When Sharlena said, "Girl, Reverend Flowers makes me want to commit a crime, just so he can arrest me," her friend said, "Oooo, chile, don't you just wonder what it sound like for your pastor to say, 'Hands behind your back—you are under arrest.'"

Before Sharlena could say one more thing on this titillating subject, one of the sincere, God-fearing church mothers walked up to their table. "How did that old Holy Roller roll up on us in this restaurant?" Sharlena's friend asked in a loud whisper.

Miss Deborah, the "old Holy Roller," rolled her eyes. The words dumb and stupid couldn't even begin to describe those two women. She said, "You two sit up in church every Sunday, and you still talk and act like alley cats working to claw your way straight to hell."

Those two were quiet during the reprimand, because they knew Miss Deborah was right, even if they wished she would take her "I love Jesus for real" self back to her own table so that they could continue with the business at hand.

"We didn't have anything to do with the bishop's decision to send a man as fine as Reverend Flowers to our church, Miss Deborah," was all Sharlena said.

"Sharlena Maxwell," Miss Deborah began, face clearly displaying that she was not buying that raggedy mess from her. "You get all beside yourself whenever we have a new pastor. And he don't have to be fine for you to do so. If you remember, our last pastor could really preach, but he was butt ugly."

Sharlena sighed and resisted a strong urge to cut her eyes at Miss Deborah. She was truly a righteous woman—even in Sharlena's book. Folk at church didn't mess with Miss Deborah, because she would get to calling on Jesus, and then mess your butt up. Miss Deborah could pray, Miss Deborah could sing, Miss Deborah could preach, and Miss Deborah could fight.

Plus, she had seven children who all spoke in tongues and liked to fight. And her husband, Mr. Lester, wasn't any better. He was always standing off on the sidelines with a big bottle of anointing oil, just waiting to assist the love of his life with any kind of altercation she might encounter as a soldier for the Lord.

And as much as Sharlena hated to admit it, Miss Deborah only checked folks who had really gone too far and were working up on some trouble that could affect the church. A member like Sharlena having a secret tête-à-tête with the new pastor would definitely cause problems in the church.

Shoot, Sharlena thought as she watched Miss Deborah retreat with relief. Ain't my fault that man stepped up in our church looking all good and sexy and tasty, and without a woman in his life. I don't know why these men think its okay to be all frolicking in the church, all alone, and think folk are just going to stand by and watch all of that. If he had somebody right, he wouldn't have even noticed my butt, and he sho' wouldn't be interested in anything I have to offer.

Miss Deborah sighed, as she went back to Lester and the children. The bishop couldn't have appointed a better pastor than Reverend Flowers. That man was full of fire. But she knew, in her heart of hearts, Pastor didn't have the sense God gave him to hook up with a good woman—the kind of woman who understood what it took to be the helpmeet to a handsome and up-and-coming pastor in their church.

Pastor was going to need her prayers. He'd been at Tabernacle all of one month, and it was clearer than clear that women loved themselves some Denzelle Flowers. Good news—the pastor was a good man. He was a great pastor, a powerful preacher, and a dedicated community servant. Bad news—he definitely had a weakness for a big round butt, stuffed into a delectable-looking church suit.

When Denzelle graduated from his third, so-called secret

rendezvous in the church the bishop stepped in and let Reverend Flowers know that a marriage was a prerequisite if he planned to keep moving up in the ranks of the ministry. Upon hearing the M word, Denzelle determined that his troubles with lust would end if he identified a woman to marry—as if marriage could be boiled down to something as calculated as putting an FBI pinpoint on a potentially suitable mate.

Against the advice of his best friend, Denzelle decided it would be a swell idea to marry one of his newest members, Tatiana Hill. Tatiana, a registered nurse, was tall, shapely, with dark micro braids, dark eyes, and an aura of mystique about her that made a brother like Denzelle curious to know what was behind that cool and controlled exterior. She had an air about her that could be misinterpreted as aloof or regal. But there were folks at the church who read her demeanor for exactly what it was—Tatiana was mean, stuck up, and thought she was too cute to be nice to people.

Once the two started dating openly, Tatiana would make it her business to stand next to the pastor while he greeted the members at the close of service. But the members wished she'd take herself to the bathroom or something, so they didn't have to pretend they wanted to be bothered with her. Tatiana barely opened her mouth when folk spoke to her. When one lady just decided that she was going to make that girl talk to her, Tatiana stood there in that high-priced, lime-green silk first lady suit and looked down at the woman like she was a piece of poop smashed up on the sidewalk.

Miss Deborah shook her head whenever she saw Denzelle and Tatiana together. She told Lester, "You know no good will come out of this. Nothing either one of them is doing has anything to do with the Lord. It has everything to do with gaining the whole world at the risk of your own soul."

Tatiana Hill believed she was supposed to have the pastor simply because she was Tatiana. As far she was concerned, Denzelle was supposed to chase after her, even though the only thing she really loved about this man was his status, his growing bank account, and the fact that she had something all of those other women wanted—him. It made Tatiana glow and purr when she felt the envy from women who would almost die to be on the pastor's arm. Sometimes she didn't even feel like being on Denzelle's arm until she spied another woman gazing wistfully in their direction.

While Denzelle's heart was as far from loving Tatiana as sunlight was from moonlight, he believed he was doing the correct thing by marrying this beautiful, cold, and conniving woman. But that boy knew he'd made a terrible mistake the moment the two of them stepped on the plane en route to a romantic honeymoon in Tahiti and fought like cats and dogs during the entire flight. By the time the limousine driver had finished putting their bags in the car, Denzelle was looking at a makeshift vegetable stand with longing, wishing he could hunker down there for the duration of the trip.

In that moment he truly understood what the old preachers had tried to explain to him when they kept talking about the Word jumping off the page and literally coming to life. Every time Tatiana opened her mouth to speak all Denzelle could think of was Proverbs 25:24: *Better to live on a corner of a roof than share a house with a quarrelsome wife.*

And it didn't take long for another scripture to practically slap him across the face. Never in a million years did a bona fide player like Denzelle Flowers believe he would be the poster boy for these Words from Proverbs 30:20: *This is the way of an adulteress: She eats and wipes her mouth and says, "I've done nothing wrong."*

That marriage lasted just long enough for them to become unqualified for an annulment. One year, two months, five days, eleven hours, thirteen minutes, and nine seconds made it legally impossible for the good Reverend Flowers to wipe his slate clean of the woman he'd sworn to love, honor, and protect 'til death did they part. In fact, those vows scared him a bit, because sometimes Tatiana made Denzelle feel as if she'd rather have their parting be a result of him crossing over into eternity.

Tatiana left Denzelle on an afternoon while he was officiating over the funeral and burial of one of Tabernacle's long-standing members. When Denzelle got home, everything connected to Tatiana was gone except the note taped to the refrigerator with her lawyer's name and number on it, along with an amount for the check Tatiana expected Denzelle to deposit into her account to cover her moving expenses.

He had always known that girl had some nerve. He just didn't know the extent of that nerve until now. He laughed, and then tore up the note and threw it in the trash.

Denzelle was relieved when the presiding bishop reassigned him, to a smaller church, after that breakup. He needed a break from the fast track, and received the assignment to the 117-member church out in Mount Airy, North Carolina, with a glad heart.

Obadiah cracked up when Denzelle told him where he had to go for a year. He said, "D, I cannot believe the bishop has sent you Mayberry."

"Mayberry?"

"Yeah, D. You know that Mount Airy is the town used as the model for Mayberry on the *Andy Griffith Show*. Remember?"

Obie was right. Mount Airy was the real Mayberry, and he was a real officer of the law. That was some funny stuff. Denzelle hadn't really laughed or found anything funny in months. Maybe going off to Mayberry for a season was exactly what he needed.

Denzelle's time in Mount Airy wasn't too long, or too short. It was the perfect amount of a hiatus to prepare him for the next appointment at the up-and-coming New Jerusalem Gospel United Church in Raleigh. New Jerusalem was a strong church, with a growing congregation, and it was in need of a pastor who could take what their former pastor, Reverend Boudreaux, had started up to and well beyond the next level. Everybody in the First Episcopal District knew that Reverend Denzelle Flowers was the man of the hour for this job.

Denzelle remembered his first Sunday at New Jerusalem. He'd learned some valuable lessons at Tabernacle and made a point to wear the most conservative suit he owned for his first day of work. He also remembered marching in with the choir feeling a distinctive turning of the wheels in his heart with excitement over this brand-new venture.

It had been a long time since Denzelle Flowers felt that kind of fire and sparkle on the inside. There were a few times when his heart was so numb, Denzelle worried that something essential had shriveled up and died on the inside. But that morning he knew the Lord had an extra-special blessing for him at New Jerusalem—something quite out of the ordinary. It would be years, along with a few knocks upside Denzelle's hard head, before he would be able to receive the complete blessing God had prepared for him.

The big, bad Denzelle Flowers could barely bring himself to imagine that this blessing was a short, no-cool-points-earning girl named Marsha Metcalf. And the funny thing was, like many men, Denzelle would be in shock that he met this blessing in church. What an irony—a bona fide church man being in denial that the Lord would bless him with the right woman right up in church. Who knew?

Chapter Four

That's how the Reverend Denzelle Flowers came to New Jerusalem, which, despite the rumors and his checkered past, welcomed him with open arms. They had really loved Reverend Boudreaux, and cried up rivers of tears when he left. But as much as they loved their former pastor, the congregation was excited to have the infamous Denzelle Flowers as their new shepherd.

This new pastor was exciting. This new pastor had serious swagger. And this new pastor was what an older church mother dubbed as sexy as all get-outs. She told one of her fellow octogenarian missionary sisters, "Honey, if I was still in my sixties, Pastor would be in *trou-bul*."

All her friend could do was laugh and say, "He need to quit wearing all of them robes all the time during service and put on some of those good-looking three-button suits with some flaps on the back of the jacket. Have you seen *that* butt on *that* man?"

Marsha Metcalf was one of the members who loved Reverend Boudreaux but found herself liking the brand-new pastor a lot. As much as she didn't want to admit it, Marsha secretly thought the good Reverend Flowers was funny, smart, handsome, and one of the best-dressed preachers in the First Episcopal District of the Gospel United Church.

She didn't talk to Denzelle a lot during his early years at New Jerusalem. For starters, she was still married to Rodney. Then Rodney left and upped and died. At that point, Marsha and

Denzelle began to talk more. There were times when the two of them would get to talking and laughing with one another and end up finishing each other's sentences. Then Denzelle would suddenly remember that he was getting too comfortable with just being himself with a woman, push Marsha away, and run from her like she was the carrier of a highly contagious and deadly plague.

Marsha wanted to haul off and slap the black off of Denzelle when he did that to her. She'd be kind to that boy, and then he'd act and talk all stank and rude, like he didn't have any home training. It didn't make sense to act like that toward someone who didn't do anything to you but treat your stank-butt right. Denzelle just didn't know how many times Marsha came close to laying down her saved card, forgetting herself, and cussing him out so badly someone would have to take her to the hospital when she finally got through.

Marsha flipping off on the pastor wouldn't be the worse thing Denzelle could experience at New Jerusalem, however. The now famous Friday night service still topped the chart for "Church Services Gone Wild." That service had gotten so out of hand, it pushed Denzelle to the point of breaking down on the altar of his own church—confessing and repenting of a problem he had struggled with for most of his ministry. From that point on the pastor was a model preacher and truly delivered of his weakness for a pretty face and a big, black-girl butt.

Only problem was that the pastor was now so good, some members feared he was about to turn into some kind of crunked version of a preaching eunuch and start acting like Reverend Larry Pristeen up in Asheville, North Carolina. While the congregation was relieved the pastor wasn't hittin' and quittin' it with the resident loose booty in the church, they thought he could quit acting like liking a woman was the worse thing in the world that could happen to him.

The congregation wasn't alone in its frustration with the pastor's stubborn refusal to acknowledge and admit he needed a good woman in his life. When Miss Deborah and Mr. Lester visited New Jerusalem to check on their former pastor, Mr. Lester saw Denzelle turn a cold shoulder to at least two bona fide Proverbs 31 women who spoke to him before the service began. As soon as the second Proverbs 31 woman walked away, clearly perplexed by the pastor's behavior over her doing something as normal as saying, "Good morning Reverend Flowers," Mr. Lester tugged at Miss Deborah's purse and said, "Baby, did you see that?"

Miss Deborah curled up her lips and said, "Umm, hmm. I saw that ignorant mess, Les."

Mr. Lester shook his head in disgust before continuing. "I get sick of some of these men walking around like they are the only people on earth who have experienced a broken heart. *Just who in the hell do they think they are?* They act like it is a federal offense to let the Lord heal their hearts of stone and bless them with some real companionship.

"Denzelle walking around here acting like he's trying to neuter his own self like that silly and self-serving Reverend Larry Pristeen up in Asheville. That brother can't even have a decent conversation with a decent woman. Has Denzelle figured out that most church folk don't want a pastor who is too stupid to find himself a good woman?"

"Probably not," Miss Deborah answered him matter-of-factly.

"First thing Denzelle needs to do," Miss Deborah continued saying, "is let go of his anger and resentment where his ex-wife, Tatiana, is concerned. I mean, why is he so upset over what went down between the two of them? Didn't he know that marrying a woman who fits your five- or ten-year life plan for success isn't the best criteria for picking a wife?

"Way too many men do that stupid mess. Then they get mad at the woman for not being the 'bone of my bone, flesh of my flesh' kinda wife. And then they have the nerve to try and cop an attitude with the Lord, as if He told them to run off and do something crazy like that."

"Well, the Lord did tell Hosea to marry that hoochie in the Bible," Mr. Lester said.

Miss Deborah just rolled her eyes and said, "Father God, give me strength." Then she turned to her husband and said, "Baby, does Pastor look like he a Hosea type of brother? He would have kicked Gomer's butt, and then pistol-whipped the angels trying to pull him up off of that girl."

"You know you right about that one, Baby," Mr. Lester said to his wife, and held out his fist for some dap. Miss Deborah tapped his knuckles with hers and kissed him on the cheek.

Mr. Lester broke out into a huge smile, and then frowned when he saw Denzelle's ex-wife, now Tatiana Hill Flowers Townsend, of all people, sashaying into the vestibule.

"What the face?"

"Lester, remember that you are saved," Miss Deborah admonished, and then had to pray to stop from saying something other than "what the face," when she saw Tatiana walking up in this church like she was the first lady.

"Pastor know she up in his church this morning," Lester whispered in a very audible voice. Miss Deborah closed her eyes and gave herself a "shaking my head" moment. Lester had always whispered like a three-year-old—loud enough to be heard by anybody standing nearby.

"No, he does not," Tatiana snapped.

She never did like Miss Deborah and her husband. They were so hood. She stared at Miss Deborah's white brocade suit with the satin collar and rhinestone buttons down the jacket that screamed "I go to church." And if that weren't bad enough, Miss Deborah was wearing a pair of white brocade, low-heeled pumps that matched her suit.

"What you lookin' at, Tatiana?" Miss Deborah said.

"Nothing," Tatiana replied.

"Then you must be looking at your own reflection in that window," Miss Deborah told her, and prepared to say more but stopped when Dr. Todd Townsend, a highly paid trauma surgeon, came into the church with his car keys dangling off of his index fingers. It was clear he wanted everyone to note that he was driving a Mercedes.

"Again," Mr. Lester began. "Does Reverend Flowers know you are here at his church with your husband?"

Tatiana cut her eyes at Mr. Lester, grabbed Todd's hand, and said, "Let's go and sit down. It's almost eleven o'clock. Denzelle is a stickler for starting service on time."

Mr. Lester and Miss Deborah both pulled out some anointing oil. They poured a little in the palm of their hands and anointed each other. An usher opened the door leading into the sanctuary and said, "You need to come on in and sit down if you want to get in before the processional."

Miss Deborah saw Tatiana drag Todd through her ex-husband's church, hissed air out of clenched teeth, and said, "She is a trifling piece of work."

Denzelle hurried back to his office. He had to make some last-minute changes on the sermon and have a few quiet moments before praying with the choir to get ready for the processional. Denzelle needed to clear his head of his immediate concerns for his three recently fired members before service started.

It was terribly upsetting to learn that three of his members had lost their jobs on the same day. Denzelle had been praying about what to do every since Dayeesha gave him the full 411 on what had transpired in the lives of Marsha Metcalf, Veronica Washington, and that mouthy and feisty Keisha Jackson. Denzelle had been upset and angry when he received the news reports on Marsha and Veronica. But he had hollered with laughter when Dayeesha told him about Keisha's escapade at Eva T.

That Keisha was one of his favorite members. But the girl was definitely on some different stuff. He wished he could have been on campus that day to watch her drive all over the Athletic Department's overly manicured lawn. Everybody who knew the university's athletic director, Coach Gilead Jackson, knew he was a yard freak and that he siphoned off some of his budget to do the department's yard better than any place on campus, including the administrative building where the president's office was. And when Dayeesha told Denzelle how Keisha chased Gilead down in her little Italian Job car, he started laughing so hard, his sides hurt.

So with all that he had to handle, which included trying to figure out something that would help those three women get employed, the last person Denzelle wanted to see or be forced to deal with was his ex-wife. He was glad Mr. Lester and Miss Deborah were here this morning and that they both texted him of Tatiana's presence.

He couldn't figure out for the life of him why Tatiana wanted to come to his church, or any church, for that matter. His ex would much rather be at the spa, or sipping on some coffee while soaking in the tub. He used to have to practically drag Tatiana to church when they were married.

"Why, Lord, why?" Denzelle thought, shaking his head. "Why did that woman have to pick New Jerusalem for her yearly sojourn to church? I don't want her here, Lord. And I sho' don't want to have to look at and be nice to that idiot she's married to."

"You okay, Rev?" the choir director asked, after having to knock on his office door several times. Something was bothering him. And she figured correctly after catching a glimpse of the pastor's ex. Plopping her wide butt on the pew of their church. She'd heard the ex was a piece of work.

"I'm fine," Denzelle answered and hurried to put on his robe.

"You sure, Pastor?"

"Yeah," Denzelle replied, knowing that answer was a big leap from the truth. He was anything but okay. Three members were unemployed. And now Tatiana had brought her raggedy, trifling tail up in his church with the man she left him for.

He'd been hearing about folks seeing Tatiana and Todd practically all week. Every time his phone buzzed, somebody was texting him that they had seen the Townsends at Southpoint Mall in Durham, Triangle Town Center in Raleigh, Kemp's Sea

Food, The Angus Barn, and the ultimate black Durham stop, The Pan Pan Soul Food Restaurant at Northgate Mall. Whatever reason had them here this week, Tatiana obviously didn't think her trip from Winston-Salem to Durham would be complete unless she came to Denzelle's church to bug the heck out of him.

Even though Denzelle was completely over Tatiana, he still didn't want to see her sitting all up under that lame Todd in his church. It was like he told Obadiah later that day, "Man, she cheated on me. Me! No woman has ever cheated on me, Obie. They may have cussed me out and broke up with me, but they never cheated on me while they were still with me. And she cheated on me with *him*, Obie. Have you seen this brother? I mean, what does he have?"

Obadiah didn't say a word. He pulled out his credit card, bopped Denzelle up side his head, and said, "He has this. Only his is BLACK."

Tatiana had timed her entrance into the sanctuary just right. She strolled down the aisle with Todd holding her arm, and plopped down in the same spot in church she occupied years ago at her ex-husband's old church.

Dayeesha Mitchell couldn't believe either one of those jokers. Tatiana seemed completely unaware that some folk were asking, "Who in the heck is she?" and others were whispering, "What is wrong with her?" And Dr. Todd Townsend was working overtime, trying to display playah credentials he knew he did not have.

Dayeesha's daddy, Dotsy Hamilton, was a stone-cold playah from back in the day. Her husband, Metro, probably wrote the manual for players under the age of forty. So Dayeesha knew what a playah looked and acted like. And this Dr. Todd character was no playah. She leaned over to her husband and whispered, "Baby, you know that sucker ain't never had a bona fide playah's card, right?"

Metro's expert, hip-hop–fashion eyes assessed the high quality of Dr. Todd's navy cashmere sports jacket, and then had to close them to stop the visual pain caused by his very expensive beige pants that had a cuff that didn't hang long enough over those brown shoes, with their thick soles. He prayed that the shirt and tie were better but sadly was not surprised when he saw the blue oxford shirt and the red, blue, and yellow silk tie.

"Daye-Daye, baby," Metro whispered loudly, "they didn't even take his application for the card. Just stamped DENIED when it fell on the desk."

He took a good long look at Dr. Todd's wife, all decked out in a gold Dolce and Gabbana suit with a black fox collar that Dayeesha had shown him on the D & G Web site, hoping he would take the hint and buy it for her. Metro had checked out that price tag, and said, "Naw, Daye Daye, we got some cash but that is too much money for that suit. Plus, I think it would look better on you in platinum."

Dayeesha had sucked on her teeth and rolled her eyes at Metro. He knew good and well that a top designer suit was not coming in an array of colors. If D & G made it in gold, they meant for you to wear it in gold.

"Metro, we can buy two of those suits in cash," was all she'd said to her very frugal husband. And his reply was, "I know, baby. But I'd like it better in platinum, and I'll tell my cousin Naye Naye to make you one. Okay?"

Metro looked at Tatiana's suit, and then at his wife's in platinum. He squeezed her hand, glad that she was just a down sister who had his back. He said, "I told you that suit would look better in platinum."

Dayeesha laughed. Metro was right. He hadn't gotten this rich making bad calls on the fashion and merchandise sold at his store.

They both watched as Tatiana struggled to keep her composure after catching a glimpse of Dayeesha Mitchell's suit, while continuing her efforts to do a church-by on her ex-husband. She had been hearing rumors that Denzelle was kind of sweet on some little church woman who shopped at Cato's Fashions and wanted to find out who the woman was.

Tatiana didn't want Denzelle, but she also didn't want the man to find some happiness. She was going to get up in the receiving line when service ended, stand with Denzelle, find that woman, and put her in her place. She had, after all, been the first lady of Denzelle's church at one time—which is more than she could say for Miss Cato Fashions.

Dayeesha was so glad that Naye Naye, who could sew her butt off, had made her that suit in platinum, with a navy fox collar and navy fox trim on the cuffs of the coat's sleeves. She didn't miss Tatiana trying to keep her cool when she saw the suit, wondering how Dayeesha could afford it, and then, how she had found it in a different color. It was clear to Dayeesha that one of this mean woman's claims to fame was her exquisite wardrobe and her ability to dress better than most women she encountered.

She sneaked a peak over at Marsha Metcalf, sitting with her very handsome son, Marcus. Marsha looked fresh and stylish in a lilac silk suit that was so pretty on her toffee-colored skin. The skirt was straight and a few inches above the knee. The jacket was a fly peplum design that accentuated Marsha's hourglass figure.

The only thing giving Tatiana's ensemble showstopping status was the hat. It was a tall hat, almost like the Mad Hatter's headpiece, if he had been a woman trying to show off at church. The hat had stacked layers that started with a black fox brim, then a band of gold rhinestones, another layer of black fox fur, another layer of gold rhinestones, and on for a good four layers. All in all, the hat was at least eighteen inches high from the base of the black fox brim, and it twinkled whenever Tatiana moved her head. It was the kind of hat that should have been trying to jump off the pages of the Donna Vinci Web site.

"Daye Daye," Metro whispered to his wife, "How much you think she paid for that hat?"

"A grand?"

"Naw," Metro countered. "I'd bet she dropped a good fifteen hundred."

Dayeesha pulled her iPhone out and sneaked and snapped a picture of the hat. Then she did a quick search and matched up that picture to a price.

Metro whispered, "Did you find the price?"

"Yes," Dayeesha answered slowly, making him wait on the answer. "I told you that this new app for the phone was worth the money. See, if I didn't have it, we wouldn't know her hat cost thirty-two hundred dollars."

"What!" Metro said. "Shoot, I need to get some of those hats for the store."

"Nahh, Baby. We don't need to push that off on our folk at Yeah Yeah—some of them might take you too seriously and start showing up at the club in one of those bad boys. Can't you just see a sister trying to get her swerve on, with a drink in her hand and that hat on her head, when they started playing some throw-back Trinidad James?"

Metro started laughing. He'd seen enough at the club back in the day to know that Daye Daye was on the money with that ob-servation. Sometimes he didn't know who was more trill, folks at church or the folks at the club.

"Buuuttt," Dayeesha said, "I think we might want to think about putting a few pairs of those Christian Louboutins she is rocking in the exclusive section of the store."

"How do you know those are some Louboutins?" Metro asked, because the shoes just looked like some regular high-price, slammin' black suede women's pumps.

"Watch her when she sits down. She will swing her feet so the red soles on the shoes will show, so we'll know she is rockin' some Christian Louboutins."

Metro studied the shoes. They were definitely worthy of go-ing in one of his stores. He pulled out his phone and pulled up the Christian Louboutin Web site.

"Dang, Daye Daye, this brother's stuff is tight! Yeah, we are definitely adding a few pairs of his shoes to the merchandise in our exclusive section. You want me to order you a pair, too?"

"Boy, if you don't order me a pair of those shoes, I'm going to tell folk you are scared of dragonflies."

Metro opened his mouth and looked at their kids to make sure they weren't listening. He didn't need them running around telling people "Daddy scared of dragonflies, Daddy scared of dragonflies," in that sing-songy tone kids used to tease folk.

Dayeesha laughed. She said, "You just get me my shoes and your secret will remain safe with me, until I want another pair."

"I'm gonna pray for you, Dayeesha," Metro told her, and pulled up a scripture on his phone. He had been bitten by a dragonfly when he was young. He didn't know of anybody else who had this experience. So how could he really explain why he was scared of them?

Chapter Five

Dayeesha wasn't the only one in church who saw those nine-hundred-dollar pumps Tatiana was wearing. Marsha Metcalf stared at those shoes for a moment, and then glanced down at her own feet in a sweet pair of black-and-lilac suede platform pumps. Her friend in the shoe department at Sebastian-Fleur had them hidden for her until the shoes were an additional 40 percent off the lowest ticketed price. That was the only way she could afford a pair of shoes like this. And she certainly could not have afforded those shoes that mean Tatiana girl was wearing. Marsha couldn't afford one of those shoes, let alone a pair.

Tatiana Townsend was the most expensively dressed woman in the church this morning. Yet, despite that millionaire's club–priced outfit, the poverty inherent in her character was evident to anyone willing to look past the red soles of her shoes. Watching that woman kept making Marsha think of the scripture in 2 Peter: *A sow that is washed returns to her wallowing in the mud.*

No matter how much money Tatiana spent on her clothes, her hair, her shoes, jewelry, car, the works, she was still a decadent sow. The sad thing was that Tatiana seemed quite oblivious to her true state of affairs. She really believed that her rich and prominent husband, her clothes, and her bank account would make folk think she was a woman of substance—a woman to lift up head and shoulders above the other women in her midst.

Service was progressing along rather quickly, too quickly,

perhaps. Marsha had been so engrossed in the Townsends that she was almost caught off guard when it was time for the meet and greet part of service.

Tatiana hurried down to the altar and made sure everybody saw her talking to Denzelle. She looked over her shoulder, eyes scanning the sanctuary with laserlike precision, in search of the woman her ex was rumored to have a crush on.

But Tatiana completely overlooked Marsha walking down front to speak to Denzelle. She was so busy looking for a replica of herself in much cheaper clothes that she didn't even notice Marsha, who was someone Tatiana would walk right by, as if she didn't exist. It was as if scales were covering Tatiana's eyes for the length of time Marsha was talking to Denzelle.

Tatiana may have missed the exchange between those two, but Metro Mitchell and Marsha's son, Marcus, didn't miss a thing. Reverend Flowers was grinning and laughing, and the twinkle in his eyes was so sparkling and bright, Metro had to fight the urge to whip out his designer shades.

Marcus Metcalf Bluefield was very protective of his mother. He had seen the pain she went through when his father upped and left her for that woman he met while off with his boys at the CIAA Tournament many years ago. Marcus was sad when his father died. But he was also scared straight when that happened. He had been in high school and was acting out over the divorce. But when Rodney passed away, Marcus got right with the Lord and turned his life completely around.

To this day, Marcus didn't know if his father got saved before he died. It was scary not to know if someone escaped spending eternity in hell. Marcus thought about all of the people who acted like they were hell bent on going to hell. He didn't want to be around people like that for a few minutes. So Marcus knew he couldn't take that kind of companionship for all eternity. He hoped his father had been spared that eternal hardship. He also didn't want his mother troubled by that same concern, and got saved.

If losing his dad was hard, learning that his father canceled the life insurance policy that was to help his mom take care of his son in the event of his death made it all that more difficult. Money suddenly became unbearably tight, and Marcus and his mom lost their home. He counted it nothing but the grace of God that they were safely situated in their town house the day the sheriff came to the old house with paperwork to throw them out.

Even worse, his father left his stepmom a million-dollar policy. His dad was so busy making sure the stepmom would continue to live well, he forgot about his own son's pending college tuition needs. But that was alright. Marsha always told her son that when it looked like there was no way out to always keep an eye open for the inevitable "ram in the bush." She always told him to trust God because He always made "a way out of no-way." And to Marcus's delight, that is exactly what God did for him.

The lady everyone said was Rev's ex-wife reminded Marcus of his stepmother. They were mean, privileged, and very spoiled women. Sometimes Marcus wondered why God let people act like that—and that included his father, Rodney. It seemed to him that people like that could do and say all kinds of bad things and get away with it. Like this morning. That woman shouldn't have been able to stroll up in this church and bother his pastor like that.

But then, Marcus reasoned silently, if the pastor reached out to a good woman like his mother, maybe he wouldn't have stupid stuff like this jumping off on a Sunday morning. It was like Reverend Flowers believed that if he swore off having a woman in his life, his troubles with women would dissolve, like salt in warm water. As far as Marcus was concerned, Reverend Flowers acted like he got upset with himself because he couldn't help wanting a woman in his life.

"That is so stupid," Marcus mumbled to himself, so deep in thought he hadn't noticed that his mother had just sat back down next to him.

"You say something, Baby?" Marsha asked her son, wondering

what caused those furrows in his brow. She reached up and ran her fingers gently across his forehead.

"Mom!" Marcus said, more upset with himself for needing the comfort of her touch like that. He sighed. Maybe he was being too hard on Reverend Flowers. He understood. Mom was so sweet and kind, she could make a brother really soften under her touch.

"Poor Pastor," he mumbled.

"Poor Pastor what?" Marsha asked, curious as to why her son was speaking as if he were in some way empathetic toward Denzelle.

"Oh, I just feel bad that the pastor has to deal with someone like that lady," Marcus said, knowing his mother wasn't buying that. He couldn't blurt out things around his mother. She heard everything, and could discern stuff you weren't ready for her to know about.

"Soooo," Marcus said casually, hoping to get his mom off of his trail, "how is Reverend Flowers doing this morning?"

"Fine, I guess," Marsha answered her son, and then looked up at him. "Marcus, why are you so concerned about Den—"

She stopped and caught herself when she saw her son's right eyebrow go up.

"Doesn't the pastor look okay to you?" Marsha said, in the most nonchalant tone she could muster up. The last person on earth she wanted to peep out her crush on Denzelle Flowers was Mr. Marcus Metcalf Bluefield.

"Umm . . . hmm. Well, actually, Mom, he looks better now," Marcus answered with a soft laugh, thinking that his mother was hilarious. So Mom has a serious crushy-crush on old boy. *Interesting.*

Marsha started reading her bulletin like it was the Bible. The worse thing in the world for a mom was a nosey child who was determined to start poking around in a mom's business. She was going to have to be extra careful when Marcus was around when she talked to Denzelle. Because Marsha knew that Mr. Man was going to be watching her like he was the daddy and she was the child.

When the visitors were asked to stand up, Tatiana hopped up and talked right over the man who had stood up first and was in the process of trying to introduce himself and his wife and family.

She said, "Good morning, Christian friends," in the fakest and most overly proper church voice.

"If she adds 'Rs' or a few 'eerrerrrs' to the ends of her words, I'm walking out of church," Dayeesha whispered to Metro.

"I am Tatiana Hill Flowers Townsend. My husband, Dr. Todd Townsend, and I are relocating here so that he can take a top position as head of the trauma center at Duke Medical Center. We are looking for a home and a church home. I knew that New Jerusalem would be a wonderful place to start, because my darling ex-husband is the pastor. As the former first lady of this church, I will be standing in the back in the receiving line to greet each and every one of you after service."

I wasn't aware that old girl has ever sat foot in this church. And now she's the former first lady? Dayeesha texted her husband, Metro.

And the Golden Globe Award for best performance by an actress playing a lunatic feigning sanity goes to that lying heifer up there, Metro texted back to his wife.

Poor Denzelle was flabbergasted over that maneuver. First, he didn't think Tatiana would ever want to come to a church he pastored again. At least, that is what she instructed her attorney to tell him during the back-and-forth nightmare known as their divorce. And even though he believed Tatiana was capable of many things, this was weird and suspect even for her.

But if Denzelle was flabbergasted, Todd was floored. He turned red, and then all of the color drained from his face, making him look even more like the, "Is he a brother?" black man that he was. Todd tugged at Tatiana's hand, as encouragement for her to slow her roll. But that only seemed to egg her on. Because when the doors of the church were opened, Tatiana walked right down to the altar where Denzelle was standing, and Todd, who personally really had no use for church, had no choice but to hurry down there to stand with his wife.

When Reverend Flowers instructed his church officers to come forth and extend the right hand of fellowship to their new members, the other folk in the pews were so happy that they were not officers. Few, if anybody, in the church wanted to shake that crazy women's hand. They felt sorry for the officers, because they really didn't have a choice but to fulfill this portion of their duties in serving the church.

"I sure hope that heifer doesn't make good on her promise to stand with the pastor in the receiving line," Veronica Washington leaned over and whispered to Marsha.

"Well, you are hoping in vain," Marsha whispered back. "Because that thang looks like she can't wait to go and stand in the first lady spot. What in the world would make a woman do something that crazy?"

"You," Veronica answered her friend matter-of-factly.

"Me? Why? She doesn't even know me."

"Technically—she doesn't know you. But she knows of you. I don't know if you know this, but that Tatiana is friends with Yolanda Richardson. Tatiana doesn't know what you look like, because Yolanda doesn't strike me as somebody capable of giving an accurate description of someone else. But the crazy skank still knows that you exist and are a member of this church."

Marsha just rolled her eyes upward. This was crazy. Why would Tatiana care about her one way or the other? Denzelle was her ex-husband, a fact made pure reality by the presence of her present husband.

"And," Veronica continued, "Yolanda has been trying to hook up with Rev for a minute. Yolanda can't stand you because she has peeped Denzelle's card where you are concerned. And that girl just wants to get some mess started at your expense to be mean."

"What?" Marsha whispered loudly. "First, I thought you said that Yolanda and that crazy woman are friends."

"They are. Well, actually, they are what I call skank buddies. You know—skanks who hang together and pretend to be friends because they need somebody to talk to on the phone and go shopping with."

"She's right, Mom," Marcus whispered, hoping this conversation would soon end. It was hard overhearing this parent-puppy-love stuff. Based on the information Marcus was able to sneak and hear, it sounded like the pastor needed to step up his game if he was so into his mom and all of this kind of drama was popping off in church. And as far as Marcus was concerned, his mother was the poster girl for being a Proverbs 31 woman, and she deserved for a man to practically beat her door down to get her as his own treasure.

Veronica and Marsha turned to look at their godson and son. He kind of shrugged and said, "I'm a junior at Eva T. Marshall University. Don't you think I've seen skanks pretending to be each other's friends just so they can get something they can't get on their own?"

"He has a point, Marsha," Veronica said, glad that her godson was able to sniff out the skanks at such an early age. A lot of men didn't acquire that skill until they were much older.

"I still don't understand why that woman would do all of this because of me. She is rich and married and wearing real designer clothes."

"Marsha, Marsha, Marsha," Veronica said, like she was talking to Marsha Brady on the old school *Brady Bunch* TV show. "Pastor has a soft spot for you, and Miss Thangy-Thang don't like that one bit—even if she doesn't know who you are."

"Her new husband is a rich doctor, Veronica. She shouldn't care what Denzelle does."

"She shouldn't but she does. That girl is one of those women who doesn't want to see a man she discarded happy and with someone else. Just because the fool doesn't want Denzelle doesn't mean that she won't get mad about him wanting somebody other than herself."

"But Roni," Marsha whispered, "ain't she kinda late on that? Denzelle has had a lot of women since she left him for that doctor of hers."

Veronica sighed and rolled her eyes. Marsha could be so slow at times. She said, "Marsha, Denzelle didn't have a soft spot for those other women. They were just some "tap that a" calls. Okay? That crazy woman doesn't care about them. But she does care about somebody Denzelle can really like. Someone like you."

"That's crazy," Marsha spat out in a loud whisper, hoping she was not showing a reaction to the second part of what Veronica said.

"Yeah, it is crazy, because that heifer is rolling way past insanity."

Marcus started coughing to stop himself from busting out laughing. His auntie Veronica was a trip. And this conversation was on its way to rolling way past insanity.

"Mom, I can't believe you and Auntie Roni have talked through the entire last part of service."

Marsha couldn't believe that they had been so busy talking that they missed altar prayer and were now watching Denzelle prepare for the recessional.

Denzelle walked out of the pulpit, followed by his associate pastors, the choir, and the members of the Steward Board who had served in the pulpit this morning. When the last steward was on his way up the aisle, Tatiana grabbed Todd's hand, and they hopped in the recessional line right before the choir made its way up the aisle. Tatiana instructed Todd to stand next to the last Steward Board member in the line, and she went and stood right next to her ex-husband, like they were still married.

The pastor was beyond being outdone by this display. This was such a ghetto move. Denzelle's first inclination was to order Tatiana and her light-skinned man to go somewhere and sit down. In fact, it had taken all of the salvation in him to refrain from refusing those two the right to membership in his church. But he decided to allow this fiasco to run its course.

Denzelle couldn't wait to see what was going to happen when folk started pouring through the receiving line. Tatiana wasn't the friendliest of people. She hated having to talk to and grin at people she thought were beneath her.

She got away with being snooty at his old church, because she had been the first lady for real back then. But this was different. Folk at New Jerusalem didn't know Tatiana, they didn't want to know Tatiana, and they didn't give a hoot who she was. Tatiana was going to get her feelings hurt if she kept standing in that line next to him like somebody who didn't have good sense.

When the first wave of folk made their way through the receiving line, they greeted their pastor, and then recoiled when they witnessed the cold and dismissive attitude of their newest member. One of the older members had extended her hand to Tatiana, who looked at her hand like it was covered with big green buggers. The woman looked Tatiana dead in the eye and said, "Why would you hop your fancy butt up in this line if you knew you were too mean and stuck-up to speak to folk right?"

Tatiana glanced over at Denzelle as if to say, Are you going to let her talk to me like that.

All Denzelle did was issue an extra blessing to his member and then greet the next person in line. He was glad she had put Tatiana in her place.

The reprimand did not help Tatiana's deteriorating mood. Things were not working out anywhere close to what she'd hoped when she first plotted this maneuver. She stood in that line looking and acting so hateful that most of the members walked right by her as if they didn't even know she was there.

These unexpected snubs from Denzelle's church members were infuriating. Tatiana tugged on Denzelle's robe. Denzelle acted like he didn't feel a thing—he just kept on greeting his parishioners.

"Do something," she hissed.

Denzelle acted like he hadn't heard his ex-wife. He continued to greet his church folk, hoping this fool would get the message and go over and stand with her man in his preppy white boy suit. If Denzelle had the kind of money he suspected Todd Townsend made, there was no way he'd show up anywhere dressed like that.

Todd had moved from his assigned spot and was now standing off to the side talking to a group of nice church women and secretly wondering if his wife still had a thing for her ex-husband. He wished his wife would come and stand with him, or at least stand somewhere other than up under Denzelle Flowers, grinning like she was the one rare person who actually won the Publishers Clearing House Sweepstakes.

Chapter Six

Marsha went to the end of the receiving line three times, because she did not want to say good morning to the pastor while that woman was standing next to him. She had too much to deal with right now and knew she would not act like a Christian if that Tatiana rubbed her the wrong way with some mean girl all growed up mess. What did the pastor ever see in that hard-hearted woman with the real cute shoes?

While Marsha kept making repeated runs to the end of the line, Tatiana was scanning that same line with great care. She wanted to find the woman Yolanda Richardson said had caught her ex-husband's eye. Tatiana knew this woman had not come through the line, because Denzelle kept staring around like he was looking for somebody. And he had not greeted any woman in a special or intimate manner.

Her predatory eyes zoomed in on the three women who kept hanging behind the last people in line. Two of the three were in Denzelle's preferred age group. They had the look of the type of woman she knew her ex-husband would find attractive—well dressed, their own hair, down-to-earth demeanor, and friendly. Both women looked like they were excellent cooks—something Denzelle prized and one thing Tatiana could not do. Even though she'd hooked Denzelle years ago, Tatiana always secretly knew that his true dream woman was very much like those two women— especially the short one.

Marsha, Veronica Washington, and Keisha Jackson were comparing notes and hoping their pastor's hincty ex-wife would hurry up and get out of the line.

Keisha looked up and saw Tatiana scoping them out. Something was seriously wrong with that woman, or she was on something and good at hiding it.

"Is she all there?"

"What do you mean by that, Keisha?" Veronica asked.

"I mean, why is she standing with Reverend Flowers like she is the first lady? And she is with her husband. That is beyond being trill. In fact, I find it kind of disturbing."

Keisha studied Dr. Todd's outfit and frowned.

"Y'all, look at his pants. Why? That's all I have to say. Why?"

Marsha stared at Todd's pants and said, "Those pants look like he purchased them from the superboring white-boy section of Brooks Brothers."

"You mean 'bought'?" Keisha said, shaking her head. It was a shame for that black man to dress like that. He looked like one of the black guest correspondents on MSNBC people couldn't stand to listen to.

"No," Marsha answered. "I mean just what I said—purchased. You *buy* what Metro Mitchell is wearing. That corny mess was *purchased.*"

Veronica started laughing. She could not believe those two were in church arguing over the semantics of Denzelle's ex's lame husband's apparel *purchases.* But maybe they needed to fuss over some minutia-laden issue to take the edge off what they were all facing as the newly unemployed. Veronica had gone over her checkbook three times this morning and didn't know how she was going to make her funds cover her until the end of the month. She said, "I have to agree with Marsha, Keisha girl. He had the nerve to have cuffs put in those pants, and they are not even long enough. His pants are barely skimming the top of where his oxfords come up to his ankles. You know brothers wear their pants longer than that, and they don't put on some butt-ugly shoes like that."

"Now, look at Pastor," Keisha added. "He is over there in a preacher robe, and he is still as fly as can be."

Marsha sneaked a looked at Denzelle. It was a shame how good that man looked in his clerical robe. She put a fingertip to her heart, as she thought, "Lord, I am so sorry to be thinking about how good that robe looks on that man."

"That's a sharp robe," Veronica said.

"Yeah." Keisha added, "Pastor is wearing that thing."

Denzelle knew he was looking exceptional this morning. Metro Mitchell's cousin, Naye Naye, had designed this robe especially for him. It was black brocade silk, with black velvet crosses trimmed in crimson and cream silk on the sleeves, along with a black velvet stole trimmed in the same crimson and cream silk. He was wearing a black silk clerical shirt with the customary white collar, a platinum chain with a diamond cross hanging on it, and some custom-made black slip-on shoes with the thinnest red trimming on them.

Tatiana had forgotten how well-dressed her ex-husband was. She could not believe he had outdressed Todd in a preacher's robe. She watched Denzelle for a moment, and then followed his gaze all the way back to the short sister with the boobs and hips, and the head full of thick, gorgeous hair.

"So, that's her," Tatiana thought, and suppressed an urge to frown.

That woman was competition and didn't even know it. She could see why Denzelle liked her. The woman struck Tatiana as sincere, and not overly concerned with status and outdoing folk.

Tatiana knew that her American Express Black Card, designer clothes, and new million-dollar home in Chapel Hill's Governor's Club would mean absolutely nothing to a woman like that. About the only way Tatiana could get at her was to mistreat the girl on the sly whenever they encountered one another. And she knew that would be short-lived. Women like that would get you straight if you came at them one time too many.

Tatiana was growing tired of Todd. He was so boring, and

most of his friends were high-ranking white people at the hospital and medical school. And most of Todd's white friends weren't even cool white people—they were just really really smart, well paid, and white. Tatiana thought she'd puke if she went to one more cocktail party with caviar, hummus, and just plain wine.

Caviar was nasty, and hummus tasted like morning breath. Sometimes she wanted to go to a party where everybody was carrying a purple Crown Royal liquor bag and eating the kind of finger foods you could only get at a well-stocked black people event. Her mouth watered at the thought of hot wings, shrimp, fried veggies with the dip, tortilla chips and homemade salsa, potato salad, deviled eggs, juicy chunks of fruit, all kinds of fancy crackers and cheeses, tuna and chicken salad, Swedish meatballs, big old cookies, chunky squares of homemade chocolate cake, and sweet tea.

Tatiana Townsend needed a change in her life, and was hoping she could work her way back into Denzelle's good graces. That is why she had schemed and plotted to get Todd to accept the job offer from Duke University. She wanted to be closer to Denzelle and all of the church action that was bound to be associated with a prominent and well-respected pastor in the Gospel United Church.

Things had changed in the years since she left Denzelle. Back then he was a small-time pastor with limits on his budget. Tatiana rubbed her hand across the smooth, black crocodile leather of her Nancy Gonzales purse. There was no way she would have been able to afford a $2,700 pocketbook on Denzelle's old salary. Only someone earning money like Todd could do a girl right in the purse department.

But things had changed. Denzelle's church had over three thousand members who were faithful in their tithes and offerings, and it showed. Plus, Denzelle was a busy pastor, and he had money coming in from all kinds of sources to run his vast ministries. What had she been thinking to let this fine, sexy man go for Todd?

Tatiana slid her hand threw the loop in Denzelle's arm like they were still a couple, and then gazed down in the direction of that woman in the lilac suit, hoping she'd see them like this. Marsha didn't miss that bold move. She also didn't miss witnessing Denzelle removing Tatiana's hand and signaling to an usher to come and take the girl to her husband.

Once Tatiana was put in her place, Marsha, Veronica, and Keisha walked up to the pastor to shake his hand. Denzelle gave both Keisha and Veronica warm handshakes. But he saved the hug for Marsha, laughing when she pulled back, being careful to give him the church hug—which was a very chaste hug, when you grabbed a person from the side and then quickly moved back and away from them.

"I won't bite, Marsha," Denzelle whispered in her ear, and then chuckled when she looked up at him, perplexed.

Keisha didn't miss a thing. And she made a mental note to call Dayeesha to get some 411 on what was going on with the pastor. 'Cause if her expert eyes served her right, Reverend Flowers had it kind of bad for Marsha and was trying to play it off like he didn't have it as bad as he did.

"Men," she whispered.

Pastor looked like the kind of brother who would run from matters of the heart. She'd bet the last few dollars in her bank account that he'd told his own-self something real dumb and stupid like "I am going to put all of my time and energy into my work. As long as I work from sun up to sun down, I won't have to worry about worrying that I am sad and lonely and with no decent quality of life to speak of."

Keisha looked at the robe Reverend Flowers was wearing and thought, "It's a shame that Rev is walking around, sharp as can be, and there is no one in his life to tell him how good he looks in his preacher uniform before he comes out to minister to the flock."

She walked down the hall to the bathroom and almost walked right into Tatiana Townsend. Keisha's first response was to show her home training and say "excuse me." But Tatiana's expression was so hard and full of venom that she decided to throw manners to the wind. Keisha stopped and stared Tatiana up and down, and then rolled her eyes at the woman when they made eye contact.

Tatiana drew back, surprised that this ghetto church girl took her on like that. She looked at Keisha's outfit. She'd seen it in a J.C. Penny's catalog. It was very cute and fit Keisha well. But it was still from J.C. Penny's.

She turned her mouth down and mumbled, "Cute but cheap" loud enough for Keisha to overhear her.

Keisha took in Tatiana's outfit. It could have paid her rent for almost three months. She said, "Frankenstein-shaped-head heifer" loud enough for everybody to hear her.

A few folk chuckled. And one little girl tugged at her mother's hand and said, "Mommy, I told you that lady in *The Young and the Restless* lady clothes looked like she is a Frankenstein lady. She's kinda pretty like. But her head is big and square and looks like it used to have bolts in it."

The mother put a forefinger to her lips and whispered, "Shhh, it's not very nice to call people Frankensteins out loud and in church, Baby."

"But, Mommy, that's how she looks. You are always telling me to tell the truth. Jesus always told the truth. And sometimes He said things people didn't want to hear Him say."

The mother didn't quite know what to say, because her baby was right. She leaned down and whispered, "It's true, but we don't want to talk about it out loud. It might hurt the lady's feelings."

The little girl smiled and said, "Let's finish this in the car. Can I text Daddy and tell him about the lady?"

"Not right now, Baby," the mother answered, wishing the Frankenstein lady would quit staring at them like that.

Tatiana wanted to slap Keisha silly, and then give what was left over to that bad little girl. She must have fell and bumped her head to think she should think about joining a church Denzelle pastored. She didn't like the people here, and it was clear the feeling was mutual. Come to think of it, the people at his old church didn't like her.

The worse part of this fiasco was coming to terms with Denzelle not wanting any part of her. Like most folk who called the shots in a painful breakup, Tatiana was having a hard time digesting that all of the stuff she did to her ex-husband made him want her as much as he wanted to wear those pants Todd had on this morning. Denzelle wouldn't be caught dead in that outfit. And it looked like he didn't want to be caught dead with Tatiana, either.

It was amazing how upset folk who rejected and dogged-out a good person became when they discovered that person didn't want them anymore. Tatiana had a big ego, and she always believed Denzelle would be so happy for her to want him back. Based on how he was acting, it was clear Denzelle didn't even want her as a member of his church.

After seeing Denzelle in that robe and watching the women ogle him, it was clear that the reason Tatiana was so unhappy was because she was married to a trauma surgeon. It wasn't a doctor that would make her happy. Tatiana needed a preacher to be happy.

Tatiana didn't know why she hadn't thought of this when she was wishing Todd would die, so she could be happy and have enough money to enjoy her happiness. It was Todd's bank account and being the wife of a well-known surgeon that gave Tatiana the illusion that her happiness was with Todd Townsend. But now she knew better and could finally see the light.

It was clear that being the wife of a prominent pastor was the answer to all of her problems. Plus, as the first lady, Tatiana would actually have more clout in her church than she would as a rich doctor's wife. And if her husband ran for bishop and won? That was like winning the Indy 500. The bishop's wife, or the Episcopal Supervisor, could be an enviable position if you worked it right.

On second thought, Tatiana was glad Denzelle dissed her. She didn't think he had any interest in running for bishop. And being a pastor's wife wouldn't suffice. Tatiana would need more prestige than that.

She closed her eyes and tried to think of a good-looking and wealthy pastor who would run for bishop in the next year.

"Xavier!" Tatiana exclaimed out loud and then started coughing, hoping no one heard what she said. There weren't a lot of Xavier's in the Gospel United Church, and somebody would figure out that she was talking about Reverend Xavier Franklin

Xavier Franklin was the perfect choice for a new husband. And with her by his side, Reverend Franklin would be a sureshot winner in that very expensive and competitive race for a place in the church's Episcopacy.

Tatiana was going to have to work fast, though. There was a lot to do if she planned on becoming the first lady of Xavier's church before the Triennial Conference rolled around. She didn't know how she was going to work that out, however. First, Tatiana was still married to Todd, who considered their union a 'til death do us part kind of deal. Second, she had gotten used to living well off of Todd's money. And third, Xavier was married, too. It was a good thing that neither of them had children.

Maybe she and Todd could separate, she would stay in the house, Todd could pay her household expenses, and Tatiana and Xavier could become an item. A legal separation would give her a legal right to have a man in her life. It would also keep the money flowing in until the divorce was final. And if Tatiana could make Todd think she was coming back to him, he'd probably be more likely to pay what she wanted him to pay.

Tatiana had walked all the way back to the front of the church in this dreamlike state, working out the details of her plan while waiting on Todd to go and get the car. It all seemed so perfect until Todd pulled up and blew the horn to get her attention.

"Babe, you ready?" he asked, wondering what put that cat who ate the canary grin on his wife's face. Sometimes Tatiana made him uncomfortable when she went off into space like that. Todd wasn't much on this God thing. But Tatiana could make him spend some time in prayer when she looked like that.

Tatiana shook her head like she was coming out of a trance. She stared at Todd's top-of-the-line Mercedes and frowned. This was not going to be easy. She would have to keep Todd in check while she dated Xavier, help Xavier keep his wife in check while they dated, plan the divorces, and get some really ruthless lawyers to suck as much money out of Todd as possible.

"This is going to be some work," Tatiana mumbled while getting in the car.

"What is going to be some work, Babe?" Todd asked, and then shivered when his wife looked at him. If he didn't know better, he could have sworn Tatiana had the hard glint of someone who wanted to kill you in her eyes.

Todd suppressed the second shiver that ran up his spine. He reached out and covered Tatiana's hand with his, hoping to ignite some warmth between them. He said, "Never thought I'd say this, but I want to come back to this church, Babe. And I don't care if the pastor is your ex-husband. This is a good church with good people in it."

Tatiana was so shocked, she started hyperventilating. One of the key parts of this plan she had just started working on rested on Todd being a man who didn't like going to church. Now he was talking about coming back here to worship again?

"Are you alright, Babe?" Todd asked.

She started sweating and rolled the window down to get some air. The attack subsided. This was not going to be easy. This man was not going to give her up without a fight.

"I'm fine, Darling," Tatiana answered weakly. She couldn't wait until she was with a man like Xavier, who could roll the word "baby" off of his tongue like it was something good to eat. She wanted to be called Baby like that so bad, it almost made her cry.

It suddenly occurred to Tatiana that if Todd wanted to come to Denzelle's church, it would be easier to figure out a way to get to Xavier's church without her husband. She was going to have to move fast to get to Xavier, make him fall in love with her, and then move toward becoming Xavier's wife.

The more she thought about planning how to make this work, the better she felt. It had been months since Tatiana felt like there was something to live for. Some days it took everything in her to get out of bed and pretend to Todd that she was happy and on top of the world. Now, just the thought of Xavier, whom she hadn't seen in over a year, made Tatiana feel all tingly and so alive.

As much as there was to do to put this plan into action, the one thing Tatiana didn't have to worry about was convincing Xavier to hook up with her. Xavier Franklin had always had a thing for Tatiana, and would jump at the chance to have an affair with the good Reverend Denzelle Flowers's ex-wife. The only thing Tatiana had to do was inform her new lover that this was not a fly-by-night thing. They would have an affair until they could get married.

The one real big problem in this plan was Xavier's wife, Camille Creighton Franklin, who had all of the money in their marriage. Camille came from money. Her mother had been a North Carolina black socialite, whose family owned the Classy Clean Car Wash Company.

Camille's father, Revered Dr. Creighton, had left her a boatload of cash when he died, too. He had been a prominent theologian and professor at Eva T. Marshall University's Divinity School. Reverend Creighton had also made a lot of money from his three cleaners—Clean Inside Cleaners.

Xavier came from people who didn't have a pot to piss in. He was smart, fine, sexy, and suave. He was not, however, a black man with good credit on his own, or some extra cash to dispose of on his other woman. Tatiana's good credit came from Todd paying off her AMX Black Card expenses on time every month. Xavier's purchasing power was totally dependent on that mean and ugly woman he married in exchange for some cash in the bank.

"Pimping show ain't easy," Tatiana whispered to herself, with a tear streaming down her right cheek.

"Babe, are you going through the change?" Todd asked, now concerned.

"Yes, Darling. I am most definitely going through a change of life," she said, and then cheered up. Change of life was the perfect way to describe what Tatiana was planning on going through.

Todd put the car in drive and glanced at his wife out of the corner of his eye. He could have sworn Tatiana had gone from a boo-hooing moment to absolute delight in less than sixty seconds. His car didn't go from zero to sixty that fast—and Todd drove a Mercedes CLS63 AMG. The el-cheapo cars in this class started at over ninety grand.

Dayeesha and Metro walked out of church with their three children skipping behind them just as the Townsends were about to pull off. Dayeesha did not miss the self-satisfied expression on Tatiana's face. She also didn't miss how quickly that smirk turned into a scowl when Tatiana's eyes locked on Dayeesha's suit.

"You know something, Metro," Dayeesha said, and pointed at Tatiana, making sure that skank saw her. "She looks like the killing girl on a Lifetime Movie Network movie. You know, the woman who comes back to a town acting all innocent, when in reality she showed up just to kill some man or his wife at the high school reunion. And nobody believes she's that evil until a bunch of weird and crappy stuff starts happening to people."

"Baby, I keep telling you that you watch way too much LMN," Metro admonished, and then said, all in the same breath. "Don't let her give you anything to eat or drink, though. I don't trust her."

Dayeesha laughed. Metro knew that lady look like one of those smooth LMN killers who plotted and schemed about everything she did—down to simple stuff, like what kind of soap she was going to put in her bathrooms.

"Metro, you know that girl looks like an LMN killer woman."

Metro tried to ignore Dayeesha. He knew his wife was right.

That woman did look like one of those crazy heifers on Lifetime. But Metro didn't want to answer Dayeesha, because then he'd have to confess to watching a few Lifetime Movie Network movies when he was home watching the kids. It wasn't like Metro didn't love ESPN or MSNBC. But sometimes a brother wanted to sneak and watch a good Lifetime Movie Network movie.

"Daddy likes watching Lifetime Movie Network when you aren't home, Mommy," their older son, Joseph, said.

"How do you know?" Dayeesha asked.

"Cuz we all like to watch them with him, too. He makes us popcorn and juice when we we watch those movies with Daddy."

"I see," Dayeesha answered her son, with a smirk on her face.

Metro looked at his children and said, "Why y'all got to front a dad off like that? Y'all don't have to tell your mama all of that."

"So you don't want us to tell Mommy that one of those movies made you cry, Daddy," their daughter, Jeneene chimed in.

Dayeesha looked at the supercool Metro Mitchell with a raised eyebrow. He said, "Okay, it was the movie about the little ten-year-old boy who hid under water, breathing though a piece of reed, so he could hide from the killers. Then he climbed out of the lake and sneaked back up to the house and found his parents, who had been beaten real bad, untied them, sneaked and started the car, and then drove them to safety before the killers, who were out looking for him, came back."

"Yeah," Dayeesha said, tearing up. "I saw that one. I cried for thirty minutes after they made it safely to the police station, and the killers got shot running up in there trying to get them. That was a good movie."

"Yeah, it was real good, Mommy," Jeneene said. "The little boy's name was Jeremiah, like our Jeremiah."

"Umm hmm," Jeremiah Mitchell said. "At the beginning of the movie, the movie Jeremiah used to walk around his house with his parents, telling them to fix their security system. He kept giving them a warning just like the prophet Jeremiah in the

Bible. They should have listened to him, then they wouldn't be all beat up and tied up like they were."

Jeremiah's older brother popped him in the back of his head.

"Oww, why you hit me?"

"Because if they listened to him there wouldn't have been a movie. They were supposed to be all hardheaded and not listen to a little boy with sense, to make the movie good."

"Yeah," Jeneene added. "See, that's why you and Mommy need to make sure you listen to us, Daddy. We might be telling you something that will keep all of us safe."

Metro shook his head and went to get the car. His three children with Dayeesha were something else.

Chapter Seven

Reverend Denzelle Flowers was at his desk studying the portfolio on the church's Pastor's Aide Club account that had only recently become available. The fund had been set up years ago by a now deceased church mother, Clara Mae Davidson, in honor of her late husband, Reverend Chuckie Lee Davidson, who served as the assistant pastor at New Jerusalem back in the 1980s.

The Davidsons had been prominent church members with deep pockets because their family owned the Clean Car Wash Company. There wasn't a black person in Raleigh, Durham, Chapel Hill, and Mebane, North Carolina, who didn't take their cars to the Clean Car Wash Company at least one time.

Denzelle almost fell out of his chair when he saw the eight-hundred-thousand-dollar account balance for the fund Mrs. Davidson had set up for New Jerusalem, only to fix it so that she controlled it until the day she died. Mrs. Davidson had been the nightmare church member every black church in America wished it didn't have to have—a mean and unsaved lifelong church member who tried to run the church and tell the pastor what to do by any means necessary.

Denzelle didn't even know how much money was in the account until Mrs. Davidson died three weeks before Marsha, Veronica, and Keisha got fired from their jobs. Clara Mae Davidson was clearly good with money and investments. But Mrs. Davidson would not give the church access to the money because she didn't like Reverend Flowers. In fact, Mrs. Davidson didn't like anybody she couldn't rule over. Rumor had it that the late Reverend Chuckie Lee Davidson didn't do anything without Clara Mae's permission. He didn't even pick out his own underwear.

So the money had been sitting in that account, collecting interest like it was dust, until Mrs. Davidson got so mad at all of the people she couldn't stand and died just to get back at them. And all of that money she sat on all of these years would now become accessible to the very man she vowed to never help— Reverend Denzelle Flowers. Imagine that: Close to a million church dollars from a woman who once bragged she had never tithed a day in her life.

When Dayeesha first told Denzelle of the three women being fired, he immediately thought of using that money to hire them to do some much needed work for the church. But that was proving to be a problem. Even in death, Clara Mae Davidson was reaching out from the grave to try and put a stranglehold on the pastor and her church. Denzelle learned that he could use the money—as long as he used it solely to fund activities for the now defunct Pastor's Aide Club at New Jerusalem Gospel United Church.

Church lore had it that Mrs. Davidson had once been the head of the Pastor's Aide Club, back in the day when those types of auxiliary organizations carried clout in the church. The backlog of church gossip, however, claimed that Clara Mae was so invested in the Pastor's Aide Club because she was having a hot and torrid affair with the man who pastored the church before Reverend Boudreaux came to New Jerusalem. The club was just a ruse for her to have an excuse to see her man.

At first Denzelle didn't want to believe that about Mrs. Clara Mae Davidson. For starters, she wasn't exactly the prettiest woman in the church. Denzelle always thought she looked like an ostrich with a tiny silver afro. And then, Mrs. Davidson was uptight, and so prim and proper he couldn't fathom her holding a man's hand, let alone sneaking off to the hotel to get her freak

on. Just the thought of Mrs. Davidson calling some man "Daddy"
was enough to give Denzelle nightmares for weeks on end.

He had been ready to jump right into using that money until
it became clear it was only for a Pastor's Aide Club that nobody
at New Jerusalem wanted back in action. Many folk in Denzelle's
age group and younger dreaded being asked to run the Pastor's
Aide Club, or having to go to one of the club's activities. They
had grown up with this organization and didn't have the best
memories of Mrs. Davidson and her club.

As one of the Trustee Board members said when they met to
discuss the merits of reactivating the Pastor's Aide Club, "Pastor,
I don't want to do any Pastor's Aide Club business. When I was
little I got tired of getting in trouble for asking for more cake and
extra punch when that haint decided to put on something for the
pastor. Miss Clara Mae was so stingy with her food that she mea-
sured out slivers of cake with a ruler."

Denzelle laughed. His trustee was right. He and his brother,
Yarborough, had grown up in Fayetteville Street Gospel United
Church under their uncle, Reverend Russell Flowers. Denzelle
knew, firsthand, the kind of terror someone running the Pastor's
Aide Club could inflict on fellow church members.

But he was going to have to get over it, where Pastor's Aide
Clubs were concerned. Denzelle needed that money, and if reactivating the boring Pastor's Aide Club was the only way to get it,
then New Jerusalem was going to have to just suck it up and deal
with it. Now that he'd made up his mind to get it back up and
running, the only thing left to do was convince those three unemployed women they needed to help him run it.

Denzelle was sitting in his office with three checks and three
tasks for the new and improved club. He closed his eyes for a moment, thinking about how to deal with all of the questions he knew
Keisha Jackson was going to shoot at him. Veronica was going to
try to reshape his proposal to suit her sensibilities. And Marsha
Metcalf was going to be real quiet—and dumbfounded when she
saw what he had instructed Dayeesha to prepare for her to do.

He flipped through the three proposals and suddenly got cold feet about this venture. What in the world was he thinking, letting Dayeesha talk him into this? It had all sounded real good over breakfast with the Mitchells. But now Pastor was getting a little nervous about enlisting these women to give him the help he needed.

Denzelle opened his Bible to find a scripture that would help him run this meeting right. He went to Psalms, Ecclesiastes, Ephesians, and 1Kings before turning to Proverbs 3 and reading verses 5 and 6. That was it. Why was he worrying? All he had to do was trust in the Lord with all of his heart and mind and soul and try real hard to refrain from leaning on his own limited understanding.

There was a hard knock on the door before it flew open. Dayeesha never knocked to ask permission to come in. Her knocks were just to warn him that she was coming in. Denzelle didn't know what to do with Dayeesha Hamilton Mitchell sometimes. She was something else—just like her crazy daddy. She was also the best administrative assistant he'd ever had.

"Reverend Flowers, Marsha is here," Dayeesha told him, and then chuckled softly. This was going to be good—watching Rev trying to be all cool, like he wasn't superhappy that Marsha was earlier than the other two women.

"Send her in," Denzelle answered, hoping he sounded preacherly. He had secretly hoped Marsha would arrive earlier than Veronica and Keisha, because he wanted to be alone with her.

"Okay," was all Dayeesha said right before Marsha walked in solo. Dayeesha knew she was so wrong to call Veronica and Keisha this morning and ask if they could come to the church twenty minutes after the time Marsha was scheduled to arrive.

Marsha walked into Denzelle's office and stood in the middle of the floor. She did not want to be in here with him all by herself. That was just too much Denzelle for her.

Denzelle got up and came around from his desk and got

himself an eyeful of Marsha—his eyes going over her like a high-powered scope.

"Yes, lawd," he whispered to himself.

"Huh?" Marsha said, looking perplexed, and quickly reminding Denzelle how uncool the girl was.

"You are looking very nice this morning," he told her in his preacher voice. Truth was, Marsha was looking better than very nice this morning. The girl was looking downright delectable in a pair of dove gray denim capris and a ruffled T-shirt in pale pink. Those pink, gray, and white–sequined Chuck Taylors added some nice flava. And Marsha's thick, chocolate-colored hair, with silver streaks running through it, was pulled up in a bouncy ponytail with a pink, gray, and white scarf that made it hard for Denzelle to refrain from reaching out and giving it a good tug.

All of that pink on that toffee-colored skin was working on Denzelle. And he deemed it totally unfair that Marsha was wearing one of the scents in the Vera Wang line of colognes. He knew those colognes well, even if he didn't know the name of each one. Denzelle had bought a lot of Vera Wang for his women before he "retired" from being a career "ho."

Marsha looked up at Denzelle, smiled, and extended her hand. She didn't know what else to do with a player like Denzelle Flowers—especially since she had a crush on the man. She hated that—having a crush on Denzelle Flowers, of all people. Denzelle was a ladies man—the worse kind of man to be sweet on, as far as Marsha was concerned.

Denzelle stared at Marsha's hand and then looked her dead in the eye, right before he got close enough to whisper, "You know I do not want to just shake your hand," in a low sexy voice.

Marsha jumped back and sat down in the first chair she saw. What was wrong with Denzelle? Why was he always messing with her like that, and then never making good on those little hints? It was frustrating, and at times infuriating.

When Marsha was reserved with Denzelle, he came after her.

If she responded in any way, he would pull back and act like she'd just talked about his mama. She couldn't understand why he did that to her. It was wrong.

Didn't Denzelle know that a good woman would petition the Lord on him about that mess? And didn't he realize this petition would include asking the Lord to send another man who really appreciated her if this man was too dumb and stupid to recognize how blessed he was to have her in his life? And why did this irritating man have to look and smell so good? Marsha wanted to pistol-whip Denzelle for looking so good.

He was dressed in navy slacks and a crisp white Tommy Bahama camp shirt, with thin caramel and navy stripes running down the sides of the tailored strip for the shirt's brushed silver-plated buttons. Marsha sneaked a peek at his shoes. She felt like she needed to call the police. That man was wearing a pair of navy, split-toe oxfords that had a strip of caramel accenting the detailing on the split-toe design. The shoes alone screamed "fine, sexy black man."

She could hear the Bose system on the credenza playing softly. Marsha strained her ears, thinking she was going to pick up some notes from Maurette Brown Clark or the newest church theme song, "Let the Church Say Amen," by Andraé Crouch and Marvin Winans.

Jill Scott and Anthony Hamilton. That is what her pastor was listening to.

Denzelle went and turned the music up on the system. He said, "I always thought you were a big Jill Scott fan."

"What would make you think that?" Marsha asked him.

"You do like Jill Scott, right?"

"Yeah, love her music. Like Millie Jackson, too," she said, hoping to wipe that smirk off of his face. Denzelle was a preacher. Marsha knew he was not expecting for her, of all people, to like some Millie Jackson.

Denzelle sucked on his tooth for a moment like he was standing on the street corner, checking her out while she walked by.

"Millie, huh. You trying to be grown and don't even know any of the infamous Millie Jackson's songs. Name two."

" 'Hurt So Good.' The ultimate, she-know-she-wrong song, 'Caught Up.' And my favorite, 'Ask Me What You Want.' Satisfied, Pastor?"

"I'm scared of you, Ms. Metcalf."

Millie Jackson. Sister tells you she likes Millie Jackson, and then starts talking 'bout the song 'Caught Up,' that's a sister who definitely got some crunk in her system. Denzelle knew Marsha had it going on. But what he didn't know was that she had it like a good plate of ribs and freshly cooked collard greens. That was the kind of woman a brother had to search high and low for.

He knew Marsha was an anointed woman of God. Now he was wondering about the extent of that anointing. How far, how much, how deep did that anointing go? Was it the kind of anointing that stopped in the church, and showed up a bit in the living room or in the kitchen? Or did that thing work its way all the way home—to the bedroom? Now, if it did. That was an anointed woman. Women just didn't know that brothers wanted that anointing to be total, complete, and quite comprehensive.

It had never occurred to Denzelle that he'd been underestimating Marsha. True, he had it for her. True, he wanted to get to know her. But one thing that was holding Denzelle back was that Marsha was so sweet and always acting so appropriate. That was a good thing—up to a point.

Denzelle Flowers was saved, and he definitely loved the Lord. But he was still a man. And he wanted a woman who could handle the real Denzelle—the one who wasn't wearing the collar, and the one who wanted to see the full spectrum of a woman's *anointing*.

So the crucial question: Was the girl really, really anointed? Denzelle wanted to know the answer to that question. But he didn't have a clue as to how to obtain this information in the right, or more like righteous, way.

Back in the day he would have gotten himself a sampling of

the answer to that question. Now he would have to rely on prayer and the Lord for the answer. And Denzelle was a good enough preacher to know that the Lord would take His own sweet time in giving him a breakthrough answer on this one.

Marsha had been passing all of Denzelle's secret tests on that secret list brothers keep close to their hearts when they were single and scoping out women. His list, however, was a bit on the ridiculous side, because Denzelle was terrified of getting hurt again after being married to Tatiana. That extreme list had helped him to get rid of a whole lot of women. And while the list hadn't helped him get rid of Marsha Metcalf, it sure did aid in his determination to keep her at bay.

Now Miss Thing had told him something simple and funny about herself that put her name high on his list, and Denzelle didn't quite know what to do. Instead of letting Marsha know how funny and delightful that little tidbit was to him, Denzelle decided that he needed to put her back in her place: at a complete disadvantage with him.

Denzelle sat back on the edge of his desk with one leg swinging down, grinning. He loved this stance. It was so mannish and gave him the upper hand with a woman like Marsha Metcalf. He couldn't take this posture with all women—some of them were bold enough to take him up on his unspoken offer. It only worked with a woman he could count on retreating into a ladylike posture.

Denzelle grinned again. He'd read Marsha like a book. She was sitting down with her hands folded in her lap, looking like she was at a job interview. He rested one hand across the leg that was leaning up on his desk.

Just as Denzelle had expected, Marsha was not comfortable with him sitting on that desk like that. She wished he would get his butt off of the desk and go somewhere and sit down like he had some sense. Marsha knew she was not going to win this particular round with Denzelle. So she opted to throw *him* off balance.

Marsha was tired of being off-balance with him. She looked

at Denzelle grinning, and then up at a picture of him in Chicago the night President Obama was elected. She stared at the picture like it was the first time she'd ever seen it, and then asked, "You were there?"

"Uhh . . . yeah, Marsha," Denzelle answered, thrown off for a second with a question he knew she knew the answer to. "I think you know that picture has been up there over four years."

"Uhh . . . yeah," she said, determined to keep the control she'd just managed to seize from him. "But sometimes I just have to ask. It was such an incredible night, you know."

Denzelle didn't even respond. Of course the election of President Obama was an incredible night. He was not going to let her win this round, though. Denzelle went behind his desk and turned up the music and began bobbing his head like he was in his car, cruising around Raleigh with her by his side.

Marsha sat back in her chair and tried to act like she couldn't hear the music.

"Girl, loosen up. I know you want to get your groove on to this song."

He stood up and began to bob his head and move his hands up and down like he was at the club. Jill Scott's "It's Love" was playing. Denzelle thought there wasn't a more perfect song than this one for this moment. He started singing the chorus all off-key.

". . . do you want it on your rice and gravy,/do you want it on your biscuits,/baby . . . Jill, you need to be my baby mama."

Marsha was cracking up with laughter. A lot of folk didn't know how silly and funny Denzelle was.

"See, that wasn't so hard," he told her, still getting his groove on to the last drop of notes on the song.

"Nahh . . . just surprised to hear it in your office like that," Marsha told him.

"Why? Do I always have to listen to gospel music? Now, don't get me wrong, I do love me some gospel music. And I always need the Word in song to feed my spirit. But there are days when a little bit of Jill Scott, Kem, the Isley Brothers, and some Earth, Wind, and Fire are what I need for the day.

"Now, if you rolled up in here and I was blasting some Rick Ross, then maybe you might need to pull my coattail a bit."

"Denzelle, you like Rick Ross?"

He grinned, picked up a pen, and held it up like the rappers did when onstage, and said in a perfect Rick Ross imitation, "I think I'm Big Meech, Larry Hoover/whippin' work, hallelujah/one nation, under God . . ."

Marsha laughed hard at Denzelle, who had the moves and the beat down. Then that crazy boy start singing, Ross's "Hustlin'."

"You are so crazy."

"Yeah, Baby," Denzelle answered, and then started on the first chords of "No Hands" by Waka Flocka Flame with Roscoe Dash and Wale. He started singing, "girl the way you movin'/got me in a trance."

Marsha held up her hand and said, "Stop, don't you sing the rest."

Denzelle was cracking up. He wasn't going to sing "girl, drop it to the floor,/I love the way your booty go," even though he was definitely thinking it, looking at the way Marsha was working those capris.

"Okay, Miss Marsha Metcalf. I'll be good, for your sake."

"Thank you," Marsha said. Marcus kept telling her that their pastor was on the trill side. And he'd also told his mother, "Mom, you know Reverend Flowers knows all of the words to good rap songs. I think it's pretty cool. Let's me know he just a man trying to make it to heaven like the rest of us."

She would have told Marcus that he was right. But couldn't. Telling Mr. Man all of that would have necessitated telling him what led up to her personal rap performance. Marcus would be all up in her grill, trying to figure out why the pastor wanted to sing a song like "No Hands" to his mother in his office at church. That would be like giving Marcus an overdose of TMI.

There was a hard knock on the door, and before Denzelle

could say anything, Dayeesha swung the door wide open, and Veronica Washington and Keisha Jackson were right behind her. The three of them had been standing right outside the door, trying not to laugh out loud when they heard Denzelle in there doing a pretty crunked Rick Ross imitation. They would have paid good money to see Marsha's face while this show was in progress.

Right before Dayeesha knocked on the door, Keisha whispered, "I told y'all Rev was off the chain. Y'all don't want to believe me when I tell you stuff like that."

"I've always believed your butt," Dayeesha whispered back. "All you have to do is look at how Rev dresses. Remember, he buys his sports clothes from Metro."

"And," Veronica added, "he left a string of frustrated hoochies when he started telling folk that he needed some time to be with the Lord."

"That is such an old church player move," Keisha said. "Brothers get on my nerves talking crazy like that. You don't have to announce that you are going to spend time with the Lord. All you have to do is do it."

"I know," Dayeesha added. "Whenever a brother starts talking like that, he is trying to get some women in his church up off of him. You let the woman he wants to get with show up, and see how fast, he will tell Jesus, "Hollah at ya' later, Homey.""

"You ain't never lied," Veronica said, and pushed the door open, hoping to see just what Mr. Denzelle looked like doing all of that entertaining. She knew he was a trip—just rarely saw him acting like the regular brother that he was. Folk made it hard for preachers—acted like they didn't have the same needs and interests as other men and women.

Denzelle heard the knock and tried to reel it in before Dayeesha or Keisha saw him trying to get a slick, "I'm mackin' on you but I'm acting like I ain't mackin' on you" on Marsha. They had to hand it to old boy—he was smooth. But he wasn't smooth enough to get past their expert eyes. They hadn't been out in the world all of those years and not know what time it was with a man.

Dayeesha couldn't wait to get back to her desk and text Metro about this. She really wanted to call him but didn't dare do so. The last thing Dayeesha needed was to be overheard giving Metro a blow-by-blow account of Rev hitting on Marsha Metcalf. Her daddy had told her how Rev was a better player than he'd ever been. And that was saying a whole lot, because Dotsy Hamilton had been a consummate player back in the day.

Her daddy said, "Baby, I got it going on. But I'm telling you, Reverend Flowers used to have women sending him pictures in the mail. And that was long before folk were sending pictures to folk over the Internet and their phones."

She had just looked at her daddy, hoping that he wasn't talking about the kind of pictures some women still sent to Metro. Big Dotsy looked back at his daughter and said, "Yeah, those pictures. What? You younguns think y'all the ones who started sending stuff like that to a man? Babygirl, some old and seasoned hoochies perfected that game long before you all were ever even thought of."

Chapter Eight

"Ladies," Denzelle said, as he gave each one a folder with her name on it and an envelope with a check in it.

Keisha put the folder in her lap and opened the envelope. She knew it was money, because she knew what an envelope felt like with a check in it. Keisha smiled at the $3,500 check with Keisha Jackson written across it. This would carry her through a whole month, with some change left over, while she continued to look for a full-time job.

Keisha had been very scared that she wasn't going to make it. It was still scary, and touch and go financially. But she could rest better at night with this extra cash in hand.

"What are you smiling about?" Veronica asked, wanting so bad to open up her envelope but didn't, because she didn't want to appear impolite.

"This," Keisha answered, and handed her the check.

"Oh my," Veronica said, and then she hurried and opened her own envelope. It was a check for $3,500. She looked up at Denzelle and said, "Thank you. I'm behind on my car payments."

Denzelle nodded and sighed. He knew they were having it rough. Didn't know they were in the down to the wire state with their finances. But Obadiah always told him to listen carefully when folk started opening up about money troubles. He said, "D, when someone gets to telling you things like 'my money real tight,' 'I'm having a hard time finding a decent job,' 'I'm struggling to get past this point,' what they're really trying to tell you in the nicest of ways is 'Look, my back is up against the wall and I can barely pay basic bills like RENT, CAR, FOOD, GAS, LIGHT BILL, and on and on and on.

"And if they keep running behind on finishing something you know good and well they want to get done, they just may be running all over the place to get money to keep a roof over their head and don't know how to tell you that! That person is doing everything they know to do to get past this point. And maybe, just maybe, you might be the one with the ability to make a difference to ease the harshness of what they are facing. God may have given you the ability to be a blessing, so He can really bless you in return."

Watching Keisha and Veronica caused Obie's words to hit home hard. Denzelle closed his eyes for a moment to hold back tears. It hurt that people were so mean and hateful that they would snatch jobs and mistreat others simply because they could. He was now curious to see Marsha's reaction to all of this. Of the three women, she had experienced the most financial hardships.

Marsha opened her envelope and wiped at the tears streaming down her cheeks. She had forty-three dollars left in her bank account. Rent was due, she needed to get her car inspected so she wouldn't get a ticket, and she had to make a payment to the IRS, so they wouldn't snatch away what little she had. Marsha needed a miracle, and she needed it fast.

She had been praying and asking the Lord to do what folk always said He did—His best work when all you could do was stand. Just yesterday, Marsha had looked up at the sky and said, "Do me a solid as beautiful as this sky is, Lord. I'm tired, and You said You would never leave me nor forsake me. Those are Your Words, Lord—not mine. Help me, Lord. Show Yourself strong. Let folk know You are the Great I Am."

Denzelle felt a quickening in his spirit and a strong nudge from the Lord to focus on Marsha. He thought the checks would lead into a lively discussion and convince the three women that their help and expertise was sorely needed by their pastor. But one look at baby girl let him know that he had to handle his business. Denzelle walked over to Marsha and took her hands in his. He said, "I'm your pastor. What has you all torn up like this?"

"Nothing," she whispered, embarrassed by the tears and the almost uncontrollable urge to break down in sobs.

Denzelle touched her cheek softly.

"It's not, nothing," he whispered so softly, Veronica and Keisha almost fell out of their chairs trying to get in on this conversation. It took all of Keisha's resolve to refrain from pulling out her phone and texting, *Gurl, you betta get in here to see this,* to Dayeesha, who was at her desk about to bust with curiosity.

"Honey, I've never seen you this upset. You didn't break down like this when Rodney left."

Veronica and Keisha turned to each other and mouthed, *"Honey?"*

"It's—it's just that I was almost out of money," Marsha said, wishing her nose would stop running. She hated it when snot ran all down in her mouth.

"I didn't know what to do. That mean IRS lady follows me all around the city. Denzelle," Marsha continued, not even realizing that she'd called the pastor by his first name in a voice that sounded like they were boos.

"Do you know that she parks all outside of my house, watching me like some serial killer on *Criminal Minds?* And one day she came in my house and acted like I had stole something from her cousins. I've been praying for a breakthrough. I've been waiting on the Lord's help. And today you gave me this check, and not a moment too soon."

Denzelle followed his uncontrollable urge to lean down and kiss Marsha on the cheek. The baby was really going through. He'd had some rough moments in his life, but he'd never had it that rough. He said, "It's going to get better. I know it doesn't feel like it will. But the Lord just touched my heart with so much joy and peace about your situation, Marsha. It's going to change."

"Okay," Marsha whispered, and wiped her face with the tissue Keisha had put in her hands.

"And," Denzelle said, as he went to sit back down. "Girl, don't you ever do that again. You hear me," He admonished.

"Do what, Denzelle?" Marsha said through a sniffle.

"Not tell me when your back is against the wall like that."

"I . . . I . . ."

"I nothing," he told her firmly. "You carrying all that around and I have plenty of money. I would have helped you out myself before I sat back and watched you suffer like this."

Keisha and Veronica were really, real quiet now. This was getting good. They hoped Marsha and Denzelle would forget that they were in the room and keep talking like they had forgotten they were in the room.

"I couldn't ask you for money like that, Denzelle."

"No, you couldn't," he told her in a very firm voice that had "pastor" all over it. "I said that you better."

I like a man who knows how to take charge. Know what I'm sayin'? Keisha sneaked and texted to Veronica.

Girl, I didn't know Rev had it going on like that, Veronica responded.

Me, neither, Keisha texted back, and then started flipping through her folder when she saw Denzelle looking over in her direction.

Veronica put her phone down and opened the folder, hoping Denzelle didn't know they were texting about him.

Marsha looked up at Denzelle and said, "Thank you." She didn't know what to think about what Denzelle had told her. A part of her was overjoyed. Another part of her felt frustrated and heavy of heart.

Denzelle told her to make sure to contact him when she needed help. What about contacting him on help with the way she felt about him? What was she going to do with all of that? And why didn't he see that as a pressing need, too?

Marsha wondered how men could be so comfortable living

in a state of deprivation. They walked around like their hearts were screaming for companionship. Then they retreated into isolation, when all they had to do was come out of that space. It was the most insane and stupidest phenomenon as far as Marsha was concerned. And sometimes she wished the Lord would roll up on them and give them a good lesson they'd never forget.

Denzelle patted Marsha's hand and smiled. He dared not say what he was thinking, which was "I will do anything for you, Baby." Then Keisha and Veronica would really have something to text each other about.

Keisha saw Marsha watching her and Veronica and started flipping through her folder to try and make it look like she wasn't all up in her friend's business. She stared at the information, frowned, and then blurted out, "Reverend Flowers, really. This is about the Pastor's Aide Club? I need some money, but I ain't doing no old boring and stuck-up Pastor's Aide Club. That's jacked up. You know those clubs have all of the mean and stuck-up people at our church all up in them. Why are you bringing this mess back to life? Huh?"

"Pastor's Aide Club," Veronica said with a frown. "Why in the world would we want to do anything like that? I don't like those things—bunch of mean church ladies trying to get in good with the pastor so they can be the boss of everybody."

"I heard that," Keisha said, and gave Veronica some dap.

Denzelle rolled his eyes. He knew they were going to balk at running a Pastor's Aide Club. But he didn't think they would try and clown a brother—especially when the brother was trying to help their unemployed selves. He looked at Marsha, who was going through her portfolio very carefully. She flipped the folder closed and sat back in her chair, obviously uncomfortable with what she'd just read.

Denzelle really didn't know what to do with that response. It had never occurred to him that Marsh might not want to work with him as closely as her responsibilities would call for. He said,

"Sooooo . . . Marsha, is there something wrong with what's in your packet?"

"No, Denzelle," she answered in a very quiet voice.

"But you look so uncomfortable. It's not that bad, is it?"

"Why didn't you tell us you were running for bishop at the next Triennial Conference?"

"He's what?" Veronica asked.

There had been rumors Denzelle would throw his hat in the ring for the bishop's race. But the Triennial Conference was a ways away, and he hadn't said anything as yet. Denzelle was a good pastor, and they all hoped that he would not get bitten by the "bishop bug" so many good pastors succumbed to.

There was a time in their denomination when it was expected that the best and brightest pastors would automatically run for bishop at some time in their career. But it was different now. Pastors like Denzelle who ran large churches that were financially sound, with large budgets and comprehensive programs, didn't necessarily need to leave their lucrative churches to run for an Episcopal post. They had a lot of influence already, including with their own bishops. It was a rare (and foolish) bishop who would risk causing problems for a pastor like Denzelle Flowers.

"He's going to run for bishop, and he wants me to put a special touch, or a unique style, to his campaign," Marsha said, wishing she didn't feel so sad about Denzelle running for bishop. He was such a good pastor, and he would be a great bishop. But Marsha didn't want to lose her pastor. This was the second time she had to go through this with a pastor at New Jerusalem Gospel United Church.

"So, why do you need Veronica and me, if you have Marsha helping you style your campaign?" Keisha asked.

"Why don't you read what's in your folder and then tell me why I need you, Keisha," Denzelle answered in a firm voice.

Keisha raised an eyebrow as if to say, It's like that, huh?

All Denzelle did was tilt his head to the side and shrug, as if to answer her with a, Yeah, it's definitely like that.

Keisha scanned the information in her folder and then started laughing. She said, "Pastor, you've got to be kidding. You want my butt to run the singles ministry at this church. I mean, do I look like somebody's running the singles ministry type of sister?"

"Yeah. You do, homey," Veronica chimed in.

"Okay, so I am to bring all of the singles in the church together to do what—go together?"

"You know that is not what you are going to be doing," Veronica said.

"Well, since you know so much about what I will and will not be doing as the head of the Go Together ministry, Missy, tell me what your butt gone be doing," Keisha asked Veronica.

Veronica hurried to flip through her folder and scanned it real quickly. She frowned and blurted out, "Uhh, naw."

"Uhh, naw what?" Keisha asked. Now that the shoe was on the other foot, Miss Perfect wasn't all down for the count.

Veronica said, "'Uhh, naw.' I am not the one to run a jobs ministry for folk coming out of jail and prison. I mean, why not just put me in some mechanic man clothes, and then hire me to head the car repair ministry, so I can go and work on your new Audi, Denzelle?"

Marsha started laughing. Denzelle looked absolutely petrified at the mere thought of Veronica, with her prissy self, messing up under the hood of his sleek black Audi sedan.

Denzelle sighed. These three were a piece of work. He said, "Veronica, you need to take a chill pill. You can handle this assignment in your sleep. It's a PR type of position to help advertise our postprison ministry and get folks to help us out with job placements and fundraising.

"And Keisha, you are the only one in this church who can run the Singles Ministry. The folk who, to date, have volunteered to help with this ministry are lame, trying to find a slick way to be church hos, and they would turn it into a hot, boiling ghetto mess."

"Like that big mess called a singles ministry run by your boy Reverend Larry Pristeen up in Asheville," Keisha told him, and then started laughing. "I can't stand Larry Pristeen. He is so full of it and needs to be slapped for running around telling singles to learn to 'bask in the glow of being alone.'"

"Then I should be glowing like I'm radioactive," Veronica said.

"You know darn well I don't want anything remotely akin to that foolishness Pristeen is running," Denzelle told them.

"Well, good for you, Pastor," Keisha said. "You do know that Reverend Pristeen has a team of women from his church who run his Glowing for Jesus booths at annual conferences around the country. Bay Bowser was at one of those conferences helping with security, and he said those women were running around in pink T-shirts with the words 'I'm glowing' up under a big-A picture of Larry Pristeen's face."

Marsha started laughing and said, "Keisha, watch your mouth. We are in the pastor's office."

Veronica was just shaking her head. That was some trifling mess, even for Larry Pristeen. She said, "I thought you all got the memo that Reverend Pristeen is a very slick undercover ho."

"Girl, be quiet," Keisha exclaimed. "That is really some news to me. 'Cause that joker don't have no game. Marsha got more game than Larry Pristeen."

Marsha rolled her eyes at Keisha. So she didn't have game. Why did folks always have to have game? Denzelle had plenty of game, and all all of that game did was get him in trouble, and then made him act stupid and annoying.

"Well, game or no game," Marsha said. "All I know is that Reverend Pristeen is running around lying about being happily single. There is no way that man is 'happily single,' with the way he flirts with a woman every chance he gets."

"He hasn't flirted with you, has he?" Denzelle asked, with a frown clouding up his face.

"Well, not really. He . . ."

"He what?" Denzelle snapped. "What did 'he' do?"

"I don't know. Larry's not my type, so I wasn't paying any real attention to him when he was . . ."

"She may not have paid attention to Larry," Veronica said, "but I sure was watching that sucker the last time our church went up to his church in Asheville. He was all up in Marsha's face, grinning and acting like she was a piece of red velvet cake. You didn't see all of that, Denzelle?"

He shook his head and said, "I don't remember seeing Larry flirting with anybody, come to think of it."

"You don't?" Keisha asked, surprised. "Rev, he was flirting with several cute women that evening. You must have been super preoccupied with your sermon that day."

"Nahh girl," Veronica said. "That's not why Denzelle didn't see Larry flirting. Girl, Denzelle didn't know that wack mess Larry was doing was actually flirting."

Denzelle frowned. He remembered how Larry kept putting his arm around Marsha's shoulder and heaping praise on her 'Proverbs 31 woman' demeanor. He even remembered Larry talking crazy in his flat, low voice, saying some crap like, "Miss Marsha Metcalf, I love how glowing in the aftermath of being single suits you. I want you to fully embrace being completely alone and without the companionship of a man. Girl, I almost envy you for the way you make this look so easy and compelling."

He couldn't believe he'd missed all of that. It didn't occur to Denzelle until now that what Larry was really saying to Marsha was, I want you in a state of isolation and loneliness. I want that state to be a bit extreme, so you will be overjoyed when I deign to pay you some scraps of attention. And I don't want you to know I'm getting my rocks off from watching you get all excited over these scraps I'm throwing your way. I don't even know if I want you. I just want to be able to make you think I want you— just in case.

Denzelle knew Larry Pristeen was very ambitious. Yet he'd

never pegged Larry for being a ho—mainly because he'd never seen him getting a true mack on a woman. And he'd also never noticed a woman who was acting like the two of them were getting their freak on in secret.

But now he understood why. Larry was such a sneaky ho that only a very observant woman would pick up on it. And Denzelle figured that Larry's women were on the QT with him, because they were dumb enough to believe Larry was working through his "anxieties about commitment" and didn't want to "scare him away." Denzelle couldn't stand brothers who ran lame games like that on women.

"So, Marsha," Denzelle asked one more time. "Do you think Larry Pristeen was trying to hit on you when we were all at his church?"

Marsha shrugged. She really didn't care what Reverend Pristeen was doing, because all she knew was that Larry Pristeen got on her last nerves with all of his cryptic behaviors. Plus, if Denzelle was so concerned that another man was flirting with her, maybe he needed to do something about it—like ask her out for lunch.

Denzelle decided it best to table that discussion. He'd have an opportunity to see for himself. He hoped it wasn't true. Denzelle would hate to have to kick the brother's butt. But right now there was a more pressing matter—getting the Pastor's Aide Club up and running so that these three women could get some money in their homes.

"So Rev," Keisha said, "I hope you don't plan on having us do what that old evil Clara Mae Davidson used to do with the Pastor's Aide club before she died. I do not intend on picking up where that scrunched-up-face witch left off."

"I do not want you all to do anything close to what Mrs. Davidson did back in that day," Denzelle answered, and then shuddered. Clara Mae Davidson had been a piece of bad work.

"So then, just what are we to do? 'Cause what I'm not doing is making any of that ice cream and ginger ale punch stuff." Keisha said.

"You do not have to make 'frappé,'" Denzelle told Keisha with a chuckle. "You don't even have to make a glass of water. I just want you to help Marsha out with a campaign project for now. And when she's off and running, you can start working on how you are going to do a singles ministry at the church."

"Denzelle," Veronica said, "how does the prison ministry business fit for pastor's aide?"

"The money has to help the pastor. That is the main stipulation. Only thing, Miss Clara didn't have any real vision. So she didn't think about defining what she thought the aid should be. It gave me a legal loophole and made it possible for me to come up with some things that I, as the pastor of the church, really need. And right now, I need help running for bishop, with the singles ministry, and with a prison program."

"How did you get a loophole for running for bishop?" Marsha asked. "If you get elected, you won't be a pastor anymore. So how exactly does that work for the Pastor's Aide Club?"

"Old girl used the club to sponsor and 'aid' her husband when he ran for bishop," Denzelle told her, grinning.

"Did he win?" Keisha asked. Reverend Davidson was dead by the time she'd gotten old enough to pay attention to church politics.

"Of course not," Denzelle said, looking at Keisha like she was crazy. "Nobody wanted him as a bishop. He was pompous and full of himself, and he had a lot of enemies."

"True," Veronica said. That was one time a man who didn't need to be elected bishop was sent home in defeat from a Triennial Conference. Most times they had to fight long and hard to get the good preachers in and keep the bad preachers out.

"So, Reverend Flowers," Keisha said, "how does what you want me to do, and what you want Veronica to do, fit with you running for bishop, and also with helping the Pastor's Aide Club?"

"He is going to use what you all are doing as bragging points on the campaign trail," Marsha said, in a voice full of authority.

"See, while you and Veronica are putting the programs in place, Denzelle can begin the conversation about how he is going to spearhead these types of programs in Gospel United churches around the country. Folk will be interested in how this works, because a lot of churches need these kinds of ministries."

Denzelle, Veronica, and Keisha were just looking at Marsha. They knew she was good, but they often forgot that she had it like that.

"What?" Marsha asked. "Did I say something wrong? I thought you wanted me to help you get a style, a special look, something that would set you apart for the campaign, Denzelle?"

"That is exactly what I want."

Veronica nodded. At first she'd wondered why Denzelle gave Marsha an assignment that was close to her own area of public relations. But she got it. This campaign didn't need PR. It needed style, flair, an image that would place Denzelle Flowers head and shoulders above the other candidates. Only Marsha could work it so that Denzelle didn't even have to say anything to promote himself and his campaign. Folk would get it just by watching how he looked, what he did, how he did it, and so forth.

Keisha got it, too. In fact, she got it so well it was practically killing her not to sneak and text Dayeesha. Marsha would definitely be able to help Pastor have the flair he'd need to run that campaign right. But she knew that what the pastor really wanted was a safe and explainable way to have some up close and personal time with Marsha Metcalf.

This was going to be very interesting. Keisha was kind of glad she'd gotten fired. She could finally do something she'd wanted to do at church for a long time—start something for the singles at church that wasn't wack. Her singles program was going to be off the chain, and they were going to have a whole bunch of fun— kind of like going to the club, only you'd be at church.

Veronica exchanged eye contact with Keisha. She was glad that somebody else was thinking what she was pondering concerning Denzelle and Marsha. It was going to take a lot of time together for Marsha to school Denzelle on how to work it with some serious game and style. It wasn't that Denzelle didn't have game—he had plenty of game. But now Marsha was going to help the brother define that game stylishly. And that would require them spending a lot of time in each other's company. Yeah, this was going to be very interesting to observe from the sidelines.

"So, are we on?" Denzelle asked.

"As long as I don't have to stand behind a table and give out cookies and sheet cake, I'm good, Reverend Flowers," Keisha said.

"We're on," Veronica chimed in.

"Bring it," was all Marsha said.

Denzelle forgot himself for a moment. He gave Marsha a sideways look while sucking on a tooth and said, "I plan to."

Chapter Nine

When Reverend Marcel Brown, Presiding Elder over the Michigan Annual Conference, saw the text from Bishop Ray Caruthers that read, Denzelle Flowers is planning to run for bishop, he sighed heavily and went and poured himself a glass of Crown Royal before answering the text. He could not believe he was up against the Theophilus Simmons/Eddie Tate faction again.

They had been fighting, and at each other's throats, since 1961. That was over fifty years ago, and in another century! But if Marcel were to be more exact in his chronology of this church war, it actually began more than sixty years ago. The folks born when this feud started had been card-carrying AARP members for a decade.

He found it hard to believe that he and Theophilus Simmons and his boy, Eddie Tate, first faced off against each other during the Gospel United Church's national basketball tournaments back in the 1950s. Theophilus was a part of the denomination's mighty First Episcopal District, which ran from Virginia all the way down to Georgia. Marcel was the star point guard for the Ninth District, representing Michigan, Wisconsin, Minnesota, and Iowa.

Every year Marcel's team would start each new basketball season on a hot winning streak, only to come up against the brick wall that was Theophilus Simmons and his boys from the First Episcopal District. No matter how they prepared, and how many games they won before the play-offs, Theophilus would meet Marcel on the court and beat him like he stole something.

Marcel always counted it his good fortune that Eddie Tate was serving as a young chaplain in the army at that time. Otherwise he would have gotten a second tail-whipping from those Chicago and St. Louis brothers in the Eighth Episcopal District. Nobody messed with the brothers from South Side Chicago, or their counterparts farther south, from St. Louis, Missouri's North Side. Back then the brothers coming out of Vashon and Sumner high schools in St. Louis would tear you up like you were a thin piece of paper.

His beef with Theophilus Simmons and Eddie Tate was almost as old as they were. And if that wasn't bad enough, the women would be all over Theophilus at the end of the championship games. Marcel couldn't understand it. Back then, lightskinned black men with a head full of curly hair were supposed to epitomize fineness in the community. But Theophilus would wipe out all of that when he showed up tall, chocolate, and grinning. Some of those women acted like they were going to throw their panties at him on the basketball court.

Even worse, Marcel didn't have a chance when Theophilus and Eddie Tate ran together. Eddie was a big, yellow brother with dark curly hair back in the day. He was also one of the best dressed young preachers in the denomination. And if that were not bad enough, the brother was smooth, and a player to the bone.

Marcel *hated* those two Negroes. He'd hated them when they were youngsters. He couldn't stand them when they were men at the height of their prime. And he positively detested them when they grew into their maturity as older men. Theophilus Simmons and Eddie Tate had been the bane of Marcel Brown's existence all of his adult life.

Now he was getting a text that Reverend Denzelle Flowers, who trained under Bishop Eddie Tate, had thrown his hat into the ring for the bishop's race. He scoffed, and then sighed. At least he didn't have to contend with Reverend Obadiah Quincey, who was a protégé of Bishop Theophilus Simmons. Denzelle and Obadiah were boys. Only one would run. The other would help with the campaign.

That's how it was done in the Gospel United Church. If your boy ran for bishop, you worked behind the scenes to get him in. There was only one exception to that unspoken rule. Back in 1986, Eddie Tate was tapped to run for bishop, with Theophilus Simmons as his campaign manager. But a fluke in their plans set things in motion that caused both men to get elected as bishops that year. Marcel became physically ill after that, and couldn't work for months, even though his boy, Sonny Washington, managed to win an Episcopal seat as well.

He read the text again, and then sent one back to Ray: *That is some messed-up mess. I would say something other than "mess," but I'm a preacher and trying to live right.*

LOL, Ray texted him back. *You a crazy negro and you know that.*

So, another text from Ray began, *are you still running our boy for that one and only, and very coveted Episcopal seat?*

Yeah, that's the plan, Marcel replied. *Rev. Xavier Franklin is the one as far as I'm concerned.*

But he's most likely going up against Flowers, Marcel, Ray texted. *Plus, how do you plan to take that on? Denzelle is a favorite. And the women still want to be his baby mama even though Denzelle has been on the straight and narrow with ladies for a while. And as much as I hate to admit it, he's a good pastor, and will make a good bishop.*

Marcel was about to respond to Ray's text, when his cell phone buzzed in his hand. Ray was on the other end.

"I know you know Denzelle has stayed on the wagon with the ladies. He hasn't been tappin' tail left and right like he used to, for a minute now. That isn't going to hurt him because sisters love a reformed player—best of both worlds as far as they are concerned. It means that the brother has the potential to fall in love with 'a good woman,' while maintaining that he still has the skills to rock a woman's world."

"Good woman, huh?" Marcel told him. "There ain't nothing a 'good' church woman can do for me but point me in the direction of one of those old school freaks like me."

"You know you a dog, Dawg," Ray said laughing.

"Wolf, wolf," was all Marcel said, to the beat of Adina Howard's 1990s hit song, "Freak Like Me."

"Ray," he continued, "the only thing I didn't like about that song was that I was on my way to being an old player when it came out. The women bragging that it was their theme song were too young for me. Ain't nothing wrong with some fresh fruit. But good fruit needs to be ripe. Unripened fruit can kill you."

"I hear you on that one," Ray told him, in complete agreement.

Ray Caruthers had crossed a lot of lines in his day. But women who were too young for him were off-limits. Ray was a player and didn't want to mack on somebody he knew he had an enormous edge on. What fun was that? A hot young thing interested in a man his age was nothing but some real trouble. Plus, a lot of those little heifers were real fertile, and would pop out a baby in a heartbeat to keep a hand in his wallet.

Whenever a young gold digger got to chasing Bishop Ray Caruthers, he stopped her, saying, "Baby, my name is Ray and not Abraham. You can't even handle expensive and aged liquor. So I know you can't handle me."

Marcel scratched at the gray stubble on his chin. His curly, dark brown hair was almost white. And it had started getting thinner, now that he was in his seventies. But Marcel still looked good and could pull plenty of women his way.

"Denzelle Flowers running for bishop," Marcel said dryly. "What are we going to do to stop that train from rolling right past us at full speed?"

"I suggest we work to stop the train before it ever leaves the station," Ray answered him.

"It's like I've told you and Sonny before. We always wait too late to deal with those jokers. That's why they always win. Once they get in the race, it's over for us. And it doesn't matter what we do or how far we go to try to stop them."

"That ain't nothing but the truth," Marcel said, in a quiet voice.

They had come up with some good schemes, backed with plenty of money, and nothing ever worked to beat out the Theophilus Simmons faction. There were times when it looked as if they were going to win the battle. But they always failed—sometimes in the eleventh hour.

"Marcel, we need to find a way to get Denzelle Flowers out of the race for bishop now. He has only recently hinted at his candidacy, and probably hasn't done a lot to promote himself yet. If we get rid of him now, few people will ever figure out that he was ever in."

"I think you're on to something, Ray. But I need to give this some more thought and do some digging. Matter of fact, I'm on my way to that Saved Negroes R Us conference in Atlanta."

Ray was laughing. He was so glad the denomination had tapped Marcel to serve as one of the senior-level ministers in the delegation representing the Gospel United Church at the conference. He said, "Better you than me. I haven't had to attend the National Consortium of Black Denominations for two years. I may not be so lucky next year, though."

"As much as I wish I was going anywhere but there, I may as well use this trip to my advantage," Marcel replied. "I'm thinking there is going to be something I can find to use against our opponents among all of those Missionary Baptists, CMEs, AMEs, AME Zions, COGIC, and Holiness ministers at the conference. Somebody doing *something* we can use."

"I heard that, Marcel, man. Be sure to keep a close watch on the AMEs and AME Zions. Their structure is real similar to ours, and both denominations have Quadrennial General Conferences that are similar to our Triennial Conference. I know they have something going on concerning running for an Episcopal seat that might be useful to us."

"Yeah, I think you're right," Marcel answered. He remembered hearing some talk on the black preacher grapevine about one of those BME denominations (Black Methodist Episcopals) voting in a policy that would affect the ability of divorced ministers to run for bishop. Denzelle Flowers was divorced, and there could be just enough meat to this policy to use against the brother in the Gospel United Church. All Marcel had to do was get the real talk from preachers in that denomination.

The National Consortium of Black Denominations was the largest ecumenical gathering of historically black church denominations in the country. The consortium meeting was held every year, and it brought ministers together to fellowship and talk across denominational lines. There were some preachers who couldn't wait to get to this event—especially if they were among the elite core of preachers invited to give a sermon at one of the main sessions.

Preaching to other preachers at a big-time preacher event could stroke a preacher's ego big time. It could get the undercover ho preachers good play from the resident church hoochies who attended these conferences almost as dutifully as the preachers themselves. And it was guaranteed to get a preacher many more invitations to preach at other big conferences for big money.

Reverend Marcel Brown, however, was not one of the preachers in need of that kind of experience and attention. Marcel had plenty of money, and he had always preferred working behind the scenes over preaching, anyway. Hooking up with a church hoochie didn't do much for him, because that kind of woman could be too much trouble.

Most of the church hoochies he knew came to those conferences to snatch up a prominent preacher, hoping that her freak behind closed doors skills would give her an opportunity to catch a husband. If Marcel wanted a bedroom freak, he'd prefer one that wasn't in church. He didn't need a woman walking around looking like Jacob's first wife Leah, was head of the Usher Board, and had detailed biblical knowledge of a fifth of the preachers at any conference on any given day.

Every time he read the story of Jacob, Rachel, and Leah, he shook his head in wonder that Jacob, the slickest brother in Old Testament land, didn't see the hoochie in Leah. It was plain as day. Whenever Marcel read that scripture, he'd get so mad at Jacob and start yelling at his Bible, "Dawg, get out, get out! Get behind the veil! She a hoochie!!!!!!!"

It would surprise people to discover that Marcel Brown read his Bible on a regular basis, and even thought about things like that. Most people assumed Marcel wasn't as sharp as he was, because he was always into some dirty dealings. But in reality, this particular Presiding Elder was a whole lot smarter and observant than people gave him credit for. He just didn't give a care that they were even thinking about him like that.

The private jet, compliments of his wife's family's business, landed smoothly. Sometimes, when Marcel was bemoaning having to remain married to his only son's mother, he thought about this jet and felt a whole lot better about the situation. He had married Tweaki, as he called her, because she was high yellow, had long hair, was good-looking, and accustomed to the kind of marriage he always hoped to have. She came from one of those old school, black moneyed families with more secrets than money—and Tweaki's family had a whole lot of money. It was more important to his wife to stay married than to be married right—an attitude that suited Marcel just fine.

Marcel wanted to stay married, too. He just didn't want to have to always be married right. One of the things Marcel loved the most about Tweaki was her ability to understand what he needed and wanted out of their marriage.

As long as Tweaki could show him off to her Junior League sisters during one of their many annual events, she was happy. Marcel always wondered why the girl didn't accept the invite to the Detroit Chapter of the Links, Inc. Personally, he preferred being surrounded by black folk—especially high-rolling black folk like the ones who were in exclusive black organizations like the Links, the Boule for black men, and the extremely exclusive Guardsmen for high-profile black men.

But Tweaki told him that her family had been there, done that for decades, and she liked going into new territory like the Junior League. All Marcel could do was kiss her forehead as he gave specific instructions to only involve their son, DeMarcus, in the upscale, black Jack and Jill activities while he was young. Since Marcel rarely made any demands on his wife, DeMarcus was exempted from having to do anything connected to the Junior League. Tweaki thanked Marcel for laying down the law on that issue when DeMarcus went off to college and brought home a beautiful young sister who'd just crossed over to be an AKA like his mother, with a 4.0 grade point average as icing on that good-looking cake.

As much as Marcel secretly wished his wife would put on some white and green, get some white roses, and leave the Junior League for the Links, he liked all of the other things she brought to the table too much to give her a hard time over that flaw. If the girl could handle working with all of those white women at one more "let's help the less fortunate than us" event, then he could handle watching her do it. Because being able to use the family jet any time he needed it was too sweet of a deal to try and convince his wife to do otherwise.

Funny thing, Marcel Brown had always wanted to make more money than he was willing to work for. But when he found and fell in love with Tweaki, he started working harder than he'd ever worked in his life. Marcel Brown didn't have millions in trust like his wife. He couldn't do much for Tweaki financially. But he could make her proud of him through hard work as the Presiding Elder in his church conference.

The plane pulled into a private hub off of the runway. Marcel finished his drink and went to the bathroom to brush his teeth and gargle, to get that liquor taste out of his mouth. Drinking didn't bother him in the least, but he knew there would be some serious Holy Rollers at this convention. Crown was the last thing Marcel needed on his breath when he embarked on his fact-finding mission to get the goods on Denzelle Flowers.

Marcel came out of the bathroom just as the plane was opening up to reveal the limo waiting on him.

"This is the life," Marcel thought, and then texted his secretary to make sure to send Tweaki some yellow roses. His wife loved roses—especially the yellow ones. Every time Marcel rode that plane, it made him want to do something nice for his wife. Tweaki loved getting what she called her "elder is out of town flowers." She never knew this gesture was connected to the great pleasure her husband derived from flying on her private jet.

"Do you need for me to get your bags, Reverend?" the limo driver asked sweetly.

She'd been ruthless in getting assigned to pick up the infamous Reverend Marcel Brown. Her coworkers said he was still fine, a trip, and the kind of man who would pay extra money on the side if you played your cards right. But no one told the girl that this old player still had plenty of game in him. What in the world was the Presiding Elder putting in his water? He had to be one of the finest old men she'd seen in a very long time.

When Marcel saw the handful of redbone wearing a chauffeur's hat, he whispered, "My, my, my. Babygirl is too young for me to mess with. But she's not too young to stop me from admiring what she's working with."

"Reverend?" she asked, trying to act like she hadn't heard what she'd heard him mumble. Her coworkers told her the Presiding Elder from Detroit was a player, and something else. But they didn't know what they were talking about. This man practically wrote the play book.

Marcel smiled at her, his eyes not missing a thing. He almost put on his reading glasses to make sure he could see everything up close and personal.

"Pardon my French, Miss, errrr."

"LaTina."

"LaTina?" Marcel asked, thinking that black folk could come up with some names for their children.

"No. It's not pronounced 'La-ti-na' like I'm Spanish. It's pronounced Le-Tee-nah."

"LaTina," Marcel repeated.

"Yes."

"And how did you come about such an unusual name, LaTina?"

"My mom's name is Tina."

"Of course," Marcel said. Black folk loved to put "La" in front of a name of a girl child who was named after her mother or aunt or grandmother. It was like calling a boy "Jr." He had lost count of all of the "Las" he'd baptized throughout his career in the ministry.

LaTina grabbed Marcel's bags, but he stopped her.

"It's my job, Reverend Brown."

"I may be many things, LaTina, but when it comes to luggage and a young lady, I still have home training."

LaTina smiled and said, "Just don't let my bosses know. You know how it is."

Marcel put his fingers to his lips, as if he were zipping them shut. He put the luggage in the trunk, and then went to the front of the limo.

"Sometimes I don't want to ride in the back alone. Plus, I want to see what a sweet little thing like you is working with when you are driving me around."

LaTina smiled. Reverend Brown was a trip. She'd always wondered why some women liked sugar daddies. Now she knew.

"The hotel?"

"Yeah," Marcel answered with a sigh. "I'd love to ride around the ATL with you, Baby. But there is some pressing church business I have to attend to."

"Anything I might be able to help you with?" LaTina asked. She liked Reverend Brown, but she also needed a big tip, so that she could afford human hair for her new weave.

At first Marcel couldn't imagine what the limo driver could do to help him, until it occurred to him that he wasn't the only person she was driving around during this conference.

"Who have you picked up today?"

"Lots of folks—mostly preachers and a few of their wives."

"From which denominations?"

"You are the only one from the Gospel United Church that I've picked up so far. Most of my people have been COGIC. And I had two runs with a carload of some preachers from the black Methodist churches. I think one of them had some kind of meeting today, and they were rushing in to get to some meeting on who should or should not run for bishop."

"Bingo!" Marcel thought to himself. Preachers and bishops involved in a controversial ruling were always rushing and uptight to do the do on something like that. This was going to be easier than he first imagined it would be.

"What hotel is that group staying in?" Marcel asked. He knew he was supposed to be at the hotel with his own church folk. But he needed to be in the one with the denomination with that new rule for who could or could not run for bishop. Marcel stood to pick up a lot of information from all of the conversations that would occur in the hotel lobby and the restaurant—especially during the breakfast hours. He'd notice that a whole lot of good talking went on during breakfast.

"The ones rushing off to those meetings are all at the Ritz Carlton. You want me to take you there, Reverend Brown?"

"Yeah. They aren't filled up are they?"

"At the Ritz Carlton in Buckhead? Reverend Brown, you are funny. You know that hotel is really high. They have some available rooms. Trust me on that one."

"Well then, the Ritz it is," Marcel told her. The Ritz Carlton in Buckhead was one of his favorite places to stay while in Atlanta.

LaTina pulled up to the hotel, and this time she hopped out to go and open the door for him. She whispered, "You have to let me do this, because you know these white folk working here are watching me. Don't need any of them calling my agency talking junk about how I handled getting you in and out of the hotel."

Marcel nodded and let LaTina handle her business. He liked her style and work ethic. Miss LaTina looked like she'd make it her business to keep him in the loop, if he let her know that a big tip was coming.

Marcel got out of the limo, let the bellman get his bags, pulled out his wallet, and peeled off two fifties. He put them in LaTina's hands and said, "There's more where that came from. I need some information. Will you let me know what you hear when you're around this group of preachers in the hotel?

"Will do," LaTina told him. "I have folks in some good spots. They will pass on information if I can put a few bills in their hands."

Marcel put five twenties in her hand. He said, "This should get you started for today."

"Yep," LaTina said, as she went to get into the car. She came back around and pulled her business card out of the breast pocket on her uniform.

"Here, Reverend Brown. Call me if you need anything. I can get you some ribs, liquor, and other good food. And I can also take you wherever you need to go while you're in the city. Just call me, okay?"

Marcel smiled at that enterprising little missy, and said, "You can count on it."

Chapter Ten

Marcel checked in, went up to his room, showered, put on some comfortable clothes, flipped on the TV, and got in the bed. He was supposed to get ready for the conference's Interdenominational All Saints Banquet later that evening, but he was tired and not in the mood to attend one more fancy church banquet.

Marcel Brown had been going to fancy church banquets since he was a little boy. He didn't want to change from his T-shirt and athletic pants into a tux just to hear one more speech on why we are here, suffer through a high-ranking preacher heap accolades on his or her great denomination in black churchdom, eat, not be able to drink some good whiskey, talk the same-old-same-old with preachers he didn't even like, and force himself to pretend like he was having a holy ghost good time.

Oh, he almost forgot about the choir he'd have to suffer through. Almost every time he had come to a banquet for this conference, they always had the stiffest, most traditional and opera-sounding local choir singing. There were so many good church musicians in Atlanta. He couldn't understand why the coordinators of this conference would not get a choir that somebody really wanted to hear.

The choir at his late father's church sang like that. There were times when Marcel wanted to throw a brick at them on a Sunday morning. He envied the pastors with those choirs that sang the

kind of songs that made an old reprobate like himself get up and
start clapping.

He got the menu off the nightstand, ordered room service,
and settled in for a quiet and peaceful evening. There would be
plenty of time to get out there to wheel and deal with preachers.
Sometimes Marcel wished for the good old days, when he could
just go out and get into some dirt with some preachers looking
for the same kind of adventure. Couldn't do that now—at least
not out in the open. Technology had changed how that game
could be played. Folk see you with the wrong people, and they'd
get to documenting you on their phones.

He did not need to be in the middle of all of that drama waiting to happen; he was glad to be off to himself. When room service came with his food, Marcel ate, drank some liquor, watched
an episode of *Scandal*, and then fell asleep.

The next morning Marcel was up bright and early and feeling real good. He picked out a gray three-piece suit with pale blue
chalk stripes running through it. He then selected a dove gray
shirt, a pale blue silk tie, and gray Detroit gators. He hurried up
and dressed, and then went downstairs for breakfast. His gut told
him that all of the information he would need would be right up
in that restaurant with the overpriced cup of coffee.

Marcel was right, too. He spotted his target audience hud-
dled over at a big round table off in a more private spot in the
room. The hostess came over to him and was about to seat him
at a table on the opposite side of the restaurant.

"Miss, it's kind of lonesome looking in that section. You
think I could be closer to my fellow preachers over there?"

"You sure can," the young woman with a head full of thick
blond hair told him, and put him at the best seat in the house.

"This better?"

"Perfect," Marcel said, and sat down at a table for two next
to the huddle of preachers. He could hear everything they were
saying, right down to the young preacher whispering, "You think

that white girl wearing a weave? She has a whole lot of hair on her head, even for a white girl."

"You over here asking about her hair, and I'm trying to fig- ure out if that is her real booty. It's sticking out pretty far for a white girl."

Marcel made it his business to look at that girl's behind. If he hadn't been so determined to get into their real business, he'd tell them the truth about all of that booty and where she may have purchased it from. But to interject that observation right now would halt the real conversation. The last thing Marcel needed was for them to gauge that he was knee-deep in their personal church business.

He ordered one of the fancy omelets on the menu, some orange juice, and coffee. The more he seemed engrossed in his meal and own business, the better. Marcel's phone buzzed that he had several text messages just as the waitress came with his coffee and orange juice. It was from his new best friend, La- Tina.

Hey, Rev. Check out these pictures I'm sending you. The preachers at the table near you are all prominent in their denomination.

My friend in the kitchen, here at the Ritz, said thank you for the forty dollars. He really needed it to buy some school supplies for his little boy.

He said to keep listening. They have been talking some serious church stuff all week. His sister goes to the church pastored by the preacher in the plain blue suit.

Marcel studied the pictures and realized that they had just been taken. He studied the picture a moment and saw himself sitting off in the background.

Yep, I'm in the hotel, LaTina texted. *Turn around real cool like, so no one will know that I'm sending you these messages.*

Marcel smiled and did as LaTina asked. There she was in her uniform, watching the preachers and texting him all of the goods.

His phone buzzed with new messages.

The preacher in the plain blue suit is Rev. Tim Ealey. Keep your ear tuned in to him. He is the ring leader. I have to go. Break over. Hollah back at a youngun.

Marcel's breakfast had arrived. The omelet smelled delicious. He spoke grace over his food and dug in. The omelet was so good, it was almost heavenly. Marcel was glad he was eating, so he could listen while giving the appearance that he wasn't in their business.

LaTina was right; that Reverend Tim Ealey did have on an awfully plain blue suit. It was high quality. But it was so plain—nothing about the suit gave it any kind of flair. The brother even had on a stark white, FBI-looking shirt with a conservative navy and royal blue striped tie.

Tim Ealey was definitely the ring leader. It was clear he was holding court with those preachers, because they were quiet and taking notes while he talked. Marcel adjusted his chair so that he could hear them better. He wanted to know why this brother had those preachers hanging on to his every word.

"I," Tim Ealey said in a deep and commanding voice, "I have met with all of our bishops, and they are going to put this matter to a vote this evening. It took a lot to persuade them that this was the right thing to do, but I managed to get them all to see the light."

One of the preachers at the table took a long sip of his orange juice. Marcel knew that move. That brother didn't agree with one word Reverend Ealey was saying. In fact, the young preacher looked like he wished he could pimp slap Tim Ealey.

Marcel was straining hard to hear this. It had to be good if those preachers were scared to oppose this brother.

"Reverend Ealey," the young preacher gulping down the juice said. "So, you are telling us that the bishops have actually agreed to overturn the bylaw that would allow divorced preachers to run for bishop and hold an Episcopal seat. I don't think it wise to overturn something like that. Folk don't need to feel compelled to stay in bad marriages just so they can become a bishop."

Tim Ealey shot the young man a deadly look, and threw back his head in a gesture Marcel was sure Ealey thought made him look deep and pensive.

"My good, young brother. I see that you do not truly understand the necessary, theological ramifications of this reform."

"With all due respect, Reverend Ealey, we are talking about reinstating an early-twentieth-century ruling for a twenty-first-century clergy. How does that have anything to do with what you just said?"

Marcel almost fell out of his chair. That young brother was going to find himself serving in the assistant pastor capacity for many years after taking on a pompous, think-he-know-it-all brother like a Tim Ealey. Preachers like Ealey liked to present that they were all noble and down with the people. But they were some of the biggest snobs Marcel had ever encountered. He'd bet some money that Reverend Ealey lived in a fancy gated community, and that "the people" had better not show up at his front door talking about hangin' out with him.

Marcel could just look at Tim Ealey and tell he had a very personal and self-serving agenda on the other side of this so-called reform and upgraded theology. Ealey was getting something out of this new law, and it wasn't satisfaction for doing the Lord's work, either. Marcel could only wonder who had Reverend Tim Ealey tucked neatly in his (or her) back pocket. Ealey was getting paid to run this game on his denomination, and he was earning every single penny of that under-the-table, tax-free cash.

Marcel Brown didn't have issues with a preacher getting his hands on some extra cash. He had practically made a career of that kind of thing. But he did have a problem with Ealey sitting up there acting like he was some kind of noble warrior for the regular people with this new law. Listening to Tim Ealey talk all of that crazy junk and representing like he used to write sermons for Jesus made Marcel want to backhand him.

"See," Tim was saying in an exaggerated and condescending tone, "you are shortsighted and do not understand why this is so important."

"No, I don't, Sir," the young man answered politely. "I don't know why our church would want to risk passing over a good candidate for bishop just because he or she went through a divorce. That just strikes me as wrong, and mean, too."

"The law, my young preacher, will not stop a good man or woman who has experienced divorce from running for an Episcopal seat. It will stop them from remarrying, therefore providing them with an otherwise unattainable opportunity to serve the Lord without any distractions."

"That's messed-up," Marcel thought. Tim Ealey was unbelievable. And that young preacher was right. That rule was mean, lacked compassion, and was purposely designed to stop some good folk from running for bishop.

The perception of bishops had been changing steadily. People did not shout them up and down like they did years ago—making bishops think they were so much more special than other people in the church. And talented preachers no longer felt like getting elected to serve as a bishop was the pinnacle of their careers. A rule like this could make some preachers who should run for bishop decide their denomination wasn't offering enough to give up being able to get married again after a divorce.

"But, Reverend Ealey. What about those good preachers who find themselves faced with a divorce they couldn't prevent? What are they supposed to do if their wife or husband just ups and walks away from the marriage? Become a eunuch?"

Marcel wanted to tell the young blood to tread carefully. Ealey was mean. But the young brother was really put out with this, and didn't back down.

"If," Ealey said in a tight voice, "a bright and talented preacher in our church finds that he or she will have to go through a divorce, they cannot remarry and run for bishop or remain a bishop if their ex-spouse is still alive when they make this kind of decision."

"Kind of like Miss America doing something folk don't like and having to turn over her crown to the first runner-up, huh," the young preacher said dryly.

"Think what you like," Ealey stated. "But if a preacher remarries and the spouse is still alive, they will have to give up that purple and all of the privileges that go with it."

"What in the world is wrong with that joker?" Marcel thought, and studied Tim Ealey for a moment.

Marcel discerned that Tim Ealey was mean and thought he knew everything because he was smart and had some kind of doctorate degree. He figured correctly that Ealey must be married to a woman he couldn't stand, but he wouldn't leave her because Tim Ealey worshipped his status in the church more than he did the Lord. Marcel suspected Reverend Ealey had secret affairs that no one other than Ealey and his secret women knew about. This fool was miserable, and he wanted everybody else to be miserable with him.

Reverend Ealey reminded Marcel Brown a whole lot of Reverend Larry Pristeen in his own denomination. Pristeen was all up in everything, acting like he was so saved and holy, and he had more room keys from churchwomen than the most notorious preacher ho. The only reason Marcel had not cussed out Larry Pristeen was because he might be useful. And he knew Larry Pristeen was so ambitious that he would align himself with an old and powerful reprobate like a Reverend Marcel Brown if he believed it would boost his status and power in the Gospel United Church.

"This meeting is over," Tim Ealey said, as he stood up, and he made sure that every man at that table was standing with him, waiting to trail behind him when he left the restaurant.

"Wow," Marcel thought. "All of this time I'm thinking the Gospel United Church was filled to the brim with crazy preachers."

That was one insane law Reverend Ealey was pushing on his denomination, but it would be a great weapon to use against

Denzelle Flowers. Denzelle was divorced, and he was also the kind of man who would want to remarry. Denzelle's ex-wife, Tatiana, looked real healthy, and not like somebody on her way to glory to meet up with the Lord. A law like this in the Gospel United Church might be just the thing to get Denzelle Flowers out of the race for bishop.

Chapter Eleven

Reverend Marcel Brown and Bishop Sonny Washington had not seen each other in over six months. Back in the day, a month wouldn't have gone by before they were hopping on a plane, en route to some fun and exotic location, up for whatever was on the social menu for the day. Marcel and Sonny had ho'd their way all over the globe. They enjoyed every single minute of it, too. Those were the good ole days, when they could run through women like crazy and not even have to drink some blue Kool-Aid to keep up with the honeys.

But that was then, and this was now. Marcel always said that whoever came up with Viagra/Cialis/Levitra deserved some kind of medal of honor. Those blue pills made an old man's life sweet.

Only thing was, you couldn't pop those pills like they were Flintstone vitamins. Taking too many would have a brother finding himself in a deep face-to-face conversation with the Lord before he was ready to sit down and talk to the Lord like that. Because as much dirt as Marcel Brown was involved in, he still did not want to die without getting saved.

Folks would be surprised to discover that Marcel looked forward to saying the Sinner's Prayer at some point in his life. But he wasn't ready to give up the world in exchange for walking with the Lord just yet. Marcel wanted to chase a few more rainbows, even though he knew he was playing with fire to keep delaying getting saved.

Marcel Brown loved the thrill of being in the wrong spaces and always finding a way to weasel out of them. He just didn't love the chronic panic, fear, and anxiety that came with being in such a risky state. Reverend Marcel Brown had been in church long enough to know he was playing with fire—literally. He secretly hoped that he didn't ride this train too far, and not be able to get back to the Lord before it was too late.

He discovered the hard way, while still at the preacher's conference in Atlanta, how much he needed to slow down. Against his better judgment, Marcel hooked up with one of those church hoochies he was always telling younger preachers to stay away from. Maybe it was laziness that made him go for a woman who was chasing him down like he was a young man. Maybe it was his ego, that some women would still do anything to be with him. But whatever it was, it caused Marcel Brown a whole lot of problems.

He wished he had listened to LaTina, who told him which women at the conference to stay clear of. LaTina saw that church she-devil in that gray St. John's with the custom-made church hat coming from a mile away. She said, "Reverend Brown, I know that thang lookin' good from where you see it as a man. But Rev, please don't tap that tail. It isn't worth the trouble you'll get after a few moments of pleasure. I'm tellin' you, don't do it."

Marcel was listening to LaTina, but he wasn't exactly hearing her. There was a strong chance she was 100 percent right. But she was trying to talk some sense into a man whose sensibilities had gone into overdrive every time that woman brushed up against him at the conference.

He didn't know what it was about this woman. Maybe it was the "do me, baby" and "anyway you like it" signals in her eyes. Whatever it was, Marcel was going to throw caution to the wind and do what he wanted to do. He was a grown man—old, too. And he purposed in his heart to hit that before he went back home to Detroit.

LaTina left her new friend alone and made sure he knew to

call her if he needed anything. She had a bad feeling about this, and wanted to be on hand in case of an emergency.

That woman had set her cap for Reverend Brown. She didn't just want him for the duration of the conference. She wanted Marcel on a permanent basis. The woman knew he was married, but that was only a minor technicality as far as she was concerned. That woman believed she had the magic touch when it came to men, and she worked what she had convinced herself was some special brand of mojo on Reverend Brown.

And during the first few days Marcel was at the conference, it looked like the woman was correct in her assessment of herself and her skills. She couldn't get enough of Marcel, who was discovering that he was getting more than enough of her. At first he reveled in the way she worked him over, and the way his named rolled off of her tongue over and over and over and over and over again.

That got old quick, however. Mainly because the woman didn't know what the word "break" meant. It was like Marcel was in a dream-come-true version of a nightmare. That woman barely wanted to eat. She had so much going on, Marcel had to pop Viagra tablets like they were Tic Tacs.

The one time he asked her to let him get some rest, she told him, "For years I've been hearing how no one can hold a candle to you behind closed doors. I've been dreaming for this opportunity, and everything those other women have said is true, with the exception of one thing."

When Marcel stared up at her with a raised eyebrow, she went on, "The older ladies from back in the day all said that they couldn't keep up with you, Presiding Elder. But I guess you are real old now, even if you are the finest thing at this conference. Because I'm not so sure you can keep up with me."

That's all that crazy woman had to tell Marcel to manipulate him into rising up for her challenge. He went against all common sense and swallowed three more Viagra tablets, heedless of the warnings on the almost empty bottle. He was able to keep up with that woman. He was also able to ride to the hospital in an ambulance, with LaTina, who was so glad he didn't croak. And even worse, he had to ride to the hospital with that Viagra still working overtime. It had been horrible to hear the paramedic laughing when he thought Marcel was out.

That incident reminded him of the time Marcel and his cronies tried to make this Viagra-like drug called WP21, from ground-up watermelon powder. That stuff was so strong, it made the whole body stiffen up. And it also killed a few folk who were too dumb and greedy to use it right. Marcel wasn't trying to go out like that. It would be a long time before he tried something crazy like that again. Tweaki would have to be enough woman for him for a while.

The whole time Marcel was in the hospital, he was praying they would get him straight, and up and running, before somebody thought to call Tweaki. It was one thing for Marcel and Tweaki to have a don't ask, won't tell agreement with each other. It was another thing for something to happen to bring all that Marcel liked to keep hidden in the dark to the light where his wife was concerned.

He was indebted to LaTina, who lied and told the hospital folk she was his niece and would make sure the family was informed of his condition. It was on the drive to the jet that Marcel hired LaTina to work for him, even when there was no work to do. When she protested, he said, "Baby girl, you are a true friend. I have plenty of money, and I want to make sure you always have what you need. Let me put you on my payroll. Okay?"

LaTina hugged her new BFF and said, "It's a deal. Just let me know whenever you need anything. I believe in earning what I'm paid. Okay, Rev."

Marcel kissed her on the cheek and said, "Deal." He climbed up the stairs to get on the jet, and felt so odd. This was the first time in his life that he wanted to do something for somebody and not want a thing from them in return. The scripture in Acts about the new Christians sharing what they had with one another became real to Marcel for the first time in his entire life. He'd never realized just how real the Bible was.

Now, just weeks after that satisfying epitome, Marcel was with Sonny at a small, private airport in St. Thomas. They were waiting for Bishop Thomas Lyle Jefferson's limo to scoop them up and take them to the bishop's plush digs high up in the hills of St. Thomas. As much as there was to get into in St. Thomas, and especially while visiting Thomas Jefferson, Marcel knew better than to ho around with Sonny on this trip.

He was still recuperating and didn't want anybody to know that he'd almost overdosed on Viagra. It was a miracle his skin hadn't turned blue from ingesting all of those tablets. Every time Marcel looked at himself in the mirror, he feared that a blue-colored black man would be staring back at him.

The one thing Marcel liked the most about Bishop Thomas Lyle Jefferson was that he didn't live like a bishop. That brother lived like a king. And now he was living even better with that new wife of his—Violetta. Lot of folk didn't understand why Bishop Jefferson wanted that ex–dance hall performer, who was also half his age.

Marcel could have told them why, after he and Sonny found some YouTube videos of Violetta dancing to her hit song, "Burn de House Down." That was a hot song back in the day. And Violetta was working it when she hopped off of the roof of a burning house in the official video, landed on the ground dancing, and started singing, "I so hot, I burn de house down. With one whip of my hip, I burn de house down, Daddy." Marcel used to be a big fan of the other famous Caribbean performer, Patra, until he saw the video by Violetta.

It didn't surprise either Marcel or Sonny Washington that the women in Bishop Jefferson's district couldn't stand Violetta Jefferson, and wanted her gone for several reasons. The first and most obvious one was connected to the women who wanted the bishop for themselves. Then there was the group who insisted that their bishop needed a saved wife. And last, there were women in the church who wished their bishop had chosen a woman who attended church at least once before she met him. Violetta didn't act or dress like she even knew where a church was before she met Thomas Jefferson.

Marcel always cracked up whenever he heard a woman in Bishop Jefferson's district talk about Violetta not going to church before she became an Episcopal Supervisor. He always wanted to tell the sister, "What in the world would an unsaved old reprobate like Bishop Jefferson do with a saved woman? Show her how to keep from skidding while backsliding?"

But as much as Marcel hated to admit it, those women were right. It was a glaring problem that Violetta Jefferson was an Episcopal Supervisor. That could be a very powerful position in the Gospel United Church, because she had charge over the wives of the pastors in her husband's district. Marcel understood completely how the pastors' wives felt about that kind of thing. His own mother, God rest her soul, would have led the pack of ministers' wives in protest against an Episcopal Supervisor like a Violetta Jefferson in their district.

The sleek Mercedes limo pulled up to a swanky, pale-brown stucco mansion. Marcel could not believe he had been so deep in thought that he missed all of the beauty of the ride up the hillside. He also didn't realize he was so tired, either.

"I'm getting too old for all of this cheating and slipping and sliding mess," Marcel mumbled to himself, as he waited for the limo driver to come and open the door for him. This brother was polite, proper, thorough, and willing to get Marcel and Sonny whatever they needed or wanted. Still, Marcel missed being driven around by LaTina. Now that was a real driver. The girl had skills, she knew all about cars, and she knew how to take good care of a high-profile preacher on her watch.

Thomas Lyle Jefferson walked out of his house to greet his guests. He was a tall, slender man with dark brown hair that had a heavy dusting of silver. Sonny Washington always said that

Bishop Jefferson looked like a taller, older, and more conservative version of the rapper Shaggy. Sometimes both he and Marcel would look at Bishop Jefferson and wonder if he knew the song "Mr. Boombastic."

Bishop Jefferson was delighted to see his old partners in crime. He missed the good old days, when they could run through some women, wash down some expensive liquor, and run through some women some more. That was the life, and Bishop Jefferson missed it a lot. Sometimes he wondered how the preachers who were really saved and for real about the Lord could stand it.

Thomas had watched his colleagues Theophilus Simmons and Eddie Tate for years, and just didn't get how they could be so happy and not be able to do the kinds of things that made him feel good. It was rare that Thomas felt happy. But there were many times when he could do something to feel good. He'd never understand what made them so excited when they started talking about the goodness of the Lord or gave a testimony.

Even worse than those two "I'm happy with Jesus alone" jokers were the preachers who used to hang tight with him, getting into all kinds of dirt, and now they were saved and all in cahoots with the Lord. And even more tragic was discovering that all of the fine women who had gotten into some good down and dirty stuff with him had gone soft, talking about how they couldn't take another second of being in the world.

In fact, the last time he was in the States, he'd called one of his women, only to discover that she couldn't talk because the woman was on her way to Bible study. Bible study? Bishop Jefferson was so upset after talking to that woman and trying to figure out what he was going to do now that he had Cialis coursing through his system, he had to go and drink a fifth of scotch to calm himself down.

And to make matters even worse, if that were even possible, that old hoochie had the nerve to start quoting some scriptures to him over the phone. He got mad and said, "You are aware that I am a bishop in the Gospel United Church? Right?"

She said, "Whatever. All I know is that I'm gone pray for you, Thomas," and hung up the phone in his face.

The house staff ran to the car to get the luggage. They were just as happy to see Marcel and Sonny as the bishop was. Those two old players were good tippers and fun to be around. The staff loved driving them around St. Thomas, enjoying all of the stuff Marcel and Sonny could still find to get into at their age.

Thomas Jefferson grabbed his friends in a big hug and said, "My man, Marcel. My man, Sonny. Lawd, you two old players are a welcome sight to me."

He turned around to the two servants standing behind him with mojitos made with homegrown ingredients. They hurried to put the drinks in Marcel's and Sonny's hands.

Sonny sipped on his drink and smacked his lips. Thomas always did have the best liquor, with five-star-hotel-quality drinks made by the bartender he had on his own staff.

"Brother, I see you are still living like your name is Big Money Grip."

Bishop Jefferson took a drink for himself and drank half of it.

"Well, my friend," Thomas answered, in the smooth Caribbean accent that always made the ladies in the States swoon like he was some kind of R&B singer, "is there any other way for a man like myself to live?"

"No," Marcel said. "I'd be disappointed if you got crazy enough to try and live any other way. I always tell folk that there are two things I can count on. The first is that I will always wake up in the morning black. The second is that Thomas Lyle Jefferson is the smoothest player in the Western hemisphere."

"Are you sure my husband is the smoothest player, Reverend Brown?" Violetta Jefferson said in a deep and sultry voice, and suppressing an urge to laugh out loud. She knew they didn't see her come out of the house.

"Men," Violetta murmured.

"Violetta," Marcel said. "Girl, you get finer and finer with each passing year. Now tell an old player how you are managing that?"

Violetta grinned, as she looked Marcel up and down like he was a big cookie in a baker's display case. As much as she relished being married to a man like her Thomas, there were times when she wished she could sample some of that urban American flavor. Reverend Brown was too handsome, and he looked like he was the kind of man who was a lot of fun behind closed doors. Violetta imagined Reverend Brown could keep a woman entertained for hours.

Marcel was hoping in vain that Thomas didn't pick up on what was going on with Violetta. He thought, "Old boy needs to step up his game."

It was not clear whether Thomas saw it, but Sonny hadn't missed a thing. He reached out for Violetta's hand, glad she wasn't attracted to a brown man like himself. Sonny felt bad for Marcel, because he knew Violetta was going to try and make a play for him. Thankfully, Marcel liked Thomas enough to respect his wife and the man's house. A brother didn't need to try and run game on a hoochie in her man's own home.

Unfortunately, Marcel would have to put up with Violetta trying to put the move on him the whole time they were in St. Thomas. Sonny felt that somebody needed to remind that woman of her place. Prior to meeting Thomas, Violetta worked fifteen-hour days dancing, singing, and filming all of those music videos that were still going viral on YouTube. By now, Violetta Jefferson should be a wealthy woman in her own right, after all of those hits her videos were getting on YouTube.

Violetta swung her long braid around in a swirl like she was getting ready to do that dance she was so famous for from the video when she jumped off of the roof and kept dancing. She grabbed Thomas's arm and started kissing his cheek, hoping to make Marcel Brown jealous.

Marcel took a swig of his drink. He couldn't believe this trick was trying to play that game on him. If it were any other man, he'd tap that tail and dare her to tell her man when he dropped her. But Marcel didn't mess with the women of men he liked—even though that list was very short.

Thomas knew Violetta was flirting with Marcel. He was just glad to know the two of them were still boys enough for Marcel to stay up off of his wife. Violetta was wife number six. His first wife, whom he truly loved, had died. His second wife went crazy and died years later while in an institution. His third and fourth wives were both living in Miami, even though they didn't know each other. Both women had caught Thomas cheating and decided that a generous deuces check was worth more than remaining the bishop's wife. He didn't know where number five was. She just upped and left after discovering his prenup was airtight.

Now here was Violetta, and sometimes Thomas wondered if there was going to be a number seven. Violetta worked his nerves. And if she didn't tread more carefully with him, he was going to forget himself and haul off and slap her silly.

A tall, brown, and well-built man who looked like a male version of Violetta came out of the house in some overpriced Bermuda shorts and a graphic T-shirt. He was wearing a thick gold chain and had tattoo sleeves on both arms. Thomas sighed and rolled his eyes.

"Vincent, these are my colleagues in the ministry and long-time friends, Bishop Sonny Washington and Reverend Marcel Brown."

Marcel raised an eyebrow. It was clear Thomas didn't like this man. He surmised correctly that Vincent was Violetta's brother.

Vincent reached out his hand to both Sonny and Marcel. He said, "It is an honor to meet you, Bishop Washington and Reverend Brown. I've heard much about your high-profile placements in the church."

Sonny coughed to stop himself from blurting our "Negro please." "High-profile placements"? He'd been described in many ways but not as somebody with a high-profile placement. This brother was a trip!

Marcel could see why Thomas didn't like Violetta's brother. Vincent thought so much more of himself that he ought to. It was clear he was used to being a kept man, too. Probably had a black book full of the names of women who would write him a check for anything he asked for.

Marcel would never begrudge another brother a good hustle. But he had never liked the Vincent types. Their kind of hustle didn't even require brains or work. All they had to do was look good and say what folk wanted to hear.

Another man came out of the house. He looked like an older, shorter, and fatter version of Vincent. Another brother?

"Vincent is Violetta's younger brother," Thomas was saying. "And this is Violetta's uncle, Raphael. He is staying in the guesthouse out back until he gets back on his feet"

Sonny looked down at Raphael's feet and almost choked on the laughter he was working so hard to hold back. He pulled out a handkerchief and dabbed at his eyes before those tears of laughter started streaming down his face.

At first Marcel didn't know what had Sonny acting like a little kid at church trying not to laugh. Then he followed Sonny's eyes down to Raphael's feet and started coughing to stop himself from hollering with laughter. This was too good to act like he hadn't noticed it. He said, "Bishop, that's gonna take a long time from the looks of things."

Thomas bit back his own laugh. He was so glad he wasn't the only one who thought Uncle Raphael looked ridiculous with his homemade cut-out shoes. It had been a long time since Thomas, Sonny, or Marcel had seen a pair of homemade sandals. Uncle Raphael was wearing a pair of beige Stacy Adams with toes of both of the shoes cut out. It looked like someone had taken a big knife and sawed the wing tip of the shoe right off. And if that weren't bad enough, Uncle Raphael was wearing a pair of dark brown socks.

"My feets can get all swole up and make it hard to wear my shoes," Uncle Raphael explained, before tottering off toward the guest cottage.

As soon as Marcel knew Uncle Raphael could not hear them, he said, "You know, I thought the only brothers with homemade sandals were down in the hood in Detroit."

"Or on some brother out in my neck of the woods in North Carolina," Sonny told them, and laughed. "Do you know how many old and retired playahs I've run across at one of Glodean's The Dollar Is King Stores, wearing cut-out Stacy Adams shoes? I even saw an old playah wearing one shoe regular, and the other shoe was a cut-out. Can you even imagine what that country mess looked like?"

"Uhh, yeah. Actually, I can," Marcel said, laughing and wiping at his eyes.

Bishop Jefferson was laughing, even though his wife was looking like she was thinking, I didn't see anything funny about the shoes. He turned to Violetta, standing there pouting with her no-good brother and said, "Uncle Raphael can go and live anywhere he pleases if there is anything about my home and hospitality he finds unpalatable."

Violetta frowned, clearly in the dark about the word unpalatable.

Marcel pulled out his phone and started acting like he was checking his text messages. He reread the one he'd received from Tweaki, and then texted Sonny.

She's not the sharpest knife in the drawer, huh?

It was killing Sonny not to pull out his phone and read that text from Marcel. The only thing stopping him was that he knew Vincent was standing there watching him intently.

That chump needs to get a job and quit worrying if we are going to figure out that his butt is a straight-up pimp, Sonny thought.

"Thomas, I don't like it when you treat my family as if they are moochers," Violetta whined.

Sonny closed his eyes and resisted shaking his head. He had seen Violetta's video, the one with her jumping off of the roof and landing on the ground dancing. And he could only imagine her other levels of expertise. But was Violetta so dense that she didn't think Thomas could see straight through her family members? Thomas Jefferson was the same man who had figured out how to skim thousands of dollars off of the tops of the budgets of most of the churches he'd pastored before becoming a bishop. He had rarely been caught, and never prosecuted or threatened with going to jail.

To his credit, the bishop didn't give his wife an answer. He just walked back into his house and let the door slam in Vincent's face. Marcel Brown wondered how long Violetta was going to be able to hold on to her only recently acquired position as this district's Episcopal Supervisor. If Violetta didn't get herself together, Marcel knew Thomas was going to strip her of the papers granting her the right to hold that title.

Bishop Jefferson needed a new wife like he needed a hole in his head. But Marcel knew he would get a new one if this girl didn't act right. Folks always assumed the bishop was just a ho who couldn't keep his hands off of other women. Nothing could be further from the truth. Thomas only cheated on his wives when he was tired of the old one and was starting to actively court the woman who would become the new one.

That is why he was going to become the poster boy bishop to help his church implement a new Episcopal law. It was a stupid law. But if ruling that a preacher could not run for bishop if he/she got divorced and then remarried while the ex-spouse was alive would keep Denzelle Flowers out of the race, it was a stupid law he was willing to live with. What did he care anyway? Marcel wasn't getting divorced, and he sure wasn't running for bishop, either.

Chapter Twelve

Marcel held his glass out for more rum punch—a refreshing way to polish off a delicious meal. Thomas had never been one to hold back on providing his guests with the ultimate in Caribbean hospitality. The only drawback in coming to the bishop's lovely home, with that cool island wind blowing across your face, was that Marcel never knew who would be standing next to Thomas with a rock on her left hand. Thomas changed wives like some men changed cars.

Sonny had once commented that it was too bad there was no special leasing program for men who like being married—just not to the same woman for any real length of time. Marcel agreed with Sonny. It would be the perfect solution for a man like Thomas Lyle Jefferson. But what would happen if the bishop married a woman he didn't want to turn in when the lease was about to expire? Would he have to take out some kind of lease option to buy policy or pay a penalty for not releasing the wife at the designated time?

Bishop Jefferson led his guests to the open porch that spread out across the back of the entire house and overlooked the ocean from high in the hills. Marcel and Sonny had often discussed where the bishop got the capital for all of this captivating luxury. They knew he had sticky fingers and had found a way to fill up his personal coffers without getting caught. But this cost way more than an unscrupulous bishop could get his hands on.

"Thomas, you live awfully well on a bishop's salary," Sonny said.

"And why does that surprise you? I've been to your estate in North Carolina. I wouldn't exactly classify it as low-income housing."

"Thomas, you have not answered my question," Sonny told him. "How do you do it? I'm looking down this hill. The view is breathtaking. The breeze is so fragrant, I want to open my mouth and taste it. This kind of thing cost money."

"You need to be better educated about your church's history," Thomas told Sonny.

"Church history? What does that have to do with this house, these servants, your cars, and even your liquor? Thomas, you serve rum that is handmade just for you. How many people do you know who can afford something like that?"

"My grandmother was one of the Caribbean Meetings," Thomas told Sonny. "I thought you knew that."

Marcel stared at Thomas. How could he have missed that all of these years? He looked a whole lot like the Meetings in North Carolina. Thomas Jefferson's people were some of the architects of the Gospel United Church—which explained why he could always get some kind of leniency when he strayed. It also explained why he had so much money that couldn't be explained by his position as a bishop in the church.

"So, Bishop," Marcel began, "your people were those so-called white folk Bethany Meeting left in charge when she left St. Thomas and came back to North Carolina before the Civil War."

"Yes."

"Are you talking about the same Bethany Meeting whose son switched places with the slave owner in the Chapel Hill area and acted like he was the plantation owner?" Sonny asked. This was amazing.

"Yes. Hezekiah Meeting was Bethany's son. His half brother, Cornelius Meeting, was a white plantation owner who lived right outside of Chapel Hill, North Carolina. Hezekiah drugged him and then exchanged places with Cornelius. Bethany left my great-grandmother and her husband in charge of the St. Thomas plantation when she left to go back to the States."

"Where was the plantation?" Marcel asked.

"You're sitting on it," Thomas answered with a short laugh. Black folks' history was something else. So many twists and turns from then to now.

"Well, it's no wonder you have a home like this. You better—with all of that Meeting money," Sonny said.

"My thoughts precisely," Thomas told him.

Violetta came in with a glass of lemonade in her left hand. The seven-carat white sapphire, surrounded with black diamonds, sparkled and glittered in the dwindling sunlight. She sat down on Thomas's lap, hoping to make Marcel jealous.

"Bad move," Sonny thought to himself. He wished he could give women a list of things that men wished they wouldn't do. And one of the first things he'd tell a woman was to never try and make one of your husband's boys jealous. Then, never ever come in and plop yourself down in the middle of a conversation that had "Men Only" all over it. What did a woman expect—that the men would capitulate because she was there looking fine, and start talking about stuff she knew they didn't want her to hear?

Thomas patted Violetta's hip and kissed her on the cheek.

"Girl, you fine," he said in a smooth and low voice that had "Playah, Play on" all over it.

Violetta blushed and tried not to giggle. She said, "Thomas, not in front of our guests."

Thomas gave Violetta the kind of smile a playah gave when he'd gone fishing and had the catch-of-the-day on his hook. He patted her hip again.

"Then, Baby, you need to take your fine, set de house on fire self off of this porch before the guests see even more."

Violetta slid off of the bishop's lap and said, "See you two gentlemen in the morning."

Thomas grabbed her hand and let it slide out of his as she walked off. He said, "Girl, you know you so fine."

As soon as Violetta was out of earshot, Marcel and Sonny hollered with laughter. Marcel said. "Player, I think I'm gonna have to give you the blue ribbon award for Pimp of the Year. That was smooth. I would never have thought Violetta to be one to fall for the 'but Baby, you so fine' line."

Thomas grinned and sat back in his chair with his legs spread apart. He knew he was the man in his home. He said, "I'm always amazed at how well that works. Your woman tries to work game on you, turn it around on her and tell her she's fine."

"I know," Sonny said. "When one of my women get mad at me for calling Glodean while I'm with her, I finish talking to my wife and then turn to the woman and say, 'Baby, calm down. You know you fine.'"

"Now, don't you two players get beside yourself," Thomas cautioned them. "It doesn't work on every woman. A woman with a good head on her shoulders will catch it, and you will get your feelings hurt."

"You ain't never lied, Thomas," Sonny said. "I tried that on Glodean one time, and she put me in my place real fast. I never tried to run game on her like that again."

"Was that before or after you stopped beating her tail," Marcel asked in earnest. He'd always wondered what made Sonny stop hitting Glodean and start having normal disagreements like normal married folk. There were times Marcel threatened to kick Sonny's behind when he wouldn't stop hitting Glodean.

"Why did you have to bring that up, Marcel man? I stopped fighting my woman decades ago."

"So, what made you stop? I really want to know, Sonny."

"She did," he answered solemnly. "Glodean started making all of that money and used her fat checkbook to shut me down. I raised my hand to her one day. She didn't even flinch—just said, 'If your hand lands on me when it comes down out of the air, your American Express card, the car, and even your credit rating

will change in a heartbeat. I make all of the money. I don't care
that I make all of the money. But you better not hit me, or even
think about hitting me, again, or else you will have to borrow
some money from the homeless man."

Marcel bit his lip. He didn't want to hurt Sonny's feelings by
laughing.

"I never hit her again—been on the wagon for decades now.
And it feels so good not to treat your woman like that. The aftermath of beating a woman is a horrible feeling—like the worse
hangover you've ever had."

"You're right," Thomas said, even though there were times
when he wanted to put his foot in Violetta's behind. He drained
his lemonade.

"So, what do you two need that would make Marcel gas up
his wife's jet to fly to St. Thomas? Could it have something to do
with the race for bishop?"

Sonny and Marcel nodded.

"How can I help?"

"Thomas," Sonny said, "are you ready to retire from being a
bishop?"

Bishop Jefferson got real quiet and still. He made them wait
a few minutes before answering the question. Marcel could hear
the wind passing all through the sheer blue curtains on the porch.

"Not really. I like what goes with being a bishop in the Gospel United Church."

Sonny sighed. He said, "Look, we need you to agree to retire
if we are going to be able to win an Episcopal seat. A retired
bishop still wields influence and clout."

"A retired bishop doesn't preside over an Episcopal district,
Sonny," Thomas said in a quiet voice. He'd never realized how
much being an active bishop meant to him.

Marcel was surprised at the bishop's response. He knew how
much clout a retired bishop had. But it had not occurred to him
how intoxicating it was to preside over a district of churches,
pastors, presiding elders, and parishioners. He didn't realize they

were going to have to do some real work to get Bishop Jefferson to go along with this plan.

Sonny was not as surprised as Marcel. He had been a bishop in the Gospel United Church since 1986, and was rapidly approaching his own retirement. Even though Sonny would appreciate being able to move at a more relaxed pace, he knew it would be an adjustment to relearn how to function without a district. It felt good to have all of those folks deferring to him when he visited churches and pastors in his district. Marcel would never be able to grasp what this felt like.

"Thomas," Sonny began, "we need your help to get our candidate in a position to get elected. I know you are tired of the Theophilus Simmons and Eddie Tate faction running things their way. What I'm about to propose is the only way we can win."

The bishop sat back in his chair. Sonny was right. He was very tired of Theophilus Simmons and Eddie Tate running everything and having the strongest influence in the church. They ran into a brick wall every time they tried to overturn anything those two implemented. It was becoming increasingly difficult for men like Thomas Jefferson and Sonny Washington to work the system in their favor when they met with the other bishops.

Back in the good old days, a bishop like Thomas Jefferson could put his cronies in key churches, he could influence the selection of Presiding Elders, and he could influence policies made at the Episcopal level. Even if folk didn't like what came down from the bishops, they would deal with it. Back then they didn't have to deal with women in the pulpit, they could come in a church and walk off with a lot of cash, and they could do what they wanted and have few worries about the church being upset and demanding answers.

All of those changes began in 1963 when the late Percy Jennings and his boy, Murcheson James, with the help of Theophilus and Eddie, stopped their opponents from putting their choice candidates in the office of bishop and demoted a bunch of pastors—Marcel Brown being one of them. Nothing had been the same since.

No matter what they did, how good the plan, and how much they fought the opposition, they always came up short. And even worse, they always lost what little ground they had gained when they were defeated just one more time. Enough was enough. Thomas knew he was going to have to man up, suck it in, and be prepared to step down from running his district.

He took a deep breath and said, "This must be a hell of a plan if you are asking me to step down and retire from my district."

"It is," Marcel answered him.

Sonny pulled a fat beige envelope out of his breast pocket and laid it on the table.

"For your troubles, Bishop."

Thomas smiled and patted the envelope. He said, "Twenty-nine thousand USDs. A thousand dollars for each year I've been a bishop."

"And one thousand to grow on," Sonny told him grinning, as he reached back into his breast pocket and pulled out ten crisp, new one hundred dollar bills.

"I like your style, Bishop Washington," Thomas told him.

"So, you want to hear the plan?" Marcel asked, now anxious to get this thing going, so he could go home. All of a sudden he was missing Detroit and Tweaki. That had been happening a lot lately. The episode with the church hoochie in Atlanta had scared him, and was making things Marcel used to thumb up his nose at more appealing.

"I'm all ears," the bishop answered, as he put the money close to his ears, just so he could hear how good it sounded.

"I know you know one of the BMEs," Marcel began.

Thomas raised an eyebrow. If this plan was connected to one of the Black Methodist denominations, he might have to back down. He fanned the money across his nose and sniffed. Maybe the smell of money would calm him back down.

"We aren't working with any of them," Marcel said. "They

are too straight-laced for my taste. Too many of them want to play by the rules. We are only going to use one of their new rulings to our advantage."

"What new ruling?" Thomas asked, wondering why Sonny and Marcel were grinning like they had just hit the lottery.

"The one where one of the BMEs ruled that if a preacher in their denomination gets a divorce and remarries while the ex-spouse is still alive, he, and now she, cannot run for an Episcopal seat. And if he or she remains single, runs for bishop, and gets elected, falls in love, remarries, and that ex-spouse is still alive and kicking, old boy, and now old girl, will have to step down."

"You are lying, Presiding Elder Marcel DeMarcus Brown," Bishop Jefferson said. He couldn't believe they had come up with something like that.

"If I'm lying, my name is Theophilus Simmons. And you know how I feel about that Dudley Do-right brother."

Thomas chuckled. "Yes, I do. There's no true love lost between the two of you." He chuckled some more, and then got a pained look on his face.

"I don't understand why they would want to come up with something crazy like that. I've been a bishop long enough to know they are courting a lot more trouble than the new policy is worth."

"I agree with you, Bishop," Marcel told him.

"But they are very adamant about making this policy something their preachers can't get around. They are claiming this ruling is needed to make sure some bad eggs don't roll under the radar to win and occupy an Episcopal seat. But honestly, I believe it's about some of those old fogeys wanting to keep the best, brightest, and most innovative of their potential candidates from becoming a bishop.

"And we all know the honest preachers will not pretend they want to be married to somebody who isn't right for them. They don't like shams and acting like stuff is all hunky-dory when all hell is breaking loose up in their home. That group would look at their bishops like they were crazy and act like they had never even heard the word 'bishop.'"

Thomas nodded. Marcel had a point. Even in their own denomination, it was the most honest and upstanding of preachers who would hunker down and weather the storm of a divorce rather than be dishonest and live a lie.

"The good preachers will remarry at some point," Sonny said. "They are not going to meet someone, start loving that person, and then risk losing them forever because they were too much of a punk-A to marry that man or woman. And truthfully, I don't blame them. I can't imagine being a bishop without Glodean in my life and by my side."

"Yeah," Marcel added. "This group is not going to run around acting like they are happy and content to remain single. They want a boo and they know the Word says that it is better to marry than to burn. They also want to be true to the one they are with, and they will want a mate."

"Which makes them extremely vulnerable to a ruling of this nature," Bishop Jefferson said with a grin spreading across his face. "We can get rid of some good candidates for bishops—preachers who would side with Simmons and Tate—with this one simple policy."

Bishop Jefferson got up and walked back inside of the house. He pushed the button on the intercom. A soft female voice said, "Do you need your cigars now?"

"And my Hennessey, and Crown for Reverend Brown, Violetta."

"I'll be right there, Bishop," Violetta answered, barely able to contain the excitement in her voice at being able to come back to where the men were talking. She wanted to see Reverend Brown, and try to get the inside scoop on their conversation.

The bishop sighed. He wished he had told Violetta to get this for him earlier. He knew she was going to do everything in her power to stay out on this porch with them.

Violetta showed up in record time. She rolled in a glass cart with an ice bucket, Fiji water, Hennessey, Crown, and a box of Cuban cigars.

"Thank you, sweetheart," Thomas told his wife. He kissed her on the cheek, winked, and said, "Girl, have I told you how fine you are today?"

Violetta gushed and grinned. She said, "Only ten times today, Bishop."

"Well, let me make that eleven times before you take your fine self on away from here. Girl, you fine."

Violetta walked away, making sure her husband (and Reverend Brown) could see the easy and smooth swing of her hips. She turned back to make sure Thomas was looking, and Marcel was sneaking a look.

She was happy when Thomas winked again, and said, "Girl, hurry up and go on with your fine self."

Violetta frowned when she saw Reverend Brown was busy texting.

When Thomas knew Violetta was gone, he put some ice in a glass, poured himself some Hennessey, and got a cigar. He twirled the cigar with his thumb and middle fingers, ran it under his nose, and sighed in delight. Thomas couldn't wait to finish snipping the end of the cigar so he could light up.

"Bishop," Marcel began, "we want to push this ruling through at the next Board of Bishops meeting in Raleigh, North Carolina. We need you to come forth as a willing example of why we need this policy. You have to confess you should no longer remain an active bishop because of your many marriages. I know you can fix this up when you talk to your colleagues and get their sympathy."

"What would I say?" Bishop Jefferson asked.

"Don't *say* anything," Sonny told him. "Just preach. You know, get up and get to whooping and hollering and carrying on. That will work just fine for me."

"Then," Marcel added, "you tell them why you know the Lord led you to spearhead the denomination implementing this rule, and to use you as the first bishop to step down as a result of so many marriages. That will carry a whole lot of weight and make your petition look authentic."

"Looking authentic is relative, Marcel. It depends on who's watching you. I might be able to sway some of the bishops. But the ones in the Theophilus Simmons and Eddie Tate camp are going to be very suspicious, because they know it's time for me to retire anyway."

Sonny sighed heavily. No matter what they did, it always boiled down to having to deal with those two. He said, "The stakes are too high to let Theophilus and Eddie sway bishops away from us. We are going to have to grease some palms to get what we want, and make promises to scratch those itchy palms from time to time."

"And how are you going to do this, and keep it up?" Bishop Jefferson asked. He knew paying off greedy and crooked preachers could get real expensive. Sometimes it was more expensive than getting rid of a wife you were tired of.

"Attorney Luther Howard," Marcel replied.

"How can Luther Howard help us?" Bishop Jefferson asked.

"Luther has a fat discretionary fund. He needs to get some bonus points for his tax situation. So he is donating his excess to us. Thomas, it's enough to work like some green cortisone cream on the right hands."

"Okay, Marcel," Thomas said. "We get all the money we need to sway folk in our direction. But that can't end with this vote. We'll need money to carry us all the way through to a win for an Episcopal seat.

"Plus, what does Luther Howard want? I've never known him to scratch somebody's back and then not turn around and demand you return the favor."

"Luther wants us to put our muscle behind Reverend Xavier Franklin. And once Xavier is elected, he wants us to buy his way into the Seventh Episcopal District, which is now under Bishop Jimmy Thekston Jr.," Sonny said.

"I'm in complete agreement with Luther wanting Xavier as the next bishop. But I don't know how Luther is going to get a Thekston to pack up his office in the Seventh simply because he asked him to."

"Luther Howard is not worried about getting Jimmy Jr. to concede to his request," Marcel said. "Luther will lay an offer on the table Jimmy will not turn down."

"Why the Seventh, Marcel?" Bishop Jefferson asked. Reverend Xavier Franklin was smart, ruthless, a good liar, and would do whatever he had to do to make it happen in any district he was assigned to.

"Money."

"Money? That's your sole answer, Marcel?" Sonny asked. "Hasn't it always been about money for us?"

"I'm talking about the kind of money you wish you could get your hands on. Like us getting a ten percent cut and walking away with a couple million. We've had some good money schemes, and made a lot of money. But we've never scored as big as we will if we do things Luther Howard's way."

"Where is Luther planning on getting all of this money from?" Sonny said.

"Right now, Luther Howard is putting together three dummy corporations that will get its hands on that 'BP "We messed up big time" oil money,'" Marcel told them.

"One corporation will handle bogus claims requests for money. The second corporation will get paid to pretend it is helping small business owners in the seafood industry continue getting back on their feet. And the third corporation will claim to be involved in making amends for the environmental damages to the area as a result of the oil spill.

"He's done this kind of thing before and made millions. But this time he needs help from the church to make it happen. People love to see the church working to set things right in the community and help get folks jobs. This will look good on paper. But all of the money will go straight into our pockets—kind of like an on-shore, off-shore account. Only thing we need is a bishop who will come in on the ground floor to help make it happen—a bishop like Xavier Franklin."

This plan was so wild, exciting, corrupt, and crazy it made Marcel Brown feel like he did when he saw a fine woman he wanted to spend the night with.

"That's a helluva plan, Marcel," Bishop Jefferson said.

"Yes, it is," was all Sonny said. He had felt such a rush listening to this, he almost started hyperventilating.

"All we need is to get Xavier elected as bishop," Marcel said.

"So, Thomas, you understand why we need you to do this, right?" Sonny asked.

"Yeah," he answered with a heavy sigh. It was going to take a lot to get used to being without a district to run. But the thought of making all of that money made him feel better. Plus, Thomas was going to make sure Luther gave him some extra bonus money up front for having to go through all of this for the plan to work.

"So, we're all in on this?" Marcel asked.

"Yep, we're in," Thomas told them, and went to stand on his open porch to watch the waves hitting up against the shore.

Chapter Thirteen

Marsha parked Lacy next to the black CTS Cadillac sedan in Denzelle's driveway. Lacy looked quite modest next to the sleek black hog, as the old players used to call Cadillacs back when she was a kid. But she didn't care how small and low-key Lacy looked next to this car. She loved Lacy and dreaded the day when she would have to get rid of her.

Marsha named all of her cars, and then drove them until the car would practically scream no more. Marcus chided his mother about how long she drove a car. He always told his friends, "I've only been in two cars my entire life—Callie, Mom's blue Subaru, and Lacy, Mom's blue Ford Escape. It would be nice to see the inside of another car before I have children of my own."

She turned off Lacy's engine and patted the steering wheel.

"Girl, I don't know why folk give me such a hard time about you. Lacy, you have made sure that I have always gotten everywhere I've needed to go."

Marsha got out of the car and walked up the fancy brick walkway leading to Denzelle's huge, double front door. She had heard that his house was so sharp it was almost off the grid. But Marsha was not prepared for a house that was so inviting and lovely.

Denzelle lived in the North Hills section of Raleigh—one of Marsha's favorite areas of the city. She always thought he would have a home in one of the newer sections, like the neighborhoods off of 540. But she was impressed that Denzelle had gone completely old school by purchasing and upgrading one of the more traditional homes, located not too far from North Hills Mall.

She really liked the deep crimson color of the front doors, set against the pale, almost cream-colored brick of the house. There were rose bushes framing the large windows and an old-fashioned red swing sitting on the porch. This house had Yvonne Fountain Parker's hand all over it. Yvonne was a premiere interior/exterior designer and landscaper in North Carolina. The swing on the front porch was Yvonne's signature for any house she worked on.

Marsha rang the doorbell, hoping she presented a cool composure in spite of the mixed feelings she had about having this meeting at Denzelle's house. Part of Marsha was secretly excited to spend some time alone with Denzelle. Another part of her was uncomfortable and hoped he would not discern she had a deep crush on him. And the worst part was that the crush was getting more intense the longer they worked together on this Pastor's Aide Club business.

She was about to ring the doorbell again, but then checked her notebook to make sure she had the right day and time. Marsha was so nervous about going to Denzelle's house, she feared she may have written down the wrong information. But that very irrational "I'm so excited to see him again, I scare myself" fear was put to rest when Denzelle's uncle, Reverend Russell Flowers, answered the door.

"It is Miss Marsha Metcalf in the flesh. I hope I left you enough room in the driveway," Uncle Russell said, with a big smile spreading across his face. He was a handsome man—an old-school, silver fox with plenty of charisma to add to his good looks.

"Hi, Reverend Flowers," Marsha said softly.

She had a sweet voice. It reminded Russell of the voices of the soloists who sang two of his favorite gospel songs, "I'm Still Holding On" and "Fully Committed." He said, "Come on in and take a seat in the living room."

Uncle Russell's keen eyes hadn't missed Marsha trying to hide the disappointment spreading across her face when he opened his nephew's front door. He'd heard there were some sparks between those two from Denzelle's older brother, Yarborough. Now it was confirmed—at least where Marsha Metcalf was concerned.

Denzelle, on the other hand, was a cool piece of work, and would be very careful to keep his true feelings hidden from his uncle. But if there was one thing Russell Flowers knew was that a man in love couldn't hide his feelings all that well. That's why some men in love actually choose to run from instead of running to the woman who touched their hearts with a gentle fingertip. They'd rather shove her away and hurt the girl's feeling than have someone see that all of the cards in their hands were hearts. Uncle Russell was making it his business to stay longer than necessary to get a read on the cards his nephew was holding awfully close to his chest.

He certainly hoped that what Denzelle felt for Marsha was the same thing she was trying to pretend she didn't feel for him. Marsha Metcalf was a good woman and had been walking around without a man in her life too long. Russell didn't know what was wrong with these younger single brothers when it came to women like Marsha. And he didn't like what he saw.

Brothers like his nephew would discover a woman they needed to spend time with and then hightail it in the opposite direction, toward one that wasn't worth the energy it took to blink your eyes. There were times when Uncle Russell, who was now retired from pastoring, would have to fight back tears when he saw all of those good and beautiful women sitting in church alone because the men were too scared to step up and claim a blessing. He hoped there was something so special about this Marsha Metcalf that she would make Denzelle think twice about running away from her.

Marsha followed Uncle Russell into a lovely and cozy, creamy-colored and brickred-accent living room. The sofa and matching chairs were brickred and had an assortment of pale gold-, cream-, and camel-colored pillows on them. The walls were a soft and soothing cream, with windows framed with shutters of a deeper cream. There were original oil paintings on the wall and huge plants in cream, gold, and deep-red ceramic pots. The room smelled good, too—like cinnamon with just an itsy-bitsy taste of lemon in it. Marsha wouldn't have thought to pair up those two fragrances, but they worked well together.

"I like this room, Reverend Flowers. Looks like one of Yvonne Parker's jobs."

"Yes, it definitely has Yvonne stamped all over it. And you can call me Uncle Russell."

"Okay . . . Uncle . . . Russell," Marsha responded very carefully. She'd never been one to try and rush to get to know folk and their families. It was always a good idea to let folk get to know you in their own good time.

Marsha sat down in one of the chairs, next to a walnut end table. There were several pictures of Denzelle as a little boy, in an assortment of gold, crimson, and light-brown wooden frames. She picked up a picture of him in a cowboy outfit, with toy guns in both holsters hanging off of his narrow, little boy hips. His chest stuck out, obviously from the pride of wearing the bright gold badge attached to his brown-fringed vest.

"That boy was always into fighting crime," Uncle Russell said with a chuckle.

Denzelle came into the living room looking so good, Marsha forgot herself and whispered, "Oh my." She prayed he hadn't heard her. But something told her Uncle Russell hadn't missed a thing.

Denzelle was wearing dark gray athletic pants that hugged that high butt like they had been sewn on his body. He had on a gray, blue, and black athletic shirt and a pair of blue, black, and silver athletic shoes. His navy baseball cap was turned backward and made him look like he was as full of mischief and playfulness as the little boy in the cowboy picture.

Marsha felt her heart skip a beat. She knew that look. It was the one of the sweet little boy underneath all of that man stuff. She saw it in her son all of the time. And she also saw how Marcus worked to hide that part of himself from most folk—especially women.

She reached out to shake Denzelle's hand.

Denzelle looked at Marsha and her hand like she was on the kind of drugs that were not available at a CVS pharmacy.

"Girl, give me a hug. I cannot believe you have walked yourself up into my home, and you have the nerve to try and reach out and just shake my hand. Do you honestly think I would let somebody I don't like enough to do more than shake their hand into my home, and on a work night, too?"

Marsha smiled. He had a point. She'd never invited anybody into her home she didn't like well enough to do more than shake their hand. She stood up, and was surprised when Denzelle reached out and grabbed her in a big hug. Marsha positioned her body so all he could get was a side hug.

Denzelle rolled his eyes and looked down at Marsha. He said, "That is the most pitiful hug I've ever gotten. I don't stank, do I?"

He sniffed up under his arms and then said, "Nahh . . . nothing but roses there."

Now Marsha was laughing out loud. All she could say was, "Boy, you are so crazy."

"Yeah, he is crazy," Uncle Russell said, waving his hand across his face like he was fanning away some serious funk. "'Cause don't nothing 'bout your behind make me think about some roses."

"Unck, why do you have to play a playah like that, huh?" Denzelle asked his uncle, grinning.

"Playah?" Uncle Russell looked at Marsha. He said, "Baby girl, do you see a playah standing in this room?"

Marsha let a chuckle escape.

Denzelle got real close up on her. He looked down into Marsha's eyes like they were the only two people in the room and whispered, "Well, *Baby girl*, do you see a playah standing in this room, or don't you?"

Marsha stepped back. She didn't like being that close up on Denzelle. The brother was dressed down and smelling up too good for her comfort. What she wanted to say is that he had the mark of a true player. Brothers who knew how to roll the dice in a game with a woman always smelled good.

"Baby, I'm still waiting on your answer," Denzelle said in low sexy voice, hoping Uncle Russell didn't pick up on the heat layering those words. He didn't want to be so sweet on Marsha Metcalf, but he couldn't help it that he was.

Marsha couldn't stand it when Denzelle teased her like that. She knew he was smug enough to think she was going to belly up and tell him that he was the ultimate player, all that, and then some. She said, "I don't see one playah in this room, Den-zelle. But I do see someone with some serious swagger—your Uncle Russell."

Uncle Russell put his fist up to his mouth, leaned down and over to the side, and said, "Ohhhh, snap, Nephew. Missy just clowned you good."

Denzelle's mouth got kind of tight. He wasn't used to Marsha getting the best of him, and especially in front of somebody like Uncle Russell. He was never going to hear the end of this unless he regained control of the situation.

Denzelle winked down at Marsha and said, "I see you got jokes," in the lowest, smoothest, playah voice she'd ever heard coming out of his mouth. She knew Denzelle was smooth, but right now Denzelle was sizzling, he was so sexy.

Marsha hurried and sat back down and started going through all of the stuff she'd brought with her for this meeting. She and Denzelle were supposed to go over the first big fundraising and publicity event for his campaign. That was the only reason why she was even at the man's house.

Veronica had warned her to make Denzelle meet her at the church. But noooooo—Marsha had to act like she had game enough to roll up on Denzelle on his turf. This had to be one of the dumbest things she'd done in a very long time.

Uncle Russell liked the chemistry going on between those two. It was plain to anybody who knew Denzelle that he was quite taken with Marsha Metcalf.

"About time," Uncle Russell mumbled under his breath.

"You say something, Unck?" Denzelle asked.

'Naw, son. Not really. Just thinking out loud about all of the stuff your auntie wants me to pick up at the store before I go home."

"If you say so," Denzelle responded, eyeing his uncle suspiciously. He didn't get why Uncle Russell was telling that kajoomba lie. Uncle Russell never went to the grocery store on a Tuesday night to get a bunch of stuff. He and Denzelle's aunt loved to go grocery shopping early on Saturday mornings. They could stay out all day, like they were on a date.

Denzelle opened his mouth to ask his uncle what was up but didn't get a chance. Uncle Russell left the house so fast he almost hurt his nephew's feelings.

Marsha finished organizing her things.

"Where can I spread this out?"

"Back in my office," Denzelle answered from the hallway. It occurred to him that he hadn't offered Marsha so much as a whiff of oxygen since she'd walked through the front door of his house.

"Can I get you anything, Marsha? I have some homemade walnut brownies."

"Did you make them?" Marsha asked him, before she remembered her own manners. It had never occurred to her that Denzelle could cook. But this house was pretty homeylike. Most men who were so settled and comfortable in their homes were usually very good cooks.

"As a matter of fact, I did," Denzelle answered, with a big smile on his face. Few folk ever thought about him cooking. But he was an excellent cook.

"Okay," Marsha said, still sitting in the living room chair. As much as she wanted to see the rest of Denzelle's house, Marsha wasn't so sure if she wanted to be introduced to the more

private Denzelle Flowers. You learned a lot about a person when
you saw their home—especially the rooms that were not ear-
marked for company.

What if his house was messy? What if this was the only
pretty part or company part of the house? What if he forgot she
was coming and had his underwear lying in the middle of the
floor?

Marsha had never thought about Denzelle and his underwear. He looked like he wore boxer briefs—especially in those
athletic pants. Marsha closed her eyes and tried to shake that
thought out of her head. What was wrong with her, thinking
about Denzelle Flowers like that?

"Are you coming, Girl?" Denzelle called over his shoulder,
wondering why Marsha was sitting there looking like she was
having some kind of fight with herself.

Marsha heard and felt the frustration in Denzelle's voice,
even though she didn't know what was making him take a trip
into what she called the cranky man space.

"I know he doesn't think he's the boss of me," Marsha mumbled under her breath, and took her time getting her stuff up in
her arms. If she ran down that hall after Denzelle Flowers after
he snapped at her, she wouldn't know.

Denzelle sighed loud enough to be heard. He could not believe Marsha was being that stubborn with him. He told her to
follow him, and she was acting like he wasn't talking to her. Then
this girl had the nerve to start singing Kelly Price's lyrics, "You're
not my daddy. You're my man," under her breath, but loud enough
to be heard by him from the doorway to the kitchen.

"Marsha!" Denzelle commanded. "We need to go over this
project."

Marsha stood her ground, staring at Denzelle like there was
something seriously wrong with him. He was talking to her like
there was something between them. That was the only time a
man got his butt all hunched up on his shoulders with a woman
for what, on the surface, looked like no good reason.

Denzelle stared back at Marsha standing there giving him the universal black girl look that clearly stated "I don't know *who* you think you talkin' to."

He couldn't believe they were acting like this. What in the world was wrong with him? Denzelle had never had so much as a mild debate with Marsha, and they were carrying on like two people in love.

"In love?" Denzelle thought, with panic creeping up in him. "I'm not in love with anybody, let alone Marsha Metcalf."

Marsha finally started to move in Denzelle's direction, walking slowly to be defiant, while at the same time trying not to be too nosy and look around at his house. She peeked into a room that could only be classified as Denzelle's man cave. His house was cheery, comfy, and neater than Marsha would have thought it would be. But the man cave was all of the parts of Denzelle he didn't want just anybody to see.

This room had the typical gigantic flat-screen TV turned on to Reverend Al Sharpton's *PoliticsNation*. There was a navy, leather love seat and two whiskey brown, leather La-Z-Boy chairs. The floor had a navy, light blue, and cognac–colored area rug sitting on top of a mahogany stained-wood floor. The coffee table had newspapers, copies of *Sports Illustrated* magazine, *Jet* magazine, *A Gun Catalog*, and *Sharp Shooter Digest* laying all over it. Denzelle's tray was in front of one of the chairs, and his Bose iPod system rested on a cool-looking steel shelf that had bottles of Fiji water and two boxes of strawberry Nutri-Grain bars on it.

"Are we going to be in here?" Marsha asked, hoping that her enthusiasm over the man cave didn't show up in her voice.

Denzelle's eyebrow went up. Marsha was such an inquisitive little thing. He saw her eyes light up when she saw his favorite room, which had all of that stuff that so defined him.

"Nope," he answered, trying not to laugh when Marsha tried to mask her disappointment. She made him think of his niece, Yasmine, who used to try and hide when she was mad and pouting when Unky D didn't let her have her way. He said, "Don't you think it would be better to hold a business meeting in my office?"

"Of course," Marsha mumbled, as cheerfully as she could. The last place she wanted to be was in a stuffy old office. Instead, she wanted to be up in *that* room. It looked like there was so much in there to see that would tell her more about Denzelle.

He opened the door to his office, secretly hoping Marsha would like his office as much as she obviously liked his den. He tried not to hold his breath while watching her standing in the doorway to the office.

"I'll be right back," Denzelle said, and then paused and turned back around. "What do you want to drink?"

"What do you have?" Marsha asked him.

"Hennessey, Gray Goose, some wine," he answered, grinning, knowing full well she would not want any liquor to drink.

Marsha gave Denzelle the impression that one whiff of the good stuff would put her out for the entire night. If she drank a glass of liquor, got tipsy, and had to be out for the night at his house, he was going to take advantage of the situation. Denzelle knew that was wrong. But he was being truthful. If that girl ended up at his house for the night, he was tapping that and going to the altar to ask for forgiveness later.

"I do not believe my pastor is offering me some hard liquor," she said, with a chuckle.

"I'm not. You can't hang drinking liquor. I just told you what I had," he said, in a serious voice.

Marsha frowned, and was about to protest. Who did Denzelle think he was to think she couldn't drink, even though she really could not drink an eyedropper full of strong liquor? But he didn't have to know that.

Denzelle stared at Marsha as if to say please. He said, "I know just the thing to give your little trying to be grown self to drink with the brownies. You make yourself comfortable until I get back."

Chapter Fourteen

Marsha sat down in the chair facing Denzelle's desk. She tried to position her body to make it look like she was cool and relaxed while waiting on him to come back with those brownies. She hoped they tasted good. It would be awful if she had to sneak and spit them out if they were nasty.

This room may not have been the true command central of Denzelle's home, like the den. But there was a lot in it that spoke volumes about who this man was. Marsha had expected it to be crimson and cream. But instead of dripping in Denzelle's K A Ψ fraternity colors, this room was earth-toned—soothing but with just enough umph to get you in the mood to work.

It had never occurred to Marsha that Denzelle Flowers would be so in to houseplants. There was nothing in his demeanor to indicate that he had such a prolific green thumb. The plants were lush, strong, and full of life, just like Denzelle. He probably grew each plant from a tender baby clipping he'd gotten from someone like his uncle Russell's wife, Miss Della.

The plants in the office were in buttery, pumpkin-colored pots that complemented the butter cookie–colored walls and whiskey-colored leather furniture. There were finely crafted, handmade, black-lacquered bookshelves, along with a very comfortable looking whiskey-colored leather chair behind the finely made black desk.

"I like this room," Marsha said to herself.

"I'm glad you do," Denzelle responded, making her jump.

Denzelle put the tray of brownies and what looked like some freshly made lemonade on his desk. He scooped up a fat brownie with a spatula onto a brickred dessert plate. He put the plate in Marsha's hand, and then poured his homemade lemonade into a tall glass with a crimson K A Ψ stamped on it. He put the glass on the Kappa Alpha Psi coaster sitting on his desk and waited for her to taste the brownie.

Marsha bit into it. It was delicious, and it also had more than chopped walnuts in it. She took another bite, and then swallowed a big gulp of the lemonade.

"What did you put in these brownies?"

"Chronic," Denzelle lied, and started laughing when Marsha looked like she was trying to figure a way to spit it out without being offensive. Marsha would pull her taste buds out of her mouth with tweezers before she let the taste of some marijuana-laced brownies stay on her tongue.

"Uhhh, Baby, where would I get some good weed to put in your brownies?"

"The police department," Marsha said gingerly.

"The police department?" Denzelle queried, laughing. "Baby, I'm FBI. I don't need to go to the Po-Po to get some weed if I really wanted it. And what makes you think the best weed is at the police department? Don't you think the FBI would have something to do with some bigger busts, and end up getting some better weed?"

She shrugged and said, "Well, whenever I hear news about the police drug bust, they always arrest a lot of weed people. But when you all get involved, all we hear about is the amount and the value of it on the streets," Marsha said, hoping she didn't sound too dumb and naive.

"Weed people?" Denzelle asked her. She was cracking him up, sitting there eating those brownies and talking seriously about the weed people.

"Yeah, you know people who sell really good weed. I'm sure

you all can tell the difference between good weed people and bad weed people."

Denzelle just shook his head. Marsha was looking so proud to be able to talk about things like street value and good weed versus cheap weed. But it was clear from this conversation that she didn't know diddly-squat about this subject. And, in fact, he remembered how Marsha acted when they were in college at Eva T. Marshall University. She was rarely, if ever, around folk who were getting high. And Denzelle should have known, since he got high with his boys on many occasions.

"Marsha, do you even know what weed looks like? Have you ever rolled a joint? That's all I want to know."

"Uhh . . . well, there was this one time when I was at a party at Eva T., and some of those weed-looking papers were on the floor, and I bent over to pick them up . . . and . . ."

Denzelle held up his hand and said, "Stop, stop. Please. You are making it worse and losing the three cool points you are barely holding on to. You don't know jack about weed, do you?"

Marsha didn't want to say, "No, actually, I know even less than that." So she took another bite out of the brownie and drank another big gulp of lemonade.

"These are so good, Denzelle," she told him, hoping to change the subject. "What in the world did you put in them?"

"Gray Goose," he answered, letting her get away with being what she thought was smooth. When would she learn that, as an FBI agent, he could see her little maneuver coming from a mile away?

"Okay. But really, what did you put in them?" Marsha asked, and took another big bite.

"Really, I put three cups of Gray Goose in the brownie batter—gives them a great taste. The helping of Gray Goose in those brownies is probably the most liquor you can handle."

"I can handle more Gray Goose than what you put in these brownies," Marsha lied, reaching for another one.

"Don't get drunk," Denzelle admonished. Something told

him that Marsha was going to get a buzz just from eating those brownies.

"Oh, don't worry about me, Denzelle. I can handle myself and my liquor."

"Girl, you are not even drinking, and you are talking like someone who has had too much to drink."

He shook his head and sighed.

"Baby, what am I going to do with you?"

"Ohhh, I don't know, Mr. Man," Marsha, or more like the liquor in the brownies, told him. "I think there is a whole lot you can do with myself."

"Oh, really," was all Denzelle said, as he looked Marsha up and down like she was one of those Gray Goose brownies.

"Well, I didn't mean it like that," she said, speaking more to the look than his actual words.

"Mean it like what, Marsha-getting-drunk-off-of-brownies-Metcalf."

"You know what I mean by that. And for the record, I am not drunk off of some brownies. Who gets drunk off of brownies, Denzelle?" Marsha told him defiantly.

"You," Denzelle answered her. She was hilarious. He scratched the stubble on his chin and gave Marsha a hot onceover. She was making it hard for him to behave. One more word on those brownies, and he was going to be all over her.

"You keep getting drunk off of my brownies and I'm sure I'll be able to do a whole lot with your fine self. Here," Denzelle said, picking up another brownie. "Eat this, so I can take full advantage of you."

Marsha stopped chewing. Denzelle was grinning, but he looked dead serious to her. She put her brownie down. Maybe she didn't need to eat something that went to her head like Gray Goose–laced brownies.

Denzelle was beginning to wonder if he was on something himself to be having this kind of conversation with Marsha. Any self-respecting player knew you did not put cards down on the table with women like Marsha Metcalf. They were serious, no nonsense, and could actually sniff out game faster than women with far more game than they would ever possess. Marsha would play the game so poorly it would force a player to put too many cards down—which, ironically, would end up giving her the winning hand.

"Denzelle, I am not drunk, I'm just a little bit drunk. And you can't handle me," Marsha told him, with a whole lot of liquor-induced bravado.

"You wanna bet," Denzelle whispered, pleased at the rose tint spreading across her cheeks.

"Oh . . . you . . . ," Marsha began, searching for a second comeback. She was tipsy and dealing with a player like Denzelle, who always had a snappy comeback.

"So," he said, trying so hard not to laugh at Marsha, "you are admitting the Gray Goose in the brownies gave you a buzz."

"Uhh . . . ," she began.

"Uhhh . . . nothing," Denzelle said, and put the other chair right in front of Marsha's and sat down. He placed his hands on the arm rests on her chair and leaned toward her to whisper in her ear.

"Are you going to lie about me being able to handle you, too?"

Marsha leaned back in her chair. Denzelle leaned in closer to her. She smelled so good. He was about to plant a soft kiss on the tip of her ear when Marsha found a way to slice through the heat and tension building up between them.

"Denzelle," Marsha began, hoping she was sounding regular, "don't you have a gun in your house?"

He moved away, disappointed that she had found a way to push him back. He waved his hand in the direction of the glass case on the opposite wall that had his FBI badge, a lightweight bullet-proof vest, a heavy-duty bullet-proof vest, a taser, and three guns in it. It looked like it should have been a display at a museum about law enforcement.

"Did you honestly think I'd have a home without my heat," Denzelle asked. "Girl, this is just the stuff I want you to see. There's a whole lot more in a few undisclosed locations in my house."

"Uhh, okay," Marsha said. She was a bit nervous to be around that much firepower. What if they had another rare earthquake like the one that rocked North Carolina in 2011? Something like that could possibly cause those guns to go off all over the place.

She was very curious to take a closer look at the weapons in the glass case. Marsha had only seen guns like the ones Denzelle owned on television. They were pretty impressive but daunting at the same time.

"How many guns do you have in the house, Denzelle?"

He tweaked Marsha's ear playfully to distract her away from pressing in on an answer to that question. Truth was—Denzelle had six different guns other than the ones in the case in the house. He knew the answer to her question would make Marsha nervous enough to make up an excuse to go home.

Folks never ceased to amaze him with their reactions to real firepower. They liked being around someone who was doing some serious packing and knew how to use a gun. But they could also be nervous and uncomfortable about being in a home with several weapons.

"Baby, I'm a retired FBI agent. I still train. I still practice at the range. And I do training and consultation with the FBI academy. I'm one of the experts on working with churches located in areas the bureau has been keeping a watchful eye on."

"Wow, Denzelle. I never thought about you in that way. Have you ever shot anybody?"

Denzelle got all nostalgic-looking on Marsha—like he needed a moment or two of silence to reminisce about the good old days, when he could shoot up a few folk. He smiled down at Marsha and said, "I'm the one who shot the second and third toes off of Rico Sneed's foot."

"Yeah," Marsha said carefully. "I remember that. Rico Sneed hasn't liked you since."

"Baby, Rico Sneed has never liked me. I just gave him a plausible reason to be open about how he always felt."

"Why didn't Rico like you before you shot him? I don't recall you doing anything—that would give the man a reason to dislike you."

"I could always see straight through that joker—even back in the day, when we were all young bloods."

"Then that explains it all. People don't like folk who can see straight through them when they are always into some extra drama."

"So true, Marsha."

"Is Rico the only one you've ever shot?"

Denzelle smiled again, but this time his eyes were hard as granite. Marsha almost jumped when she saw that deadly, steel glint slice across his round brown eyes. She'd always heard about how Denzelle could change from being the pastor to an FBI agent with a killer instinct in a heartbeat. It was one thing to listen to someone else talk about it. It was another thing to witness it up close and personal.

"Have you ever killed anyone?" Marsha whispered, almost afraid to let those words come out of her mouth.

Denzelle stared into Marsha's dark brown eyes and said, "Would it upset you to know that I did?"

Marsha shrugged. She honestly didn't know how she would feel to know this man, whom she struggled so hard not to love, had taken someone's life.

"No, I've never killed anyone. I thank God for that each and every day. Because there was always a chance I would have to pull the trigger for a life-ending shot when I was a field agent. Baby, I've gone after some very dangerous and scary people. There was no way I could go up in some of those situations and not be prepared to shoot to kill."

"I see," was all Marsha said.

"But Marsha, I want you to understand that I have shot more than one person. And I shot them to stop them, so I would not be forced to kill them. I'm a sharpshooter. I will hit, with record precision, any place I aim my gun at."

Marsha didn't want to smile right now. This was such a serious conversation. But she couldn't help it.

"What in the world is so funny?"

"I was thinking about how folks talk about those two spots where Rico Sneed's toes used to be on his foot. The few who've seen it say that shot was so good, it looked like you took those toes off with a surgical knife. And you took off two toes with one single bullet."

Denzelle sucked on his tooth, and winked. He said, "Well, you know how it is, sweet thang—that was some of my best work."

"You are so wrong, Pastor. I mean, Bishop."

She put her plate with the brownie crumbs on the desk and stood up.

Denzelle was facing her and didn't move back when Marsha got up out of the chair. In fact, he made it his business to stand where it would be impossible for Marsha to avoid brushing up against him. It was the closest they had ever been to one another, and it felt good.

The space they were in made Denzelle feel like he had just come home. But as much as he was digging on this space, it also made him very uncomfortable. Denzelle was not ready to feel like this about a woman. He had been running from feeling like this for years and couldn't understand why he couldn't get rid of this feeling when Marsha was concerned.

Marsha picked up on his discomfort and moved away from him. She wondered what triggered the sudden chill between them.

"Did I say or do something to offend you, Denzelle?" Marsha asked, in her firm business voice.

"It occurred to me that if I am elected to be a bishop, I won't have a congregation. I like being a pastor, Marsha." He went to sit in the chair behind his desk. He needed something to take his mind off of the fact that Marsha Metcalf was in his house and the two of them were alone. Back in the day he would have taken her by the hand and walked her down the hall to his bedroom.

Why did she always have to look so good? It didn't make sense. The girl wasn't even dressed-up. She had on some jeans, a peach-colored graphic T-shirt he remembered seeing lying up on a shelf at Walmart, and some blue, graffiti-painted canvas flats. But Marsha still looked good to him—so good he wanted her right in his office.

If Denzelle thought for one moment that he could get away with it, he would knock everything on his desk on the floor. Then he would grab Marsha and put to rest the questions he caught flashing across her face when she didn't think he was paying attention to her. He knew she wondered what he was like behind closed doors. Right now it was taking considerable restraint to refrain from answering every single question she had about him.

He put himself back in control of the situation by assuming preacher posture. Denzelle had watched the seasoned preachers use it on folk for the past thirty years, and it worked. It was a way of pulling rank, by acting like you operated on a higher level, because you had a license to be a preacher and was sanctioned to wear a clerical collar.

Marsha sat back down. She watched Denzelle behind his desk, positioning his body and acting like the textbook, black-denomination preacher. Did they train preachers to act like this? Did they make them take some kind of preacher test, where they had to make sure they stood and walked and sat and looked and talked a certain way before they were allowed to wear the clerical collar?

It sure did feel like that was the case sometimes. Marsha always knew when she was walking up on a group of black preachers at a conference, because they always found some kind of way to let you know they were preachers. She'd always hoped the women in the ministry would be different when more of them started joining the ranks of the clergy. Unfortunately, some of them could rep they were clergy as hard as the men.

"Why do ministers at church conferences stand in huddles, and then make sure everyone who is not a preacher feels uncomfortable about stopping and talking to them?" Marsha asked Denzelle in earnest.

"What do you mean?"

Marsha sighed and blew a heavy puff of air out of her mouth. He knew what she meant—he just didn't want to break rank and tell one of those dumb clergy secrets. She said, "Whenever I'm at a church conference, and I walk up on a group of preachers, you guys act like I need some kind of note from God just to speak to you. You know, it can feel kind of mean. And I hoped it would be better when more women were in the ministry. But some of them aren't any better. I don't understand why you all have to act like that."

Denzelle did not want to answer that question, because it was like breaking some kind of unspoken rule. But she was right. Preachers could act like they were the cat's meow at conferences. They stood off in those groupings making folk feel like they needed a donkey, some palms, and a few coats thrown on the floor just to walk up and say good morning.

Marsha's expert eyes didn't miss a thing. She said, "So you do know what I'm talking about, huh."

"I don't know what you are talking about, Marsha," Denzelle responded, knowing that he was telling what his brother would call a bald-head lie.

"Yes, you do," Marsha pressed, and shook her head. Preachers and cops could be so guarded and overly protective of themselves and others in the ranks. They acted like it was a crime to admit when they were wrong and doing stupid stuff.

"Okay, Marsha," Denzelle said. "You're right. Preachers intimidate folk on purpose when they are in those huddles acting like they're talking about some important church business. A lot of times they aren't talking about anything worth standing there listening to.

"And there are times when the brothers in collars are in deep discussion about some fine sister with the perfectly shaped butt who walked by the group. They don't want you all to know somebody's trying to find a way to get baby girl's digits. So they act like they are standing there trying to figure out the next game move on behalf of the Lord."

Marsha smiled back. It was reassuring to get confirmation that she was right about those preacher huddles. She always thought some of them were nothing more than some brothers standing around like they were on the block, taking note of the sisters they wanted to hook up with.

Chapter Fifteen

Marsha reached down into her tote bag and pulled out information she knew Denzelle would need for his upcoming campaign for bishop and laid it on his desk. He had given her the green light to put together a plan that would profile his natural style and swagger. But she also knew he needed these profiles about the other preachers who had announced they were running.

Denzelle could not believe the folk who had filed the paperwork to become official candidates in this race for an Episcopal seat. Most people assumed there were a lot of serious and highfalutin prerequisites to establish a candidacy for bishop in the Gospel United Church. Most people also assumed a lot more was required to file an application to run for president of the United States.

The truth was that the requirements to make the initial claims were not as difficult to reach as folk generally assumed they were. Yet while many could fill out a form to enter the race, it was an extremely rare number of people who were truly qualified to run for an office as noble as the United States presidency. Equally so, many could join the race for an Episcopal seat. But few men or women were truly qualified to even run for bishop.

It surprised Denzelle to learn that running for bishop was just as much of a calling as getting elected and serving. When folk ran for bishop, they articulated a campaign agenda that was in effect the groundwork for policy and the governing theological tenets of the denomination. That was serious business. Once those agendas were put forth on the campaign trail, they could affect the spiritual, financial, social, psychological, and Christian-based educational life of the church.

As far as Denzelle was concerned, there were too many preachers eager to hop in the race feet first without giving a single thought to the true nature of the office they were aspiring to hold. Twenty-six men and nine women had thrown their collars in the ring for one Episcopal seat. It was going to be a nasty, mud-slinging, get-down-and-dirty race as far as he was concerned. When Denzelle read over this list of candidates, he wished he could run up in a big preacher's meeting with one of those huge clown canes and snatch as many of those jokers off the stage as possible.

Out of the crowded pool of candidates, Reverend Xavier Franklin from Winston-Salem would be Denzelle's most formidable opponent. Xavier Franklin was handsome and charming. Franklin presided over a large and popular church. Plus, the brother could preach a good, old-fashioned hand-clapping and foot-stomping sermon. Those attributes could carry a preacher a long way with delegates—especially many of the lay delegates, who made up half of the population of those selected to vote in the new bishops.

But Xavier Franklin was also a big crook. And lately he was making Denzelle wonder if he needed to contact the bureau and have Xavier put under FBI surveillance. The last time he encountered Xavier Franklin, Denzelle kept feeling like he had when he was around suspects who had committed a very serious crime.

This race for bishop was going to be real hard on a brother. Denzelle needed something that would set him far away from the scrimmage zone occupied by the other candidates. He sure hoped Marsha would come through with the right stuff for his campaign.

Marsha's first plan was to give Denzelle a makeover and re-define his style as a pastor. That idea had come as a surprise to her. It had never occurred to her that Denzelle needed the make-over, because he was a real cool brother with great style.

The only thing was, Denzelle's style, no matter how cool, still marked him as a preacher. Most of the folk at New Jerusalem rarely saw Reverend Flowers dressed in something other than a sharply tailored suit. Her strategy was to get him out of the suits and into some clothes that would make folk want to relax around him more than they did. One problem most bishops had was being perceived as aloof and unapproachable. The more connected to the folk Denzelle appeared, the more he would become endeared to the delegates.

Marsha pulled out a folder with pictures of clothes and swatches of materials and laid it out in front of Denzelle. She said, "You are going to need a fashion makeover."

Denzelle thought he was hearing things. Did Marsha just tell him some girlie-man–sounding nonsense about needing a fashion makeover? He was running for bishop, not for a spot as a contestant on *The Bachelorette*. He laughed, leaned back in his chair, and said, "Have you lost your mind? Do I look like a brother who thinks about makeovers? Next thing, you are going to pull out some Mary Kay samples of man makeup."

Marsha rolled her eyes up toward the ceiling.

"Look, Denzelle. I have to make you more approachable to all of the delegates who are not preachers. You are intimidating, just like a whole lot of your colleagues are intimidating. The delegates need to feel comfortable coming up to you to talk and find out where you stand on some key issues for the church. They are not going to do it if you are walking around like you are going to arrest them if they don't know all seven verses of 'Amazing Grace' by heart."

"Oh, really?" he asked. Denzelle ran a church the size of a small corporation. He'd better have a firm presence that made folk tread carefully with him.

"Yes, really," was all Marsha said. She was not backing down.

She had a good plan, and Denzelle Flowers was going to listen to her.

"Look, candidates for bishop can talk a good game and say what they think the delegates want to hear. Then they can make it difficult for the delegates to come up to them and discuss matters important to the church. They need to know where you really stand when you are not standing behind a podium, Denzelle."

"I like folk being scared to roll up on me, Marsha."

"That's cool if you are running for FBI agent of the year. But it's not if you are running for bishop in the Gospel United Church. People don't need to be too scared to come up to you at church and at the conferences."

"You know something," Denzelle said, "I want to hear something better than this to help you earn your keep."

Marsha could not *believe* he went there. That hurt, and it exemplified exactly what she was trying to tell Denzelle about himself and his ways. She felt tearful. But Marsha would pluck out her own eyeballs before she let Reverend Pastor Special Agent Denzelle Flowers see one teardrop fall from her eyes. She said, "I think you better watch how you are talking to me. I may need this job real bad, Re-ve-rend Flo-wers. But I will go out there and spread hot tar on the road with my bare hands before I sit here and let you talk to me like that.

"I know what I am doing, Denzelle. And if you didn't think I knew what I was doing, you would have given me something else to do."

Denzelle knew he had gone too far with Marsha. But his emotions were running rampant, and he was trying to keep some control over this situation. He hated not being in control. And he hated it that Marsha got under his skin.

When Marsha felt Denzelle was taking too much time to apologize for being a butt hole, she began gathering up her things to leave. She didn't know what she was going to do about a job.

And she hoped he didn't ask for the money, because she didn't have it to give back to him and the church, anyway.

Denzelle came from behind his desk and put a firm hand on Marsha's shoulder to stop her from leaving.

"I'm sorry," he said in a low, soft voice. "If you say I need a makeover, then I need a makeover."

Marsha blinked back tears. Denzelle was so difficult to deal with at times. And this thing she had for him was only made worse by all of this interaction with him. Why did she have to like him? As a matter of fact, why did she have to like anybody? Why couldn't she just be likeless?

Denzelle felt like the big bad wolf. Why was he being so mean to Marsha? Last thing he wanted to do was hurt Marsha and make her cry. He opened his arms, hoping she would come to him.

Marsha held her ground, even though his arms looked so inviting. She feared if she went over there to that man, she'd never leave that spot. She sniffled and tried to sneak and wipe her nose on her sleeve.

Now it was Denzelle who had had enough of nonsense. He came over to Marsha, grabbed her, and held her close.

"Marsha," Denzelle whispered. "I am so sorry. You have been through the wringer, and I am making it worse for you."

He could feel her holding back on him, and knew she didn't want to break down in his arms. But that is exactly what Denzelle Flowers wanted from Marsha Metcalf—a meltdown in his arms.

"I'm not a punk, Denzelle," Marsha said through the tears. "I . . . I . . . I . . ."

He stroked her hair. It was soft and smooth to the touch. He kissed the top of her head and said, "You are the last person I would think of as a punk. That's part of your problem, Girl. You are strong, resilient, and sweet. Some men can't handle that combination very well."

Marsha sniffled in his arms. Denzelle was in good shape, but she'd never thought his arms were so strong they would feel like an iron grip. And he smelled so daggone good, it should have been against the law.

Denzelle closed his eyes and wished that he could hold a crying Marsha in his arms forever. She felt so good—just a firm handful of fine woman. Rodney had to have been out of his mind to leave a woman like Marsha. It was taking everything in him not to lean down and kiss her. But Denzelle knew that if he started kissing Marsha, he'd be a goner. And he had not come this far in keeping the upper hand with women to lose out in the game to a Suzy Saved like Marsha Metcalf.

"You better?" he asked, smiling, hoping the smile made him look like he was in complete control of the situation.

"Yes," Marsha answered, hardly believing she had broken down in Denzelle Flowers's arms. Keisha kept telling her to be careful about losing her edge when she was around this man. She had told Marsha, "Girl, you got it bad for that man. And don't let Pastor fool you, either. He got it just as bad for you. Only problem is that you know you got it bad and can pray on it. Pastor doesn't quite know it yet. And he is going to cut the fool with you to try and not feel like he does where you are concerned."

As true as those words were, they didn't give Marsha much comfort. Why did she have to be the one who had to deal with a man who liked her but didn't want to deal with her because he didn't want to like her like he did? Just thinking about that—like that—was making Marsha's head hurt.

"Denzelle," Marsha said, hoping her voice was sounding stronger and more in control to him than it did to her.

"Yeah," he responded, voice all soft and tender. It made Marsha think about what a man sounded like when he was wrapped around you, spoon fashion, and the two of you talked in a dark and quiet room.

"I'm sorry to get all upset in your office like this."

"Girl," he said, laughing, "you can get all upset on me any time you please. Okay?"

She wiped her face and said, "Okay," with a smile. Marsha

hoped her face didn't look crazy. She could feel the sticky specks of mascara under her eyes.

"Uhh, yeah, you do have raccoon eyes. But they are cute raccoon eyes," Denzelle told her, thinking she looked absolutely delightful with her mascara running under her eyes. A woman who still looked good to you with damp mascara on her face was some fine workmanship.

He pulled a few tissues out of the Kleenex box on his desk. "Here, this might be better than the backs of your hands."

"Yeah," she answered, trying not to sniffle. "The tissue is better. Where is your bathroom? I think I'm going to need a mirror to get my face back right."

"It's down the hall on your right."

Marsha went into the guest bathroom, impressed by how cozy it was. Denzelle was full of surprises. This bathroom complemented the decor of the living room, and he had plenty of toilet paper on the roll.

She looked in the mirror and squelched the urge to shriek. She looked like a hot mess. Her mascara was running, and her eye shadow was all smudged down on her cheeks, too.

"I can't believe that I came to this man's house and cried myself into looking like the upset girl psychopathic in a Lifetime movie."

Marsha wet a paper towel and fixed her face as best she could. She wished she had her purse, so she could add some liner and put on lipstick. Right now she was looking rather plain with practically no makeup.

"Oh, well. This will have to do."

She patted her hair, used the toilet, washed her hands, and went back to Denzelle's office. Marsha saw an open door leading to what had to be Denzelle's bedroom. There was a pile of clean underwear on the bed.

"Lawd, he has more draws than a woman," Marsha whispered. She sneaked and counted at least fifteen pairs of different-colored boxer briefs.

Chapter Sixteen

"So, tell me more about this makeover, Marsha."

"It's just part one of my strategy. See, I want you to look more chilled and accessible to the regular folk, like me. I want folk to walk up to your booth at the conferences and want to talk to you. And I want them to get comfortable enough to really listen to your agenda and ask you some questions. I want them to take notes and take the message back to their friends. I want to build up, expand, and strengthen your base."

"I see," was all he said. She had a point. A lot of church folk were not always comfortable rolling up on a prominent preacher. And he had an excellent agenda. Denzelle and Obadiah Quincey had worked on it for close to six months before he formally announced his candidacy for bishop.

"Now, you are still going to be the sharply dressed, Reverend Flowers, but with a more casual twist to your style. I liked what you were wearing when we first met with you about the Pastor's Aide Club. I want you to do more dressing like that for the campaign. It will set you apart from the other candidates. Most of them are going to wear an assortment of preacher suits."

"I see," he said again, thinking about the suits some of his colleagues could find and wear. He knew there would be an abundance of suits with the pocket on the back, placed carefully between the shoulder blades. Denzelle didn't know who came up with that style and what the pocket was supposed to accomplish.

He rarely saw that style of suit worn anywhere other than at a black church conference and by a member of the clergy. He said, "So, you liked what I was wearing, huh?"

"Yep."

"And this evening? You like what I'm wearing now?"

"Yep. Show do."

"Well, then, I guess I'm going to get a newer look for this campaign. What else?"

"What do you want your campaign colors to be?"

Denzelle just looked at Marsha. He said, "Do you really think you need to ask me that question?"

She laughed. "Okay. I was being kinda slow. Crimson and Cream it is."

"I'm glad I didn't have to spell that one out for you—Ms. Royal Blue and White Extraordinaire."

"Well, we could use royal blue and white," Marsha said, cracking up at the horrified look on Denzelle's face.

"What? You worried that somebody will mistake you for a member of Phi Beta Sigma? I mean, what's wrong with that? I think the Sigmas are alright."

"You would, Miss Zeta Phi Beta, Inc. They are your official fraternity brothers. But if you suggest that my campaign colors go blue and white again, I'm gonna . . ."

"Gonna what, Denzelle? At least I didn't suggest you go purple and gold!"

"Now, see, you're about to get put out of my house right after I beat you with my Kappa Kane."

"Cane with a C or a K?" she asked with a soft chuckle.

"What do you think, Missy?"

"K cane it is, Mr. Kappa, Sir."

"That's right. 'Sir' it is, and you better not forget it, either," he said.

"Whatevahhhhhhh!"

"Okay, now that we are straight on my campaign colors, as if we ever needed to ponder that, is there anything else?"

"Well . . . yeah," Marsha began carefully. She'd been work-ing on an idea for the campaign kickoff and hoped Denzelle wouldn't hightail it and run when she told him what it was.

"See, it's like this."

"This sounds like something I better sit down for," Denzelle said, and sat down in the chair facing Marsha's.

"We are going to do some fun and different promotional events that will also be big fundraisers."

"Okay . . . ," Denzelle said carefully, knowing there was a whole lot to fun and different. He'd been a pastor for a long time and knew when someone was getting ready to spring something on him.

"See, most folk think of a bishop's campaign as being stodgy and not always exciting."

"Well, that's because I'm running for an Episcopal office and not homecoming king, Marsha."

"You are not making this easy, Denzelle."

"I'm not doing anything but sitting here waiting on you to tell me about fun and different. Something tells me that I am not going to be jumping for joy after you share this with me."

"Oh, it's not bad or anything like that."

"I know," he told her. "It's just something that I may not be game for. You are taking way too much time prepping me for this. I'd really appreciate you just spelling it out. I'm going to do one of two things—say yes, or hell no."

"Our first event is a ballroom-dancing contest at the church," Marsha said real fast. She hoped her words sped by fast enough to stop the "hell no."

Denzelle lifted an eyebrow and said, "A what?" It was taking considerable restraint to refrain for saying a "hell no."

"A ballroom-dancing program—kinda like *Dancing with the Stars*."

"And I'm presuming I'm going to be some kind of blend between your Sigma brothers Emmett Smith and Jerry Rice, huh."

"Denzelle, come on," Marsha said. "It will be fun. It will raise a lot of money. And it will help folk connect with you."

"How are they going to connect with me doing a bro-man version of the rumba? And how in the world did you come up with this? Veronica help you think of this? 'Cause the last thing on Keisha Jackson's mind is even the word 'ballroom.'"

"Yeah, Veronica did help me think of this," Marsha answered him. She was beginning to wonder if this was a dumb idea after all. It had seemed pretty cool when they first came up with it and worked out all of the details.

Denzelle laughed. Marsha Metcalf was hilarious, and he was being too hard on her. He wished another brother could have pulled Marsha and Veronica's skirt tails, and told them that despite Emmett's and Jerry's enthusiastic participation on the TV show, most brothers were not trying to get out there to dance the fox-trot. But he would go with the flow and see where this ended up.

He grabbed Marsha's hands in his and smiled.

"As crazy and 'shee-shee, foo-foo' as this is sounding to me right now, I know you and Miss Veronica do know what you are doing. And you both have a good feel for what works. So break it down and school me, Baby."

Denzelle wanted to laugh at Marsha for trying to act like his calling her baby didn't matter. This was fun, and it was refreshing for a woman to respond to him like that.

"Veronica and I wanted to do something that would get our whole church and the sister churches in the area—like Fayetteville Street in Durham—involved and enthusiastic about being a part of this campaign. We wanted them to come to the event, have fun, and learn all about you. We also wanted to do something that no other candidate had thought to do.

"You do know that Reverend Xavier Franklin is in this race. He might prove to be a formidable opponent, Denzelle. Reverend Franklin will play some nasty and dirty politics, and Franklin will cheat in any and every way he can.

"Second, Franklin is the choice pick of Bishop Sonny Wash-

ington and Reverend Marcel Brown. They have a lot of denominational PAC money from the Mother Benson Missionary
Affiliates. And everybody in the Gospel United Church knows
that old stuck organization run by Bishop Washington's wife, Glodean Benson, ain't about nothing but trying to get some more
crooks in some high places."

Marsha shook her head at just the thought of those people.
"Denzelle, will they ever stop what they do every time we have a
race for bishop? They've been acting like a bunch of unsaved
bugaboos since I can remember."

"No, I don't think they plan to stop this craziness anytime
before Jesus cracks the sky," Denzelle told her.

"They have a lot of money—some of it coming from under-
ground sources with some very deep pockets," Marsha said. "And
they will try and do anything to win."

"Yeah, they are going to try one more gain. And just like in
the past, they are going to make this a hard race with their craziness. But think about it. Have they ever really won the fights they
start, Sweet Thing?"

Once again, Marsha tried not to smile at hearing that endear-
ing term being addressed to her. It had been a long time since a
man talked to her like that, and honestly, it felt awfully good.
She wondered if it felt as good to Denzelle to say it as it felt to
hear it coming out of his mouth.

Denzelle held back a smile. It felt so good to say that, mean
it, and to get such a warm and sincere response from a woman.
Women just didn't understand. Talking what his uncle Russell
would call "sweet talk" did wonders for a man when it was well
received by the right woman.

"Well," Marsha began carefully, "Reverend Sonny Washington did win that Episcopal seat in 1986."

"Yes, he did. It was a fluke win, though. I still don't know
how Sonny Washington was voted in. But win, he did."

"So we can't take Xavier's run for bishop lightly, Denzelle.
We are going to have to go for the jugular on him. He's ruthless,

dishonest, and very mean. Plus, his wife, Camille, is just as bad as he is. She'll do anything to be at the top of the heap."

"You'd be mean if you had all of that money and it still didn't do a thing for you. I've seen some sisters wearing outfits from Kmart who looked more fly and fabulous than Camille Franklin dressed in a suit she purchased in Paris, France."

"I know," Marsha said with a giggle. "I shouldn't be saying this, but her weave is jacked up. You can look at Camille Franklin and tell that she has never had hair like that."

Denzelle snapped his fingers. Marsha looked confused. He snapped his fingers again and said, "That's how long her hair is."

"WRONG!"

"Then why are you laughing?"

"Okay," Marsha said, and held out her hand. "Here, tap my wrist. I repent."

Denzelle tapped her wrist lightly, and then frowned.

"You okay? Did I . . ."

"No, nothing to do with you," he told her. But I'm the one who needs to be repenting, he thought, because your wrist isn't the only thing I want to tap.

"You sure you're okay, Denzelle?" Marsha asked again. He was acting like he was having a private war with himself.

"Couldn't be better."

Marsha would never understand men.

"How is this dance going to give me an edge over Xavier Franklin?" he asked, to get Marsha up off of what was bothering him.

"It's a dance contest, and not just a dance."

"Okay, Marsha. How is doing a church folk *Dancing with the Stars* going to help me and the campaign?"

"It is going to bring a lot of folk out to the church, we are going to have a ball, we are going to raise a lot of money, and folk are going to see you in a more laid-back way. We want people to really believe our campaign slogan: "No More Business as Usual."

"No More Business as Usual,' "Denzelle repeated softly.

"I like that. And a dance, no, dance contest, as the kickoff event is different, and definitely not business as usual. I think I get where you are going with all of this."

"Glad to know that. I had hoped that when you hired me to take on this task, you trusted I knew what I was doing."

"So, do I have to dance?"

"Of course you do!"

"What about my official campaign manager? Does he have to dance, too?"

"He doesn't. But do you honestly think Obie and Lena Quincey are going to sit on the sidelines while everybody is out there dancing and competing and having a ball?"

Denzelle thought about that for a minute, and then said, "Naahhhh."

"Denzelle, the contest will be held in the gymnasium at New Jerusalem. Keisha Jackson is putting the decorating committee together. Veronica is busy handling advertising and getting contestants all signed up. We've already earned enough money to clear all expenses and have some left over in the kitty. We are also working on getting donations—cash and gift cards—for the winning prizes. Veronica said that we are going to start turning a hefty profit in the next two weeks."

"I'm impressed."

"Me, too," Marsha said. "Veronica is so good. And she had a lot of help from Charles Robinson, who makes money when he goes to the bathroom."

"Good point," Denzelle said, and then frowned again.

Marsha stared at him, wondering what in the world was wrong with Denzelle now. He sighed out loud and said, "Why are you making me dance?"

"Why wouldn't I make you dance, Denzelle? This is a dance contest for your campaign for bishop. Somebody is going to expect you to dance. And you are going to meet that expectation by doing the fox-trot."

"You are kidding me," he said and rolled his eyes. "It's my

party, and I have to do a dance as lame as the fox-trot. Why not the rumba, or something real cool?"

"We want everybody to do different dances. Obie and Lena have the rumba."

"How nice," Denzelle returned. "They get the cool dance, and all that's left for me is some old man looking fox-trot. Really, Marsha. Have you seen that dance?"

"Of course I've seen the dance. It's a good dance," she said, hoping Denzelle would quit whining and agree to the dance. When he didn't respond, Marsha said, "Look on the bright side. At least you will be able to pick your own dance partner."

"Well, then, Baby," Denzelle said, "I guess you better get some extra lessons 'cause you are doing the fox-trot."

"I'm the . . ."

"I don't care if you are Jesus' second cousin on his mama's side. If I have to do the fox-trot, you have to do the fox-trot. I just hope we don't have to dance to some old man music."

"No. We all have good music. You, I mean, we will dance to Charlie Wilson's 'Life of the Party.'"

"Isn't that kinda fast for a fox-trot?"

"It is. But it will be different and fun to learn the dance to that song," Marsha answered. She started to collect her things.

"Here, let me help you with some of that stuff," Denzelle told her, and grabbed an armful of her belongings.

"Thank you, Denzelle."

"You are welcome, Honey," he said, and leaned down to kiss Marsha on her cheek. "Do you have your keys, Marsha?" Denzelle asked. He had heard Marcus fussing about his mother and her keys always being stuck somewhere down in one of her big purses.

Marsha held the keys up and followed Denzelle to her car. He opened the door, put her things on the passenger's seat, made sure she was in the car, and closed the door. He waited until she got her seat belt on and started the car.

"You call me when you get in your house. And call me from the house phone—not your cell. You understand, Marsha?"

"Umm . . . hmm."

"So what did I just say?"

Kelly Price's "You're Not My Daddy, You're My Man" was playing on the radio. Marsha turned up the volume, looked at him, and said, "I'm grown, Denzelle. I heard you and will do as you asked."

"You think you grown. One day I'm gonna show you some grown, Marsha."

All evening Denzelle had been putting down one player card after the other. Marsha had always known he had a way with the ladies. But she'd never really gotten more than a passing glimpse of that side of Denzelle Flowers. Tonight, he was all the way live. She wondered how they were going to fare getting ready for the competition, if he kept this up. Learning to compete in a dance contest was going to put them together a whole lot. It was also going to put them in very close physical proximity with each other.

Marsha tried to shake the image of dancing close to Denzelle. She put her car in drive and said, "Dayeesha will give you all of the dates you'll need. She'll catch up with me if there are any problems with the schedule. I hope you can dance right, Denzelle. Because you are going to have to bring it, if you are expecting to do that dance with me."

"So, you know how to do the fox-trot?"

"Yes, Denzelle. I've been taking ballroom dancing for several years now. Remember, I'm single, and I don't have a man. So I have a lot of time to do lots of different kinds of things."

"Well, maybe I need to think of some ways to trim that busy bee to-do list of yours," Denzelle told her.

Marsha backed out of the driveway, thinking, "He is a pistol."

Denzelle stood in his driveway watching the back of Marsha's car until her red lights were no longer distinguishable from the lights on the other cars. He looked up at the midnight blue sky. Tonight was so clear. The air was fall crisp, with just enough of a hint of a warm breeze flowing underneath.

The artistry of the sky practically took Denzelle's breath

away. He began to try and count as many stars as possible—a game he had started playing between himself and the Lord when he was a little boy. It always fascinated Denzelle that he couldn't count even a tiny fraction of the amount of stars in the sky. Yet the Lord knew the exact number, location, name, and a host of other statistically oriented data about each and every star in the sky. Imagine knowing all of that like someone knew their phone number.

"What a mighty God we serve," Denzelle whispered.

He strained his eyes down the street, knowing Marsha was well on her way home. Denzelle sighed. He wished she wouldn't have left so fast and early. It would have been a good thing to be able to sit with her in his family room and watch a good movie.

A good movie with his arms around an A+ girl. Denzelle hadn't had that kind of experience in a very long time. He'd been out with a lot women. And before he got himself back right with the Lord, Denzelle had slept with a lot of women. But it had been eons since he was able to sit back and relax and enjoy the company of a good woman. He had no one to blame but himself, though.

Back in his playah days Denzelle avoided a woman like a Marsha Metcalf like he would have avoided a full-blown Tea Party rally. Now he wished he hadn't been so rash and fearful of the very thing he needed. He surmised that being a Marsha Metcalf type of woman couldn't be easy—not even for the genuine Marsha Metcalf.

Denzelle had noticed that women like Marsha had to spend more time alone than some of the other women he had encountered. And he knew why. Men ran from Marsha until they were ready to commit.

He looked up at the sky one more time before going back in the house.

"Lord," he whispered. "I'm going to need a whole lot of help from you to keep my hands off of Marsha. Lord, the girl makes me want to wrap myself around her right before I fall asleep at night."

Chapter Seventeen

Tatiana ran her heel up and down the sheet on the bed. She thought it a lovely color, even if it was rough on her foot. Dove gray with navy satin piping added a classic touch to fine linens as far as Tatiana Townsend was concerned. She reached under the cover and rubbed her heel.

"What's wrong, Baby?" Xavier Franklin asked his woman.

He had been involved in many affairs during his twelve years of marriage to Camille. Not one of those women (including Camille) had managed to do what Tatiana Hill Flowers Townsend had done—make Xavier wish he could fall in love with her. Reverend Xavier Leon Franklin was forty-seven years old, and he had never, ever been in love with any woman. He had fallen in love with himself over and over and over again—but never with any woman in his life.

If asked, Tatiana would have sworn Xavier loved her almost as much as she loved herself. She knew no man's love could compare or come close to the intense emotions she felt for herself. But Xavier had managed to make Tatiana feel like his love was so great, he wouldn't even notice that she was incapable of loving him as much as she believed he loved her.

If asked, Xavier and Tatiana would have declared they were soul mates of sorts. They were two of a kind—ruthless, unprincipled, unscrupulous, and greedy. Xavier had never encountered a woman who, like him, would do any- and everything to get what she wanted out of life. In fact, Xavier secretly believed Tatiana could go way past anything he was capable of to seize what she believed was her due.

Xavier couldn't figure out why Tatiana kept scraping her foot across the sheet and tossing around like she was in great distress. He touched her leg to stop all of that movement and asked again, "Baby, what is wrong?"

Tatiana sighed. This was not going to be the easiest thing to share with her man. She was going to have to choose her words carefully.

"Xavier, you know I love you, right?"

"Yeah," he answered carefully, not sure if he was going to like where this was going.

"Well," Tatiana began with another sigh and some trepidation in her voice. "I thought you told me that this was a five-star hotel. Remember, I kept asking you and asking you, Xavier, to be sure and pick a five-star hotel."

Xavier sat up in the bed and looked around the room. They were in an executive suite at a premiere hotel and spa in Cary, North Carolina. It was hard to top this hotel and its amenities.

"Baby, we're at the Umstead for the day. What part of five star and luxury don't you get, Tatiana?"

Tatiana took the edge of the sheet that made her wonder if the Umstead was really all that it was purported to be, and dabbed at her cheek.

"Well," she began with a tiny sniffle. "These sheets. They are not Frontgate's Roma Luxe Sheets, Xavier."

Xavier ran his hand across the sheet. Tatiana did have a point. Roma Luxe sheets were six-hundred-thread-count sheets that were made in Italy. These sheets were a far cry from a Roma Luxe.

"You are right," he said, now feeling a twinge of guilt. Xavier had bragged about the Umstead, and worked hard to convince Tatiana to meet him here rather than at a fancier hotel out of state.

"This can't be more than a Fleur-de-Lis sheet. Baby, you would think a hotel like this would be able to spend the minimal seven hundred dollars for a bare basic like Roma Luxe."

He wrapped his body around Tatiana's. "I'm so sorry, love."

Tatiana dried her eyes. It had been very upsetting to think Xavier would have her lying up on some cheap, three-hundred-dollar sheets. But she knew he would never, ever do anything like that intentionally. That is what made him such a wonderful man—he understood the importance of such things.

Xavier would never act like her ex-husband, Denzelle, who would have asked Tatiana if she was crazy to get all bent out of shape over some sheets. A good set of sheets from Target worked just fine for Denzelle. Neither would Xavier act like her current husband.

Todd would let her rant and carry on until she got tired. When he grew weary of listening to Tatiana's tirade, he would pull out his iPad and load up her American Express Black Card with some bonus cash. Then he would tell her to go and buy the darn sheets if it would make her happy, and end all of that fidgeting in bed.

The worse thing about Todd was that he wouldn't even notice the new sheets were on the bed after she bought them. He would have come home after being in surgery for ten hours and collapsed into a deep sleep. At least Denzelle would have known there was something different about the sheets. But that would be right before he raised hell about Tatiana spending what was a month's rent for some folks on some sheets.

That's why, more and more, Tatiana wished that she could be married to Xavier. But there were two huge barriers to fixing that problem. First, Tatiana was already married, and to a very wealthy man who gave her everything she wanted.

There weren't a lot of men out there with the kind of resources Todd Townsend had. Xavier wasn't exactly broke by most people's standards. But Todd had the kind of money most people only dreamed about. His petty cash checking account was probably quadruple the amount most folks had in their family savings account.

The other major problem facing Tatiana about marrying Xavier was his wife, Camille. She had a whole lot of money and used it to help her hold on to Xavier. Tatiana knew one reason Xavier stayed with Camille was because he craved living the good life. The second reason keeping the Franklins together was the clout that came with being married to the late Dr. Creighton's daughter, and an heir to the Classy Clean Car Wash Company fortune.

There were very rare times when Tatiana wished she and Xavier had met when they were younger and unencumbered by legal ties to other people. That would have been before she met Denzelle Flowers. They would have been some kind of team, and a force to reckon with in the denomination.

The only couple Tatiana knew of with the kind of power and presence she wanted in the Gospel United Church was Bishop Sonny Washington and his wife, Mother Glodean Benson Washington. Tatiana had always admired Mother Washington. And she often wondered why people in their church were always saying negative things about Mother Washington, and avoiding her like she had some kind of plague disease.

As nice as it would have been in theory for them to get together earlier, it wouldn't have worked too well in practice, however. Tatiana and Xavier didn't have the kind of financial resources they craved. The only way they could get that kind of money was through their marriages to Todd and Camille.

While life with Denzelle Flowers had been good on many fronts, it fell short where the money was concerned. Denzelle made a good living, but he didn't, at least not back then, have an income that could afford the American Express Black Card.

The hardest part about leaving Denzelle for Todd was giving up those warm and passionate nights (and days and afternoons and mornings and daybreaks and sunsets) Tatiana had shared with her first husband. No man had skills like Denzelle. He was the best lover she ever had—better, in fact, than her soul mate, Xavier. Now, Xavier was no slouch behind closed doors, but he was no Denzelle Flowers, either. *Nobody* was a Denzelle Flowers behind closed doors.

"Talk to me, Tatiana," Xavier said, in a soft and loving voice.

The one thing he adored about Tatiana was her ability to make him talk sweet talk without ever having to ask that from him. Xavier never felt this way about Camille. Even though he'd talked a good game of sweet talk with his other other women, none inspired these heartfelt words like his Tatiana. More and more he wanted this woman in his life twenty-four/seven, and wished that she, and not Camille, was the one standing by his side when he began his official run for bishop in the Gospel United Church.

"Oh, Xavier," she answered him in the sweetest voice. "I wish we didn't have to sneak around in a hotel with substandard sheets like this."

Xavier kissed Tatiana's shoulder. It was so soft and such a beautiful color—like a shade of light-brown sugar. It tasted like brown sugar, too.

"You're wearing my favorite scent," he said, and kissed her shoulder again.

"Brown Sugar and Vanilla Body Butter," Tatiana replied, and turned to face Xavier. She kissed his eyelids.

"Xavier, it's getting harder and harder to live without having you with me like you're all mine. I don't like sharing you with Camille. And I hate it that she is the one who gets to stand by your side at church events."

"I know, love," Xavier whispered in between planting more kisses on Tatiana's shoulders. "Do you think it's easy for me to know you are with Todd?"

"But I'm always thinking of you. I tried to pretend he was you but couldn't. Todd doesn't have it going on like you do, Xavier."

"Don't flatter me like that, Tatiana," Xavier told her, with deep anger lines buried in his forehead. "Why don't you start doing like I told you to do, and cut him off at the knees?"

"I can't do that, Xavier. Todd can't know I'm not true to him—not right now. He just let me buy my Black Diamond Cadillac CTS-V Coupe."

Xavier frowned and rolled away from Tatiana. He said, "So what did you have to do to get that car?"

"The exact same thing you did to get yours, my love," she spat out at him. Xavier could be so dense at times. He worked overtime to please Camille to get what he wanted. She remembered how Xavier went MIA on her for close to two months when he was working to convince Camille to sign him up for the coveted American Express Black Card.

Xavier sighed. It was getting harder and harder to keep up this affair. He was tired of sneaking around and wished he could find a way to get rid of Camille in exchange for Tatiana and still run for bishop. But it didn't seem like he was going to find a viable solution to this problem any time soon.

"Where are you on the divorce?" Tatiana asked, hoping he was somewhere in the vicinity of having asked Camille for a divorce. She had never done well with sharing.

"I'm running for bishop," Xavier answered her in a solemn voice.

"What's that got to do with it? The Gospel United Church has some divorced bishops, right?"

"No," Xavier said. "We've never elected a man who was divorced—even though the current bylaws don't prohibit a divorced preacher from running for and being elected to serve as a bishop."

"But Denzelle Flowers is running for bishop, right? I know he's divorced, because I divorced him."

"Yeah, he's running, love. But the difference between Denzelle and me is that he has been divorced for a long time, and everybody in the church knows you left him for Todd. So some folk don't hold that against Denzelle. They feel like he was left with no choice in the matter."

"So, I'm still confused. Denzelle can run divorced, but you can't?"

Tatiana sat up in the bed and grabbed the bottle of champagne off of the night stand. She looked for a glass, and then decided to take a few swigs out of the bottle. She wished there was something stronger to drink to help her brace herself for this conversation. Something told Tatiana she was not going to like what was about to pop out of Xavier's mouth.

"If I run as a divorced candidate, I'll be running as a newly divorced man. It'll be clear I left Camille for you, Tatiana. Plus, I won't even be divorced when I announce my candidacy. I'll be separated but still legally married to Camille.

"You know as well as I do, Camille is not going to let me run a race like that in peace as long as we still have legal papers on each other. She is going to make a big stink and tell everybody you broke up her marriage. She is also going to force folk to deal with her as long as we are still married."

"I don't care what the cow says about me, Xavier," Tatiana told him, and took another swig out of the champagne bottle.

"What Camille says may not matter to you, Tatiana, but it will matter a lot to the women in the church she says it to. Some of them are delegates and have voting power. Some of them are married to delegates, or have family members who are delegates. They will get real angry and cast their votes for someone other than myself.

"As long as I am still legally married to Camille, she will have the right to enjoy all of the privileges of being the candidate's wife. Many of the church's women's organizations are not even going to recognize you until after the divorce decree is issued. And unfortunately, some of them are not going to recognize you then."

Tatiana drained the champagne bottle with tears streaming

down her cheeks. This was so unfair. Most of those women didn't even like Camille Franklin.

Xavier sat up and grabbed Tatiana in his arms. He kissed her on the mouth and held her tight.

"Please don't cry. We'll think of something."

"But Xavier, if what you are saying is true, that's all the more reason to hurry up and ask Camille for the divorce."

He kissed Tatiana again. Only this kiss, unlike the previous one, was not full of love—it was about lust, pure and simple. Xavier knew he was wrong. But being forced to tell Tatiana the truth about what was going on turned him on.

At first Tatiana was falling for this version of the okey-doke. But Xavier had run that game on her one time too many for her not to figure out this play in his game book. She pulled away from him before things got too heated and said, "Things aren't going as planned. Correct?"

Xavier nodded, and lay back on the pillows with his hands behind his head. How was he going to tell Tatiana that "things aren't going as planned" was an extreme understatement? Tatiana had a delicate disposition and didn't do well with disappointing news. Xavier saw how upset she was over being in his arms while laying on upper-middle-class instead of rich-folk sheets. How would Tatiana react when she learned he didn't know when they could be together as husband and wife?

Xavier knew Tatiana would not be able to stomach them simply going together year after year after year. Tatiana couldn't stand the thought of Camille getting accolades as his wife. She hated it when Camille called Xavier to discuss some pastor and first lady church business, and Tatiana had to sit in the background quiet, as if she did not exist. The last time that happened Tatiana stomped on his Rolex, and then sobbed for hours. Telling Tatiana the truth about his situation was going to be painful and unpleasant.

"Baby," he began carefully. "Some powerful preachers are behind my run for bishop. In fact, they are the ones who convinced me to run in the first place. Bishop Sonny Washington and Reverend Marcel Brown are in my corner one hundred percent, and they are going to put together the PAC money needed to run this campaign."

Tatiana sat up in the bed and clapped her hands in delight. If Bishop Washington and Reverend Brown were behind this, it meant Xavier was rolling high in the Gospel United Church, and big things were in store for her man. Sonny Washington and Marcel Brown may have some shaky reputations in the church, but they were still powerful players—not to mention very, very rich. She said, "Honey, that is wonderful! Now I really can't wait for us to be together."

She put her hands to her cheeks and exclaimed.

"Oh my! I need to get up to New York to find an exquisite purple ensemble to wear to the Episcopal consecration ceremony!"

This was going to be harder than anything Xavier could have imagined. They were not even separated from their spouses, and Tatiana was planning a trip to some overpriced store in New York to find a purple, church lady's suit for the new husband she couldn't even marry. The consecration ceremony was a ways off— and he had to get elected bishop to participate in it. Tatiana was making his head hurt.

His mentors, Sonny Washington and Marcel Brown, always told him a woman could be light-years ahead of a man when it came to envisioning plans for the future. He had shrugged that observation off as some old player rumblings. Now he understood exactly what they had tried to warn him about—especially when it pertained to hot and torrid relationships with his other women.

Xavier took Tatiana's hands in his and looked her in the eye. He said, "Tatiana, I can't divorce Camille and be able to run for bishop."

Tatiana stared at Xavier like she wasn't hearing him right.

"Baby, the Board of Bishops is planning a meeting to vote in a policy that prohibits a man or woman who runs for an Episcopal seat, or is holding an Episcopal seat, from remarrying if the ex-spouse is alive.

"If I were to divorce Camille and marry you, I couldn't run for bishop. If I win an Episcopal seat and then marry you, I'd have to step down. I could divorce Camille and remain a pastor, but I wouldn't make the kind of money bishops in the Gospel United Church are pulling these days."

"Xavier, what kind of money are you talking about? I always thought bishops earned modest six-figure salaries."

"That has changed in the last ten years. Bishops presiding over the smallest and poorest districts in the Gospel United Church make at least $275,000 a year. Bishops who preside over the more affluent districts make even more. And that doesn't include the perks and salary bonuses that come with the job."

"How much are we talking about for you, Xavier? And what district do they want you to preside over?"

"At least half a mil. And they want to send me to the Seventh Episcopal District."

"So, Bishop Jimmy Thekston Jr. is stepping down so you can win and preside often the Seventh District."

Xavier sat up and frowned. He had asked the same question when Bishop Sonny Washington and Reverend Marcel Brown first told him that he was needed in the Seventh District, which covered Louisiana, Texas, Oklahoma, and Arkansas. He'd never known anyone who was able to get that district from a Thekston. But Bishop Washington had assured Xavier he didn't have to worry about Jimmy Jr.

"Tatiana, preachers with more clout than the Thekstons told me I won't have to worry about them when I am assigned to the Seventh District."

"Why do they want you there?"

Xavier got real quiet. He knew he was not supposed to trust Tatiana with the real plans involving the Seventh Episcopal District. Bishop Washington, Marcel Brown, Bishop Jefferson, and the attorney, Luther Howard, had warned him to never breathe a word of this plan, which was worth tens of millions of dollars, to anyone.

Luther Howard was a high-profile black defense attorney who had made his name representing corrupt politicians, mafia bosses, and CEOs of major corporations who had done things to bring them on the brink of a very ominous stint with the law. Rumor had it that Luther was the brains behind the defense team that represented the famous Dinkle brothers of the Dinkle brothers drug cartel.

Xavier was afraid of Luther Howard, even though he always acted like he could hold his own whenever Luther was around. Attorney Luther Howard was the coldest, hardest, and most ruthless and calculating man Xavier Franklin had ever met. It didn't even seem to bother Luther that he represented some of the most dangerous and evil men in the United States. Xavier wondered how the man slept at night, knowing he had gotten so many frightening people acquitted after they had done some pretty bad things.

Luther Howard wanted Reverend Xavier Franklin elected bishop and assigned to the Seventh Episcopal District because he needed a preacher to serve as a reputable-looking front man for the dummy corporation he planned to run out of Louisiana. The corporation would be designed to help Luther get his hands on money that would be channeled through churches in the district to help with the lingering environmental and financial problems caused by the Gulf Coast oil spill. It was going to take a lot of skill, cunning, and ingenuity to pull this off, and Luther had warned everyone of the peril that could befall anybody foolish enough to mess with these plans at any time, on any level.

Xavier knew Tatiana was waiting on an answer from him. He also knew that if he told her the details, and she revealed anything about what they were planning, they would both end up down in the gulf, absorbing all of the oil that was still having an impact on sea life at the ocean's surface.

Tatiana was watching her man intently, trying her best to

figure out why he was being so cagey and secretive about his plans to run for bishop. She knew Xavier was hiding something from her.

Xavier was not going to say anything that would get them killed. But he also had to get Tatiana off of his back and off track on this. Xavier rarely used this tactic, because it was so down and dirty. But it was foolproof and worked every single time.

He closed his eyes and rubbed the side of his head like he was trying to get rid of a really bad headache. When Xavier was confident Tatiana was watching him intently, he let his head drop down until his chin rested on his chest, and then released a noise that sounded like he was trying to hide a sob. Xavier kept his eyes closed until he felt Tatiana's fingertips on his chest. Before she could say a word, Xavier lifted his head up slowly and looked deep into her eyes.

"I can't believe this," Xavier said in the softest and sweetest voice Tatiana had ever heard coming from him.

"Believe what, Xavier?"

"I . . . I . . . I . . ."

He stopped and coughed, like he was choking back another sob.

"I'm in shock over this, Tatiana."

"In shock over what, Xavier?" Tatiana asked him with worry creeping into her voice.

It took everything Xavier had in him to stop the grin that was deep down in his chest from popping up on his face. Xavier knew he had Tatiana in the palm of his hands, and went in for the kill.

Xavier bowed his head and kept it down for a few seconds. He needed some time to think of something real sad (like wearing a cheap suit and driving a small domestic car) to make him feel like crying. When the misery of those sad thoughts hit home, and the tears began to well up inside, Xavier knew it was safe enough to raise his head back up.

Tatiana got real upset when she saw a single tear trailing down her man's cheek.

"I can't believe I'm so deeply in love with you, Tatiana," Xavier said with a voice about to break into a heavy sob. "How did I get you? What have I done to deserve you and your love?"

Xavier began to cry, and reached for Tatiana. She could barely believe he figured out a way to love her so deeply and with so much passion, he would break down in her arms. Tatiana didn't need and didn't want to ask her man anything about these plans. As long as he loved her like this, it would be alright.

Xavier held on to Tatiana and braced himself for some good loving. He had outdone himself. An old army superior officer taught him this trick when he was stationed over in Germany.

His superior had said, "Young brother, whenever you need to gain control over a situation with your woman, remember this foolproof tactic. Think of something that makes you feel so sad, it's all you can do to stop yourself from bursting into tears."

"Like someone dying?" Xavier asked with some hesitation. He wasn't comfortable pretending somebody was dead long enough to make you want to break down and cry.

"Nah," his superior answered with a casual wave of his hand. "No need to take this game that far. In fact, that's going too far. You don't want to pretend like something like that has happened.

"What you need to do, young blood, is think of something that messes you all up."

Xavier had stood there in Germany, cold, practically covered in snow, trying to think of something that would get him that upset. As he was standing there, thinking and freezing his butt off, an ugly woman from his unit walked up to him. She said, "Xavier Franklin! I thought you were going to call me after last night. You know, the way we were carrying on, we could have made ourselves a baby if you hadn't used three wrappings of protection."

His superior was trying hard not to laugh in that woman's face. It was clear Xavier didn't want anybody on the base to know he even knew the woman, let alone had slept with her. Xavier was standing in the snow looking like he wished a missile would land right on top of his head.

Xavier stared at the woman, wondering what would make her think he wanted a baby with her. That baby would come out looking like a jacked-up ghetto fox—a real fox, like the ones in the woods, only it would probably have a mouth full of gold fox teeth. Just the thought was painful enough to make him want to cry. What if his boys found out he had gotten desperate enough to sleep with her?

"So, are we on for another date, Xavier?"

"No, Private, you and Xavier are not on for another date. Because he will have his hands full doing all the work I'm giving him for sleeping with you. And if you know what's good, you will forget that ever happened between you and Franklin here. Are we clear, Private?"

"Sir, yes, Sir," the woman said, and then moped away. She had been plotting and scheming to get with Xavier Franklin since she first saw him walking across the base. Now his superior officer had shut it down. Life sure did suck sometimes.

"Thank you," Xavier whispered, so relieved there were tears in his eyes.

"See, you have something to think about that will bring you to tears, young blood."

Tatiana ran her expensive, twenty-four-carat-gold-tipped, French-manicured nails across Xavier's chest. She knew how much her man loved the feel of real gold on his body, simply by the way Xavier relaxed and then tensed up almost at the same time. She'd bet Camille never elicited a response from him like that.

Tatiana snuggled up in Xavier's arms. She said, "How much time do we have left?"

"How much time do you need, Baby?" Xavier answered, hoping Camille wouldn't call or text him and spoil everything.

He wondered how long he could keep Tatiana content to remain his other woman on what was beginning to look like an indefinite basis. Getting elected bishop meant everything to Reverend Xavier Franklin. And he realized, in this very moment, that he was willing to do, and capable of doing, anything to get that position.

Until experiencing this in-the-moment epiphany, Xavier hadn't known he was also willing to give up the only woman he almost ever loved to get what he wanted. Now Xavier Franklin had a new problem resting on his shoulders. He was going to have to convince Tatiana to divorce Todd without the imminent prospect of marriage to him. Even though Xavier couldn't get divorced so he could marry Tatiana, he still didn't want to share her with her husband.

"Xavier?"

"Yes, Baby."

"The new law for the church. You can marry and be a bishop if your ex is dead, right?"

"Yeah," he answered.

"Okay, good," was all Tatiana said. She had been thinking about how she could get out of her marriage to Todd and keep the money for months. Tatiana had been thinking about how to get rid of Camille, too. She and Xavier needed their freedom, and they also needed their incomes.

A shiver went up Xavier's spine. He knew Tatiana was thinking the same things he'd been thinking about for a while. It was a relief to know he was not all alone in pondering if there was another better, swifter, and more economically feasible way for the two of them to be together.

Chapter Eighteen

"We may have a problem," Marcel said.

"Problem?" Luther Howard asked in a voice that was so cold and hard it made Marcel Brown nervous. In fact, everything about Luther Howard made Marcel nervous.

Luther Howard was amused over the effect he was having on Marcel Brown and Sonny Washington. It was crystal clear that both men were afraid of him. But then, they needed to be afraid. Luther didn't have any qualms about ordering hits on people he considered a useless nuisance.

"Are you okay, Marcel?" Luther asked with a smile that was so menacing, Marcel and Sonny began to have some serious doubts about working with this man.

"Yeah, man. I'm good," Marcel lied.

"Well, you look paranoid to me," Luther said.

"Naw, nothing paranoid here," Marcel lied again. He was more than paranoid. He was petrified. Luther Howard was mean and he dealt with some terrifying people.

Whenever Marcel knew he had to meet with Luther, he always came up with an escape plan, just in case Luther got mad and tried to kill him. He even practiced holding his breath, keeping his eyelids from fluttering, and lying completely still, as if he were dead when he was at home alone. It never hurt to be prepared when dealing with a man like Luther Howard.

Marcel Brown had spent over half of his life being unprepared whenever he was knee-deep in some dirt. This time he was not going to get caught, he was not going to get hurt, and he definitely was not going to get himself killed.

Xavier Franklin's phone buzzed. He hit the end button. The phone was silent, then it buzzed again.

"Are you going to respond to your wife, Reverend Franklin?" Luther asked, with a great deal of impatience.

"How did you know it was my wife?"

"From the look on your face that said, 'Why is the B calling me,'" Luther answered, and got up out of his chair.

"Handle your business while I'm handling my business in the toilet, Franklin," Luther said. "I don't want to be bothered with you and your woman when I'm done."

Xavier nodded and started to text his wife. Luther snatched the phone out of his hand and pushed the end button on the phone. He said, "Call that woman," and hurried into the toilet.

Xavier took the phone back, and got up and went over to the window. This hotel suite overlooked Lake Michigan. He hadn't been too keen on coming to Chicago from North Carolina in December. But this view was so incredible it was almost worth his teeth chattering every time a gust of arctic air rushed over him in the Windy City.

"What do you want?" Xavier snapped into the phone.

Sonny Washington looked at Marcel. Shaking his head he said, "Man, Franklin is dumber than I thought he was. How is he going to talk to his woman like she's his 'I need to call somebody ho' and think that crap is gonna fly?"

Marcel shrugged and shook his head in disgust. He stared at Xavier over by the window trying to make Camille get off the phone without provoking her to throw one of those good old if you loved me tantrums. He hated it when a woman did that. It was so stupid to act out with a man you knew did not love you. Because if he did, he wouldn't do the kind of things that provoked such a volatile emotional response. When would women learn that when a man truly cared about you, there were things he wouldn't dream of doing?

"If playa had it going on like he says he does, he would have had this in check as soon as that girl said hello," Marcel said to Sonny.

"I know," Sonny replied. "I still don't know why Xavier married Camille Creighton. I tried to tell him that girl was spoiled rotten and a pain in the butt. And she doesn't even look like much to me. Does she look good to you, Marcel, man?"

"Hell, naw. She looks like a brown Twizzler."

Sonny started laughing. He'd heard Camille Creighton Franklin called many things. But nobody had ever called her a Twizzler.

"You know she looks like that because you are laughing too hard," Marcel said with a chuckle. "And you know why Xavier married that girl. Her old man was the dean of the Divinity School at Eva T. Marshall, and both of her parents left her a toilet-bowl load of money."

"Well, obviously it wasn't enough money, if that conversation is any indication of the amount," Sonny said.

Marcel looked in the direction of the bathroom. Luther had been in the toilet for a good ten minutes. He hoped he stayed there until Xavier finished his phone call.

"What do you want me to do, Camille?" Xavier snapped, resisting a powerful urge to push end on his phone. "I want you to love me," Camille whined loud enough to be heard by Marcel and Sonny. "I want you to admit you wouldn't be the great Reverend Xavier Franklin without me and my daddy's clout and my mama and my daddy's money. I want you to kick Tatiana to the curb and quit taking her to the Umstead Hotel."

Xavier was quiet. He rubbed his ear. Camille was talking real loud. He looked over at Marcel and Sonny. They were deep in conversation and appeared oblivious to Xavier's conversation with his wife. When Xavier went back to talking to Camille, Sonny and Marcel went back to listening to that conversation.

"Did you hear me, Xavier?" Camille screamed into the phone.

"Not really," Xavier lied, hoping Camille would drop the issue. His response made her get angrier and louder.

"I thought you were stupid enough to think I didn't know your newest woman was Denzelle Flowers's ex."

"But, Sugar . . ."

"Don't you say that to me, Xavier Leon Franklin! I want you out of my house, out of my bank account, and out of my life!"

Xavier started sweating. Just last week Camille told him if he left, it would be over her dead body. Now she wanted a divorce. What had influenced this decision? He was going to have to play this play better than when he ran it on Tatiana. He hated doing this over the telephone. Women responded better when the game was run face-to-face.

"How am I going to live without you, Camille?" Xavier asked.

"You should have thought about that before you bought that heifer some nine-hundred-count sheets with my money."

Marcel watched the bathroom door, hoping Xavier would get off of the phone before Luther came out of the toilet and heard this craziness.

"Nine-hundred-count sheets," Sonny whispered. He glanced back at the bathroom, too, but not for the reasons Marcel was watching the door. He said, "I hope he took some Lysol in there with him."

Marcel nodded.

Xavier's first ploy wasn't working, and he needed to modify his line of attack. Camille wasn't the only one walking around with information you didn't want someone to have. He said, "I strongly advise you to remain in this marriage if you know what is good for you."

"Really?" Camille yelled.

"Well, why don't you let me send you a little somethin' somethin'?" was all Xavier said, as he pulled up a picture of Camille sitting in a man's lap and kissing him in a silk bathrobe.

He waited a minute, and then smiled when heard his wife gasp.

"How . . . ?"

"How did I find this?"

Xavier smiled at his phone. He wished Camille could see the smug expression on his face.

"Did you honestly think I wouldn't find out you were sleeping with Jimmy Gordy?"

"Jimmy Gordy," Sonny whispered to Marcel. "Isn't he the head of the Usher Board at Xavier's church?"

Marcel nodded. Everybody knew Jimmy Gordy. In addition to heading up the Usher Board, Jimmy Gordy was also in charge of transportation when a major Gospel United Church meeting was held in North Carolina.

Jimmy Gordy had made quite a name for himself, and he should have been pretty well-off. But the curious thing is that Jimmy Gordy walked around looking and acting like he was barely making minimum wage. Marcel always believed Jimmy Gordy was the front man for that transportation business. Somebody way up, with a whole lot of money, needed a huge tax write-off. That is the only way they would set up a man like Jimmy Gordy as the so-called owner of their business.

"What woman in her right mind would go with Jimmy Gordy?" Sonny was saying, thinking that if Glodean ever went with Jimmy Gordy, he'd take his Bentley and run her over, flat as a pancake. That was just disrespectful to your man—for a woman to go and lay up with the likes of a Jimmy Gordy.

"I don't know," Marcel said. " 'Cause for starters, the brother is butt ugly."

Sonny nodded. Jimmy Gordy was a gold-colored man with freckles that were so big he looked like he had spots on him. His eyes were a weird black color—they looked like animal eyes. He was hairy and had a low hairline—he looked like his forehead was always trying to touch down on his eyebrows.

"I always thought Jimmy Gordy looked like a hyena in a cheap suit," Marcel said, and then stopped the conversation when

Luther came out of the bathroom looking a bit pale. He was so glad Xavier had finally gotten off the phone with Camille.

"So, where are we with this?" Luther asked, hoping he sounded better than he felt. He should not have eaten that lobster salad.

"Xavier, I hope you got your wife straightened out. I would hate to see something happen to her because she didn't get with the program."

Xavier was superquiet. He didn't like the threat. But he was in too deep to get out now. Men like Luther Howard didn't let go of folks who knew too much about what going on.

"Can he stomach this deal, Sonny? I told you and Marcel to choose our candidate carefully." Luther knew Marcel's 'we may have a problem' was about Xavier being weak, squeamish, and scary.

"I'm fine," Xavier said to Luther. "and Camille will be on-board, or deal with the consequences."

Xavier wished he could wipe that smug grin off of Luther Howard's face. Even though he constantly wished Camille would keel over and die, he still didn't appreciate another man threatening his wife. Camille was his problem, not Luther's.

Camille Franklin sat in her million-dollar home staring at the phone. She did not know how Xavier had found out about Jimmy Gordy. Camille wasn't even all that enamored of Jimmy. She only fooled around with him because he had mad skills behind closed doors, and she knew Xavier would be pissed off that she was sleeping with the head of the Usher Board at his own church.

Plus, Camille knew Xavier would get mad because Jimmy was ugly. Xavier would not be able to figure out why she was attracted to the man. He would never figure out that the main attraction was simply that it would make him mad.

She swung her feet back and forth, admiring the black-suede platform pumps with the rainbow-colored soles. Nobody had a pair of shoes like these, because they had been handmade especially for her by a cobbler in Spain. Camille liked the shoes so much that she purchased four more pairs—blue, chocolate, red, and gray. Five thousand USDs a pair—and the shoes were worth every single penny spent on them.

Camille Creighton Franklin was rich. She wasn't in the 1 percent, but she certainly had enough money to put her a little bit ahead of 15 percent of the population. Who cared about being a 1 percenter? Didn't folk realize that folk in the top 5 percent had some serious cash? A 1 percenter like Warren Buffet had lunatic money. A 5 percenter had stupid money. And a 12 or 15 percenter had enough money to wipe their butts with a C-note on special occasions.

Despite her wealth, Camille was miserable and in a very painful marriage. Spending money on things most people couldn't afford to even think about made life more bearable for her. About the only overpriced purchase Camille regretted making was Xavier. Sometimes she wished she had made better use of her cash and gotten herself a cheaper man.

"Xavier, I am going to tell you this one time and one time only," Luther Howard began.

"Discipline your wife. When the new ruling goes through, you will not be able to divorce and run for bishop in the Gospel United Church. And you can't divorce your wife once you've been elected to the episcopacy and hold on to that seat.

"We cannot succeed in our plans without you. So Mrs. Franklin had better get with the program, and fast. And tell her to end it with that ugly, hyena-looking man she is sleeping with to get back at you."

Xavier's mouth fell open. That was Camille's reason for sleeping around with Jimmy Gordy? Xavier knew he was fifty times better looking than Jimmy. And Camille was walking around acting she was boo'd-up with somebody who looked like Idris Elba.

"What? You believed there was something about Jimmy Gordy that Mrs. Franklin was attracted to, Xavier?" Luther asked.

Sonny and Marcel were superquiet. While they agreed with

Luther, they also knew that there was another reason for that affair. Jimmy Gordy was an ugly brother who was tappin' that tail on the wife of a fine brother. He had some skills in the bedroom that probably should have been packaged and marketed on a TV infomercial.

Xavier was upset and didn't want to show it. He went to the bathroom, hoping it had cooled down since Luther's extended stay in it.

Luther stared at the closed bathroom door. He knew Xavier wasn't the sharpest preacher around. But the brother had been in the clergy business for a while. He should have a better handle on what motivated people to do things.

He hoped this plan wouldn't end up being a messed-up scheme that disintegrated into a fiasco. Because the people he worked for were meaner, scarier, and way more evil than the people he defended in court. They wouldn't even just kill them. They would kidnap and torture their entire families and *then* kill them.

Chapter Nineteen

It was sad that the only preachers Luther Howard liked and respected were the ones he had to work against. Luther wished it were different. He wished he could respect Sonny, Marcel, and Xavier as much as he found himself respecting Denzelle Flowers and Denzelle's best friend, Reverend Obadiah Quincey.

Even though Luther Howard needed the help of wayward preachers, a part of him secretly wished there was something in these men that made them want to get him to turn from wrong to right. But he knew they were too dumb and greedy to even do that right.

People like Sonny, Marcel, and especially Xavier Franklin were always stupid enough to believe they could shift directions and be allowed to swim back upstream, because they had an epiphany midways through a corrupt business deal. The last man Luther ordered a hit on had signed the contract, taken Luther's money, spent it, and then had the nerve to try and make the contract null and void when he discovered he didn't like all of the terms. Luther would never forget the conversation with the man—it was just that funny.

That brother had driven up to Luther Howard's legitimate office suite in the laser red Saab 9-5 Sedan he bought with Luther's down payment money, looking ridiculous in a blue velvet Hugo Boss suit. The brother was built like a football player, and he had a gut. To this day Luther would never understand why that man thought it okay to stuff himself in a Hugo Boss suit. Anybody who knew anything about Hugo Boss suits knew they were not user-friendly to big, thick brothers with a gut.

The man had walked in Luther's office and said, "Howard, I want out. I had my cousin, Lil' Jeronimo, look over the details of the deal, and he told me some innocent people would lose their jobs, and maybe even get kilt."

"You mean 'killed'?" Luther asked him, wondering what possessed the brother to risk his life by blabbing that he consulted with a family member named Lil' Jeronimo on a man like Luther Howard.

"Yeah, dawg—kilt. Somebody could get kilt."

"Is Lil' Jeronimo your cousin's real name?" Luther asked quietly, hoping the answer was no, even though he knew that was wishful thinking at best.

"Nahh. Lil' Jeronimo's real name is Jeronimo Jenkins Jr. He a junior. That's why his nickname is Lil' Jeronimo."

"So his father, your uncle, is Jeronimo Jenkins Sr."

"Nahh. His daddy ain't my uncle. Lil' Jeronimo is my play cousin. So technically we ain't kinfolk, but we still family. His daddy's name is Jerry Jenkins."

Luther didn't know why black people always had to have a play mama or a play daddy or play cousin. He'd never met a white person who talked about his play mama. And why would anybody tell a play person about a deal like this?

"I see," was all Luther could say. He was relieved to know Jeronimo Jenkins Jr. would probably be easy to find and get rid of. There was a strong chance Jeronimo Jenkins had a rap sheet, and there were folks in the community who had beef with him. How could that not be the case with someone named Jeronimo Jenkins Jr. and whose daddy's name was Jerry Jenkins?

"So you and your cousin."

"Play cousin."

"My bad," Luther said, and then continued. "You and your *play* cousin have discussed this. And the two of you came to the conclusion that you want out because this is too down and dirty even for you? Right?"

"Correct," the man said.

"So why come to me after spending my hard-earned money on your new Hugo Boss suit and brand-new Saab? Did it occur to you that I might take issue with that?"

The brother grinned and said, "You know what a Hugo Boss suit is? I knew you had some class, Luther. But this ain't no real Hugo Boss. It's a knock-off. Them suits cost too much."

"Is the car a knock-off, too?" Luther asked with a frown. Did this joker really think he looked like a brother who didn't know his way around a hip designer suit?

"Dawg, you so crazy. Of course this ain't no knock-off car. It's a Saab, dawg. I bought it because it's one of those upscale types of cars. It screams old money. 'Cause old money thangs don't bring too much attention to you—know what I'm sayin'?"

If Luther didn't have to order a hit on this fool and his cousin, no, play cousin, this mess would have been downright hilarious.

"So, what you're telling me is that a bright red Saab isn't noticeable. And that a car made by a company that has filed for bankruptcy and suspended making new cars spells old money?"

The brother got quiet. He didn't know all of that about his new car. No wonder he was able to name his price when he bought it from the man who owned the chop stop. Who knew?

"Dawg," Luther began in a cold and hard voice. "*You* called *me* with this deal. My agent told you from the beginning the potential casualties associated with this kind of situation. I know she also asked if you were down for this, because that's how she rolls.

"So, here is what I suggest. You and your play cousin, Lil' Jeronimo, better get me my money. And then, you might want to get ghost."

"I'll have your money back to you in six months."

"Not good enough," Luther countered. "I want my money in six hours."

The brother's face went gray. He didn't know how he was going to get ninety-four thousand dollars in six hours. He didn't even know how to get it in six months. He was just talking trash to buy some time.

"You look kind of upset, dawg," Luther said. "You don't think you can make it happen?"

"Naw. Oh, hell. What I mean, what I mean is, yeah. Yeah, I can make it happen, dawg. They don't call me the Wiley Coyote of Charlotte for nothing."

Luther rubbed that spot between his eyebrows. He sighed. The brother may have been the Wiley Coyote of Charlotte, North Carolina. But he was going to have to turn into the Roadrunner to outrun the bullet that was going to be aimed at him very shortly.

"You a'ight, dawg?" the brother was saying, breaking up Luther's concentration. He hoped what he said would make sense to Luther Howard. But it didn't look like he was making much headway with the man. His cousin had told him to pray before he came to the office. He was so glad he brought the Bible his cousin's baby mama's sister's boyfriend had loaned them.

"I'm fine," Luther responded in his courtroom voice. "I guess I'm a bit worried about you and your cousin."

"No need to worry about us, dawg," the man said nervously. "Look, I want to read you something from the Word. It will make you feel better, and it will help you understand where I'm comin' from. Know what I'm sayin'."

Luther didn't blink an eye.

"I tell you what," the brother said. He was sweating hard and had dark spots under the arms of that ill-fitting, velvet "Hugo Boss" suit. "Why don't you tell me what scripture you'd like to hear me read?"

"I want to hear the verse that talks about when you have to walk through a valley with some death shadows following you all around. You know which one I'm talking about?"

"Yeah. Yeah, dawg. You talkin' 'bout the Twenty-third Psalm. And shadows don't follow you in that scripture, it's—"

Luther raised his hand and said, "Just read it to me."

"Okay. I'm gone read from the New Living Translation Bible. So it will sound a little different to what you might expect, dawg."

"I always thought the King James version was the one people liked."

"Not always, dawg. Some folk like it broke down for them in another version. So, here goes: 'Even when I walk through the valley of death, I will not be afraid . . . for you are close beside me. Your rod and your staff protect and comfort me.'"

"I want you and your cousin to remember that scripture just like you read it to me. You will find it a great comfort to you in the coming days."

"Luther, you still with us, man?" Sonny asked. Just moments ago Luther was looking like he could chew a handful of nails like it was some chewing gum. Now the brother was acting like he wished one of them would go straight preacher on him and bring a word or a sermon up in this room.

"I'm fine. Just processing some information."

Luther studied Xavier. He said, "How much does this other woman mean to you? Can we help you keep her close but still in the honey on the side spot? Or will it take a whole lot more?"

"Well, I guess I could . . ." Xavier began.

"Xavier," Sonny said, not in the least bit interested in hearing about Xavier and that skank, Tatiana Townsend. Right now, he was sick of Xavier and his women. He continued, "You are aware that Denzelle Flowers is running for bishop? He has money, he has a campaign team, and Obadiah Quincey is his campaign manager. Theophilus Simmons and Eddie Tate are his fundraisers. Right now, they are planning the first major fundraising and promotional event. And from what my spies have told me, it promises to be a big hit."

"So what does that have to do with me?" Xavier snapped.

"Everything," Luther answered in a very calm and quiet voice that had deadly chill laced through it. He was glad for the change in venue. They were focusing on Camille and Tatiana like some women gathered around the kitchen table. And that was starting to get on Luther's nerves.

Xavier was about to offer an apology but was stopped by Sonny Washington's firm hand on his shoulder. He got the message fast. The worse thing he could do was let on that Luther Howard frightened him.

"You see," Luther continued, satisfied that he had gotten his unspoken message across to Xavier. He hadn't missed the transaction between Xavier and Bishop Washington. Luther had to give the bishop some points. Sonny Washington couldn't be punked easily.

"Denzelle Flowers has everything to do with you. There is only one Episcopal seat that will become available at your Triennial General Conference."

"I thought there were two," Xavier asked, now looking to Sonny Washington and Marcel Brown for some answers.

"There were," Marcel responded evenly. "Bishop Conrad Brown in the Twelfth District decided to stay through one more term. And Bishop Jefferson is still stepping down, but he has been granted special permission to continue to serve as bishop for another year. He will share his responsibilities with Sonny, who has three years left before he'll have to retire."

"How and why?" Xavier said. He raised his hands up in the air. This was getting wilder and crazier by the minute. But he'd been warned. One of Bishop Conrad Brown's protégés told him that he could find himself in some very hot water if he got tangled up with Bishop Sonny Washington and Reverend Marcel Brown.

Marcel, Sonny, and Luther Howard stared at each other for a moment. Xavier felt strongly that they were weighing in on how much to tell him. He figured this must be a very lucrative, sure-shot deal if they were willing to share more than need to know information.

"Son," Marcel began, "we cut a deal with Bishop Jefferson.

We paid him a lot of money to become the 'poster boy' for why preachers who run for bishop do not need more than one wife. The bishop has been married more times than I care to count. His wives are a poor example of what an Episcopal Supervisor is supposed to be. In fact, I don't think his newest wife, Violetta, even knew where a church was before she met the bishop."

"Yeah," Sonny chimed in. "Did you know Violetta Jefferson used to be one of the hottest dance hall singers and dancers in St. Thomas? That girl could put Patra to shame?"

Luther grinned. He used to love himself some Patra. He said, "Is Violetta Jefferson the same Violetta from the video 'Burn de House Down'?"

Xavier raised an eyebrow. He used to love that video. He didn't know Bishop Jefferson had it going on like that to snag Violetta.

"Yep," Marcel said. "One and the same. She is also the worse Episcopal Supervisor the Gospel United Church has ever had. The pastors' wives in their district can't stand Violetta. And there is always some mess brewing whenever she brings any member of her family with her. Have you seen that uncle?"

"Yes," Luther said laughing.

It had been a long time since he had seen some ghetto sandals. He didn't know what made brothers cut up their Stacy Adams and make some sandals out of them. That had to be the countriest, craziest, and most ghetto mess he'd ever witnessed.

"Okay," Xavier said with a shrug. "So the bishop doesn't know how to pick the right kind of Episcopal Supervisor. What does that have to do with me, or any other preacher who faces divorce, for that matter? There a lot of Episcopal Supervisors the women in the church don't like.

"I mean, let's just get real. Do you all honestly believe Camille is the kind of woman who will endear herself to the women in my district if I am elected bishop?"

Sonny winced. Xavier had a point. Nobody liked his wife—not even Xavier.

Marcel couldn't stand Camille, either. But Camille Franklin was in a completely different category of women people couldn't stand than a Violetta Jefferson. Camille was stuck-up, mean, nasty, and haughty. But she still knew how to handle herself around church folk. Camille would not defy basic minister's wife protocol when in public or while involved in some Gospel United Church business.

Even the bona fide church hoochies would have trouble with a Violetta Jefferson. Church hoochies may be on the prowl for a preacher or prominent church man—but they still played the church game, and played it well. Marcel rarely encountered a card-carrying church hoochie and she wasn't dressed head-to-toe in a Donna Vinci church suit. Violetta, on the other hand, never wore appropriate church-lady outfits like that.

Every time Marcel saw Bishop Jefferson's wife, he always expected her to pull a portable stripper's pole from her Prada bag. And ironically, most church hoochies couldn't even afford any of Violetta's clothes. Tweaki once told Marcel that Violetta wore a lot of Donatella Versace pieces. But those expensive, couture outfits still had "the club" written all over them.

As exciting and entertaining as Violetta Jefferson was, she could not get the women in the denomination to listen to a word she said, let alone follow her lead for some bishop's wife program. As unpopular as Camille Franklin was, she, unlike Violetta Jefferson, could exert some leading-church-woman power and influence in the denomination. She had grown up the daughter of a very prominent preacher in the Gospel United Church. And she was rich and very well connected.

"Can you control your wife, Xavier?" Luther.

"You know I can," Xavier replied, with a whole lot more bravado than he felt.

"No, actually, I really don't know that about you, son," Luther told him. "And this is what I'm going to do to help a brother out. If Camille doesn't stay in this marriage with you, I'll take matters into my own hands."

Luther pointed his index and middle fingers toward his fore-head.

"So, are we on the same page?"

"Yes," Xavier answered.

"Don't look so glum," Luther said, with a chilly laugh. "Think of it this way. If Camille doesn't want to play this game, you'll be free to marry Tatiana. And you'll have some extra cash on hand. Because I know you've taken out a very hefty insurance policy on your wife."

Marcel and Sonny exchanged quick glances with each other. They hoped Xavier could handle Camille, because her life depended on it. Luther Howard was proving to be more than they bargained for.

Chapter Twenty

Marsha signed for the FedEx envelope, opened it, and said, "Thank you, Jesus," when she saw the second Pastor's Aide Club check. Marsha had been praying, and told the Lord she trusted Him. But her money was still unbearably tight, and she barely made it from the first check to this one.

Marcus was remaining in school on her prayers, because Marsha was barely able to pay the monthly bill for his tuition. He had some scholarship money, but it wasn't enough. She was so glad Marcus was okay about not being able to remain in the dorms. Marsha knew how much he liked living on campus. But right now, they could not afford that extra expense.

She had been late on the rent payments twice. But thankfully her landlord couldn't afford to lose them as tenants. It was hard right now. And it was only by the grace of God that Marsha was doing as well as she was. She counted it a miracle that she and Marcus were still able to laugh and have joy in their hearts. The scripture about the joy of the Lord being your strength had never been truer in their lives.

Veronica and Keisha kept telling Marsha to have the money deposited into her account. But Marsha was old school when it came to payroll checks. She preferred to have a check put in her hand. She came close to learning a very painful lesson about going completely high-tech/new school when it came to convenience and money while married to Rodney Bluefield.

Her late husband, Rodney, almost managed to wipe out her entire bank account through an almost online bank transfer. Marsha would have been out there broke and turning her pockets inside out, looking for lint, if her mother had not gone super-old school and said, "Baby, you better move your money to my account, just in case that ex-man of yours takes a notion to dip his hand in the till."

Right before Marsha was scheduled to receive a hefty bonus, she went straight to Human Resources and asked that her check be put in her hands. Sure enough, on the day the check was supposed to hit the account, Rodney ran out to handle business with a practically defunct debit card. It took that fool a minute to realize that he was very short on cash when he kept trying to buy gas, pay the electric bill, pay the water bill, and buy groceries with the complimentary $117.47 Marsha left in the account.

Rodney was livid. And it was just a matter of time before he figured out that Marsha wasn't answering the phone and decided to confront her face-to-face. Rodney rolled up on Marsha one evening just as she was about to go outside to roll the trashcan to the curb.

Marsha counted it nothing short of a miracle that she followed an urge to look out of the living room window before going outside. It was in that moment that she saw Rodney's car pulling up into her driveway. Marsha hurried and got her brand-new stun gun, dropped it in her jacket pocket, and walked outside when she heard Rodney's car door slam.

"You know I needed that money to pay the bills," Rodney yelled at Marsha.

"What money to pay what bills? I thought you had it all together the day you left me to be with . . ."

Marsha looked up and snapped her fingers, trying to remember Rodney's exact parting words the day he woke her up at four a.m. and said, "I'm leaving you for my soul mate." She looked him in the eye.

"Now I remember. You said you were leaving me for your soul mate."

"Don't try and get cute with me, Marsha Bluefield."

"Metcalf. I'm changing my name back to Metcalf."

"Whatever," Rodney snarled. "All I know is that I'm over two thousand dollars in the hole, thanks to you."

Marsha popped her head to the side, curled up her lips, and said, "Whatevveerrrr, Rod-ney."

"You," Rodney said, with his finger in Marsha's face, "better give me my money."

"Get your stankin' finger out of my face, and get off of my steps, Rodney Bluefield," Marsha told him in a low voice.

"And what if I don't," he retorted. "What you gone do?"

"You just better move your old funky finger out of my face. I don't know where you ole nasty finger been. You could've been diggin' in your *soul mate's* nasty booty for all I know."

Rodney stuck his forefinger in Marsha's face again—this time right up under her nose.

Marsha looked at that finger on Rodney's left hand, with the tip missing from an old army accident, and bit it as hard as she could.

Rodney screamed and pushed at Marsha. She lost her balance and fell up against the front door. She was so mad at that man, she could hardly breathe. Rodney came toward Marsha again. But this time she was ready for him.

When Rodney tried to stick his finger in Marsha's face a third time, just to make a point, she took her stun gun and tapped it on his shoulder. He screamed and fell down on the porch. He reached up to grab Marsha's ankle, but she dodged his hand and tapped him with the stun gun again.

Rodney was pissed, his finger was hurting, and he felt like he was being electrocuted. Marsha stared down at him and said, "Don't you ever come near me with some mess like this again."

Rodney struggled to get up. He was about to start cussing.

Instead, he screamed, because she ran up to him and stunned him right up on the crack of his butt.

"I ought to get you good, one more time, Rodney Bluefield—just because you're making my new stun gun smell like fried booty."

She walked back into her house and slammed the door. Rodney was standing at the bottom of the porch, massaging the crack of his butt with a bit-up finger.

Marsha closed her eyes a second to block out the Rodney memory. She looked at the $7,500 check and whispered, "Thank you, Jesus," again.

It felt so good to have some money. Marcus still couldn't stay on campus. But now he would be able to get all of the extra materials he needed for the big project he was working on in his building design class. Marsha felt like she was finally beginning to experience a break in this storm she'd been in for years.

The cell phone was jumping with Beyoncé's "Love On Top." Then the house phone was practically ringing off the hook. Marsha ran and got the house phone right after she flipped open her cell.

"Where are you?" Keisha yelled into the cell and Veronica yelled into the house phone. Marsha's ears hurt. She'd been dumb enough to put one phone up to each ear.

"At home. Where else would I be?"

"Did Veronica call you?" Keisha asked.

"Yeah, Keisha," Veronica yelled loud enough to be heard over the other telephone. "I'm calling her now!"

"Why don't I put y'all on speakerphone on both phones," Marsha said. "That way, you can yell at each other and quit busting up my eardrums."

"Whatever," Keisha said. She could not believe Marsha was still at home. They had to rehearse this *Dancing with the Stars* thing later today. And the pastor was already at church going over his steps. Reverend Flowers could be so competitive.

"Again," Veronica said, as if she had been the one to bring this up in the first place. "Where are you, Marsha?"

"Okay, Roni. You are yelling at me through my home phone. Where else could I possibly be?"

"You could be at church to rehearse with Denzelle for the dance event," Veronica told her.

"Roni, our rehearsal doesn't start until five. It's three-thirty."

"Well, your pastor is over here practicing and stuff," Veronica said. "Girl, he is working it. I didn't even know Denzelle could dance like that. You all are still dancing the fox-trot, right."

"Yes," Marsha answered. "That's still the plan."

"And you all are still doing the fox-trot off of Charlie Wilson?" Keisha asked in a flat voice.

"I know you know that is just wrong, Marsha," Veronica said. "I'm shocked Denzelle agreed to that. I knew you could talk him into dancing. But the fox-trot?"

"Well he did," Marsha said softly. She was feeling less and less confident about this whole *Dancing with the Stars* event by the second. It had seemed like a wonderful idea when they came up with it. But more and more she wondered if it was kind of hokey.

"I'm shocked, too," Keisha said. "You know the fox-trot isn't exactly the coolest dance and especially for a cool brother like Denzelle Flowers."

"Well, be shocked, Keisha," Marsha said, with a taste of attitude steeping into her voice. "Because Denzelle is doing that dance. And it wasn't easy convincing him to go with the flow of the plan."

"I bet it wasn't," Keisha said with a soft chuckle. "But I'm sure you, Miss Lady, had all that was needed to convince the pastor to get out there and dance off of Charlie Wilson."

Veronica was cracking up. Poor baby. Marsha tried so hard to pretend she didn't like Denzelle like that.

"This is a cool project even if Denzelle has to do the fox-trot," Marsha told them. "Plus, we have raised a lot of money and sold a lot of tickets."

"It is a good project," Keisha conceded. "But I won't lie. I can't wait to see how you are going to pull off doing the fox-trot of all things to 'Life of the Party.'"

"Well, whatever you plan on pulling off, Marsha," Veronica added, "you need to get over here before five p.m. Everybody has gone through their numbers but you and the pastor. Denzelle has been here at church warming up, trying to remember all of the steps to the dance, and trying to look all cool while he is messing up."

Marsha laughed. She didn't know if she wanted to know what Denzelle looked like over at the church trying to do a "Who's Your Daddy?" version of the church version of *Dancing with the Stars*. She said, "I'm on my way."

"Hurry and get here as fast as you can," Keisha said. "Because now, Pastor is acting like he is going to try and weave in a sermon with you all's dance number. That is not going to go over well at all."

"I better hurry," Marsha said, and sprayed herself with Coco Chanel before she left the house.

Chapter Twenty-one

Denzelle was in the church's gym admiring its transformation from the place where good basketball games were played into a dazzling showpiece for the dance competition. Keisha Jackson, with the help of Bay Bowser, contracted with Yvonne Fountain Parker and her team of design students to decorate the gym. They outdid themselves with this project.

Denzelle always thought Keisha and Bay made for a good team. He also thought they needed to get together. He and Charles Robinson both agreed Keisha was the perfect woman for Bay. Only thing, neither knew how to tell the brother that. So Denzelle put it in prayer, laid it on the altar, and left it with the Lord. He figured God made Keisha and Bay. And God knew exactly what was needed to get those two together.

He looked up and smiled—crimson and cream balloons covered the entire ceiling. Keisha and Bay promised to replenish the room with a batch of fresh balloons the day of the event. They thought filling the ceiling with balloons now would help build up anticipation for the competition. They were right, too. Folk would come in the gym, see the decorations, look up at the balloons, and go and buy some more tickets. At the rate they were going, this was going to be a sellout crowd.

This event had been widely publicized, thanks to Veronica Washington, who worked tirelessly to secure corporate donations, get a whole bunch of church folk to buy those ten-dollar tickets, and encourage the different auxiliary ministries in the church to provide in-kind service to make this event a big success. Thanks to those ministries, they had saved a lot of money on catering, supplies, and food. This promised to be a great kickoff for Denzelle's campaign for bishop, and not to mention a whole lot of fun.

Now, if only the architect of this thing would show up, so they could learn this dance. Fox-trot to Charlie Wilson's "Life of the Party." Whoever heard of doing the fox-trot to a hot number like that? Denzelle liked the song. He just wasn't sold on the notion that it would work for that dance.

One of the side doors opened. Denzelle smiled, and then tried to hurry and look preacherly, and like he was solely about the business of the Lord when Keisha Jackson and Dayeesha Mitchell walked in. They knew he thought they were Marsha, and was clearly disappointed when he saw them.

"We're here to observe how Marsha is going to do that dance to that song," Dayeesha said, and then went and took a seat. She pulled out a bag of red Twizzlers and started chewing on them like she was at the movie theater.

As much as Denzelle didn't want to do the fox-trot to a Charlie Wilson song, he was looking forward to learning this dance with Marsha Metcalf. Having a legitimate excuse to hold her in his arms would make dancing in front of his members a worthwhile endeavor. Marsha in his arms—that was about the best thing he'd thought about all evening.

"What are you smiling about, Pastor?" Dayeesha asked, chewing on a Twizzler. Keisha held her hand out for one and started laughing. It was pretty clear Pastor was thinking about *something* with that kind of look on his face.

"Uhhh," Denzelle began in the voice he used when meeting with his Trustees or Stewards. "Just so pleased about the way things are going. The event is in a few days, and I'm blown away at how it has all come together."

"Well, if you ask me," Veronica said, "you have the same

look on your face brothers have when folk start talking about Janet Jackson or Beyoncé or somebody like Angela Bassett."

"What look?" Denzelle asked in his preacher voice.

"The look that was plastered across your face before Dayeesha called you out," Veronica told him, laughing.

"I see you have jokes, Ms. Veronica."

Marsha walked in carrying the shoes she'd dance in during the competition. They were some black velvet, Mary Jane–styled shoes with a decent heel and rhinestones all over them.

"Oooo, love those shoes, Marsha," Keisha said. "Where did you get them?"

"Miss Thang's Holy Ghost Corner and Church Woman's Boutique," Denzelle said while stretching out his calves.

All of the ladies turned to look at their pastor.

"What? Y'all think the only folk shopping at that store are women? I have a mom. I have cousins. And . . ."

"You used to have a bunch of women who were high maintenance and expected gifts from Ms. Theresa's store," Dayeesha said. She could only imagine the tab their pastor used to run up trying to keep his women happy and in check.

Marsha didn't know what to say on that matter. Dayeesha was probably right. But it was weird hearing it put out there like that. She'd never thought about how much money Denzelle had to spend back when he was waving the playah's card all over the place.

She sat down and started putting on her shoes. They were sharp and very comfortable. Theresa had called in a shoemaker to design these shoes for her. Denzelle stood off to the side admiring how good those shoes looked on what he surmised were size six feet. His eyes wandered from the sexy shoes up to Marsha's calves. A part of him wished she needed someone with strong and firm hands to knead out the kinks in one of those calves.

Denzelle noticed both Dayeesha and Keisha watching him intently. Those two were too busy and inquisitive for their own good. He was going to have to tell Metro that he was falling on the job with Dayeesha. She had what he always described to his boy Charles Robinson as "too much freed-up mental space." It was dangerous for a brother when a woman had that kind of thinking time on her hands.

As far as Denzelle was concerned, women loved to sit around and think about and figure things out anyway. And when one had that kind of luxury to mull over her thoughts extensively? Watch out—especially if she was smart, observant, and had the gift of discernment like Dayeesha. If Metro put *something* on Dayeesha's mind, she'd be sitting around thinking about *that* instead of trying to figure out if he wanted to go with Marsha Metcalf.

"Again," Denzelle said to Marsha, "why are we dancing the fox-trot, of all things, to Charlie Wilson's 'Life of the Party'?"

"Denzelle is right," Veronica said. "Why the fox-trot and 'Life of the Party'?"

They were getting on Marsha's nerves about the dance and song selection. She knew what she was doing. The fox-trot was a great dance if you did it right. Most folk had only seen watered-down versions of the dance, performed by mediocre dancers, with mediocre songs. When she got through teaching Denzelle Flowers their routine, he would need a great big bowl of crow to munch on.

She didn't even deign to give any of them a response. As much as she loved them, they could really get on her nerves. Marsha knew she could be goofy and off-beat at times. But they always acted like they were so hip and cool—especially Dayeesha and Keisha. Those two acted like they taught a graduate-level course called "Swag" up at the college.

Marsha nodded toward the DJ box and Marcus put the song on, anxious to witness what he was hoping and praying would not be a hot mess. Marcus loved his mother. But sometimes she could take the dance to the beat of a different drummer position too far. Who ever heard of doing the fox-trot off of Charlie Wilson's "Life of the Party"? Next thing you know, his mother would be teaching folk how to do the waltz off of Trina's "Long Heels Red Bottom."

Marcus started cracking up at just the thought of his mother's reaction to that song at this dance event. He played it for a second, just to get a rise out of his mom. As soon as the first beats thumped out, Denzelle looked up at Marcus and said, "Come on, Son. You can't rock some Trina at church. What you trying to do? Get us all jolted-up with some lightning?"

Dayeesha was rolling with laughter. She said, "Keisha. Girl, who knew Rev was up on some Trina? Girl, Trina?"

"I know," Keisha answered. "Who Rev been playing that song for? You know if a brother is listening to some Trina, his mind ain't nowhere near thinking about some church."

"I heard that," Dayeesha said, still laughing. Their pastor was a trip. Dayeesha couldn't even imagine what Reverend Flowers was like back in the day. She figured that he and Mr. Charles Robinson ran some serious game on women when they were in college. And they were Kappas, and smooth, and fine? They probably had notches all over those Krimson and Kream Kanes.

"Marcus, put on Charlie Wilson," Marsha said in her mom voice.

"Yes, Ma'am."

"What's wrong, Marsha?" Denzelle asked, with a soft laugh. "You don't wanna do this dance off of some Trina?"

"Trina?" Marsha said. "That's who made the 'Black Pumps, Red Soles' song?"

"Lawd. Lawd. Lawd," Keisha mumbled out loud, shaking her head. She said, "Pastor, would you tell your member the real name of the song?"

"'Long Heels Red Bottom.'"

"Huh?" Marsha said, looking at all of them like they were the ones who were off base.

"'Long Heels Red Bottom' is the name of the song by Trina. Not, 'Black Pumps, Red Soles,'" Denzelle told her.

"You know the real name of this song? You like this song?"

"Yeah, and yeah," he said and looked over at Marcus, as if to say, That is *your* mama.

Marcus just shook his head and did what his mother asked—put on the Charlie Wilson CD. When the first notes on the keyboard rang out loud and clear, Marsha started to move to the beat. It had never occurred to Denzelle that Marsha could really dance. He liked the way her entire body caught and held on to the beat. It was like the notes were wrapping themselves around her hips and shoulders.

"Gone, Shawty," he said, with a wink. "I didn't know you had it like that, Girl."

Dayeesha and Keisha exchanged looks, as if to say, *Shawty?*

Denzelle stood back and watched Marsha work the song, and put together the basic parts of their dance steps. It hadn't occurred to him that she had done the choreography and was going to teach him the steps.

"See, this is how we will start off," Marsha was saying. "We'll begin in the traditional position for the fox-trot, do the actual dance, separate . . ."

She did a lovely pirouette, and moved back toward Denzelle.

"Then we'll fox-trot across the floor, using all of the space with movement and energy."

Marsha bounced across the dance floor so smoothly, they all wanted to just sit back and watch her do the fox-trot with herself. She did the tiny leap and foot movements that so defined this dance like a professional dancer. Her movements were beautiful.

"I never really thought about how nice this dance was," Veronica said to Dayeesha and Keisha. "It has some real pizzazz to it."

"I know," Keisha responded, head bobbing to the song and Marsha's dancing.

"I never knew Marsha could move like that," Dayeesha said, and sneaked and videotaped it on her phone. There was no way she was going to be able to fully describe this to Metro.

"*Dancing with the Stars* ain't got nothing on Miss Thing over there," Keisha said, amused at how captivated the pastor was with Marsha and her fox-trot.

"So, is that it?" Denzelle asked Marsha with more cool and confidence than he felt.

Marsha made every step performed appear effortless. And why did she have to look so doggone cute doing it? He had been so mesmerized by those dancing shoes, he had not taken in her dance outfit. No one but Marsha Metcalf would have been able to glide across the dance floor in some skinny jeans and a white, graphic T-shirt with glittery black stars all over it.

"Uhh . . . yeah," Marsha told Denzelle. "I think that's enough. Don't you?"

"It's sufficient," Denzelle said, knowing he was fronting big time. Because all he could think was, "How in the world am I going to learn those steps and then do the dance without looking like Masta P when he was on the real *Dancing with the Stars*?"

"Pastor looks like he is getting cold feet," Dayeesha said.

"That's because," Veronica began with a heavy sigh, "old boy is acting like he is in control, and he's not."

"Including his feelings for Marsha," Keisha asked.

"That, and discovering how good a dancer she is," Veronica said.

"Denzelle thought Marsha was going to do a relatively competent—'I just learned how to do this dance correctly'—version of what she just performed. He didn't know she was going to work it like that. Denzelle is out of his league with Marsha right now, and he ain't happy. Last thing on his mind was a Marsha holding a version of some cool points he is incapable of earning."

"Can Pastor even dance?" Dayeesha asked them

"Yeah. Denzelle's a smooth dancer," Veronica told them.

"But he ain't quite got it like Marsha. And that's the problem, right?"

"Dayeesha, he ain't even got it close to 'like Marsha.'"

Veronica was about to say some more but stopped short when she saw Denzelle coming toward them. That cool bravado was gone. Denzelle was frowning and scratching the back of his head like he was trying to figure out the answers to a midterm exam he hadn't studied for.

"You think you have it all down, Pastor?" Dayeesha asked, with mischief lighting up her eyes.

She thought he was getting just what he deserved. Pastor was always acting like he was too cool to like Marsha. And Veronica was right. Reverend Flowers was mad because Marsha could run circles around him in a coma when it came to dancing. And while Denzelle could get out on the floor and look good, Marsha could get out on the floor and give Charlie Wilson himself a run for his money. And Charlie Wilson could dance his butt off.

"So," Marsha said, bouncing up on them, "are you for ready this thing?"

"I'm always ready, Baby," Denzelle answered, trying not to laugh when he observed Marsha's discomfort and efforts to remain cool under his fire. He knew he was wrong to say that but couldn't help it. Plus, the expressions on Veronica's, Keisha's, and Dayeesha's faces were so priceless, it made him want to say some more. But he knew that would not be appropriate. He was still their pastor and had to honor his commitment to being a good shepherd.

"You'll be ready, Denzelle," Veronica put in. "Today is Monday. You have close to two weeks to get this thing wrapped up."

"Yeah, you'll be ready, Denzelle," Marsha said, acting like she hadn't heard all of that heat and sizzle in his voice.

Chapter Twenty-two

"I gave you specific instructions to sign us up to compete in the *Dancing with the Stars* program at Denzelle Flowers's church, Camille," Xavier yelled at his wife.

"Why are you hollering at me like that, Xavier?" Camille Franklin screamed back. "It's not like your tired, cheating, no-good, I-can't-stand-you self can dance. You cannot even clap on the white people beat."

"What in the hell is the 'white people beat,' Camille?" Xavier said through clenched teethed. He was seething, and the more he looked at his wife the more he hated her. He couldn't stand Camille.

"Xavier, if you have to ask me a dumb-butt question like that, it confirms you can't clap right. I should have known something was wrong with you when you told me that you didn't like Al Green, Eric Benet, Teddy Pendergrass, Mary J. Blige, Stephanie Mills, or En Vogue. What black man on this earth does not like En Vogue, for goodness sake?"

"I like Fergie," Xavier said calmly.

"Fergie of the Black Eyed Peas?" Camille asked. "I like Fergie, too. But we are talkin' 'bout sistahs. And the last time I checked, Fergie was white."

"Well then, how about Joss Stone?" Xavier said.

"Joss Stone has great music. But can you dig around in your gray matter and pull up one good-singing black woman?"

"Kathleen Battle."

"As in the opera singer, Kathleen Battle, Kathleen Battle?"

"None other," Xavier answered in the middle of sending a text to Tatiana.

"I'm not going to stand here and pretend like you are not texting that skank you are screwing around with, Xavier."

"I'm not expecting you to pretend anything, Camille. You can read the text if you want to."

Xavier hit send on his phone and said, "We wouldn't even be in this predicament if you had listened to me. I tried to get you to pay me for a divorce a year ago. Now that I'm running for bishop, we are stuck with each other for who knows how long."

"I wasn't paying you to leave me," Camille told him.

"I don't know why not," he told her in a hard and nasty voice. "Your daddy wrote a pretty big check to get me to marry your ugly behind."

Camille bit her bottom lip to help her hold back the tears. She'd always known she was not the cutest woman. But it had never occurred to her that she was ugly. She looked just like her father.

"He was ugly, too," Xavier said, as if he heard her thoughts.

Xavier didn't know what part of "you ugly" his wife didn't get. He must have been awfully broke to take that little measly fifty grand Dr. Creighton put in his account on his wedding day. He ran through that money like it really was water. Xavier didn't even have sense enough to put it in a CD account to collect interest and grow a bit of capital. It wasn't like he needed the fifty thousand to live off of. Camille's father had given his baby plenty of start-up money for her new marriage.

"I'm not staying married to you, Xavier. And I'm not paying you a dime. We have an airtight prenup. So I guess you and 'ho-ella' will just have to make do on the cool million you are to receive for being my husband all of these miserable years."

Camille started laughing at the thought of Xavier and Tatiana trying to have a good life off of $1 million. Heck, they were living off of $1.8 million a year right now. That was only her annual trust fund payment. Did Xavier really think that a Creighton—no, better yet, a Davidson—was going to let go of some cash? She'd rather stay ugly and die first.

Xavier stared at Camille for a moment. She wasn't really what he'd call ugly when in a benevolent mood. Camille was actually what most church folk would describe as plain. She just had a bunch of spoiled and nasty ways that helped to bump her up from plain to ugly.

He had met some very plain women in the churches he pastored who had lovely hearts. Few if any folk would have called any of those women ugly. Even the women who wore painfully plain outfits with those flat shoes that practically screamed "I'm saved" had something special and beautiful about them.

But Camille and women like her? There was little hope of them ever becoming someone's beauty—even with a closet full of incredibly beautiful clothes. Camille had a bedroom-size closet filled up with some of the most beautiful designer clothes Xavier had ever seen. Xavier was a man, and he gaped every time he went into Camille's closet.

However, those fancy clothes didn't do a thing to flatter the girl. Half the time they didn't even fit her right. Xavier didn't know what his wife was doing when she went shopping for clothes. But whatever it was, she needed to quit.

Camille once spent fifteen hundred dollars on some mustard, olive green, and gray–stripped leggings, a mustard-colored tunic, and olive green suede ankle boots. Who wore a mustard-colored shirt next to brown skin with a heavy dose of yellow in it?

"Camille," Xavier said to distract her. He didn't appreciate the way she was texting and laughing at the responses to the texts she had sent.

"Umm . . . hmm . . . ," she responded halfheartedly, and then started laughing and murmuring, "You are too crazy," when she read the next text message.

Xavier walked over to where his wife was standing and reached out to snatch that iPhone out of her hand.

"I wish you would, Xavier," she snapped, and then sent another text.

"Your little boy toy can't be all that amusing." Xavier could not believe he caught Camille having affairs with two men—Jimmy and Ramon. He found out about Ramon first. Then, there was Jimmy. And Ramon's dumb, young self had the nerve to fall in love with his wife. How in the hell did a man fall in love with Camille's evil self? And why did the brother talk about being in love with her so much it got back to Xavier?

"I don't have a boy toy," Camille said. "He is a grown-tailed man. More man than you are."

"Are you going to stand in my face and tell me that Ramon Brown isn't a boy toy?"

"Ramon and I broke up," Camille said calmly, sounding like she was talking to a close girlfriend.

Xavier wondered why she would break it off with a man who he believed made her happy. Camille hooked-up with Jimmy to get back at him, but there was something special about Ramon.

If Ramon wasn't going with his wife, Xavier probably would have liked the brother. She didn't follow Xavier around so much when she was with Ramon. Camille starting making his life absolutely miserable again, when she started fooling around with Jimmy. But when she was with Ramon? Camille was happier and left Xavier alone when she had been with Ramon.

"What did Ramon do to make you break it off with him? I mean, why keep Jimmy and get rid of Ramon?"

"Ramon and I didn't have anything in common, for Pete's sake," Camille answered.

"And we do?" Xavier asked. "And better yet, you and Jimmy have something in common?"

"No, you and I don't have anything in common either, other than we can't stand each other. But really, Xavier, Ramon and I are worlds apart. And Jimmy? Well, Jimmy is Jimmy. Plus,

Ramon and I grew apart when he started going to church on regular Sundays—not just Easter Sunday and Mother's Day."

"But you go to church on regular Sundays, my dear. What is wrong with that? I would think you'd appreciate that quality in a man. Plus, Jimmy's ugly behind is always up in church. Sometimes I wish that joker would stay home on Sunday mornings so I don't have to look at him."

"Jimmy is different, Xavier. He only goes to church like some people go to a job they don't really like but like the salary and benefits enough to tolerate it and not quit. He's a big church devil. And church devils LOVE to go to church."

"Camille, that still doesn't help me understand why Ramon's going to church bothered you enough to push him away from you."

"Ramon was getting too real about church. He was listening to the sermons and starting to read his Bible everyday. Do you know he had the nerve to call me and ask me to pray for him?"

"Imagine that," Xavier said, trying not to laugh. This was hilarious. Who knew Camille didn't want a church-going man to be her man on the side?

"And do you know that Ramon put his hands on my head and started praying for my deliverance? And get this, he is saved. I mean, really—the man is genuinely saved and loves the Lord. He wanted me to make up my mind and chose to be either your wife or his wife. He got to quoting Paul, talking about it was better to marry than to burn."

"So, you're telling me that you don't want to be involved with a saved man."

"Yeah, that's exactly what I'm telling you," Camille said. "He can go to church, but I don't want him to be saved. Like you, Xavier. You are always doing something in church, but you are about as saved as I am."

Xavier just nodded. No use trying to argue with his wife on that one. Bishop Washington once told him that wives, even the ones you wanted to get rid of, knew you in a way no other woman did. One day he would have to tell Bishop he was right.

"But Camille, I hate it that you broke up with Ramon. There was a tiny part of me that kind of liked the brother. He always seemed so in love with you."

"Yeah, he did. But I couldn't stay with him—especially after he joined Apostle Grady Gray's church. You don't mess with folk at Grady Gray's church. They are saved for real. And you don't want to have to deal with God for trying to mess over one of those people."

Xavier nodded. Camille was right. It was dangerous to try and mess with folk at Jubilee Temple Holiness Church II.

If Ramon was saved and a member of Grady's church, it was best to let him go. Plus, Camille couldn't get divorced and marry Ramon anyway. Well, she could—but if she did, chances were great that Camille would be resting in that fancy tomb next to her parents before the official separation papers were signed and printed out.

He got a text from Luther Howard asking if he had more information on the *Dancing with the Stars* event at Denzelle Flowers's church. Xavier was about to answer that text when it occurred to him that if Ramon was out of Camille's life, how long had he been gone? And who was she doing all of that texting with? She rarely texted Jimmy when he was around.

Camille was sitting on the love seat in the solarium having a good time texting.

"If Ramon is gone, Camille, and Jimmy won't text when I'm around, who in the hell is it that you are so engrossed with?" Xavier snapped.

Camille looked up at Xavier. He was back to normal. For a moment she had enjoyed being around him. She said, "Do you really want to know?"

"Were you with him when . . . ?"

"When you were with your ho?"

"Don't you talk about Tatiana like that—you understand me, Camille?"

"I am your wife," she spat out. "My money is what made it possible for you to drive that Aston Martin V8 Vantage your skank is always drooling over. So I can and I will talk about your broke ho anytime and any way I please."

"Tatiana is far from broke," Xavier said testily.

"She is a broke ho, and that is the real deal," Camille told him calmly. She knew Tatiana's husband made very good money. But Todd Townsend didn't have the kind of money Camille Franklin had.

She and Xavier had an official annual couple's income of $1.8 million. But there was another fund that belonged only to Camille. Her trust, which Xavier couldn't touch, paid $4 million a year. They had a disposable income of close to $6 million a year.

Camille was very good with money. Most years they only lived off of $3 million. The rest she invested in a fund that was separate from her trust. She was building up some serious capital from that fund. Camille knew Tatiana didn't have anything close to the kind of money she was used to dealing with.

"You are so stuck-up, Camille."

"Get over it."

"Who is your new man?" Xavier asked her. He wasn't comfortable with his wife's new man being all up and about in her world without him having a clue about the man's identity.

Camille sighed heavily. She did not want Xavier to know who her new man was. But she was not in the mood to fight with him. She said, "It's Conrad Wilcher."

Before Xavier could catch himself he ran over to Camille and knocked her off the love seat. He snatched at the collar on her new shirt and pulled her face up close to his. Camille was so angry that she almost forgot to be afraid.

"Why Conrad Wilcher, Camille? Wasn't it bad enough you were with Jimmy? What is wrong with you?"

"Why not Conrad? Who do you think you are to tell me who to date? Conrad . . ."

"Is my head trustee and you are having an affair with him behind my back! That's what's wrong with Conrad, Camille."

"Well, for starters, I am not having an affair with Conrad, I just like to text and screw him. And second, it's not behind your back, because I just told you."

"How could you?"

"How could I? HOW COULD I? How could I not? Conrad is better in bed than you, Ramon, and Jimmy put together."

Xavier wanted to punch Camille. But he just turned her loose. Conrad Wilcher was a loser. Ramon had just been broke. But he'd never been a loser. Conrad wasn't about anything. He could not believe Camille was sleeping around with Conrad on the side when she was supposed to be going with that butt-ugly Jimmy.

"Camille," Xavier said in a serious voice. "I approved of your relationship with Ramon. I stomached your relationship with Jimmy. But you cannot be with Conrad. I'm ordering you to break it off with him."

"Okay," Camille told him cheerfully. "I'll be happy to do that when you tell your skank her services are no longer needed."

"I'm not living without Tatiana," Xavier said, in a tight and very mean voice. "She is the most wonderful woman I've ever met. No woman compares to Tatiana."

Camille looked at Xavier like he was crazier than he was. She said, "I don't know what you've been smoking. But you might want to try and clear your head long enough to understand that you can't tell me who I can't date and then insist on hanging on to Trashiana."

"I will, I can, and I did just tell you who you cannot be with, Camille. Now, I'm asking you one last time. When are you ditching Conrad?"

"If I ditch him, it will be because I found a new man. And right now, Conrad is the only man I want. You act like I can't just walk out of this door and get myself another man. I can go to the grocery store and pull that off."

Xavier wanted to dispute that point but knew he'd better leave it alone. He didn't know what men saw in his wife, because she was never without a man. Camille had a man on the side the first time she found out he cheated on her.

"So when are you breaking up with Conrad? When are you getting us a spot for the dance contest at New Jerusalem? And when are you calling your lawyer to call off filing divorce papers?"

Camille was shocked. How in the world did Xavier know that? Her lawyer was one of the most discreet folks in Raleigh. Plus, his retainer was so high, he knew better than to risk losing her as a client.

Xavier was cracking up. That look on Camille's face was price-less. He said, "Baby, I'm not playing with you. I have resources, and I know about the meeting with your attorney. So be a good girl and do exactly as I tell you, so this will not get ugly. We are not getting a divorce. You are breaking it off with Conrad. And we are going to that *Dancing with the Stars* mess Denzelle Flowers is all pumped-up about."

"If I have to live with Tatiana being in your life, you have to live with Conrad being in mine. So please quit bugging me about my man. I'll get rid of Conrad when I'm good and ready.

"Xavier, I know your dancing is piss poor. But I will get our tickets and find a way to get us a spot in that competition. And, for the record—I can't stand you, and this divorce is going through."

"I'm stopping the divorce, Camille," Xavier said quietly.

"Over my dead body."

Xavier really wished she had not said that. Luther had made it clear that Camille had to get with the program, or else. Xavier felt a dull ache in his chest. As much as Camille got on his nerves, he didn't want Luther to put a hit on her. He wished it could be dif-ferent. But she was the one who drew a line in the sand. Running for bishop was a trip. Who would have ever thought it would come to something like this?

Chapter Twenty-three

"What about Todd, Luther?"

He put his hands behind his head and stared up at the beautiful evening sky. They were lying in a great big hammock in Key West, Florida, watching the sun go to its final rest. It looked like the sun was being dipped into the ocean by some huge invisible hand. As much as Luther wanted to answer Tatiana's question, he didn't want to talk until the sun went down.

He brought Tatiana down to Key West with him because he thought she would appreciate some of the real finer things in life—things you couldn't buy, like a breathtaking sunset. But, unfortunately, Tatiana Townsend was just like his other women. That was a big disappointment to Luther. He had a secret hope she would be different somehow. He didn't understand why his women weren't able to enjoy simple things like the sun displaying blues and pinks and soft purples across the sky.

Luther loved the way color was displayed in natural ways. He grew up wanting to be a painter but had to surrender that dream to please his father and grandfather. His mother had been an incredible artist. His father had been one of the best defense lawyers in the West Indies. His grandfather had been a judge.

His father and grandfather always insisted that Luther's mother was so good at her craft because his father earned so much money defending the indefensible. It was the money, his grandfather insisted, that made it possible for his mother to have

the time and supplies needed to make art. Luther always felt he
might have become a better man had he been allowed to study
art when he was accepted to the Sorbonne when he was young.

Tatiana pushed at Luther's rock-hard shoulder. He had the
firmest, most ripped body of any man she'd ever been with. And
even though she was desperately in love with Xavier, few men
could compare to Luther and his skills. Tatiana couldn't believe
her good fate when Luther called and invited her down to his
condo in Key West for a weekend-long business meeting.

She pushed at Luther's shoulder again. He grabbed her wrist
so hard she could feel it bruising and swelling. He said, "Push me
again and I'm going to break it."

Tatiana had never known a violent man. She couldn't even
process the chill that went through her body when he grabbed her
and said that. Luther's voice was so calm and regular sounding, he
could have been asking her to pour him a glass of sweet tea.

When the sun was gone, he swung out of the hammock so
fast, Tatiana almost toppled onto the balcony's concrete floor.
She barely managed to get her balance, stood up, and followed
Luther back into the condo. He poured himself a shot of some
superexpensive Russian vodka from somewhere near the Caspian Sea, where Russia and Iran met up with each other. He pulled
out another shot glass and was about to pour Tatiana some but
stopped.

"I forgot," Luther said. "You are a terrible drinker." He
poured himself another shot of the vodka. "Too bad you can't
drink this. It is smooth as silk."

Luther downed one of the shots and said, "You wanted to
know about Todd."

Tatiana nodded. She had been on pins and needles since stepping off of Luther's private jet to find out how he was going to get
rid of her husband. She had known what kind of payment was
required for a deal like this, and came prepared to rock Luther
Howard's world.

"Here is your contact for the hit, Tatiana," Luther told her.

"I have to make the contact?" Tatiana asked incredulously. It had never occurred to her that she would be forced to become involved in Todd's death. She had wanted this to be neat and distant.

"You cannot have your cake and eat it, too, Tatiana," Luther said. "I will not be involved in a hit you have nothing to do with. You really believe I would have a hand in this without your initials on it? I don't want or need you to get a conscience and talk to the feds.

"Remember, your ex is a retired FBI agent. You might want an old times' sake booty call with the brother and get diarrhea of the mouth during some pillow-talk time. This way, you'll watch your mouth. That way I won't be burdened with the blood of three hits on my hands.

"Three?" Tatiana asked. "There's only Todd . . ." She gasped.

"No, it will be Todd, Denzelle, and you if you stray from my instructions in any way," Luther said, in that same calm voice he'd used while grabbing her arm.

She wondered what it felt like to be able to be so calm and nonchalant about having people killed—especially people you knew. The only thing was, as bad and scary as Luther was, she didn't think he could take down Denzelle Flowers. Her ex-husband had been a bad boy in his day. Based on what she'd witnessed, he was still a bad boy, and very deadly, too. Tatiana hoped her face didn't betray her

"What's wrong? You think I can't take on the big, bad Agent Flowers?" Luther asked, with a whole lot more bravado than he felt. He honestly didn't know if he could take out Denzelle. There was something unnerving about going after a man of God who was also a man of the law—and had a mean streak and some scripture to back it all up. That was a scary dude in Luther Howard's policy and protocol handbook.

"Luther, you are the kind of man that few wise men would want to have to face off with. And that includes my ex," Tatiana told him truthfully. The reason Denzelle was so deadly was because he always respected his adversaries. Denzelle never underestimated anybody. About the only person who had gotten by him was Tatiana.

Luther liked what Tatiana said. She may not have enjoyed the sunset the way he'd hoped, but Tatiana did know what to say to a man. He walked up behind her and wrapped his arms around her waist. He buried his nose in the nape of her neck and inhaled her perfume.

"You know you smell lovely."

Tatiana looked back at Luther and smiled. At first she'd been excited about a daring weekend with the rich and dangerous Luther Howard. Now she wished she could be with Xavier.

Luther sensed the change in Tatiana immediately. He said, "Xavier is at a church conference with Camille trying to make it look like they are the happy couple. So you might as well forget about your man this weekend and love the one you're with."

He felt her tense up even more. Only this time it was due to hurt and anger with Xavier. Luther let go of Tatiana and moved away from her. She needed a few minutes of space to reel in her emotions and pull herself back together. Women just needed time when they heard that their man was all up on another woman—even when the other woman was the man's own wife. He was a good trial lawyer and always knew when to back off of a witness right before going in for the kill.

Tatiana's phone buzzed.

"Hey, Baby!" she said to Todd, hoping to sound happy to hear from him.

"How are you doing, Sweet Thing?" Todd asked, hoping this phone call would not be too long.

He had been happy and relieved when Tatiana told him she was going to a workshop to get certification as a telephone triage nurse. She'd only recently gotten a certification in emergency room care, and would soon be qualified to train nurses in this area. Todd had cheerfully paid for all of these workshops, because he knew Tatiana would need to earn more money when he finally filed for his divorce.

Todd had given Tatiana a generous payout in the prenup agreement. But he knew his wife loved money and status and would drag out the divorce if she didn't have a way to earn extra money doing something she loved.

Todd Townsend had been planning this divorce every since he met Shanna Webster, who was a cardiology resident at Duke. It was the introduction to Shanna that helped Todd make his decision to take the job at Duke Medical Center. He had been mesmerized by Shanna's lovely red hair and the fact that she was practically a dead ringer for the actress Debra Messing in the movie *The Wedding Date*. Todd couldn't believe his woman looked like a very pale brown version of one of his favorite actresses.

"The workshop was the best, Todd," Tatiana told him in earnest. She really had gone to a workshop to get certification as a telephone triage nurse, and was looking forward to completing her training. But that workshop had been for only one day. Tatiana told her husband she would be in training for a week.

Tatiana had always been a good liar. But she perfected that skill after listening to Denzelle's FBI agent stories about criminals who were proficient at lying. The best liars always put a good dose of the truth in their stories. That way they had a better chance of coming across as authentic. What Tatiana didn't know was that the best liars were the ones like her husband, Todd—the ones who were so slick and sneaky you never even suspected they were involved in something that would require a high level of lying.

"Well, you just enjoy Miami for a few extra days, Sweetheart. Get some good shopping in and relax."

"You sure you don't need me back home, Babe?" Tatiana asked, hoping the answer was no. She loved Miami and Key West.

"No, love. I'll be here plugging away making money to pay for all of that good stuff I know you'll buy."

"Okay," Tatiana said and blew a kiss in the telephone.

Todd pushed end on his phone and looked toward the bathroom door. He loved Shanna's house in Durham's old-school Hope Valley neighborhood. It was small and homey and lovely. Todd felt so good every time he walked through the door and said, "Honey, I'm home."

Shanna came out wearing a new bra and thong set. The salmon-colored lace set off her pale brown skin and shimmering red hair. Todd studied Shanna's hair for a minute. It occurred to him that it was a very good weave. Tatiana had taught him well. A weave always had some minor puffiness on hair that should have been lying real flat on a woman's head.

She also told him that, when in doubt, try and run your fingers through a woman's hair. A sister with a good and expensive weave would stop your fingers cold. There was no way you were going to mess with that weave and mess up that hair she'd paid good money for.

"You like?" Shanna said to Todd, and turned around so he could get a full, panoramic view of the thong.

"Me like . . . me like," Todd answered grinning. "Looks like somebody paid a lil' visit to the booty doctor. Come on over here, so I can examine that newfangled silicon correctly."

Todd was really glad Shanna had gone and gotten something done to her butt. It was too much like a white woman's behind for his taste. As stiff and proper and Ivy League–acting as Todd Townsend was, he still had a black man's affinity for a big juicy behind on a woman.

Shanna bounced over toward Todd and put her new butt right in his face. She loved the way she looked. Only problem with this new butt was that she had to go up two sizes with her jeans. Now she finally understood what her cousins were talking about when they lamented that jeans were not cut for black women. They said they always wore at least one size larger to make room for their hips, behind, and thighs.

"Arrrhhh," Todd growled, and took a bite off of Shanna's cheek. He was impressed. The silicon was of high quality.

Shanna swatted Todd's hand and said, "Down, boy."

He said, "You sure that is what you want?"

Shanna bit her lip and thought about what her man was saying. She grinned and said, "Nahh."

Todd laughed and reached up to grab a handful of Shanna's hair. He wanted to touch her hair, and he also wanted to give it the weave test. Shanna moved Todd's hand real fast, and then touched her hair.

He couldn't believe how right Tatiana had been when she told Todd, "You know, Dr. Shanna Webster wears a hellavu good weave. I wish I knew where she gets her hair done. Her weave specialist is off the chain."

"Does your husband suspect anything," Luther asked, and wrapped his arms around Tatiana again.

She shook her head. It was clear Todd was settling in for the evening, probably pulling his favorite TV show, *Grimm*, up on demand.

"Good," Luther said with a smile. "And you have some extra time down in Florida?"

"Yeah," Tatiana said and placed a kiss on Luther's cheek. "You smell awfully good."

"Thank you, Ma'am," Luther said, and started taking off Tatiana's T-shirt. "You know," he murmured in the nape of her neck, "You make sure Xavier doesn't try and back out of participating in that *Dancing with the Stars* business your ex is doing at his church. From what I've heard, it's going to be a hit, and Denzelle is going to get a whole lot of play with the folks voting for the bishops."

"Luther, have you ever seen Xavier dance?"

Luther shook his head.

"He is horrible—moves like he has a stick up his butt for real," Tatiana said.

"Is he really that bad," Luther asked, "or are you comparing him to Denzelle Flowers, who gives the impression he can handle himself on the dance floor."

"He's worse. Plus, I don't want him doing any more than he

has to with Camille at a big Gospel United Church event. I don't want people to associate the two of them as the bishop and his wife when I am going to be part of the bishop and his wife."

Luther wondered if Xavier had that little talk with Tatiana about not being able to marry her if he was going to be a bishop. He would have texted Xavier to get some clarity on the issue. But that wasn't smart. Xavier would sense something was wrong, unlike Todd Townsend, who seemed to buy Tatiana's BS hook, line, and sinker.

The last thing Luther Howard needed was Xavier Franklin figuring out he was doing Tatiana. Xavier thought he ran a tight ship where his women were concerned. Luther knew that fool would challenge him like they were some brothers on the corner over his thing with Tatiana.

On second thought, Luther did remember Xavier sharing that he'd talked to Tatiana. So she was just being stubborn and entrenched in some wishful thinking. He wasn't going to waste time trying to get Tatiana to accept she wasn't marrying Xavier. It was best to push her gently off of this subject before she got all riled up, and then pissed-off enough to cause trouble for everybody. He said, "If you don't want Xavier out there dancing with Camille, why not get him to challenge Denzelle to a debate, like the ones the Republican candidates did before Romney became the favored son in their race? That will be a great way to get folks interested in what each candidate is about."

"Those debates were pretty lame, Luther. Plus, Denzelle will annihilate Xavier in a debate," Tatiana answered, and then said, "Ooops, sorry." She'd almost forgotten Luther Howard was a staunch Republican. But then again, so was Xavier.

"You have problems with my party affiliations, Tatiana?" Luther asked with a soft chuckle. He was well aware of the disdain most black people had for the modern Republican Party. But when had Luther Howard ever cared about what most black people felt?

Luther Howard lived his life by the edicts of one of his favorite books, *The Prince*, by Niccolo Machiavelli. He especially loved chapter eight in the book. That chapter sanctioned using immoral tactics to get what you wanted. A quick and ruthless decimation of an opponent was the way to go, according to old boy Niccolo.

Tatiana held her peace. There was no way she was starting a fight with Luther Howard over his party affiliation.

Luther held Tatiana tight, and then let her go. He said, "We can't do this, love."

"Huh?" Tatiana said. She was surprised, relieved, and scared at this turn in the program.

"I'm not going to hurt you, Tatiana. I'm not going to sleep with you, either. I like you and don't want to ruin a potentially good friendship with us sleeping together. Plus, I want to keep the air clear between Xavier and me. You are his woman, and I don't want you bad enough to tamper with that."

"Thank you?" Tatiana said with a raised eyebrow.

"You're welcome."

"Sooooooo."

"Yes, I put a hit on Camille," Luther lied. He wasn't bothering Camille as long as she played the game according to his terms. Even though he understood why Xavier would want Tatiana over Camille, Luther knew Xavier would not get elected as a bishop with Tatiana Townsend on his arm. Church folk hated her more than they did Bishop Thomas Jefferson's wife, Violetta.

Tatiana was staring at him with a pained expression on her face.

"What?" Luther asked.

"It won't be painful for Todd, will it?" Tatiana asked carefully. She didn't want Todd to feel a lot of pain when the hit hit.

"How sweet," Luther said with a hard laugh. "No, it won't hurt too much, even though I'm sure it will be a bit uncomfortable to be murdered. Most people don't like getting killed, you know. At least, that has been my observation."

"You make it sound like Todd is going to the dentist for a root canal," Tatiana told him.

"Well, it probably is kind of on that order," Luther answered with a shrug. "Is he saved?"

"I don't know," Tatiana said with a worried expression on her face. It had never occurred to her how important salvation was until now. She couldn't help that Todd needed to die for things to work out for her. But she didn't want him to die without at least saying the sinner's prayer.

"Pity," Luther said. "But at least he'll die with a real big smile on his face."

Tatiana frowned. What in the world was Luther talking about? The only time she thought about a man dying with a big smile on his face was when he died while being with a woman. Tatiana's eyes got real big. Todd? Cheating?

"What, Tatiana?" Luther scoffed. "You honestly believed that your husband was being true to you while you ran off and did whatever you wanted to do? That's why he let you do what you wanted to do. He needed you away so he could be with his little honey on the side, Dr. Shanna Webster."

"I knew that wannabe white–looking heifer was after my man," Tatiana snapped. "When I get back to North Carolina, I am going to—"

"Possibly be a very rich widow with a very explainable death kind of murder," Luther replied matter-of-factly. "Todd went and got himself some of that WP21 folk think is off the market."

"You mean that watermelon powder stuff men use with their women like some kind of super Viagra? That stuff that killed those men back in the 1980s at the Gospel United Church conference?"

"Ummm . . . hmmm," Luther said. "Shanna got it for him from one of my cousins. As soon as the order was placed, I got a call, and I ordered a special dose for your husband. Now, the only thing they are waiting on is the call from you giving the final okay."

Tatiana took in a deep breath. She was in this way too deep. But it was too late and too dangerous to turn back now.

"What about Camille? Does Xavier know that you are going to put a hit on her?

Luther thought about that question, and then shook his head. He said, "Xavier still believes he's stuck with Camille and will have to figure out a way to live with her, and then find a way to be with you. I want him in the dark on that, because he'll play the game better if he believes he's stuck with Camille," Luther told her, like he was really going to do this this way.

"So," Tatiana began carefully. "How are you going to . . . you know . . . ?"

"How am I going to have Camille Franklin killed?"

Tatiana nodded.

"That plan, Sweet Thing, is quite elaborate, and might require some help from you," Luther told her, and went and poured himself some more of that expensive, Caspian Sea Russian vodka.

Chapter Twenty-four

"You ready for this?"

Denzelle sighed. Who in the world did his best friend think would be ready for "this"? He said, "You need a refill, Obie?"

"Nahh. I have to drive back to Durham. You know I can't hold my liquor like you."

"Yeah, you can be pretty lame on that front," Denzelle said with a chuckle.

"So, are you ready, D?"

"How ready can a preacher get to be in *Dancing with the Stars*, Obie man?"

"I'm not talking about the event. Are you ready to get out there and run for bishop?"

"I guess I'm as ready as I'm going to be for this bishop's race. The other candidates have already started putting out negative campaign ads on each other. Man, this is the church, and they are out there airing all of the denomination's dirty laundry. What's next?"

Obadiah closed his eyes for a second and said, "D, this is what's next," and pulled up his iPad and the YouTube video of Denzelle's women going rogue at that infamous church service years ago.

Denzelle stared at something he kept praying would just go away. But this thing was like a horror movie. Every time he thought that monster was gone, it came back to do more damage.

He said, "I cannot believe this video is titled *Church Gurls Gone Wild.*"

"Yeah, Lena and I were cracking up when we saw the title, and you have a lot of hits . . ." Obadiah stopped when he saw the pained expression on his friend's face.

"It is what it is, D. And it happened. You can't mess with women's emotions, run game on sisters, and not expect to pay for all of that dirt you sowed."

Denzelle raised his hands up. Obadiah was right.

"Well, at least you've learned your lesson," Obadiah said. "There are brothers out there, like Reverend Larry Pristeen, who are working up on a very hard and painful lesson in this area.

"Larry has been going all over the country preaching and flirting and talking trash to some of these church women. It's only a game to build up his ego and garner support for that weird singles' ministry he has started getting so much attention for. Personally, I don't know why church folk are getting all excited over Pristeen and his new program, D."

"Me, neither," Denzelle responded, shaking his head. "You know Larry tried to hit on Marsha the last time we were at his church in Asheville."

"You lyin'," Obie said and laughed. "Larry ain't got no game. What kind of pitiful pimp concoction did he come up with to try and hit on your girl?"

"Marsha is not my girl," Denzelle said in a tight voice.

"My bad," was all Obie told him, thinking, *She needs to be your girl.*

Denzelle sighed. Larry was quite fortunate he didn't know he'd hit on Marsha like that. Because if that were so, Denzelle would have put his foot so far up the brother's tail, he would have needed a trauma surgeon like Todd Townsend to get it out.

"That was some sneaky mess Larry tried to put down on Marsha, Obie. You know the game some brothers run on women to make them think they are above trying to hit that when that is exactly what they are trying to do."

Obadiah nodded. He knew exactly what Denzelle was talking about. He said, "Larry better stop while he's ahead. Because one day he is going to do that to the wrong kind of woman—one of those unstable stalkers."

"That's exactly what is going to happen," Denzelle said. "And if he gets a really crazy one, he'll wake up in that hotel room all tied up, crying and wondering if he's in that movie *Misery* with Kathy Bates and James Caan."

Obie was laughing. He said, "That is exactly what is going to happen if Larry doesn't stop playing these games on church women."

"But you know something," Denzelle continued, "I don't understand how Larry keeps his women in check. Even a good sister will go off on you if you play her too hard. Know what I'm sayin'?"

"He picks 'em real well," Obie said with a frown. "He only zooms in on the sweet ones—the ones who don't sleep around, want a sincere and steady relationship, don't tell all of their business, and think they are supposed to be patient and wait, because they don't want to scare Larry away while he is getting himself together."

"The ones who are kind of like Marsha, huh?" Denzelle said, looking like he wanted to pistol-whip Larry Pristeen.

"Well, D, not exactly a Marsha. He made a mistake when he tried to hit on her. He is also trying to pick the ones whose self-esteem is a little low. Marsha is going through and having it hard, but she feels fine about herself—even in this harsh storm. She just looked vulnerable because of her trials."

"True that," Denzelle answered. What Obadiah was saying made a lot of sense. Women like Marsha Metcalf could come across as being vulnerable and with low esteem because what they were going through was so hard it could wear on them. Having it hard was very hard to deal with, and it took a lot of inner strength and courage to go through. A person wouldn't always be or look at their best while in a season of having it hard.

"I wonder, Obie, if the women know that Larry doesn't have any game."

"Oh, they know it. That's part of his appeal—he comes across as a church man who is interested in them but doesn't have any game. They think that makes him sincere."

"I have never respected or liked a brother who gets tail by pretending he's not in the game. That is the worse kind of player," Denzelle said.

"Yeah, he is. And Larry is not just dishonest with church women. I've discovered that he is also very calculating where the church leaders are concerned. He is working to get the Board of Bishops to promote his singles' program for the entire denomination at the Triennial Conference.

"Larry ain't about nothing but money, prestige, power, and attention. He walks around dressed in those plain, old man suits, looking all low-key and humble. That's nothing but a ruse."

"You think Larry is planning on running for bishop, with all of this scheming and plotting he's into?"

Obie nodded and said, "Absolutely. But Denzelle, unlike Larry, folk are genuinely excited about you, and they are excited about this event. Lena said our congregation can't wait to see you dance. Marsha came up with the perfect event to get folks to see you as a fresh and different kind of candidate."

"Well, it's definitely time for a change," Denzelle said. That change was one of the main reasons he agreed to run in this race.

"Yes, it is," Obadiah said. "But as popular as you are, it is going to be a nasty, low-down, and dirty fight."

"We've had nasty fights for Episcopal seats in the past."

"Yeah, we have. But D, we've never had to come up against folk like Luther Howard in a bishop's race."

"Luther Howard? What in the hell is he doing messing around in a race for bishop in the Gospel United Church? Does he even go to church?"

Denzelle paced around his den for a few seconds, and then went and got his favorite piece out from under his favorite chair.

He reached for a clip and was about to put it in when Obie said, "Whoa, player! You can't go out and shoot up Raleigh over that chump."

"That *chump* is the one who made it hard for us to nail the Dinkle brothers cartel to the wall. I've wanted a piece of him for over twenty years."

"Well, it looks like he wants a piece of you, too," Obadiah told him. "I have it on good authority that Luther has pumped a lot of money into Xavier Franklin's campaign. He is real chummy with Marcel Brown and Sonny Washington. And get this: Word on the church parking lot has Washington and Brown in cahoots with Bishop Thomas Lyle Jefferson."

"Now, why would they want to work with old boy?" Denzelle asked. "What in the world could that old coot offer anybody? Jefferson is slimy."

"Yeah, he is. Lena can't stand his butt. She said that when he looks at women his eyes start twirling around, and he starts panting."

"Like Pavlov's dog?" Denzelle asked. "Remember that dog our psychology professors were always talking about."

"How could I forget Pavlov getting that dog to do stuff through association with that daggone bell," Obie said, rolling his eyes.

"You think somebody rang a bell to make Bishop Jefferson pant like that every time a sister with a big booty walked by?" Denzelle asked, laughing.

"Nahh," Obie answered. "Lena said he did that every time a big boobed sister walked by."

"But his new wife has a big butt," Denzelle said matter-of-factly.

"Yeah, Violetta has some sexy legs, too," Obadiah said.

Denzelle started cracking up. He said, "Don't tell anybody, but I love Violetta's video."

"'Burn de House Down,'" Obie said laughing. "That is still one of the baddest music videos I've ever seen."

"I know. Old girl was working it on that roof. Then, when she jumped off, landed on her feet, and started dancing. I was, like, work it—*work it*, baby."

"D, you know you still got some dawg in you, right?"

"Woof, woof," Denzelle barked, and laughed. "You know how it is. I have to keep a lil' dawg in me. And I have to keep my player's card activated. Never know when I'll need to swipe it."

"Yeah," Obie was saying. "You never know when you'll wanna swipe it where Marsha is concerned."

"Why did you have to go there, Obadiah?"

"Oh, I see. It's O-ba-di-ah when I bring Ms. Marsha Metcalf into the conversation. You got it bad for that girl, D."

"I don't have it bad for anyone," Denzelle retorted.

"Don't get testy on me, dawg," Obadiah replied evenly. "Personally, I don't understand why you keep running from Marsha, because she is your Ruth."

"For the record, I don't run from a woman. And I don't have to rush and put my mark on Marsha. She is not the kind of woman a brother will chase down and try to pull in his direction."

"That's mighty cavalier of you, my brother. Do you really think it is okay to leave Marsha on the shelf until you are ready to take her off of it? I wish the Lord would teach you a lesson about taking a blessing like a good woman for granted."

"Why you going so hard on me, Obie?"

"Because you need to stop this mess, and quit leaving Marsha out there like that. You don't want to have regrets from playing this game."

"Regrets? What? You think there is a risk of Marsha being in the arms of another man?" Denzelle blurted out. "She's mine. God told me Marsha was mine. I don't have to rush, because she is mine—all mine."

Obadiah just stared at Denzelle. He was telling the truth and talking crazy at the same time. Lena told him Denzelle was in love with Marsha, and the reason that joker was acting a fool was because he knew he could get away with it.

"God told you that about Marsha? That she belonged to you."

"Yeah," Denzelle snapped back.

"Do you plan on letting Marsha in on this little secret? I'm sure she'd appreciate knowing you feel that way about her."

"This is about my heart, not hers," Denzelle said in a hard voice. "Marsha's heart is in good condition. I'm the one with the heart trouble."

"D, don't you think it would do your heart good to be with Marsha and feel sweetness coming from her heart to yours? Plus, she's been alone for a while and needs your company, too. You are being so unbelievably selfish about this, it's downright sinful."

Denzelle was not going on talking about this with Obadiah. He was used to being in charge, and he wasn't ready for his heart to run off and jump in Marsha's hands. It unnerved Denzelle that Marsha made him feel things inside he hadn't felt since he was a young man.

Marsha made every part (*every part*) of his body react like it had when he was in his twenties. Sometimes Denzelle couldn't even sleep for lying up in bed thinking about Marsha Metcalf and wishing she was cuddled up under him, spoon fashion. Sometimes he felt like God wanted him to go after Marsha as if there was no tomorrow. But he was too afraid and too proud to get enough sense to do this on God's and not his carefully constructed man timetable.

Chapter Twenty-five

"Have you seen this mess?" Veronica asked and put the engraved invitation addressed to Reverend Denzelle Flowers, Senior Pastor, New Jerusalem Gospel United Church, in Marsha's hand.

"What?" she asked with a frown. "Is it for the Singles Shouting for Jesus Festival Reverend Larry Pristeen been all over the church TV and radio stations talking about?" Larry Pristeen was getting on her last nerve, running around from church to church acting like he was the guru of all singles' ministries.

"No, not that bad," Veronica answered. "It's Xavier Franklin. He has a super PAC for his campaign that is run 'independently' by Luther Howard."

Marsha took the envelope and turned it over several times She said, "I hope they haven't done a YouTube video ad talking junk about 'I Am America.'"

Veronica started laughing and singing the "I Am America" theme song from the infamous Herman Cain presidential campaign ad that went viral. She kept singing, and then started dancing and acting like she was going to drop it like it's hot.

"Ooops, wrong commercial," Veronica said, still laughing. "I was about to get the Cain ad confused with the drop it like it's hot soda commercials."

Marsha pulled the engraved invitation out of the expensive, white linen envelope. She ran her fingertips over the charcoal-colored letters and said, "Luther Howard, with his unsaved and suspect self, is the head of Xavier's super PAC. And he has the audacity to challenge Denzelle to a special candidates' forum at Denzelle's own church."

"So, what do you think *Denzelle* should do with this invitation?" Keisha asked. "You know I'll need a few weeks to pull everything together. No way Xavier, and that thang he's married to, coming up in here and we're not rolling hard like the ballers that we are."

Marsha acted like she didn't hear Keisha's reference to her reference to Denzelle. Right now, she was too through over Xavier Franklin's attempt to horn in on all they had done with Denzelle's campaign for bishop. He was ahead of all of the candidates in the church polls, and everybody was showing up for their *Dancing with the Stars* event.

"You know this forum will be like a debate," Veronica said. "I don't know what Xavier hopes to accomplish with this, because Denzelle will eat his tail up alive. Xavier can't handle Denzelle in a debate."

"Wait a minute. How do you issue an invitation to someone on their own turf?" Keisha interjected. "That is so presumptuous."

"Well, Xavier issued Denzelle this invitation as a challenge," Veronica continued. "If we advise the pastor to refuse, it could make it appear as if he's threatened by the Franklin camp of supporters."

"And if we accept," Marsha said. "It'll look as if Xavier Franklin and his super PAC chair, Luther Howard, can waltz up in this church and give marching orders any time they feel like it."

"Good point," Keisha said. "Pastor is running for bishop and not public office. We cannot get distracted with mess. If Luther Howard wants to do a debate, then he can do one with Xavier and them at Xavier Franklin's church. We don't serve Luther Howard. This House of God serves the Lord."

Veronica took the invitation, tore it to shreds, and threw it in the trash. "Our pastor will appreciate this decision."

"Show you right," Keisha said.

Marsha's cell buzzed, and Denzelle's name popped up on her plain little Walmart phone.

"Pastor's ears must be burning 'cause we're talkin' 'bout him," Veronica said with a grin. She wondered how long Denzelle's number had been buzzin' up his name on Marsha's phone. Marsha was terrible about putting folks' names and numbers on her contact list, and now Denzelle was in a place it took most folk months to get to.

"Why don't you get a fancier cell phone, so Rev's picture can pop up when he calls you?" Keisha said.

"You better answer that, Marsha," Veronica said with a hearty laugh. "You know how men are when their women don't answer the phone in time."

"I heard that," Keisha echoed, tickled at the embarrassment spreading across Marsha's face.

The phone stopped ringing right before Marsha tried to pick up on the call. It buzzed up Denzelle's name again. She hurried to flip the phone on.

"Hello," Marsha said, as if she were trying to figure out who was on the other end of the telephone.

"Did I catch you at a bad time?" Denzelle asked in a low and sexy voice.

"No," Marsha squeaked out.

"Are you okay, Honey?" Denzelle asked.

"Yep," she answered, hoping she sounded more relaxed and casual than she felt.

"What time do I need to be at church?"

"It starts at eight p.m. and . . ."

"Baby, I know what time everything starts up," Denzelle said. "I just want to find out when I need to be there. And do I need to pick up my tux?"

Marsha sucked up that deep breath she almost took in when Denzelle said "Baby." And to make it worse, he had on Foxy 107.1 . She could hear the Isley Brothers' "Make Me Say It Again Girl" in the background.

Veronica and Keisha were watching Marsha so intently she feared their eyeballs were going to pop out of their heads like they were some cartoon characters. She turned away from those two so they couldn't get such a good read on her facial expressions.

"My cousin Lil' Too Too is picking up your tux. And be at the church by four-thirty p.m. I'll have something for us to eat, and we can relax before the program starts up."

"Solid. I'll see you tomorrow afternoon around four-thirty," Denzelle said and hung up.

He sipped on his Fiji water and whispered, "How in the world am I going to get through that dance with all of that fine hanging in my arms?"

"So, what he say?" Keisha asked, eyes all lit up like a thirteen-year-old trying to get the scoop on the boy one of her friends just got through dancing with.

"'Solid.' And 'I'll see you tomorrow afternoon,'" Marsha said, hoping she sounding cool and nonchalant.

"Oh, I see," Keisha said, thinking, "Rev must have really put it down with his sexy brotha phone voice to get Marsha this bent out of shape over 'solid' and 'I'll see you tomorrow afternoon.'"

"So what time do we need to be at the church?" Veronica asked. "And what else do you need for us to do?"

"Be here around five p.m. And check on the caterers. Make sure the youth choir finishes folding the programs and knows where they are to be when they get here. I asked them to serve as hosts and hostesses."

Marsha looked up to make sure she had everything covered.

"Make sure the floor is clean and dry and that there are plenty of towels, fresh fruit and crackers, and bottles of water for the contestants."

"Do you have the final number on who is competing?" Keisha asked.

"Dayeesha and Marcus have all of that information. They will give out the final numbers and give us the order of performance for each set of contestants."

"You think Xavier and Camille Franklin will be there tomorrow?" Veronica asked.

"You know they will," Marsha said. "Xavier Franklin is not going to let Denzelle get this much attention and not be around to try and steal some of it away from him. Plus, I know he thinks Denzelle can't dance and is hoping he will make a fool of himself."

"Well, he is in for a rude awakening," Veronica said. "I saw you all putting the finishing touches on the dance day before yesterday. That dance is tight."

"Sexy, too," Keisha added, grinning.

"It's not sexy. It's full of energy and spunk," Marsha said defensively.

"I guess Rev isn't really 'sexy,' just full of 'energy and spunk,'" Keisha said. "Gee, I never knew 'energy and spunk' was the 'new sexy.'"

"Me, neither," Veronica chimed in, laughing, and then said. "Marsha, quit running game on your own self and admit that Denzelle is fine and sexy and makes you want to give him some."

"VERONICA!" Marsha said. "That is so wrong."

"Even if it is a correct assessment," Keisha mumbled under her breath.

"Girl, we know you are the *savedest* woman in the Triangle," Veronica said. "And I know you are not lusting after that man. I also know he is the one man who can get next to you. But you get up under that man's skin, too. And Denzelle Flowers definitely doesn't like that, because he is not in control whenever you are around."

"Yeah," Keisha said. "Rev is so scared you will capture his whole heart. And you know a reformed player like Rev can't go down on a technicality. That's why he fights you so, Marsha."

"It's deeper than that, Keisha," Veronica told her. "Denzelle is afraid Marsha will discover she has already captured his heart. Remember, this is a brother who has been fighting against and running from love for years."

Marsha was quiet. This conversation made her uncomfortable. She had such a sweet spot for Denzelle Flowers—but thought she should leave that matter in God's capable Hands. Because God was the only One who could truly deal with Denzelle on this matter. The best thing Marsha could do about him was pray.

If the Lord led a man to a woman, she had to trust the Lord to handle all of the behind-the-scenes details about this matter. That was easier said than done, however. Some men were running from a woman and the Lord so hard, they were going to end up facing off with a talking donkey, stuck down in a whale's funky belly, or going back and forth with the Lord over fleece that was wet when it should have been dry and dry when it should have been wet.

Marsha had discerned that Denzelle was running from the Lord like that. Sometimes he could play the game of running so well, she wanted to GPS him directions to the town of Nineveh in the Bible. Other times Marsha wanted to go off on Denzelle. Then sometimes she wanted to just ignore him and act like he didn't even exist.

"You okay?" Veronica asked her friend.

"I'm fine. Just thinking."

"I hope you're ready to kick some butt on the dance floor tomorrow. Because you sure do look like you are ready to kick somebody's butt right now."

"Yeah, Roni, I'm ready," Marsha answered solemnly. She honestly didn't know if she were more ready to kick Denzelle's butt or just plain ready to tear up that dance floor with Denzelle. Marsha was not in a mood to deal with Denzelle trying to keep a distance from her while being all up on her when they did their dance.

"I think you're very ready, Marsha," Keisha said. She wondered if Marsha had a clue as to how beautiful an experience it was for others watching her dance with Reverend Flowers. It had to be one of the best dances she'd seen in a long time.

Chapter Twenty-six

"Don't forget to get Reverend Flowers's tux, Lil' Too Too."

"I'm at the tux shop right now, Cousin Marsha. I'll be at the church in about forty minutes."

The store clerk came back up to the register counter as soon as Lil' Too Too finished talking to his cousin. He raised an eyebrow when the man walked up to him empty-handed.

"Did you say Reverend Denzelle Flowers? That's the name for the tux?"

This was unbelievable. The man just told Lil' Too Too he took Rev's tux order, and how much he liked the tux Reverend Flowers's selected. He said, "Dawg, why you askin' me a dumb question like that—as if we haven't already had a detailed conversation about Reverend Flowers and his tux? I can't imagine you had two people with a name like 'Denzelle Flowers' coming up in this joint to get a Dolce and Gabanna tuxedo."

"Well," the man began nervously, "I have been all over the back and there is nothing there. I don't know what has happened."

"Whatever happened, you better fix it fast," Lil' Too Too told the man, and started texting one of his girlfriends to see if she would fix him something to eat.

"I've got this, Kenan," an older black man said with a smile Lil' Too Too thought was too smooth to be trusted. Plus, the brother's teeth were too even and way too white. That man didn't look like somebody who should have teeth that white. His teeth looked like he colored over them with some dollar store chalk.

Lil' Too Too, who had a handsome smile and great teeth, stared at the brother's mouth again. He wondered why the brother wasted money on caps and whitener and didn't do anything about those spaces in between each tooth. That man had enough spaces between his teeth to put an extra set of teeth in his mouth.

"So, what can I do for you, young brotha?"

"I'm here to pick up the tux for Reverend Flowers over at New Jerusalem. You know they are . . ."

The man raised his hands to stop Lil' Too Too from continuing. He was sick of hearing about Reverend Denzelle Flowers. If he never, ever heard the name Reverend Denzelle Flowers again, it would be too soon. And it had been horrible over these past weeks with all of the radio announcements about this *Dancing with the Stars* mess at Reverend Flowers's church.

Truthfully, Zeus Nance had never met Denzelle Flowers. But Zeus had met Denzelle's big brother, Officer Yarborough Flowers, from the Durham Police Department. Yarborough had arrested Zeus for beating up his wife, and then for slapping his new girlfriend around on the parking lot of The Place to Be Night Club, and after that for attacking his baby mama with a stun gun. The stun gun incident landed him a year's vacation in the Durham County Jail, thanks to the hard work and dedication of Yarborough Flowers.

Zeus swore to never use a stun gun again after serving jail time. It wasn't because of the jail sentence, either. Zeus discovered just how serious a weapon a stun gun was after Yarborough used it on him as many times as he could without having to explain himself to his superiors.

Zeus Nance swore he would get Officer Flowers for that. He didn't have a clue concerning how he was going to get Yarborough. But it sure did feel good to go around Durham County talking trash about all he was going to do to Yarborough Flowers.

Zeus was presented with an opportunity to get Yarborough when he was approached by one of Luther Howard's flunkies to help Mr. Howard with a small job. The only problem with the offer, however, was that Zeus would have to settle for Yarborough's little brother, Denzelle. It was about as close to getting Yarborough back as he was going to come. And the most unsatisfactory part about this offer was Zeus couldn't even plan his own method of attack. All he could do was mess up the tuxedo order for that *Dancing with the Stars* program.

"Are you going to go and find the tuxedo, dawg? Or will you refund Rev's money?"

Zeus didn't want to have to give up a refund for this tux. It hadn't occurred to him that a refund would be demanded when he messed up this order to get back at Yarborough Flowers. A refund demand could get a Lil' Vincent employee fired, because there was usually little room for error with folks and their tuxedos.

Lil' Vincent's Tuxedo Wear had been the main tuxedo shop for brothers in Raleigh, Durham, and Chapel Hill for over fifty years. The store prided itself on getting things right the first time. Black men loved going to Lil' Vincent's for a tuxedo, because they knew the staff would not mess up their orders. It was also a store tailor-made for them—just like Durham's Miss Thang's Holy Ghost Corner and Church Woman's Boutique was the perfect store for black women in the area.

Lil' Vincent's was a well-kept secret in the community, and few if any white folk knew it even existed. The store was located in Raleigh's black community. And from the outside it looked like a traditional mom-and-pop operation. But nothing could be further from the truth. On the inside, Lil' Vincent's was the black man's store heaven—with some of the sharpest tuxedos at the best prices in the entire Triangle.

You could find a tuxedo in every style, color, and fabric, and by every designer (known and unknown) imaginable. The most popular tuxedos were the ones made out of material with famous NCAA, NBA, and NFL team logos printed all over them.

Many a high school prom had a young blood strutting up into the dance decked out in a tuxedo made out of material with his favorite team's logo all over it.

"Let me go in the back and see what is going on," Zeus said, and he walked back to where he had hidden the countriest red tuxedo in the world.

He hoped Denzelle Flowers would not demand that refund, because he'd just gotten out of jail and needed this job real bad. But for the moment, he was getting great pleasure from handing over this ugly mess. Zeus Nance knew Denzelle would dance in some old man Bermuda shorts, black socks, and brown sandals before he wore this outfit.

Zeus came back with a black satin bag across his arm, grinning like he'd just gotten over on somebody. There was something wrong with this tux. Lil' Too Too was sure of it. He couldn't figure out what it was, because everything looked normal. But something was wrong.

Lil' Too Too was getting ready to inspect what was in the garment bag but was stopped by his phone buzzing.

"Where you at, Cuz?" Marsha asked. It was five p.m., and they would need to start getting dressed soon.

"I have Rev's tux," Lil' Too Too told her, while walking out of the shop. "Cuz, do you want me to check it out? I don't like the way the joker in the store handled this situation. Something ain't right."

"We don't have time for you to do all of that. Denzelle's been doing business with Lil' Vincent's Tuxedo Wear for years. He's never had any trouble with them."

"Okay, Cuz. I'm on my way."

Denzelle was standing in the back door of the church when Lil' Too Too pulled up in a black Volkswagen Bug with rims and spinners. He didn't remember ever seeing a Bug with rims and spinners before. But then again, this was Lil' Too Too. Marsha's family was a trip. Lil' Too Too was her baby cousin, and he was always into some extra stuff.

Denzelle always felt that Lil' Too Too would make a good cop. Lil' Too Too had a lot of street sense, he was smart, he could sniff out crap, and he was always game for a good fight. While Lil' Too Too had experienced some skirmishes with the law, he'd never committed the kind of offenses that would keep him from joining the police force. At some point, Denzelle was going to have that hard conversation with Lil' Too Too about answering the calling on his life to serve and protect his community.

And then there was Marsha's other cousin, Sweet Red, who recently stopped dancing at Rumpshakers Hip Hop Gentleman's Club to enroll in their management training program. Sweet Red could put a hurting on a pole, and she was fine. There was nothing more exciting than a sister who could dance and was fine, too. Denzelle understood why some of Charles Robinson's most loyal patrons had been in tears when they were told Sweet Red was stepping down from the pole.

Marsha's people were a trip. But you couldn't help but love them. They were some hardworking and loyal folk who would be there for you when you needed them.

Lil' Too Too hopped out of the car and got the bag with Denzelle's tux off of the back seat. He said, "I hope this tux is okay, Rev. I kept thinking something was wrong. But Cuz said you've always done business with them and everything was always okay. They had this new guy. A Zeus Nance. I didn't like that joker."

"Zeus Nance works at Lil' Vincent's?" Denzelle asked Lil' Too Too. "My brother has arrested him several times for beating on his women. Last time Yarborough made sure he spent some time in Durham County Jail. Didn't know he was out."

Denzelle put the garment bag over his arm. Lil' Too Too was right. Something wasn't right about this. Nothing was ever right if Zeus Nance was involved.

Marsha met Denzelle at the door, eager to see the tuxedo. They were both dressing in Denzelle's campaign colors of crimson and cream. She made sure he had the smoothest tuxedo— black, with a white shirt with red stud buttons, trimmed in black, and a red-and-black jacquard silk tie and matching pocket handkerchief. It looked so good when she and Vincent put it together online.

"Let's see what you have, Denzelle," Marsha chirped, trying so hard to contain her excitement.

Denzelle walked back to his office, laid the garment bag on his desk, and unzipped it. He frowned, "I thought you said my tux was black."

"It is," Marsha answered.

"Then why do I have this?" Denzelle told her, as he pulled out the crimson-colored tuxedo, a red ruffled shirt with black trim, and a red cummerbund and matching tie.

"Oh, dear. That is hideous," Marsha said, before she could catch herself.

"You ordered it," Denzelle snapped.

"No, I didn't. I sent you pictures of what I ordered," Marsha told him, and made sure he saw her roll her eyes at him.

"So what the hell am I to do with this mess, Marsha?"

"I don't like the way you are talking to me, Denzelle. You ought to know I would never order anything this ugly for you."

"Sorry," was all he said. "Your cousin was right. There is nothing about this that is right. Somebody got the other tuxedo. And I'll bet some money we'll see my tuxedo waltzing around the dance floor in just a few hours."

Marsha sighed heavily and said, "You think somebody stole your tux."

"Not think, I know. This reeks of Xavier Franklin."

"But how could Xavier get away with something like this? Vincent would never allow this to happen knowingly. I don't even think Vincent likes Xavier enough to even speak to him."

Denzelle nodded. Marsha was making a good point. Few if any people liked Xavier Franklin. He'd known Vincent for many years, and that brother had never been cool with brothers like Xavier. There had to be another source.

"Baby, hit your lil' cousin up and let me talk to him," Denzelle said. His voice had the tone a man used when talking to his woman.

Marsha pulled out her cell and was about to push Lil' Too Too's number on her speed dial when she saw Denzelle staring at her plain little Walmart phone. She said, "What?"

"You know what? That phone? Looks like it belongs to Betty Rubble."

Marsha frowned. "Why not Wilma Flintstone?"

"Because," Denzelle said, "Wilma would have the most up-dated phone available in Bedrock. Betty Rubble, on the other hand, would be just as happy with *that* cell phone."

"Forget you, Denzelle," was all Marsha said, and then dialed Lil' Too Too.

"Yeah, Cuz. What you need?"

"Pastor wants to talk to you, Too."

Marsha cut her eyes at Denzelle and gave him her cell. She said, "You might want to run around the church real fast while you're talking on my phone. That's the only way you can charge it up."

"Too, tell me some more about the brother who gave you this tuxedo."

"Rev, I don't know where that brother came from. He didn't act like any of the other folk working there, but he was all up in everything—bossing folk around and taking over. You know what I'm sayin'?"

"Yeah, Too. I know exactly what you're sayin'," Denzelle said, frowning.

"I can go back and handle the brother," Lil' Too Too said. "If I punch him in the mouth and knock out a few teeth, nobody will know that happened to him."

"Why not?" Denzelle asked. Lil' Too Too was resourceful and smooth. But Denzelle couldn't figure out how the young brother was going to accomplish that.

"His teeth are messed up. They already look like somebody punched them out."

Denzelle laughed. Lil' Too Too was right about how Zeus's teeth looked.

"Rev, not only are his teeth jacked up, but I'm sure the tuxedo he gave you is hellacious in appearance. You want me to come and get it and find you something else? Metro Mitchell might be able to hook you up with something from Yeah Yeah?"

"Thank you, Too. But Metro doesn't do tuxedos. I'm going to have to wing it for the performance."

"Cousin Marsha can help you fix the situation, Rev."

"I hope so," Denzelle said, shaking his head at that hideous tuxedo Zeus had stuck him with. But that was okay; Denzelle knew how to fix this situation. He put Marsha's phone on a table and pulled his out of his jacket pocket. He said, "Yarborough."

"Why are you calling me with less than two hours before your gig, Denzelle?" Yarborough said with some irritation. He was trying to hurry up and finish his paperwork at the station so he could get off work and get to the program on time.

"Zeus Nance is working for Vincent."

"Really," Yarborough asked with some mild interest. He remembered Zeus being very difficult to place in the Triangle's new Post-Prison Job Placement Program, because most people didn't like him. Not being liked by most people was bad enough with a regular person who'd never been in any trouble. It could spell disaster for an ex-con nobody liked. People were very suspicious of folk who had done jail time, had attitude problems, and were just plain old unlikable.

"Yeah, Big Bro. I don't know how that dude got assigned to Vincent, but he needs a serious reality check."

"Don't worry, I've got this," Yarborough said. As soon as he hung up the phone, he was calling Zeus's parole officer and having him reassigned. Zeus Nance didn't even have the qualifications to work at Lil' Vincent's. He had horrible taste in clothes and was clueless about what colors went together. Yarborough was a guy's guy and completely unconcerned about making fashion statements. Nonetheless, he still knew when a brother didn't know how to dress.

"So tell me, Marsha. What are you going to do about this fiasco? I hired you because you are supposed to be the big-time stylist."

Marsha put her hands on her hips and stood looking up at Denzelle with her feet apart. He was acting like she was the one who slapped that mammy-made tuxedo on him.

"Don't look up at me like that," Denzelle snapped. "This whole thing is your—and not my—idea, Marsha."

That statement stung, and it hurt. It was also so thoughtless and unnecessary.

"It's a good idea," Marsha told him. "And do not snap at me like that again."

"Or what?" Denzelle asked her. There was no way he was going to let Marsha Metcalf get the best of him. What if one of his boys walked in his office and saw Marsha having the upper hand? He'd never live that down.

"Or I'm gonna tell you, you'd better not do it," she said, in a voice that sounded like a little girl telling somebody off and then stomping her foot to emphasize her point.

He started laughing. Folks were always getting on Denzelle about pursuing Marsha. But one of the reasons he was reluctant to grab a hold of her was because he feared she could not handle him. Denzelle didn't want a woman who wasn't confident standing up to him.

"You talkin' bad for a person who is not going to do anything, Girl."

"I don't have to put up with this mess from you, Denzelle Flowers," Marsha said, and she collected her things and started walking off, mumbling, "Who does that boy think he is, my daddy?"

"Marsha, calm down and help me figure this out."

"Oh, you want my help now, Mr. Man."

"Girl," he said.

"What, Denzelle Flowers? What are you going to do?" Marsha shot at him. She couldn't handle Denzelle's mess right now. Marsha felt like everything she'd dealt with over these past years was suddenly crashing down on her head. She didn't have the capacity to be calm, to be nice, or to even respond to him in a civil manner.

Denzelle had never experienced Marsha like this. The girl was always so mellow and didn't get her feathers ruffled easily. But she was anything but mellow right now. In fact, if he didn't know better, Marsha was looking and acting like she wanted to put her foot up his behind.

He, on the other hand, could get riled up real quick. And he wanted a woman who could handle him when he wasn't at his best, or simply when he was just being cantankerous and showing the crack of his butt—which Denzelle was prone to do. This was especially true when he was tired and had packed up his schedule with meetings with folk who made him feel even more exhausted, mean, and cranky.

Marsha walked over to the door of his office suite and struggled to open it with all of that stuff in her arms. Denzelle rushed over to help her. He said, "You know you can't open this door with all of this stuff in your hands."

Marsha ignored him and kept trying to open the door. Denzelle took her things out of her arms and put them on his desk.

"I'm sorry."

She looked up at him and didn't say anything.

"I'm sorry, Marsha."

Marsha still didn't acknowledge Denzelle's apology. He took her hands in his.

"I was wrong. Baby, I'm sorry. Come on, Girl."

Marsha looked down at her feet. She needed a moment to regain her composure. This was a part of Denzelle she'd never experienced, and it was getting to her.

Denzelle reached out and grabbed the back of Marsha's head. He leaned down and kissed her cheek.

"Come on, Honey. Give me another chance to get this event thing worked out," Denzelle whispered in Marsha's ear, sending a few shivers down her back.

He kissed the tip of her ear.

"Are you going to forgive me?"

Marsha remained silent. Denzelle kissed the side of her neck and whispered. "Come on, Girl. Help a brother out. You know you want to."

Marsha felt herself melting into Denzelle. It had been years since a brother whispered something that sounded good in her ear. She loved a good, low whisper from a man who knew exactly what to say. Marsha looked up at Denzelle, and before she could catch herself, wrapped her arms around his waist. She wished she could move, but holding on to Denzelle felt so normal it was scary.

Denzelle stared down into Marsha's eyes. He was mesmerized by the sweetness of her gaze.

"I need you, Marsha," Denzelle blurted out, and then lifted up her chin and kissed her lips. It was a soft and tender kiss—perfect in length and the pressure of the touch of his lips on hers. He kissed Marsha again. It was a sweet kiss that ended with a soft "smack."

"I know what we can do about your outfit," Marsha said, hoping she didn't sound as lame to Denzelle as she sounded to herself.

Denzelle kissed Marsha's cheek again, and said, "I can't wait to discover how you are going to work this thing out."

Chapter Twenty-seven

Marsha hurried back to Denzelle's office to give him a first and private viewing of her outfit. She twirled around a few times so that he could get the full effect. Denzelle could not believe how well she had fixed the tuxedo disaster. No one would ever know that this was not the original costume for their performance. Denzelle's expert player eyes swept over Marsha, taking in every single detail of how she looked. He sucked on his tooth and grinned. "You look like my dessert," he said in a low and dangerously sexy voice.

Marsha blushed.

Denzelle chuckled. Marsha was going to make pursuing her so much fun. He loved the chase, and it was a long time since he'd wanted to go full throttle in chasing a woman down. He closed his eyes for a few seconds. He could not believe he'd just committed himself to chasing Marsha Metcalf.

"I did a pretty good job of hooking us up," Marsha said with a smile, hoping that placing attention on their attire would diffuse the heat coming from him.

"Yeah, Beautiful, you did just that."

Marsha stared at Denzelle, admiring her own handiwork. He looked better in this outfit than what she'd first planned for him to wear. Instead of the elegant Dolce and Gabbana attire, Denzelle was wearing the tuxedo jacket like it was a red sports coat with dark blue jeans. She found a starched white dress shirt hanging in his office closet, and instructed him not to tuck it in. In place of a pocket handkerchief, Marsha tucked the tuxedo's red bow tie in the breast pocket, leaving several inches of the tie hanging out of the pocket. The red jacket, white shirt, jeans, and the sleek, black Cole Haan leather oxfords made for a sharp complement to what Marsha had done to her own outfit.

She decided to keep on her black silky leggings, and put Denzelle's ruffled tuxedo shirt on over them. The shirt was large and covered her whole body, like a minidress. She gave the big shirt some shape and definition by putting the bright red cummerbund around her waist. She pulled her hair up into a high ponytail, and was wearing her fancy, black suede, Mary Jane pumps, with the rainbow-colored rhinestones all over them.

Denzelle couldn't take his eyes off of those prissy little shoes. He wondered what Marsha looked like in just those shoes—*just the shoes*. A mannish grin spread across his face at the thought. Women didn't know how much that kind of mental imagery could work a brother over.

Marsha twirled again, hoping Denzelle was feeling okay about how she'd revamped their outfits. She thought he would like this better. The jeans and shirt would be more comfortable to dance in.

Denzelle picked up on Marsha's uncertainty and quickly surmised it was in response to his own lack of response to her. He smiled at her. Marsha was such a sweetheart. He tweaked her ear, resisting the urge to nibble on it, and said, "What are you wearing?"

"Your shirt and cummerbund."

Denzelle sighed and gave a soft chuckle. That girl was so concrete. A brother didn't need to be too smooth with Marsha, because all of those Mack-Daddy words would go to waste and right over her head.

"Girl, you smell good," he said, and kissed her cheek.

Marsha moved back, and Denzelle reached out and pulled her back to him, only this time he was holding her in his arms.

He planted another kiss on her neck, and then stroked it lightly with his fingertips.

"Mmmm. . . . You taste even better."

Denzelle slid his fingers up to the nape of Marsha's neck. He pulled her head back gently and kissed her lips.

"My Honey," was all Denzelle could say in between several kisses. He tried to keep the kisses light but couldn't help himself. He held onto Marsha tightly and kissed her deeply, and with so much heat and passion, it made her feel like she was going to melt.

He kissed her deeply again, and then planted several soft and warm kisses on her lips.

"We can finish this later," Denzelle said and tweaked Marsha's ear playfully. He grabbed her hand and pulled her in the direction of the gymnasium.

They walked into the gymnasium thirty minutes before the program was scheduled to begin. It was packed to full capacity with folk from every Gospel United Church in the North Carolina Conference. Marsha had expected the regular church folk to turn out for this—especially the ones living in the Triangle. She had not, however, been prepared for the high representation of Gospel United Church preachers and their wives present tonight. The only reason that group was here was to find out what they were doing and take the information back to their own candidates for bishop.

"Veronica worked that marketing thing, didn't she?" Denzelle said, with a huge grin spreading across his face.

Folk didn't know how much it warmed a pastor's heart when his members did wonderful work for their pastor. A lot of people didn't realize how much flack pastors could receive on any given day. There was always a member who wanted to give his/her pastor a piece of their mind, or to complain about another member or assistant pastor. It felt good when someone did a good work on the pastor's behalf.

"Yeah. I am amazed at the number of folk who bought tickets and came."

Denzelle pointed across the room to where the contestants were seated.

"Did you expect that many folk would want to compete in this?"

"No," Marsha answered. "But I did expect it to be a lot of fun, and I'm confident it will be just that."

"I agree," Denzelle said, and grabbed her hand, leading them across the room to the other dancers.

"Don't forget that you have to give the opening prayer."

"I didn't know I was doing the prayer."

"Aren't you the senior pastor of New Jerusalem?"

Denzelle shrugged, and then asked, "Who is doing the welcome address?"

"Keisha."

He laughed and went up to the podium where the microphone was. Judging from the looks of all of the contestants, this was going to be some kind of shindig. Denzelle couldn't wait to witness some of the dances he knew were going to be the talk of black-church Raleigh. He hoped he could keep it together and not fall out on the floor rolling with laughter.

Veronica Washington and Keisha Jackson walked up to the podium and stood next to Marsha and Denzelle.

"So, Pastor," Keisha said. "How do you like me now?" She waved her hand around, gesturing to the entire room.

"I'd say I like you pretty well, little sister," Denzelle said, and stuck his fist toward her for some dap.

"This is going to be a whole lot of fun," Veronica chimed in smiling, and then she started frowning. "Why are they here?"

"Who?" Marsha asked, following her friend's gaze over to where Veronica's ex-husband, Robert, was standing with his arms around his current wife, Tracey Parsons Washington, whispering in her ear and laughing like he was having the time of his life.

"That is the biggest crock of poop I've ever seen," Keisha said, rolling her eyes. "Robert knows he is not all that into Stewie."

Denzelle started laughing, and then tried to stop. He was not supposed to laugh at his own parishioners like that. Even though he did not like Robert Washington and his wife, they were still a part of his flock. And as their shepherd, he was as responsible for them as he was for the members he liked. It was hard work being a good and upstanding pastor.

While Denzelle had the love of Christ in his heart for all of his members, he didn't like all of them. That had been a difficult issue to come to terms with when he was a new pastor. He used to think something was wrong with him, because there were some folks in his church he just didn't like. And when Denzelle confessed this shortcoming to his mentor, Bishop Eddie Tate, the bishop hollered with laughter, saying, "Is that all you are having trouble with—not liking some black people who need to be pimp-slapped on general principles? Young Blood, you need to be shouting and praising God if that is all you have to deal with as a pastor."

"I wonder what that dance is going to look like?" Keisha whispered. "And where did she find a hat to fit her big head?"

"Why are Robert and Tracey dressed in army fatigues?" Veronica asked.

"Again," Keisha whispered, "where did she find that hat to fit her big head?"

"We need to start," Denzelle said in his best preacher's voice.

They were not the only ones who had some serious questions about Tracey Parsons Washington and her husband. Denzelle's fraternity brother Charles Robinson had come to support Veronica, and he wanted to know the same thing. In fact, he was surprised Robert had come out for an event for Denzelle Flowers. Robert Washington was not a Denzelle Flowers fan—especially after Denzelle gave him a dress down at the last Board of Trustees meeting.

Charles came and stood by his frat, and said, "Look at that joker standing over there looking like a broke-down G.I. Joe doll. He is still pissed that you took him down at the last trustees meeting."

"Well, he's going to have a hissy fit when I replace him with you on the Steward Board."

Charles raised his hands and said, "Whoa, Player. I'm still adjusting to the Trustee Board. I'm not so sure I'm Steward Board material."

"Yeah, you are," Denzelle told him. "You are a dutiful member of the church, you tithe, and you attend service regularly. I'm the pastor, I make these appointments, and I need you on the Steward Board."

"D, dawg, it's me. I'm not like your other church members—know what I'm sayin'."

Charles was not used to being a trustee, and he was nervous about an appointment to the Steward Board. While he was a dutiful tithing member of New Jerusalem, Charles was still the owner of Rumpshakers Hip-Hop Gentlemen's Club. And he wasn't planning on giving up that title any time soon. He wondered what was going on with Denzelle that would cause him to give him any of these appointments.

Denzelle knew where Charles was coming from. And Denzelle also knew what he was doing by appointing Charles to those positions in the church. He'd prayed about this and was surprised when the Lord led him to appoint Charles. When Denzelle looked upward in the middle of his prayer, he felt a peaceful tug at his heart, and was led to read the second chapter of Mark, verses 14 to 17.

Levi, or Matthew, was a rich tax collector who fellowshipped with rich and corrupt tax collectors. Yet Jesus called him to be a disciple, and even had dinner at Levi's house, with many of Levi's boys in attendance. Levi, unlike the Pharisees, gave up his profession to follow Jesus. The Lord made it clear to Denzelle that it was just a matter of time before Charles Robinson gave up his hold on the world to follow Him.

"Frat, you are saved—unlike some of my most dedicated so-called holy rollers at New Jerusalem. I know that is a well-kept secret, but you are saved nonetheless. Being saved is one of my primary prerequisites to hold major offices in my church. My stewards need to be saved. All of them are not right now. But they need to be, and I'm making some much needed changes on that front."

Charles scratched at the stubble on his chin for a moment.

"I always wondered why certain folk were not trustees. It surprised me when you didn't appoint him."

Charles pointed discreetly to a distinguished-looking brother sitting toward the back of the gym. The man was extremely well dressed in a black, chalk-striped suit, crisp white shirt, and navy silk tie with black velvet dots on it. He looked like he should have been waiting to give some kind of expert testimony at a congressional hearing.

"Who? Morris Palmer?" Denzelle asked.

"Yeah, Palmer," Charles said. "Why isn't he a steward, D?"

Denzelle sighed heavily. Folk were always asking him about Morris Palmer and the appointment, or rather, the lack of his appointment to either the Trustee or Steward Boards at New Jerusalem. He said, "Morris Palmer is rich. Now, he's not as rich as you, Frat. But I think he is worth about eighteen million dollars.

"He has a fine wife, a fine woman on the side, no children, and a very lucrative cardboard-box factory in Butner, North Carolina. He has also been arrested four times for beating his wife and twice for throwing his fine woman out of his car while it was still moving. Palmer loves to make his wife come to church with him and pretend she is happy, and that he is the perfect husband."

"Why is she still with him?" Charles asked.

"Money and status. That is the only reason because Morris is mean, and he doesn't have any game. That old man over there on the Hoveround with the oxygen tank and mask hanging off of the back of it has more game than Morris Palmer," Denzelle answered.

"You're right on that one, Denzelle," Charles said. "Genevieve is snooty, and stuck-up, and treats women who are not in her social group really bad. I would think that constant butt whippings and all of those other women would serve as some kind of wake-up call. But nothing has worked to convince Genevieve she can do better than Morris Palmer."

Denzelle looked down at Marsha, who was studying Morris Palmer with great intensity. He was about to ask her what was wrong when Morris got up and walked across the gymnasium to where they were standing. His expert ho eyes scanned Marsha better than anything the TSA could use at the Raleigh/Durham airport.

Marsha shrank back when she saw the cold glint in Morris Palmer's eyes. She didn't like this man. He was horrible.

Denzelle moved Marsha behind him so that Morris could not stare her up and down. He was about to say something when Keisha pointed across the room and said, "What in the world are they doing here?"

They all, Morris Palmer included, followed Keisha's finger pointing at Reverend Xavier Franklin, Camille Franklin, and Tatiana Townsend. Keisha could not believe Tatiana was walking up in here, hot on the heels of her married man. She also couldn't believe the girl came in here acting like she and Todd would be able to get on the list of dancers at the last minute. Keisha was so glad she had a time limit on the registration dates.

"Please tell me that Xavier Franklin and his wife are not in the competition?" Denzelle asked. He could tell by looking at Xavier and Camille that they couldn't dance. Denzelle didn't want to be so uncouth that he would practically laugh in Xavier's face when they did whatever stupid-looking dance they came up with.

"Lord, Patra is in the house," Marsha blurted out—glad that mean Morris Palmer was on his way back to his seat. The last thing they needed was for him to overhear her comment about Bishop Jefferson's newest wife. Morris Palmer was a tattletale and would report everything said about Patra to Bishop Jefferson just to get back at Denzelle.

"Patra?" Veronica asked. "What about Patra? Who is like Patra?"

"Is that Violetta?" Charles Robinson asked. He was looking like he was ready to run and get her autograph.

"Violetta who?" Veronica asked Charles. She was curious to know who had him riled up like that.

"You know, Violetta, Violetta," he said.

"And?"

"Veronica, did you ever see the music video, 'Burn de House Down'?" Denzelle said, when he realized she needed some help with understanding why Charles, or any man for that matter, would get so excited over seeing Violetta, the dance hall queen, at a church event.

Veronica shook her head.

Charles said, "'Burn de House Down' is a video with the bishop's wife on it, from before she was the bishop's wife. It made Violetta famous. And I have to tell you, old girl was working it on that video."

"Yes, lawd, she was 'wurkin' it,'" Denzelle said, cracking up. "I hope she is going to dance tonight."

"Me, too, playah," Charles said, and held his hand out for some skin old-school style. "I tell you, if the 'supervisor' works it like she did on that video, she'll have every old playah in this room trying to get her number."

"Don't wish that on us, Charles," Denzelle said in a serious voice. "Last thing I need is for Bishop Jefferson to be more put out with me than he already is."

"Rev," Keisha said. "We need to get this party started."

Chapter Twenty-eight

Keisha hit the microphone at the podium, and then blew into it to make sure it was on. When the "bloooosh" of her blowing sounded out around the room, she said, "Good evening!"

"Good evening," the people in the audience echoed back.

"Are you ready for some good dancing?"

"Yeah!!!!!"

"ALRIGHT!!!!" Keisha said with a whole lot of pep and excitement in her voice.

She took a quick survey of the room and stifled the urge to sigh with relief. Bay Bowser was able to get off at Rumpshakers early. She saw him watching her and found herself blushing.

Charles Robinson saw his employee, Bay, come in. He hadn't missed the way Bay's face lit up when he saw Keisha. But Keisha's blushing came as a surprise to him. Charles had never seen Keisha Jackson blush about anything.

"I'm glad Bay is really, really saved," Charles whispered to Denzelle. " 'Cause old boy would hit that if he weren't."

Keisha tried not to stare at Bay too long. He was looking so fine in charcoal slacks and a light gray polo shirt. She wanted to fan herself when she noticed his biceps in that polo. Bay looked like a slightly older and browner version of the actor Laz Alonso from the TV show *Breakout Kings* and the movie *Jumping the Broom*.

She patted her freshly done hair. It was looking good, with reddish-blond streaks running through the new cut—a chin-length bob, with a heavy bang falling in her face. Keisha stuck out her leg, with the shimmery navy stockings and navy glitter platform pumps, so that Bay could catch a glimpse.

Keisha smiled when she saw Bay watching her legs. She blushed when Bay winked and licked his lips. When Bay grinned and winked again, Keisha took in a deep breath and said, "My name is Keisha Diane Jackson, and I am your 'hostess with the mostess' tonight. I want to welcome you all to the first annual Ballroom Dance-off, or what many of you have been calling *Dancing with the Stars*, at New Jerusalem Gospel United Church. And before we get started, I want to ask our senior pastor, Reverend Denzelle Flowers, to say a prayer."

Keisha moved away from the podium and stood next to Marsha. She said, "So, how did it go?"

"Perfect," Veronica said.

"Yeah," Marsha added. "It was short and sweet. I'm so glad you didn't go old-school church on us and start introducing folk in the audience and asking the bishop and his wife to stand."

"I know," Veronica said. "And Keisha, if you had added some 'eerrrrerrrs' to your words, I would have slapped you."

Marsha was laughing. There was nothing worse than being at a fun church event with everybody anxious for it to start and the Master/Mistress of Ceremony keeping on talking. Even worse was if they began to give a testimony. And the ultimate torture was when they started singing and then solicited the members of the congregation for testimonies and songs. That could only be topped by the MC shouting and doing the holy dance.

Denzelle, too, was relieved Keisha kept the welcome address short and sweet. He placed his hands on either side of the podium and said, "Let us pray. Father, in Heaven Above, we come before You with heads bowed in complete reverence and awe of You. We are thankful for all You do in our lives, all that You have done, and all of the blessings You have waiting in the wings for us. You are a good God, and we want to take a moment to say Thank You."

"Thank You," echoed around the room.

"So, Lord," Denzelle continued, "bless this evening's event. We bless Your Holy Name. In Jesus' Name, I pray, Amen."

"Amen," everyone in the gymnasium said.

"Well, now that we are ready to rock and roll, I am going to turn this program over to our lovely MC, Ms. Keisha Jackson."

Keisha stepped back up to the podium and said, "Thank you, Reverend Flowers. And now . . ."

Before she could continue, one of the older ushers walked up to Keisha with a piece of paper in his hand, like they were in the sanctuary during a church service. Keisha had practically begged the members of the Usher Board to refrain from wearing their regular uniforms. But those pleas had fallen on deaf ears.

Keisha didn't even want the regular Usher Board to help out with tonight's program. At Marsha's suggestion, Keisha asked the members of the youth organizations to help in this capacity. But when they arrived at the gymnasium, just an hour ago, the head of the old people's Usher Board had taken over and assigned the teens to helping to set up the chairs. Now she had to deal with annoying Usher Board stuff.

The ushers were in generic usher spots around the gymnasium. The men were wearing navy suits, white shirts, navy-and-white striped ties, and white cotton usher gloves. The women were wearing navy blue suits with navy-and-white striped scarves around their necks and white cotton usher gloves. They looked like they were doing duty for an annual conference.

She read the note and frowned.

"What's the problem?" Denzelle asked.

"This," was all Keisha said, and put the note in Denzelle's hand.

He read it and sighed. Church folk were a trip. Whoever heard of folk participating in a dance contest marching in like they were in the processional at the opening of a church service? He almost vetoed this request but thought it best to let this play itself out. The only thing Denzelle was not going to do was grab Marsha and walk in the processional with them.

Denzelle glanced over at Marsha's son, Marcus, and then texted him, Put on some funky, bluesy instrumental church music so that these fools can march in like the choir is getting ready to do a concert.

Marcus started laughing. He said, "Would all contestants for the dance program gather at the back of the gym so the processional can begin."

All of sudden there was a whirlwind of movement as folks hurried to the spot in the back of the gym. One of the women ushers rushed over to the contestants and gave instructions about how everybody was supposed to stand and line up. Denzelle stood at the podium thinking that this was the craziest thing he'd seen at church in a long time. And he had seen some wild stuff in his day.

When everybody was in place, Marcus put on Al Green's rendition of "Too Close." He knew Al Green was one of Reverend Flowers's favorite singers, and that his pastor would appreciate hearing this if he had to watch a processional at a dance competition. As soon as the first cords of "Too Close" began, Denzelle looked up at Marcus and mouthed the words, "Thank you."

The head usher gave the contestants the signal, and they started marching in, church processional style, dressed in dance contest costumes like they were in the offering promenade at a revival. Marsha didn't dare look at Veronica and Keisha, because she knew they would all burst out in hysterical laughter and be no more good for the rest of the evening. What possessed the head of the Usher Board to march those folk in like that?

Dayeesha and Metro were sitting in the back hollering with laughter. Metro leaned over and said, "Baby, the only thing wrong with this picture is that we are technically at church, and I can't go and grab myself a glass of Crown to sip on while I enjoy this moment in the annals of Gospel United Church history."

"Whew, baby," Dayeesha said, wiping at her eyes. "My stomach is hurting. This thing is so good."

Charles Robinson and his boy Pierre Smith were about to bust wide open, they were laughing so hard. Leave it to Denzelle to have something happen at his church that a playah could truly appreciate.

"Dawg," Pierre said, "am I really seeing this with my own eyes? Check it out."

Charles whipped his head around just in time to see the old player in the Hoveround "marching" in the processional with his boo walking next to him in a matching outfit.

"Isn't that Mr. Arvelle?" Pierre asked. "You know, the old playah who had to use his oxygen mask when he used to watch Miss Hattie Lee Booth dance at Rumpshakers?"

Charles nodded and said, "Umm, hmm—one and the same. But who is that old hoochie he's marching with?"

Pierre took a long look at the old lady marching next to Mr. Arvelle in his Hoveround. He said, "That looks like Miss Roberta—the old lady who owns the Ethnic Peoples Dollar Store with her son."

Bay Bowser, who was standing with them, kept wondering how black folk could turn a dance contest into a semichurch service. His mother always said black people could have church anywhere. She was right. Bay said, "Boss, I know you've heard the Ethnic Peoples Dollar Store commercials on *Grady Gray's Hour of Holy Ghost Power*. Those commercials are so hood, if you google 'ghetto fabulous' a picture of Miss Roberta and her son will pop up."

"You can buy stuff there you didn't even know was still being sold in a store," Pierre said."

"Like what?" Charles asked.

"For starters, every kind of Now and Later flavor you can imagine," Bay answered. "And you can find Mary Janes, Boston Baked Beans, those pink, white, and chocolate coconut bars, Red Hots, and Lemonheads."

"Do they sell more than candy?"

Bay nodded and continued, "They have those silver change things people used to put on their waists, coin purses, rain scarves, and rubber covers for men's dress shoes when it's raining and snowing."

"They also have a special section in the store where you can buy Cold Duck, and Boone's Farm wines," Pierre said, with a look of nostalgia.

"How does a dollar store qualify to sell liquor?" Charles asked.

Pierre and Bay just looked at each other and shrugged an "I don't know." Charles thought about the business side of things way too much.

"You know something, boss," Bay said, "you need a woman, and you work too much."

"You still haven't told me how Miss Roberta and her son, Thaddeus, are able to sell wine at the dollar store."

"I don't know how they do it," Pierre said. "All I know is that if you go down to their store, off of the north part of Alston Avenue in Durham, you'll find all kinds of stuff you like."

"I should have known the store was in Durham," Charles said.

"And what is that supposed to mean?" Pierre asked. He loved Durham—didn't know why folks were always hating on the Bull City.

"It means you can find all kinds of good stuff in Durham— like some Cold Duck and a pack of green apple, grape, or strawberry Now and Laters, or a lap dance that won't quit at Rumpshakers," Charles told him. He was a Durham boy, born and bred, and proud of it.

"Shhh," Bay said. "The processional just ended."

Keisha was dabbing at her eyes with a tissue. Watching Mr. Arvelle on his Hoveround in the processional was more than she could take at the podium. She leaned over and whispered, "What made Mr. Arvelle and Miss Roberta think it was cool to get in this contest?" to Veronica.

She'd bet no one knew a Hoveround could do all of that—not even the other people who owned one of those motorized scooters. All it took was one resourceful black person to give their Hoveround the hook-up. Mr. Arvelle had that scooter looking good, too.

His Hoveround had a customized black leather seat with gold dots on it. The base of the scooter was gold with black trim, and the tires had custom-fitted, gold-spoke rims. The back had a black leather sack that held his oxygen tank and mask. The handles of the scooter were gold with black leather on the handles. Mr. Arvelle's Hoveround was so smooth and tight, he could have driven it around the gymnasium and picked up some women just like brothers worked it with a fancy car.

"I'll try and answer the question about Mr. Arvelle and Miss Roberta if you all can answer this question for me," Veronica said. "What made Bishop Jefferson's wife, Episcopal Supervisor Violetta Jefferson, think it was okay for her to dance with that man in those shoes."

"What man in what shoes?" Marsha asked.

"That man right over there, standing with Supervisor Violetta in a semimatching outfit and those shoes," Keisha said, pointing directly at the man.

Marsha and Veronica found the man who was next to Supervisor Violetta. He kind of looked like her, only where she was long and slender, he was medium height and stocky in build. They were wearing violet-colored outfits.

Supervisor Violetta was dressed in a violet-Spandex dress, with just enough flair to the short skirt to enable her to dance without showing more than what was already being put out there for all the world to see. She had on violet satin pumps, and there were violet streaks throughout her long, swinging braid.

Her dance partner was wearing a shiny violet suit with black pinstripes running through it. He had on a black shirt and tie, as well as a black hat with violet trimming around the brim of the hat. But it was his shoes that capped off the outfit.

Marsha, Veronica, and Keisha could barely believe what they were witnessing with their own eyes, concerning those shoes and the man's feet. It had been a long time since they met and knew anyone who wore shoes like that. Talk about a throwback. The man had on violet patent-leather shoes, and the entire toe part had been cut off like he tried to make himself some sandals at the last minute.

"I thought those shoes went out with *The Mack* and *Shaft*," Veronica whispered to Keisha, who said, "I thought there were no more easily accessible bottles of curl activator floating around."

"OMG," Veronica said, "It's Souullllll Gllllow."

"Stop. Just stop," Charles Robinson whispered in Veronica's ear.

"But he has curl activator loaded up in his hair, Charles," Veronica began, trying to act like she didn't feel his lips brush across the tip of her ear.

"And he is your brother in the Lord, Sister Washington," Charles told her, with a smirk on his face. "So behave."

"You can try and get all mighty and holy on us if you want to, Mr. Rumpshakers," Keisha said. "But that is Soul Glow in a pair of homemade pimp sandals."

At this point Denzelle, who was getting a bit nervous about having to dance in front of his parishioners, fellow preachers, presiding elders, and a bishop, just wanted to get this thing started, so it could end. He adjusted the red bow tie hanging out of his tuxedo jacket.

"You know you are sharp, Frat," Charles said. "I wouldn't have thought to wear that combination. But it works."

"Marsha put it together, after somebody messed with my original outfit," Denzelle answered.

"All things work together for the good of them that love the Lord, Frat," Charles answered him, a bit shaken at how fast that Bible verse had come to him. It seemed like each and every day he was moving further and further away from business as usual and taking more pleasure in "walking up the King's High Way."

Denzelle nodded. Charles was right. Just about every other contestant had on some version of a tuxedo. He had come in looking for somebody in his tux. But it didn't matter now, because his outfit stood out. Denzelle knew he was looking good. He pulled out his cell and texted Marcus, *Dawg, can we please get this started?*

Marcus texted back, *Who do you want to dance first? I have a lineup list. But Rev, a few of those folk need to go first so that we can concentrate on the real dances and not on what I fear will jump off on the dance floor with some of the "contestants."*

Denzelle glanced up at Marcus in the DJ's box and nodded in agreement. He texted, *Let Mr. Arvelle go first.*

Got it, Marcus texted, and went and found the music Mr. Arvelle had given him for his dance with Miss Roberta. He could not believe that frisky old man had selected "Smokestack Lightnin' " by Howlin' Wolf for his dance.

Chapter Twenty-nine

Mr. Arvelle whirled his Hoveround out to the middle of the gym floor. He couldn't believe they let him and Roberta set this thing off. Roberta stood by the Hoveround with her hand on the back of Mr. Arvelle's chair, full of herself and Mr. Arvelle. She believed they were the best-dressed couple—especially since their outfits matched Mr. Arvelle's Hoveround.

Roberta was wearing a black leather miniskirt, black lace tights, flat black suede boots that came up to her calves, a black leather jacket, and a gold satin tank top. Mr. Arvelle was dressed in black leather jeans, a black leather jacket, a gold satin shirt, and black gators. He was also wearing a gold chain with a medallion hanging off it and a black leather Kangol hat.

"Bro man looks like Johnny 'Guitar' Watson's little cousin," Charles whispered to Denzelle.

"You wrong, Frat," Denzelle said, and then asked. "Who told Miss Roberta she was sexy enough to rock a miniskirt?"

"Mr. Arvelle," Marsha answered. "She has some very pretty legs for a woman her age."

Denzelle gave Miss Roberta's legs a once over. Marsha was right. Old girl had some sexy legs.

"Shhhh," Veronica said. "They are getting ready to dance."

As soon as the first *bem-dem . . . duh-du-de-duhm . . . duh-de-duhm* chords of Howlin' Wolf's "Smokestack Lightnin'" blasted out over the system, some of the old heads got up out of their seats and started getting in the groove of the song.

"This has to be the ultimate, old-playah theme song, if I ever heard one," Denzelle whispered to Obadiah, who, with his wife, had come to stand with his best friend to witness this.

"I heard that," was all Obadiah could say.

"Shhssh, Obie," his wife, Lena, said. "It's getting ready to get good."

The song busted out into those classic lyrics, "Ahhh ohhh, smokestack lightnin'/shinin' just like gold." And then the best part of the song came on, "whu . . . ooooh . . . . hooo . . . whu . . . ooooh . . . hooo . . ."

"Whew," Keisha said, fanning herself. "I love myself some rap and hip-hop. But I declare, the late, great Howlin' Wolf is working that thang."

"I think he would have called it 'wurhkin','" Marsha said, with a soft laugh laying low in her voice.

Denzelle looked down at Marsha. He liked that sound coming from her. It was the kind of laugh that would make a brother kiss all down her neck just for the privilege of hearing that laugh.

"Y'all are missing this dance," Lena Quincy said, her expert eyes not missing a thing about the unspoken exchange going on between them. Denzelle was in love with Marsha and not ready to admit it.

Mr. Arvelle had his hands on the control button on the Hoveround. He was moving it back and forth to the beat of the song. Miss Roberta was dancing all up on the chair like she was on the stage of a strip club. When the song got to the part that said, "ahh . . . wuhhh . . . ohhh . . . /stop yo' train and let ahh po' boy ride," Miss Roberta put her back on the side of the chair and shimmied on down to the ground.

"Wurhkk it, guhl . . . wurhkk it. Show Big Daddy what you wurhkin' whit," Mr. Arvelle called out from his chair, right before he pulled a harmonica out of the breast pocket of his leather jacket and started to play on it with the song on the CD.

Miss Roberta backed off of the chair and turned to face Mr. Arvelle. She stood before the chair holding a fancy scarf above her head with both hands. Then Miss Roberta shimmied down to the ground and stayed there a few seconds.

All of the old men in the gymnasium were up, some holding onto fancy hats, giving out catcalls to Miss Roberta's provocative, old lady dance. Somebody yelled out, "I sho' do wish you wuz my woman!"

Miss Roberta looked in the direction the voice was coming from and frowned. She had broken up with Mister Quincey over a year ago, and he was still trying to find ways to get back with her. Mister was too slow for Miss Roberta. She needed a man who could keep up with her, like Arvelle.

"Isn't that your uncle yelling down at Miss Roberta, Obie?" Denzelle asked, laughing.

Obadiah closed his eyes and said, "Lord, give me strength." His uncle Mister was the child Obie's grandfather didn't know he had until his children with Obie's grandmother were all grown. Mister's mother, Miss Mary, had been Mr. Quincey's woman in the cut for years. Obie's grandfather had been so slick with that affair, nobody knew about it until Mr. Mister showed up at Grandpa Quincey's funeral with Miss Mary. That funeral had been so wild and crazy it could have been a reality TV show.

"Obie," Marsha said, "what is Mister's first name?"

"Mister."

"No, his first name," she asked him again.

"Mister."

"Mr. what?"

"Mr. Mister, Marsha," Obie said. He hated his uncle's name. What kind of fool gave their child a title for a first name?

"And his name is Mister because?" Keisha asked.

"Because his crazy mama wanted to make sure white folk couldn't get out of calling her son Mister," Obie told them.

"Roberta, Baby. Why come you dancing like that for him?

Why come, Baby? I want you to dance like that for me," Mister shouted out again. He knew Roberta was trying to act like she didn't hear him. But Mr. Mister Quincey wasn't having any of that. Arvelle had stolen his woman from him, and that joker was going to pay.

"Shut up, Mister!" Roberta hollered out. Miss Roberta was standing in the middle of that gymnasium floor looking like she should have been standing down on the steps of a liquor house, waiting for her man to come outside after she caught him up in there drinking with his other woman.

Mister was too through, and he was not going to let Roberta front him like that in front of all of these people. He should have been on that dance floor with Roberta, not Arvelle, who had to do the dance in a Hoveround.

Mr. Mister started coming up to the dance floor. Mr. Arvelle swung the chair around to face off with him. Miss Roberta pulled some hot pink lipstick out of her skirt pocket, put some on real quick, and posed next to the Hoveround.

Denzelle was about to go out on the dance floor and tell those old playahs, and that geriatric hoochie they were fighting over, to act like they had some daggone sense and get off the floor so that the real competition could take place. Miss Roberta and Mr. Arvelle were not even doing any of the dances that were on the list for the competitors.

He started walking forward when Charles put a hand on his shoulder and said, "You are going to have to let this play out, Frat. You stop this, and folk are going to get up and leave."

"But this is a church function," Denzelle began.

"That it is," Charles told him. "But when has the Gospel United Church ever had an event for a campaign for bishop and something crazy didn't jump off? Does 'WP21' mean anything to you, Denzelle?"

"I hope nobody gets cut out there," Marsha said. " 'Cause all three of them look like they are carrying a switchblade. You know, that kind with the fancy mother-of-pearl handle."

"Nahh, those two old men are carrying a straight razor," Keisha said.

"I can't wait for this to start up," Pierre whispered to Bay, who slapped his palm. "This puts the G in ghetto and a capital H in Hood."

The Howlin' Wolf song had finished playing in the midst of all of their ruckus. Marcus started the song again, so the dance could continue. As soon as the first cords of "bem-dem . . . duh-du-de-duhm . . . duh-de-duhm" and the Wolf proceeded to start singing, "Ahhh ohhh, smokestack lightning, shinin' just like gold," the whole gymnasium started swaying and clapping and getting down with the song.

"Are we at church or the club?" Denzelle asked.

"How 'bout asking if we're at the liquor house?" Obadiah said.

Denzelle sighed, and then looked up and whispered, "Lord, please be patient with us this evening, 'cause it's all the way live up in here."

The folk were clapping and hollering out and laughing, watching those three seventy-somethin's work that old playah song. As much as Denzelle and Obadiah hated to admit it, the beat was wurhkin' and the music was sounding good.

"You know, some of these old and funky blues songs have the same feel as some of the hot, old-school gospel songs," Veronica said, while shaking her shoulders back and forth to the beat.

Charles couldn't take his eyes off of Veronica. He didn't know she had it like that. Charles always thought Veronica was a bit too much on the prissy side to really get down—especially on a song like "Smokestack Lightnin'." But the way the girl was working that rhythm with her head and shoulders was making him want to find out how she worked that kind of beat with the swing of her hips.

By now Miss Roberta was walking one of those back in the day hoochie mama struts between Mr. Mister, who was standing, facing opposite of Mr. Arvelle, who was staring Mr. Mister down from his chair. Marcus, who loved all kinds of music, searched his computer for another song to kick in when this one ended. He found the perfect one—"Shake It Baby" by John Lee Hooker.

Miss Roberta heard the first set of chords of the song and hollered out, "That's my song." She put her hands on her hips and started shaking down to the floor and back up, in perfect sync with the music's liquor house beat. She looked from man to man, shaking her shoulders back and forth, waiting for them to catch up with her dancing.

Mr. Mister started doing the cool, old-black-man dance walk. He stared at Miss Roberta real hard, pursed his lips together, and pointed at her. He then moved his shoulders up and down, and then back and forth, one shoulder at a time. Mr. Mister got to walking to the beat and moved his feet to the beat, heel to toe, one step at a time. He looked like he was doing the old playah's version of the Crip Walk.

"Gone head, Mr. Mister," one cute old lady in an usher uniform called out from her post. She was waving her white gloved hand all around and dancing in place.

Obadiah looked up and said, "Lord, Lord, Lord. Please forgive these old people at this church."

Not to be outdone by a man who could walk good, Mr. Arvelle reached back and got a good whiff of his oxygen. He gave Mr. Mister a stern look and maneuvered the Hoveround so that it scooted forward in the direction of where Miss Roberta was standing to the beat of the music. Then he backed the scooter up and turned it around. After that, Mr. Arvelle moved his feet off of the scooter's foot guards and started dancing in his chair like he was standing up on the dance floor. He moved his shoulders back and forth and shook his narrow hips around in that chair.

Mr. Arvelle was working it so until Miss Roberta danced back up to the chair and shimmied down to the ground. She shimmied back up and took Mr. Arvelle's hand, and started dancing with him like they were at a sock hop.

The crowd went crazy when John Lee Hooker's voice rang out, "Shake it, Baby./Shake it, Baby./Shake it, Baby./For me./For me./One time./One time./For me./Come on heah!/Come on heah!" They were up dancing and jumping around like they were on *Soul Train* or *American Bandstand*.

Denzelle would have tried to get control of the crowd if they were not having so much fun, and at church. He looked down at Marsha, who was getting it and shaking her head and hips to the beat. Mr. Mister, Mr. Arvelle, and Miss Roberta finished out the song by walking together to the beat. Folks started clapping and whistling and gave them a standing ovation.

"Okay," Obadiah said. "Soooo, what dance were they doing? Or, to be more precise, what dance did they put on the registration form? Rumba? Jitterbug? The Bop?"

"The Hoveround?" Lena said, and started laughing.

"No, all joking aside," Obadiah continued, "folk are ready to crown them the queen, king, and kang of the dance, and we don't even know what the heck they were out there doing?"

Chapter Thirty

The crowd was still up laughing and clapping several minutes after they walked off the dance floor. Keisha looked at the program and said, "Yikes."

"Yikes," Marsha said. "What do you mean by 'yikes'?"

"You and Rev are next."

"To dance?" Marsha asked, hoping in vain the answer was a flat-out no.

"Naw, to ride around the city of Raleigh in matching Hoverounds," Keisha answered and rolled her eyes upward.

Marsha's flip-phone cell buzzed. It was Marcus.

"When are you going to get a real cell phone?" Keisha asked Marsha.

Marsha shrugged and flipped open the cell. She liked this phone and was going to keep it as long as she could.

"Mom. I can't find the music you gave me."

"It's the Charlie Wilson song, 'Life of the Party.'"

"It's not in my system, and the backup CD is gone," Marcus said.

"What about YouTube? I don't think it will be that noticeable."

"The signal isn't that good in the gym, and I don't want the song to freeze right in the middle of you and Rev dancing."

"I thought you checked all of that before the event."

"Mom, I did. And you know me. You know I take my DJ work seriously. Somebody tampered with it."

Marsha sighed. This was the second time something had happened to mess with them and their performance. At first she thought it was Tatiana. But as crazy and a trip as Tatiana was, this was not in her bag of tricks. She looked around the gymnasium, searching for someone who was watching Marcus and looking amused.

Xavier Franklin was sitting in the back next to Camille, wishing he were sitting with Tatiana. He dared not try and sneak a look over at her. Camille was watching him intently, and he didn't want a scene.

Xavier noticed the back and forth line of communication between the DJ and Marsha Metcalf. They looked a whole lot alike.

"Must be her son," Xavier murmured.

"You say something, Sweetheart?" Camille said in a sweet voice.

Xavier always marveled at how sweet and melodic his wife's voice was. In spite of all of her haughty and ugly ways, the girl still managed to have one of the sweetest voices he'd ever heard on a woman. In fact, he always thought Camille sounded a whole lot like Janet Jackson. While Xavier hated to talk to Camille for any length of time, he loved to hear her voice, especially over the telephone.

"No," Xavier answered. He continued watching Marcus search for something and smiled. Morris Palmer had done him a solid, messing with the music like that.

First, he and Luther Howard had made sure that Denzelle Flowers's tuxedo was not available. And now the DJ could not find the music for Denzelle Flowers's and Marsha Metcalf's dance. This was going to be good.

Xavier knew those two had practiced and practiced on Charlie Wilson's "Life of the Party." And now, they didn't have the song. The chances of them finding a suitable new song for their dance before it was time to perform were pretty slim to unlikely.

Mom, Marcus texted. *Do you think you and Rev can do your dance to "Night to Remember" by Shalamar?*

Let me talk to Denzelle and find out, Marsha texted back.

I hear ya', playah, Marcus texted. *Gone head and ask your man what he wants to do.*

Marsha looked up at the DJ box. Marcus was staring at his mom and laughing. He was so enjoying watching her deal with liking a man. Reverend Flowers was a good brother and liked his mom a lot. That was a good thing, because Marcus didn't want to have to kick the pastor's behind for trying to play his mother.

"We need to get on the dance floor, Marsha," Denzelle said.

"Marcus can't find our music. And the signal for YouTube is not that good."

Denzelle scowled and looked around the gymnasium for Tatiana. She had the natural nerve to tamper with their music. But the tux? She wouldn't have gone through all of that trouble to mess up his tux. Tatiana may have known about this, but she was not the culprit.

He looked around the gymnasium a few more seconds and saw Xavier Franklin watching Marsha, Marcus, and him intently.

"What does he have to gain from sabotaging a dance number?" Denzelle speculated out loud.

"A lot," Marsha told him.

"Well," Denzelle said, "Now that our music is missing, what song does Marcus want us to use?"

"Shalamar's 'Night to Remember,'" Marsha told him. "Do you like it?"

"Love the song," he told her. "Marcus is the man."

Denzelle grinned down at Marsha. He gave her ponytail a tug and said, "You know what, Honey? We can definitely make this happen."

"Oooo," Keisha said. "Did you all hear that? Pastor just

called Marsha 'Honey.' And he sounded like he was talking to his woman."

"Maybe because he is talking to his woman," Veronica said.

"Yeah. 'Cause D sho' 'nuff is standing next to Marsha like she's his woman," Lena said in a very quiet voice.

The last thing she wanted to happen was for Denzelle to get cold feet about Marsha. As much as Lena loved Denzelle, there were times when she wanted to slap the Kappa Crimson off of his behind. He had been a big player back in the day. Now here he was, with the audacity to get scared over a woman who would take better care of his heart than he did.

Lena had to pray to hold her peace with Denzelle, because he was too smart and smooth for his own good. And that was part of the problem. The big, bad, smooth, Denzelle Flowers could not believe he had fallen for a little Miss Priss, on the goofy side woman like Marsha Metcalf. But as far as Lena was concerned, Marsha was exactly the kind of woman Denzelle needed in his life.

Marsha would love Denzelle the way he needed to and deserved to be loved. She would take good care of him. And she would have his back.

Marsha was sweet and on the goofy side. But she was also a mighty woman of God, and not one to mess with. Lena had seen Marsha take down a few folk, and she had barely raised her voice. But when she was done, the person looked like they had been in an altercation with somebody who had been trained by Special Ops.

"You got cold feet," Keisha said.

"In more ways than one," Denzelle said, as he watched Marsha getting ready for them to dance. He wasn't sure how he was going to feel dancing in front of folk, even though he was a very good dancer. But even more, Denzelle wasn't sure how he was going to handle dancing so close and intimately with Marsha.

He looked across the gymnasium. His enemies were sitting there hoping he would fall flat on his face—literally and spiritually. But he reasoned that they had to be awfully worried about him to go so far as to mess with his tux and then try and jack up the music.

Denzelle looked upward and smiled. He touched his heart with his hand and thought, Thank You. Sometimes the Lord lets you experience some trials at the hands of your enemies, just to let you know they were there, and also very afraid of you. Experiencing their antics was one way to alert you to the extent of their feelings where you were concerned.

"Keisha," Denzelle said. "I think it's time you introduced me and my dance partner."

Denzelle grabbed Marsha's hand and slid his fingers through hers. He marveled at how his fingers could fit into her tiny hand. It took considerable restraint to keep himself from kissing all five of the fingertips on Marsha's sweet little hardworking hand.

"And now for our second contestants," Keisha said, and gave Denzelle and Marsha time to get out onto the middle of the dance floor. "Dancing the fox-trot to Shalamar's 'Night to Remember' is our pastor, Reverend Denzelle Flowers, with his partner, Ms. Marsha Metcalf."

The whole gymnasium went up in a roar of whistles, hand claps, stomps, and cheers.

Marsha gazed up at Denzelle's surprised expression.

"What?" she asked. "You didn't know your folk loved you like this, Boy?"

He closed his eyes for a second and nodded. It had never occurred to him that he was so loved.

"Sometimes," Marsha said, "church folk don't always know how to let you know that they are crazy 'bout you, Boy."

Tatiana glanced over at her husband, Todd, and clenched her teeth together. There was Denzelle out there looking fine and sexy in a red tuxedo jacket, some dark jeans, a white shirt, and his red bow tie hanging out of the jacket's breast pocket like it was a pocket square. Tatiana gave herself a moment to reminisce about what was behind that attire—a whole lot of swagger, and then some.

She fanned herself with the program and sighed, "Whew" out loud.

"Are you alright?" Todd asked his wife. He followed Tatiana's gaze to Denzelle standing with Marsha and frowned. He said, "You left him for me, remember."

Xavier was watching Tatiana go gaga over Denzelle, too. He didn't like it any more than Todd did. Women always did that to Denzelle—acted like they wanted to throw their thongs at him. He couldn't stand the way people, especially women, went all crazy over Denzelle Flowers.

That is precisely why he was going to make sure the bishops voted to ban divorced preachers from being a bishop if they remarried while the ex-spouse was alive. That policy would fix Denzelle, and fix him good.

Camille locked eyes with Tatiana in a staring match. Tatiana got tired of looking at Camille. She rolled her eyes to break the stare, and then turned away so Camille couldn't roll her eyes back.

But Camille was not in the mood to be bothered with Tatiana and her mess this evening. She pulled out her iPhone and texted, *He is still my husband, B. Don't hate 'cause my man is fine and yours is—well, I don't know what we would call your man.*

Tatiana's eyes got big. How had Camille gotten her number? She knew it wasn't from Xavier, because he was very careful about that. She got ready to text something nasty back, and almost swore out loud. Camille's number was private.

Camille stared back at Tatiana and grinned. When she knew Xavier wasn't paying any attention to her, she licked her finger and wrote an invisible point in the air. Then Camille gave Tatiana the finger and acted like she was scratching down in her weave when she saw some church folk looking at her.

Tatiana sucked on her teeth as quietly as she could. The last thing she wanted or needed was Todd all up in her grill. She was going to let Camille enjoy and savor this moment. But what Camille Creighton Franklin didn't know was that her days were numbered. Tatiana wished she'd be able to see the expression on Camille's face the morning she woke up dead.

"You look wonderful," Denzelle whispered in Marsha's ear.

He wasn't the only one who thought Marsha looked wonderful in those leggings, those sparkling shoes, her hair and makeup, and the big tuxedo shirt hugging her body in all the right ways with that cummerbund she had tied around her waist. Reverend Larry Pristeen couldn't get over how good Marsha Metcalf was looking to him out on the dance floor.

Reverend Pristeen liked Marsha a lot more than he'd ever admit to anybody. He thought she was fine and sexy and the kind of woman a brother couldn't keep his hands off of. Larry was furious that Marsha was getting ready to dance with Denzelle Flowers. And he was pissed off over her looking so happy standing on the dance floor in Denzelle's arms.

Larry assumed Marsha would respond favorably to the stale, dry crumbs of attention he tossed at the women he found himself liking. He didn't care that his game was self-absorbed and unkind where the other person was concerned. In fact, when Larry Pristeen tried to play Marsha with that game, all it did was earn him a special spot on her list. That day he said, "You could make a man fall hard for you, Marsha Metcalf. But I don't want to make the mistake of falling for you. I want to bask in being single and in how that makes my ministry and the national singles' program I'm building better. You are single, but you want to go out on a date or talk to a man on the telephone. I don't see you striving to sacrifice enough to earn enough points to be with me."

Marsha had stood there listening to Larry, thinking about all she'd sacrificed and done without over the past few years. She thought about her long work hours and tight budget, losing her home, wanting a new car but having to wait to buy it, and being so completely alone because the so-called good brothers didn't have sense enough to try and get to know her.

And here was Larry Pristeen, with his six-figure-plus income, top of the line BMW, and three-thousand-dollar plain black suit, standing up in her face talking mess about sacrifice. Marsha was sacrificing alright. She was making a huge sacrifice to stop herself from beating Larry Pristeen down to the lowest common denominator that he was.

But she took the high road that day and simply walked off and away from Reverend Pristeen, determined to never, ever have anything to do with him again. Even when he came to her church to preach, Marsha didn't give Larry the time of day. In fact, as soon as he got up to preach, Marsha got her purse and walked right out of the sanctuary. She went down to the church's dining room and helped the Culinary Committee set the tables for the church's special dinner for their so-called guest preacher.

Now Larry was looking at Denzelle Flowers holding on to Marsha Metcalf like he'd perish if he let her go. And Larry Pristeen didn't like that one bit. Reverend Pristeen, a man who pretended he was above basic human emotions like passion, jealousy, and resentment, decided right then that he was going to get Denzelle Flowers, and get him good.

He was going to the upcoming Board of Bishops meeting in Raleigh, and would be lobbying for them to vote in a policy that would make it impossible for Denzelle to have his cake and eat it, too. Larry wanted to see just how good it would feel when Flowers realized he couldn't have Marsha and run for bishop, too. That would fix both of them. Marsha would have to be alone, and Denzelle would become a bishop without having someone wonderful by his side.

Chapter Thirty-one

Denzelle saw Larry watching them. Many years ago he had a healthy dose of respect for the brother. But that respect ended when he discovered Larry was a self-serving, power-hungry ho underneath that fiery-looking evangelist persona.

Marcus saw the frown flash across Denzelle's face and followed his gaze to the source.

"That fool," Marcus mumbled, and nodded at Keisha, who said, "Are you ready to Rrrruuummmmbbbbllllle, Pastor?" in her best imitation of a TV wrestling announcer's voice.

"Do yo' thang, Rev!" one of the teens in the audience shouted out.

Denzelle and Marsha positioned themselves to break off into the very first move of the fox-trot. Marsha held her breath. She had practiced alone and with Denzelle. They had worked hard to put those steps in place to Charlie Wilson's "Life of the Party." It had been hard to figure out how to do that particular dance to a song like that. Now they had to figure out how to make this work to Shalamar, and without any time to redo the steps.

"It's now or never, Beautiful," Denzelle whispered in Marsha's ear, when the first chords of the song came on.

Marsha looked in Denzelle's eyes and whispered, "Wait," when they heard buhdah dadadada da-dahh da duhdahda duhdahda . . .

"Move very slightly to this beat," Marsha whispered, and smiled when Denzelle swayed his body in sync with hers. She then whispered, "Go," when Jody Watley's voice came on with "So, now, my love to you, baby, I surrender./Get ready, tonight, gonna make this a night to remember."

At that point they moved smoothly and effortlessly across the dance floor in a very funky and bluesy rendition of the fox-trot. Denzelle and Marsha looked like they were gliding across the floor on some roller skates, they were so smooth. Marsha stared up in his eyes and smiled, and then blushed when he winked and took them across the floor in another rep of the dance.

Denzelle stopped and moved back from Marsha, twirled her around and pulled her back in his arms. She hesitated coming back, and laughed when he tugged at her, all to the rhythm of the song. As soon as she got close to him, Denzelle snatched her tight and did two more reps of the dance.

Folks were up on their feet, quiet, with their eyes glued on the couple dancing on the floor. Denzelle and Marsha forgot all about their audience and concentrated on the feel of each other's movements. At that point, Denzelle slowed down their pace and swayed them back and forth like he'd seen it done on the real *Dancing with the Stars*.

Marsha got so caught up in that movement, until she brought her leg up to his waist. Denzelle caught her leg underneath the thigh and dragged her across the floor with him. The crowd was cheering and whistling.

Then Marsha extended her arms out very gracefully and let them fall up and over her head. Denzelle slid his hands down her back to her waist, just in time to catch Marsha arching her back and falling in his arms like she was on a swing. The crowd went crazy.

Denzelle pulled Marsha up to him, and then they both broke away and started dancing free-style. Folk at the church knew Marsha could dance. They weren't prepared, however, for their pastor's skills on the dance floor. Marsha switched around to stand in front of Denzelle and did the Beyoncé booty bounce.

Folk yelled out, "Get it, Girl! Work that thang!"

Denzelle, not to be outdone, pretended to spank Marsha to the catcalls and whistles from the audience. Marsha started doing the Crip Walk with Denzelle Crip Walking hot on her tail. Then she stopped, turned back around to face Denzelle, and started doing the stanky leg dance. Again, Denzelle joined in on the dance.

By now they were down low on the floor. As the song started nearing the end, Denzelle stood behind Marsha, real close. He put a hand on her waist and grabbed her extended arm. They danced the fox-trot off of the dance floor, in perfect step with each other, with Denzelle standing behind Marsha. They danced like that until the dance ended.

When the music stopped, Marsha turned back to face Denzelle, who wrapped his arms around her and held her until the standing ovation ended. When she was about to pull away, he whispered, "Do you dance like that in private?"

Marsha laughed and whispered, "You are such a nasty boy."

"You like it, Girl."

They walked back over to the MC podium, trying to act like they had not felt the heat and passion of that dance. Their friends were eyeballin' them like they were trying to find more evidence of the feelings those two were running from where the other was concerned.

"Soooo," Lena began, "I take it that you two really, I mean really, like really-really-really enjoyed that dance."

"I'll say," Obie added. He was having a hard time keeping it together. The expression on Denzelle's face alone was priceless. Obie couldn't believe Denzelle and Marsha were dumb enough to believe no one was picking up on their feelings for each other. But then again, this was Denzelle and Marsha. The first one was running from love like it was some kind of monster on *Grimm*. The other was working overtime to convince herself that what she felt was just the residual effect of an outstanding performance.

"It was a wonderful experience," Marsha told them in her best church-girl voice. She hoped that would stop the looks and the speculation, and temper some of the conversations folk were prone to have about the two of them.

"I bet it was," was all Veronica said.

"I know it was," Lena said and pointed toward the crowd. "And there's your proof."

While members of New Jerusalem Gospel United Church were still basking in the afterglow of their pastor's riveting dance performance, several of his known, and now newly known, enemies were up and walking out of the gymnasium as if this were some kind of protest.

Xavier Franklin, Bishop Thomas Jefferson, his wife, Violetta, and her uncle Raphael, Tatiana, and Larry Pristeen were all walking out together, deep in conversation. Xavier's wife, Camille, and Tatiana's husband, Todd, were still sitting down in the gym looking perplexed by what had just transpired. The group walked out via the exit that was closest to where Denzelle was standing. On the way out of the door, Violetta's uncle was overheard saying in a rich Caribbean voice.

"Neeecee, I am not pleased at this turn of events. We have worked on our routine for over a week, and I am anxious to show these smug Americans what we are capable of."

Violetta ignored Uncle Raphael, whom she wanted to leave in St. Thomas but didn't because he needed to see a specialist at Duke Medical Center about his feet. She was glad they had decided to forfeit their place in the competition. His feet were too much of an eyesore and source of ridicule for this particular crowd. Plus, she liked being the showstopper in a dance event and knew they would not beat that fine preacher and his dance partner.

"When did Larry Pristeen start hanging out with 'them folk'?" Obadiah asked.

"When he saw me dancing with Marsha," Denzelle answered evenly.

"And jealousy would make him want to hook up with that pack of rabid wolves?" Obadiah asked him.

"I've come to learn that Larry talks a good game when he is

wearing a robe and feeling safe behind his or somebody else's pulpit. But he's not all he's cracked up to be. He is not that much better than Xavier Franklin—just better at making folk think he's a better man and preacher."

"Well, he's not getting anywhere worth going, hanging around with them," Lena told them. "I don't like the way I felt when they walked by."

"Me, neither," Veronica said. "They are up to something, and it's bad."

Denzelle's first reaction was to get upset. He knew whatever it was had to do with him making a bid for an Episcopal seat, and their desire to destroy any chances he had to get elected as a new bishop. But he had to trust God—he couldn't waste precious time worrying about something that was better left in the Father's Hands.

He looked around the gymnasium. Camille Franklin was sitting alone looking sour and bitter. Todd was sitting alone looking pissed. Denzelle tilted his head to the side and studied Todd for a moment. He'd never seen a pissed-off Todd Townsend. And if he didn't know better, Denzelle would wager that Tatiana's days with Todd were numbered.

"Your ex's husband is really pissed," Charles Robinson said. He'd been studying Todd, too. "I sure hope Xavier Franklin is putting it on Tatiana so good she forgets what she will give up when Todd divorces her."

"Yeah," Denzelle said. "Todd looks like a man who has had enough."

"Rev," Keisha said. "Did you bring the ballots for the ballot machines in the back of the gymnasium?"

Denzelle shook his head. He knew there was something he had forgotten to do.

"Come on," he said to Marsha. "Help me get the ballots loaded up on the cart."

"Okay," Marsha said, and followed him out of the gymnasium to his office.

Chapter Thirty-two

"Be careful, Honey," Denzelle said to Marsha and grabbed her hand. "It's dark. I don't want you to bump into something and hurt yourself."

He swiped his electronic key in the slot on the door. As soon as the door swung open, Denzelle said, "Office lights," and the room lit up. He looked around the office until he found the ballot box and said, "Roll that red cart over here. We can load the ballot boxes on it."

Marsha pushed the cart right next to Denzelle and pulled at one of the heavy ballot boxes.

"Stop, Marsha," he commanded. "That's too heavy for you."

She nodded and stood back while Denzelle loaded up four boxes full of ballots.

"Baby," Denzelle said, "get those boxes of pens off of that shelf over there."

Marsha grabbed the boxes and put them on the bottom shelf on the cart.

'Thank you, Honey," he said, and smiled when Marsha blushed through the most delightful smile. He reached out and tugged at her curly ponytail.

"You know you look adorable and sexy in that outfit," he said. "That can get you in trouble with the right man."

"Boy! It's just my dance outfit."

"Just your dance outfit," Denzelle said in a light, falsetto voice that was meant to mimic Marsha's. He tugged at her pony-tail one more time.

"Marsha, I knew you could dance. But I didn't know you had it going on like that."

"Thank you, Denzelle," she answered. "You're not too bad yourself."

"Yeah," he said with a chuckle. "I've been told I could moon-light as a male stripper, if I ever need to make some money on the side, when you all try to hold back on your tithe money."

"You know you are wrong," Marsha said.

"You don't think I could be a male exotic dancer, Miss Marsha?"

"Well, I can't imagine you doing the exotic dance, dance, Denzelle. I mean, you don't look like you can drop down and do that grind baby dance male strippers do."

He raised an eyebrow and said, "What do you know about how a male exotic dancer moves? What have you been doing when you're not at church?"

"Denzelle, I'm a grown woman, with a grown son. I've seen some male dancers. I know how they move and carry on," she told him.

"And where did you see all of this?"

"Veronica and I went with Keisha to a fashion show Dayee-sha Mitchell sponsored at the opening of Metro's newest Yeah Yeah Hip-Hop Store last year. She had male dancers and food, and it was fun."

"Ohhhh really," Denzelle said, laughing. "Going to Yeah Yeah to make it rain for some male dancers is your kind of outing, huh?"

"No, silly."

"But you sound like you were having a lot of fun over at Yeah Yeah, making it rain."

"Of course I was having a lot of fun. I was with my girls. And I always have a lot of fun when I'm out rolling with my girls."

"Soooo, if I start dancing for you, will you make it rain for me?" Denzelle asked in a low whisper.

Marsha laughed.

"I cannot imagine you doing the make it rain dance, Denzelle."

"Oh really," he said, with a mannish grin spreading across his face, and he turned on his Bose iPod system. "Let me see if I can find some make it rain music for you, Girl. I hope you have enough cash on you, because I don't take checks or credit cards—just cash."

"You that good, huh?"

"You tell me, Baby," he answered, and started rapping and bouncing around to an old-school number—Petey Pablo's "Freek-a-Leek."

Marsha could not believe that Denzelle knew every word to this song. And it had never occurred to her that his voice was a bit similar to the rapper, Petey Pablo. Denzelle was dancing around in the office, moving with smooth precision. He rolled right up on Marsha, who was standing off from him.

"Don't move now, Baby," he said. "I'm just getting warmed up."

Denzelle raised his hands up in the air and moved from side to side. Then he took his hands and danced them around Marsha's body. She moved back, and he moved back up on her, like one of those fresh brothers at the club who believed they had enough game to get any good-looking woman in the room.

He bit his bottom lip, grabbed at the waist of his pants and started dancing down toward the floor, rolling his hips like the younger hip-hop dancers would do on a song like "Freek-a-Leek." Marsha let a giggle escape. That only made Denzelle dance some more. She moved back, and he rolled right back up on her. This time Denzelle was licking his lips and winking at her. He did that dance until the song ended.

By the time the music stopped completely, Denzelle had backed Marsha up on his desk. She tried to move but he held his position.

"Denzelle."

"Yeah, Baby," he answered, and ran a fingertip across the tip of her ear.

"We're at church and in your office."

"And?"

Marsha searched for the right words. But before she could say anything, Denzelle lifted her chin up and touched his lips to hers.

She sighed and lowered her eyes away from his. Marsha wasn't sure how she was supposed to respond to this kiss. She knew how she wanted to respond. But what did a girl do when the man she was crazy about was also her pastor, and on top of that, kissing her in his office, which was the church office? Honestly, how did a sister run that play? There was nothing in the playbook to help out with a situation like this one.

"What's wrong?" Denzelle whispered in her ear. "Am I making you uncomfortable?"

"No."

"Then talk to me, Honey."

Marsha tried to think of a nice way to tell him and opted for the truth. She said, "I don't know how to respond to you."

Denzelle backed up off of Marsha. He'd never heard that line before. He frowned and said, "What are you talking about?"

She said, "Well, see, it's like this, Denzelle. You started doing that dance and jiggling all up on me, and I didn't know you had it like that with the moves. Then you got close and started kissing on me, and I liked it a lot. And I wanted to give as good as it looked like you were about to give. But I don't want to give you the wrong impression of me . . . and . . ."

Denzelle raised up his hands and said, "Stop. Stop. Stooppppppp! That is way too much information to digest. Come at me again."

"You are a minister, you are my pastor, this is the church office, and you are kissing me like . . ."

". . . like I'm trying to be your man?" Denzelle asked her softly, with laughter laced through his voice. He knew Marsha was at a loss as to how to handle him right now. The girl was straight up with no chaser, and not good at playing courtship games. She was what he and Obadiah called the real deal.

"Baby, you don't ever have to be concerned about my reaction to you wanting to be all up on me. 'Cause, Girl, that's what I want—you all up on me."

"You know you are something else, Denzelle."

"So I've been told," he said, and got all up on Marsha. She tried to back away from him. But there wasn't anywhere for her to back away from to, since she was pressed up on his desk.

Denzelle grabbed the back of Marsha's neck and kissed her deeply and with so much passion, she was scared she wouldn't be able to stop him if he decided to take this matter further.

"I want you, Marsha," Denzelle said in a low and husky whisper. He slid his hand down over her hip and brought her knee up to rest on his hip. He pressed her back on the desk.

"You feel that."

Marsha nodded. She didn't know what to do with *this* Denzelle.

He moved on Marsha and said, "Do you feel that?"

"Yes," Marsha said, hoping he would back down.

Denzelle kissed Marsha again. He had so much heat in him, she could feel it all over his body. If they had been outside in the cold, his body heat would have kept them both warm.

His lips trailed down her neck. She sighed in an effort not to moan. He found that spot on her neck. Marsha guarded that spot like folk clung to their purses in a large crowd. She didn't know how that boy found that spot, and so fast.

Denzelle caught on real quick that he had hit the right spot on Marsha. He had always wondered where the hot points were on this woman, and how to find them. And here was one, plain as day and his for the taking. He kissed her neck again, and ran his fingers across that spot. Marsha moaned softly and said, "What are you trying to do to me, Boy?"

At that point, Denzelle lost all control. He tightened his grip

on Marsha and pushed her back on the desk, knocking everything in the way on the floor. He pressed his body on her and
kissed her neck again. It tasted like Coco Chanel perfume.

"Ummmm. I want you, Marsha. Right now, right here."

Marsha knew this was not the time or place or moment for
that, but she was having a heck of a time getting out of this situation. It never occurred to her that she wanted Denzelle this much.
About the only thing helping her keep it together was that she was
scared to death of crossing that line with a man. It had been a long
time since she'd made love, and this felt like the very first time.

"I'm scared, Denzelle," she said, in such a sweet voice that he
had to get off of her and pull her up in his arms.

"Ohhh, Baby. I am so sorry. I didn't mean to scare you like
that."

He kissed her lips gently and said, "Honey, I would never
hurt or scare you over something like this."

Marsha rested in Denzelle's arms. It felt like heaven to be in
that spot. She wrapped her arms around his waist and found that
she couldn't fight the tears that were now streaming down her
face. Marsha thought she'd never be in a man's warm embrace
again. And sometimes she wondered how she was going to live
out the rest of her life never, ever feeling this again.

"What's wrong, Baby? I didn't hurt you, did I?"

"No."

"Talk to me, Beautiful," he told her.

"I'm scared that once I let go, you will back off from me, because you're worried I'm responding to you too deeply and too
fast. It's a hard and painful place to be in, Denzelle. And I don't
know why men create it. You push and do everything to win this
kind of affection from a woman. And when we feel safe enough
to respond, you run away—as if we did something wrong.

"I wish God would deal with you all on this. I wish He would
do something to make it hurt real bad for you to run, and then
only give relief when you turn back and do right by grabbing us to
you."

Denzelle's heart ached listening to those words. Marsha was saying what so many women felt. He was hearing what scared so many men—the truth.

It hurt to know how much hurt brothers had doled out on sisters when they didn't want to handle the raw truth of a woman's feelings about them. You couldn't reach out to a woman, woo her, talk all sweet to her, whisper low and sexy words in her ear, grab and hold her in your arms, kiss her with heat and passion, let her feel your manhood brushing up against her, and then get surprised because she cared enough about you to respond with the passion you poked at in the first place.

What in the hell did a so-called reasonable thinking man expect from a woman? The fact that she even allowed the conversation to begin meant she liked you and thought enough of you to talk to you. Why would a man be surprised or scared by a woman's response to him? It was crazy. And men were engaging in this insane behavior every day.

Obadiah was right. God needed to roll up on every man who'd ever played this game and deal with him in as harsh a manner as that man dealt with the woman in his life. Some of these brothers needed to be forced to watch a good woman bask in the love and arms of another man who had the sense God gave him, when it came to being blessed to find a true treasure. Some of these men needed to suffer like women were out there suffering.

"Marsha, I am so sorry for doing whatever it is that I do to make you feel like this," Denzelle said, blinking hard to hold back his own tears. His heart was so torn up and convicted. How in the world could he have been so deceived to act like this with a woman who would treat his heart like it was a rare and precious mineral? Men sure did need some serious wake-up calls. And church men needed them more than ever.

Chapter Thirty-three

The door to the pastor's office opened, causing Denzelle and Marsha to jump and try to assume a more neutral position with each other. They both sighed with relief when they saw Lena and Obadiah coming through the door.

"Obie, man, you scared the mess out of me."

"I'm sure I did," Obadiah told him, as his well-trained preacher eyes took in the landscape of the office. They landed on the empty desk.

"What happened to your desk, D?" Obadiah asked with mischief dancing in his eyes. He didn't dare look at Lena, because he would have lost his composure.

"Nothing, man. You know."

"Nahh, playah. I don't know. So why don't you school an old preacher like myself?"

"You wrong, Obie. And you know it."

"Denzelle, what's wrong is that you are so in love with Marsha, you were about to try and make love to her on the desk in your office at church while a big program is going on across the way," Lena said.

Marsha was both mortified and relieved to hear someone say out loud that Denzelle was in love with her. She knew this deep in her heart but sometimes second-guessed herself on this truth.

Denzelle didn't protest. He held his hands out to the side

and said, "Guilty as charged." He turned to Marsha. "How long have you known this?"

"Known what?"

"That I'm in love with you," Denzelle told her, shocked at how easy it was for him to say it, now that he had been called out.

"For a while."

"And that means?" Denzelle hated it when women did that.

"Since you started the Pastor's Aide Club."

"I see. And you didn't do or say anything? Why?"

"Because it wasn't my place to try and help you know that you loved me. And it certainly wasn't my place to try and help you tell me, Denzelle," Marsha said in a very firm and soft voice. "I'm not telling a man that he loves me. Not happening."

Denzelle held out his hand and said, "Come here, Beautiful. You are right. No woman should ever have to tell a man he is in love with her. I don't care how much she knows that man loves her. He needs to say it and lay claim to her."

"Then tell her, Denzelle," Lena said. "Tell Marsha how you feel."

Denzelle held both of Marsha's hands in his. He said, "Marsha, I love you. I've loved you much longer than you've known I love you. Baby, I not only love you, I adore you, Girl. I want you in my life."

"I love you, too, Denzelle. And I've loved you longer than you've known, too."

"Marry me, Marsha."

She looked at him like something was wrong. He said, "Is there a problem with me asking you to marry me?"

"We've never even been on a date."

"And? Whoever said that things have to always work in accordance with a plan or playbook? Sometimes the Lord does things differently. You have to go with what you know works in your heart—the part of your heart the Lord is pulling at.

"So marry me, Marsha. Marry me right now, right here,

right at this moment. We have a preacher, and one witness. We can do this now and then go and get the license tomorrow. Obie will sign it in the morning. Just think of it as us postdating the ceremony."

"I . . . always . . ."

"You always thought you would have a wedding when you remarried, right?" Lena asked her.

Marsha nodded.

"Marsha, you have had to wait a long time for a good man to come into your life. Marry Denzelle right now. You can throw a big fancy party later. But right now, you need to marry this man."

"Okay," Marsha said. "I'll marry you right now, Denzelle. But I don't have a ring for you. And it's okay that you don't have a ring for me."

"I have a ring for you, Marsha. I bought it during a lucid moment when I was able to admit to myself that I loved you. And I can tell you that it was one of the most frightening moments I've ever experienced. Getting shot at during an FBI rumble was never that scary. Girl, I even figured out your ring size."

Denzelle went to the other side of his desk, unlocked and opened the drawer, and dug down in it. He pulled out a royal blue silk box and flipped it open. In it was the most beautiful wedding ring any of them had ever seen.

"I had this made special for you."

The ring had a platinum band with six sapphires—a blue stone, two pink stones, two lavender stones, and a blue stone— bordered with high-quality diamond chips.

"It's lovely," Marsha said through tears, and held out her hand for him to slide the ring on her finger.

They both turned to Obadiah, who pulled a Bible off of Denzelle's bookshelf and turned to the marriage ceremony. He began to read, "Dearly Beloved, we are gathered here . . ."

It took fifteen minutes for Denzelle and Marsha to become husband and wife. Obadiah, who was now a second witness, and Lena signed a makeshift license he created and printed out.

"This is your license for your personal journal. You can get the other one tomorrow."

Their impromptu marriage license read:

This marriage is ordained and sanctioned by the Lord on the 19th day of April in the year of our Lord, 2014. It is signed by two witnesses, who also bear witness for the Lord, Jesus Christ. These two, Denzelle Flowers and Marsha Metcalf, are joined in Holy Matrimony by the laws that govern the saints of God. They will sign an additional license to adhere to the laws of the State of North Carolina, Wake County, in the United States of America.

Signed and witnessed by: *Obadiah Quincey and Lena Quincey of Durham, North Carolina.*

"Don't put this in a journal. You all frame this as a reminder that this is about a marriage and not just a wedding. People have wonderful weddings. You want an incredible marriage," Lena said. "And you all need to leave."

"But we have to get the ballots out there, so they will be ready at the end of the program," Marsha said. She had worked so hard on this and wanted to see it out to the end.

"We've got this, Marsha," Obadiah told her. "You go with your groom and take care of some much needed business."

"But, Veronica and Keisha and Dayeesha. And Marcus! What about Marcus? He's my baby, and he wasn't here. Oh, dear!" Marsha put her hands up to her face. She couldn't believe she'd gotten married without the most special man in her life being present. She started to cry.

"Honey," Denzelle said. "It's okay. It's okay. Marcus knows."

"Huh?"

"I texted him and tried to get him back here. But he said," Denzelle reached inside of his coat and pulled out his phone. Here, you read it for yourself:

Handle your business, Rev. I know Mom wanted me to
be there for something like that. But, the Lord spoke to
my heart and told me to stay put. Said this was real private between you and Mom. And trust me, Rev, I don't
have those kinds of conversations with the Lord very
often.

Tears streamed down Marsha's face. Her baby was a man.
This text was proof. And he approved of the marriage. She said,
"This has to be the best wedding present anyone has ever re-
ceived."

"I'll say," Denzelle said. "Marcus is a cool kid. I'm proud to
call him 'son.'"

"Ohhhh, snap, D," Obadiah said. "You just became a dad.
Man, you work fast!"

"What can I say, Obie? I got the right touch," he replied, and
then tweaked Marsha's ear. "Ain't that right, Baby?"

"I guess so," she said and then immediately wished she had
not opened up that can.

"What do you mean by 'I guess so,' Woman?" Denzelle queried, knowing full well what his wife meant. But he also knew he
wanted to mess with her a bit—especially since he could now
finish the business he was about to start.

One reason Denzelle had such trouble being around Marsha
was that he always struggled to keep his hands off of her. The
reason he never asked her on a date was because he knew that he
was not going to stop at a chaste peck on the lips and a good
night. Denzelle knew he was going to make good on his reputa-
tion for being smooth, persuasive, and irresistible if he were
alone with Marsha.

It had taken everything he had in him to back up off of her
that night she came to his house for the dance contest. But tonight he didn't have to hold back on nothin'. Tonight he could
pull out all the stops and make Marsha completely his.

"Well, you know . . ."

"Nope," Denzelle said, trying not to laugh. "I don't know 'nothing.' You are going to have to school a brother on this one, Honey."

Marsha looked at Denzelle and tried to talk to him with her eyes, saying, Are you kidding me? He looked back and talked with his eyes, saying, Do I look like I'm kidding you?

"Denzelle," Marsha began, in a very formal and proper, Miss Priss voice, "I wouldn't know about your touch because you haven't touched me."

He slid his hand down her arm and said, "I'm touching you now. So is it the right touch?"

"It's a . . . a . . . good touch," she replied, with a lot of Priss in her voice.

"I see," Denzelle said, and advanced on Marsha, relieved that Obadiah and Lena knew when to leave. As soon as the door to his office closed, he grabbed her close and let his new wife feel the entire length of his body.

"So, you think I'm touchin' you right now?"

Marsha coughed and struggled to maintain her composure. She said, "I'd say that you are doing a very good job of, you know, touching me, Denzelle."

"I just bet I am, Baby," he whispered in her ear, right before kissing it. Denzelle nibbled down Marsha's ear to her neck and said, "I want you, and if you don't get your prissy self out of this office with me, I'm going to have you on this desk."

Marsha said, "Where's my bag?" pushed past her husband, and headed toward the door.

Chapter Thirty-four

"Where are D and Miss Marsha?" Charles asked.

"On their way to D's house," Obadiah said.

"But what about the ballots and the rest of the program?" Keisha asked. "Don't you think they need to be here? I'm sure they are going to win this contest."

"Well, then," Lena began, with her face all lit up. "I think you all better choose the runner-up couple and tell everybody that the pastor didn't expect to win and wanted the prize to go to that couple."

"What are we supposed to say about the pastor not being here?" Veronica asked her. "This is, after all, an event to help him get elected bishop. It has gone so well. He needs to be here to say something."

"I'll handle the crowd," Obadiah said. "We'll tell them there was an unexpected emergency."

"And what would that be?" Charles asked. "I mean, we want the unedited version of this, Obie."

"Denzelle just married Marsha in his office."

The whole *Dancing with the Stars* program team was so stunned, they couldn't even move. No one knew what to say. In fact, what could they say to this kind of news?

"Did they even have a license?" Bay Bowser asked. "I mean, I didn't get the impression that they were planning to tie the knot after a dance number. I knew they were crazy about each other.

But the pastor acted like he was scared to take Marsha out for a glass of juice, let alone up and marry her."

"They are getting the license tomorrow," Obadiah replied evenly. He knew he was going to have to do a little fancy foot-work to explain this to this crowd.

"So, this means what?" Veronica asked. " 'Cause this doesn't sound like a real marriage to me."

"Why not?" Obadiah asked her.

"Well, there wasn't a wedding or an engagement or an an-nouncement or even a text message saying, 'Y'all come on back to the pastor's office 'cause we are getting married.' Know what I'm sayin'?"

Obadiah was cracking up. Veronica had a point. He said, "Look, this didn't have anything to do with how Denzelle or Marsha may have wanted this thing to go down. They were very skeptical about doing it that way. But the Lord laid it on my heart, and Lena's heart, and He touched Marsha's heart. Most importantly, He got through to Denzelle's heart. And . . ."

"Baby, tell them about the ring," Lena interjected.

"What ring?" Keisha and Veronica asked in unison.

Obadiah rolled his eyes upward and let out that hah-hah laugh that was so uniquely his.

"The ring Denzelle had been carrying around on him for a while. Seems like your pastor knew Marsha was the one long before he was able to 'fess up to anybody else, sometimes, even to himself."

"All I wanna know is what the ring looks like," Dayeesha said. She was the jewelry expert and could tell if a ring was qual-ity simply by listening to the description.

"Platinum band, one inch in width, six quarter-carat-size sapphires in blue, pink, and lavender. The sapphires were sur-rounded by gorgeous diamond chips that sparkled when any kind of light hit them," Lena said.

"Prisms of color?" Dayeesha asked, ignoring Metro shaking his head for her to stop.

"Absolutely," Lena told her. "Girl, this is Denzelle Flowers. You know he had that ring custom-made and spared no cost. That boy even had the ring in the right size for Marsha's little bitty fingers."

"Did they sign a prenup?" Charles asked. His frat had some deep pockets.

"Against Marsha Metcalf?" Obadiah said.

Charles sighed and nodded in concession.

"You have a point, Obadiah. Denzelle will be fine. Plus, D survived Tatiana, so I know he'll be fine with this one."

"This one?" Veronica asked. "What brought on calling . . . ?"

Charles gave Veronica a look that clearly said, "HUSH."

Veronica was about to open her mouth but closed it fast when Tatiana, who had returned to the gym, came over to where they were standing and asked, "Where is my husband?"

"Todd is right over there looking real pissed, Tatiana," Dayeesha said. She curled up her lips when Tatiana rolled her eyes.

"I wouldn't go there, Girl," Dayeesha cautioned.

"And what if I do?" Tatiana retorted, obviously feeling exceptionally bold and brave.

"Then I will mop this floor up with your triflin' behind, ho."

"Baby, don't go there. We're at church," Metro said.

"Metro, I didn't start this. But I will end it. So if you don't want this skeezer to get her feelings hurt and her butt kicked, you betta get this ho out of my face, and right now."

Metro turned to Tatiana and said, "You better get to steppin' if you want your weave to stay in your head."

"You betta watch yourself, ghetto rat," Tatiana shot at Dayeesha.

"I'll be waiting on you, Tatiana. In fact, we can settle this on the parking lot this evening. Come to think of it, let's go out there right now. I'm sick of your stuck-up behind walking round here like you the queen of Ethiopia, and you ain't no better than a two-dollar crack ho.

"So, you betta watch your mouth when you talk to me—

looking like you got some custom-made knee pads in your purse."

At that point Charles hollered with laughter. He'd never heard anybody talk to Tatiana Hill Flowers Townsend like that and get away with it. He felt kind of bad that his frat wasn't here to enjoy the show. Witnessing Dayeesha Mitchell put Tatiana in her place would have made a sweet wedding present for Denzelle.

Tatiana walked away. They did not know who they were messing with. She had just come back from finding someone who could make up a forensic-safe poison to take out Camille Franklin.

And she wasn't the only person who was going to get it. The Board of Bishops's meeting was being held at the Raleigh Hilton this year. And in just two days a vote would be cast that would make her ex-husband think twice about hooking up with that little Marsha Brady–acting woman. Every time Tatiana saw Marsha Metcalf she wanted to find a football and throw it right at her nose.

"You know that girl is crazy, right?" Bay said. "She acts like somebody who jumped right out of a Lifetime Network movie."

"Yeah, she does," Veronica said, wondering why she'd never noticed it before. If Camille Franklin were not so hateful, she would have been inclined to tell the girl to watch her back. But Veronica knew that if she even tried to speak to Camille, the woman would snub her and be downright hateful acting. She didn't know what it was with women like that—just mean.

Chapter Thirty-five

Denzelle eased that smooth-riding black Audi into his driveway. He turned off the engine and was about to get out of the car when he saw that he had a text from Charles Robinson.

Veronica will drop off some things for Marsha tomorrow. Keisha and Bay will make sure everything's okay with her car. Congrads, Frat. You got a good woman.

"Everything alright, Denzelle?" Marsha asked. She was overjoyed, excited, overwhelmed, and downright scared. They had never even been out for a cup of coffee, and now she was going to this man's, no, her husband's house. It had felt so right in the office. Now Marsha wondered if she had experienced a momentary lapse in her sanity.

"Everything's fine. That was Charles. Veronica will bring some things by for you in the morning."

"Wow. This is so fast, unexpected, and a bit overwhelming. I haven't even thought about where we will live."

Denzelle put his hand over his wife's. He knew she was scared. Heck, he was scared himself. But he knew that poor Marsha was petrified.

"Baby, it is going to be just fine. Don't overthink this. Be prayerful. Talk to me. Be honest. And trust God. He is the one who led us to do it this way. We have to trust Him and know that all is well. If God led us to get married like this, He had a reason, and it is for our ultimate good."

She sighed with relief. This was a good moment to be with a man who knew the Lord and loved the Lord and listened when God said, "I want to talk to you, Son."

Marsha looked relieved, and then petrified again. It occurred to her that she was going to "sleep with" Denzelle Flowers. After all of these years of wondering what he was like behind closed doors, now she was going to find out, and the girl was scared. What was wrong with her? She had a grown son and had been through a lot. Why was she scared of something like this?

Denzelle had gotten out of the car and was walking around to Marsha's side. He could tell from the way she was sitting, like she was waiting on a cop to give her a ticket, that the girl was scared to get of the car and go in the house with him.

"You scared, Baby?"

"Ohh, no, I'm just fine, Denzelle. I'm not scared. What do I have to be afraid of? You are my husband, and you love me, and you are going to take good care of me, and you are going to help me out of the car, and we are going to walk in your house, and you are going to turn on the lights, and we are going to walk on down through your lovely home and to your bedroom, and we are going to turn on that light, and you are going to say . . ."

"STOP!!!!! Baby, it's okay to be afraid. But it's not okay to ramble on like you forgot to chew on some kaopectate for your mouth. Come on and get out of the car."

He held out his hand and helped Marsha out. They held hands all the way into the house. Marsha could not believe how wonderful and comforting Denzelle's hand felt. She felt the touch of his hand all the way down in her heart.

Denzelle walked Marsha to the bedroom. No use making any stops in any other room in the house. He wanted to be in the bedroom with his wife. Wife. It seemed so natural to be walking in this house with Marsha as his wife. He would have never figured out how it would feel to have a wife—a true wife. But this feeling was so wonderful and rich and lush, Denzelle wondered what took him so long to get the courage to take Marsha to his heart as his wife.

Marsha looked around Denzelle's bedroom. It was a soothing Mediterranean blue and white. The bed was sleek and modern, like it had come from a store like IKEA. Queen-size and ebony wood, with a matching ebony wood dresser, a chest of drawers, and a wardrobe.

There was a skylight that gave a great view of the stars twinkling in a jet-black-blue sky. The windows were long, with white wooden blinds, and were draped by Mediterranean blue and white–striped cotton curtains that had tiny crimson stars on them. The curtains matched the comforter, which had crimson and blue accent pillows on it.

Marsha's feet were tired from all of that dancing, and she longed to run the soles of her feet across that inviting, dark wood floor. She wanted to sit down on the bed so badly but didn't know if that was the proper thing to do. So she opted for the cozy, crimson, ultrasuede chair resting against the wall.

"You like this room, Honey?" Denzelle asked.

"Yes, a lot," she said in a quiet voice. Marsha wasn't sure what to do with her new husband. New husband. It seemed so strange and so natural at the same time. Now what?

Denzelle walked over to the chair, reached down, and removed Marsha's shoes. Her feet were so small and dainty. He placed one foot in both of his hands and began to rub deep in the arch. He could tell they were sore and achy by the way Marsha winced when he pressed his fingers in the arch in her foot.

"Marsha, I'm not trying to hurt you. Sit back and relax and let me rub these aches out."

She sat back in the chair and tried to relax. It felt good, and just a tad weird, for Denzelle to rub her feet. She wished she could close her eyes and enjoy this man rubbing out the kinks in her feet. But that was too uncomfortable. Marsha couldn't remember ever having her feet massaged by the man in her life.

Denzelle didn't want Marsha to be this nervous with him.

It had never occurred to him that she would be scared to cross that line with him. He knew she loved him. He knew she wanted him. But he didn't know how to get his new bride comfortably from point A to point B.

Denzelle stopped rubbing Marsha's foot. He grabbed her hand and pulled her up out of the chair, guiding her to his bathroom.

Marsha's eyes lit up. Denzelle's bathroom looked like a fancy spa. It had black, blue, and white tile on the floor, a black, blue, and white custom-made countertop, a navy tub, and black, blue, and white tile shower. The tub was deep and was made in the new walk-in design. The shower had about eight spouts and a place to sit. There was also a cedar wood sauna, as well as a bidet next to the toilet.

Denzelle walked over to the tub and started running the warm water. He opened the cedar wood linen closet and pulled out a bunch of towels and a soft, white terry-cloth robe.

"I know this is big, but I also know you are not going to wash your face and walk around this bathroom naked while I run our bathwater," Denzelle told her.

He bent down and reached inside of the cabinet under the sink, pulling out some good-smelling bath salts, and tossed two hefty handfuls in the tub. The bathroom was steaming up and began smelling so good when the whiff of ginger and citrus scents hit the air. Denzelle looked around the bathroom and frowned.

"Everything alright?" Marsha asked. She was just starting to relax, and now she was back to being on her guard with Denzelle.

"Baby, relax. I want to be here with you. I just forgot a few things," he said, and hurried off toward the kitchen.

Denzelle came back carrying a large tray with two glasses, a bottle of Dom Perignon champagne, two bottles of Fiji water, a bowl of fruit, a plate with crackers and cheeses on it, and a plate with some really fancy cookies.

"I'm hungry, and I know you have to be hungry," he told her.

"Do you always have this kind of 'I'm gonna hit that, girl' food conveniently prepared?" Marsha asked him.

Denzelle stood there trying to find the right way to answer Marsha without telling her, "Yes, I do." Then he decided to just tell his wife the truth. No good would come from him trying to sugarcoat his past.

"Yes. Always. 'Cause a brother never knows when a sweet woman will marry him, come to his house hungry, and need some 'I want some, Baby' food on hand."

Marsha was laughing. Denzelle was so crazy.

He went and checked the tub and the temperature of the water. He then walked over to Marsha and said, "Let me help you out of that."

Marsha stood in front of her husband debating how to hand him the robe. She had hurried out of her clothes when Denzelle went to get the food. Now, she was in this big robe, naked underneath, and wondering if it would look crazy to get in the tub with the robe on.

She was kind of scared about Denzelle seeing her without her clothes. What if he didn't like the way she looked naked? She hung her hands on the belt of the robe.

Denzelle couldn't wait to see all that was being hidden by his robe. He was a man, and a man wanted to see what his woman looked like naked. If he thought he could have gotten away with it, he would have asked Marsha to put on those dancing heels of hers to make things even better when she took off that robe.

Marsha was still standing in front of Denzelle, holding onto the belt on the robe like she would collapse if she loosened her grip on it. Denzelle tugged at the belt and pulled her over to him. When she was close to him, Denzelle grabbed the collar of the robe and kissed Marsha on the lips. When she relaxed a bit, he kissed her again, and loosened the knot on the robe. Marsha put her arms around Denzelle's neck, and he slid the robe off of her shoulders and onto the floor.

She hugged his neck tighter, hoping that would stop him from taking a closer look at her without that big robe.

Denzelle's expert player eyes scanned Marsha's unclad body

faster than anything the TSA could use at the airport. His hands dropped below her waist to rest on Marsha's shapely hips. It was taking considerable control to keep his hands from slipping over that round and luscious butt.

He'd always known that Marsha had a sexy figure. The way her clothes hugged her curves in the most perfect manner offered proof that that assumption was a solid truth. But to see all of this, up close and personal, was almost too much for a brother. For a moment Denzelle thought he was going to need a whiff off of Mr. Arvelle's oxygen tank. And to think—not only was this woman fine, naked, and in his arms—this woman was his wife.

W-I-F-E. The good Lord sure did have a remarkable sense of humor. Denzelle had been running from even having a girlfriend or a special woman in his life. And the Lord fixed it so that he was running to make a woman he had run from for years his very own wife.

Wife. What an incredible gift. Proverbs 18: 22: "He who finds a [true] wife finds a good thing and obtains favor from the Lord" came to life for Denzelle in this moment. He had been married, but it occurred to Denzelle that Tatiana was never his "true wife."

He wondered how many brothers had experienced what was ocurring in his heart at this moment. How many brothers understood the difference between getting married to finding a true wife? Some, like his boy Obadiah, got it early and were blessed with years of a good life. But some men had to find out the hard way the difference between marrying a woman and finding a true wife.

And this delectable woman, who was running Denzelle's pressure sky-high, was his wife. He kissed Marsha's neck, and kissed it again when she took in a deep breath and let it out, like a long and satisfied sigh. Denzelle ran his fingertips across the spot between her neck and shoulder. He noticed that she had almost forgotten she was naked in his arms, and was trying to get as close to him as she could.

"Marsha, Marsha, Marsha," Denzelle whispered in her ear.

"I cannot believe that your little busy self has been hiding all of this fine from me all of these years. Baby, what am I going to do with you?"

Marsha blushed and smiled up in Denzelle's eyes. She knew the answer to that question but wasn't quite bold enough to put it into words.

Denzelle did something he had wanted to do all evening. He slapped his wife on that luscious butt.

"Ouch," she yelped.

"You know that did not hurt that thang," he said, and tapped that fine butt one more time.

"Why did you pop me on my behind, Denzelle?"

"'Cause it's my behind," he answered, with a very mannish twinkle in his eyes.

Marsha opened her mouth to say, It's my behind, but was stopped in her tracks when Denzelle said, "Are you going to try and tell me that all of this isn't mine?"

Marsha was silent. It had been a long time since she had conversations like this with a man, and had almost forgotten how much fun they were. There was nothing like some naughty bantering between you and your man.

"Your bathwater is going to get cold, Honey," Denzelle said. He let go of Marsha, taking a moment to get a full-body scan of his wife.

"Umph, umph, umph," he said, ran his hand around in the bathwater, and turned on the hot water to heat things up again. As soon as the bathwater was a perfect temperature, Denzelle said, "It's just right, Baby."

Marsha sat down in the soothing warm water with the good-smelling bath salts and laid her head back on the tub pillow. She closed her eyes and swirled her fingertips around in the bubbles. She loved baths. They felt so good.

Denzelle pulled up a small table he kept in the bathroom for food and drinks. He poured some champagne into two glasses and handed Marsha a plate with cheeses and fruit on it.

"I know you are hungry."

She nodded and popped some cheese in her mouth, following it with some small, juicy chunks of fresh pineapple. Denzelle poured her a glass of champagne, and then started to strip down. Marsha eased up in the tub, intent on getting as much of a view of him as she could without letting on that she was intently interested in what her man, no, her husband, looked like without his clothes. It occurred to Marsha that she had never seen Denzelle in an undershirt. Now he was standing right next to her, getting ready to take off his black boxer briefs.

"I knew he wore boxer briefs," she mumbled out loud, forgetting that Denzelle was watching her while he undressed.

"What about boxer briefs?" he asked, now standing in front of the tub without a stitch of clothing.

"Nothing," Marsha squeaked, not knowing what to think about seeing Denzelle in his full glory. She'd always liked his deep, caramel brown color. But she'd never thought about how extensive that caramel was.

Marsha's eyes traveled slowly from the top of Denzelle's head to his smoldering eyes, across his broad chest, down to his waist, down his stomach, and stopped at his hot spot. Marsha tried to will her eyes to keep going, so that she could get a full view of her very handsome husband. But her eyes were acting like they had a will of their own and simply refused to move from that particular spot.

She knew that women were always trying to get with Denzelle. She knew that they acted like the world was about to end when he ended his affairs with them. She knew that they thought he had it going on behind closed doors. She knew Denzelle was very handsome and sexy. She didn't know that he was packing caramel like he owned the PayDay candy factory.

Denzelle poured himself a glass of champagne and swallowed it all in two gulps. He poured another glass and got in the tub.

"Scoot over and quit hogging my tub, Girl," he teased, and sat down next to Marsha. He laughed softly and poured some more champagne. Denzelle knew Marsha would be thrown off balance when she felt his bare hip next to hers. That's why he thought it would be good for them to sit in the tub together. There was something about warm water swirling around your body that helped a person like his wife relax and let go of her fears and bashfulness around a man.

Denzelle finished off the champagne and positioned his body so that Marsha was sitting between his legs.

"That better?" he asked.

"Yeah," Marsha squeaked out. "It's fine." She could feel all of him against her bottom. It was a good feeling. It was also unnerving.

Denzelle grabbed the bottle of champagne and drank the rest. He positioned his body to maximize the feel of Marsha resting up against him.

"You didn't drink too much champagne, Denzelle," Marsha asked quietly.

He stroked Marsha's shoulder gently. She was sexy and sweet and just a bit naive. The poor baby was sitting up in this tub with him trying to be grown and just as scared. Denzelle had forgotten that Marsha had barely seen him take a sip of wine. And here he was gulping down champagne right out of the bottle.

Denzelle kissed his wife's shoulder and said, "Honey, I pledged back in the day when we were online for an entire semester. You know I can hold my liquor."

"Denzelle, I don't think I've ever seen you drinking anything other than communion wine."

He started cracking up and reached for her chin, pulling her face around to his. He kissed her lips softly.

"You taste mighty good, Mrs. Flowers."

"Huh?"

"Mrs. Flowers. That is your name, right?"

Marsha's eyes got wide. It was true. She was Mrs. Flowers.

He kissed her again, only this time with more heat and insistence. Denzelle knew he couldn't rush Marsha. But he honestly didn't know how much longer he could hold out like this. He dipped his hand down in the water and ran his hand up his wife's thigh. He could feel her holding her breath as his fingers trailed up her leg. Just as he was going to lay hand on his treasure, his cell buzzed and Marcus Bluefield showed up on the phone.

Denzelle lay back on the tub and laughed. Now they were truly married, with a child interrupting parents getting busy with each other. He said, "Everything okay, Son?" in the calmest, most regular-sounding voice he could muster up given the circumstances.

"Yeah, Rev," Marcus said, wondering if Rev was appropriate, since Reverend Flowers was now his stepdad.

"You can call me Denzelle, Marcus."

"How 'bout Pops?"

Denzelle smiled in pure delight and said, "Pops is just fine by me. So, everything okay?"

"Oh, everything is just fine. We gave the grand prize award to Mr. Arvelle and Miss Roberta. You and Mom got the most votes, but we knew you didn't want to take the prize. I don't think anything could top the wheelchair face-off dance."

Denzelle laughed softly. Marcus was right. Nothing could top that.

"Where's Mom?" Marcus asked, kind of nervous about the potential answer. He was so happy for his mother, but also uncomfortable about why she was at Denzelle's house. Kids wanted their parents happy with someone who loved and cherished them. But kids didn't want to have to contemplate all that went with that loving and cherish stuff.

Denzelle knew Marcus wanted to talk to his mom, but he also knew the young brother didn't want to talk to his mom right after his new stepfather handed her the telephone. He understood how Marcus felt. Sometimes he felt that way when his father gave his mother the telephone in the middle of the night. He could tell by the way his mom answered the phone that she was all hugged up with his dad.

"I'll get her and make sure she calls you right back," was all Denzelle said, glad he had handled it that way when he heard Marcus sneak out a sigh of relief.

"Oh, one more thing," Marcus told Denzelle.

"Yes," Denzelle answered.

"You and me—we cool. Okay?"

"O-kay?" was all Denzelle said.

"And I know you love my mom and you will try to do right by her. But Rev, I mean, Pops, I will hurt you bad if you ever do anything that will hurt her like my dad hurt my mom. You the man and all—but you'd better not get stupid and make me come after you. And I know you are FBI and can fight and shoot. But none of that will matter to me if you don't do right by my mom. You feelin' me, Rev?"

"I'm feelin' you, Son."

"Was that my baby?" Marsha asked, hoping all was well with Marcus. It had been the two of them for years, and she wanted to make sure he was alright with the way she married Denzelle.

"Yes, and he wants to talk to you. I thought it best not to just give you the phone—especially since he called my cell and not yours."

"My cell is in the other room," Marsha said and got out of the tub, trying to ignore the heat from Denzelle's eyes. She reached for a huge towel, wrapped it around her body, and went to dig her cell out of her purse.

"Mom," Marcus said in a voice that made her think back to when he was nine years old.

"Yes, Baby."

Marcus smiled. He was still his mama's baby. Funny, he was always so determined to make sure she knew he was a man. But tonight he needed to know that he maintained his spot in his mother's heart.

"I just wanted to hear your voice. And I wanted to tell you that I'm glad you married Rev, I mean, Pops. He loves you a lot, Mom. I hope you know that."

Marcus was being so sweet it made tears well up in Marsha's eyes. She was happy to know he believed Denzelle loved her, and that he cared enough about her husband to call him "Pops."

"But there is something missing in all of this for you, Marcus."

"Yeah, Mom. I had always hoped that I would be the one to give you away whenever you remarried. Now, don't get me wrong, this marriage had to play out like it did. I understand that. But now I'm feeling like something was lost in all of this for me."

"I hear you, Baby," Marsha told her son. "Tell you what. Denzelle and I have to go get the license tomorrow. Why don't we meet you in Reverend Quincey's office in Durham, and round up a few of our folk, and do this ceremony with you, so you can give me away?"

"Okay. Thanks, Mom. I love you."

"I love you, too, Baby," Marsha said, and hung up.

"You raised a fine young man," Denzelle said, and kissed Marsha's cheek. "We will definitely get up with Obie tomorrow and do this right, with Marcus giving you away."

"Thanks, Denzelle," Marsha said, and walked into his outstretched arms.

Chapter Thirty-six

Denzelle held Marsha close to his heart. She could feel the beat up against her shoulder. It was comforting.

He kissed the top of Marsha's head and wondered why it had taken him so long to get to this point. Denzelle didn't even know how lonely he'd been until this moment. All of these years he'd spent running game on women, running from women, and running from Marsha. In the words of the R&B singer Sunshine Anderson, Denzelle believed that he "musta fell and bumped [his] head" to have been so intent on avoiding his own blessing.

"Honey," Denzelle whispered, and laced his fingers through Marsha's hair. He felt her body tense up and said, "What's wrong?"

"Nothing," Marsha said. She didn't have a clue as to how she was going to tell this man she was scared to get into that bed with him. Denzelle was not a small man, and she had not been with a man in years.

Denzelle looked down into Marsha's eyes and read her like an open book. He said, "I won't hurt you, Honey."

"You won't try and hurt me," she told him, "but I don't know how you can avoid me feeling some discomfort. It's been a very long time since I've been with a man."

"How long is long, Marsha?"

"Five years," she whispered, almost embarrassed to tell him that. How in the world could she explain that she had been so supersingle all of this time? She hadn't even been faced with the dilemma of struggling with her beliefs over this issue, because no man had been remotely interested in her during that time.

"Why so long?" he asked.

Marsha just looked at Denzelle. She thought that he'd know that part, since he was a pastor.

"Okay, let me ask this another way. Why is it that no one ever tried to get with you? Or, better yet, why is it that you never had to struggle with wanting to be with someone who was trying to get with you?"

Marsha sighed and went and sat on the edge of the bed. She could not believe that she plopped down on what had always been "her" side. She smoothed out a wrinkled spot on the sheet and looked around with a tiny frown on her face.

"Is there a problem?" he asked.

"I like this side of the bed, but I hope that it isn't your side, you know," Marsha told him.

"I sleep all over the bed," Denzelle said, and went to the other side. He pulled back the covers, and took off the towel that was around his waist.

Marsha hugged her own towel to her body. Her eyes traveled across his chest, with the sprinkling of coarse, dark hair on it, down to where everything was just sitting there, as if it were looking straight at her.

"Girl, what is wrong with you? You're acting like you've never seen a man's stuff before. I know you had to have seen it at least one time, since Marcus is walking around, living proof that you saw something."

She sighed. Sometimes a man like Denzelle Flowers could work your nerves. It was obvious to Marsha that he was not the type of man, or person, for that matter, who was used to going without, doing without, and being without what he wanted or sought to have. He was always in a position to do what he deemed necessary, and in a timely manner.

For years that kind of command over circumstances had

been anything but Marsha Metcalf's experience. And that could be frustrating and hard to explain to someone who had been privy to the opposite experience.

"Denzelle," Marsha began in a firm voice, "I haven't seen a man's stuff in years. Until you kissed me, I had not been kissed or hugged by a man who wanted me in years. In fact, I have not felt a man bulging up against me in a hot hug for years. And I definitely have not seen a naked man, with all of his stuff waving all up at me like some kind of magnetic wand.

"Now, I cannot tell you why no man has seen fit to call me on the telephone, text me, e-mail me, tweet me, take me out for coffee, take me out for dinner, try to hug up on me, try to kiss me, and then try to convince me that I need to sleep with him. I don't have an answer for you, because I don't have a clue. There is nothing wrong with me, and yet nobody came my way—not even you."

Denzelle sat up straight in the bed, and was about to say something. Marsha didn't even want to hear what he had to say, because she knew it would only make her mad. She was cold and slid up under the sheets and pulled the comforter over her. She sat up as much as she could without causing the warmth of the covers to slide off.

"Don't open your mouth, Denzelle," Marsha commanded. "You were sweet on me, and you persisted in running from me and pushing me away. All I was doing was being a woman you were trying not to be in love with—as if that were my fault. You acted like you had beef with the Lord for choosing a good woman to present to you so you could be blessed.

"Sometimes I wanted to get you told. And sometimes I wanted to beat you like you stole my money. But you know what I did? I put it in the hands of the Lord. And I hope with all of my heart that the Lord dealt with you on my behalf for acting like you did."

Denzelle bristled at those words and was about to tell her a thing or two. But Marsha had held her peace on this matter for way too long. And she wasn't going to hold it another minute, and she didn't care if he stayed mad until Jesus cracked the sky.

"Oh, yeah, Denzelle, you were crazy about me, but you didn't want to like me. In fact, you didn't want to love me or let me care for your heart. Did you think I would hurt you? Didn't you know that I would take good care of your heart? I sure did pray for you long and hard enough over these years. And guess what? I didn't want to like your old smooth daddy, got-it-going-on, Kappa Alpha Psi self, either. I used to get so mad at myself for liking you like that."

Marsha was mad now. She didn't know she had been so angry at Denzelle until now. She sat up in the bed and pulled the sheet over her bare breasts.

"Who do you think you are, Denzelle Flowers, to question me about why some dumb-ass brothers didn't see the jewel that I am? Who are you to ask why I haven't seen a naked man in years? How the hell would I know? I didn't create that damn situation. Brothers like you did. So don't ask me that question. Ask your own damn self!"

Marsha was breathing hard, heaving air in and out of her mouth. Her chest was tight, and it hurt to take in real deep breaths. She calmed herself down, took in shallow breaths, and gradually got more air into her lungs.

Denzelle was pissed. No woman, not even Tatiana, had ever talked to him like that. He wanted to snatch those covers off of Marsha and let her be cold. He said, "Who do you think you are?"

"Your wife," Marsha told him so firmly, it shocked her. "Not the woman you married. Not the woman you ran game on and screwed. I am your wife. And as your wife, there are times when I have to just tell you like it is. I love you, Denzelle. But I'm not going to take away from me just so your behind can be comfortable with your tired, Big Daddy mess."

Denzelle started laughing out loud. That little miss was right. She was his wife. And every good, loving, and passionate woman who loved her husband right got that brother straightened out at some point. He scooted over to Marsha's side of the bed and wrapped his arm around her.

"Yes, you are my wife, with your sweet and sexy self. Sitting over here with your feathers all ruffled, cheeks all flushed, and looking ripe for the picking."

Marsha tried to squeeze back the blush that was betraying her and spreading across her cheeks. She tried not to lean back into her husband's body, but Denzelle just got closer to her and ran his hand over the length of her left hip.

He kissed her shoulder.

"How long have you loved me, Marsha?"

"A long time—only I didn't want to admit that I loved you. I thought it was crazy to love a man who didn't seem all that interested in me. There were times when I prayed for the Lord to take that love away and help me to just appreciate and love you as my brother in the Lord."

Denzelle was cracking up with laughter. He got closer to Marsha and wrapped his body around her, spoon fashion.

"You like that, girl?" he said in a low, husky whisper.

"Yes," she said in a real soft voice.

"You sure?" Denzelle asked his wife. "You sound like you're kinda uncomfortable with me all up on you like this."

"I am. But not for the reason you think," Marsha told him. "I love being all up on you like this. Just not sure what to do next, Baby. Remember, I've had to keep this part of me contained for years. Kind of hard to let go, just like that, you know."

"I think I know, Honey," he said, and stroked her cheek. "It must have been real hard to carry on like you did all of this time. And you really did have to keep a part of you on lockdown and inaccessible to men."

Denzelle kissed Marsha's shoulder again.

"You are a strong and very beautiful woman. I want you bad, Girl."

He turned her around to face him. Marsha wrapped her arms

around Denzelle's neck. He kissed her lips gently, and then pulled her to him real tight while kissing his wife deeply.

"Ummm, Baby, Baby, Baby," Denzelle murmured.

He slid his leg through hers and cupped her behind.

"You are going to make me start talking dirty with all of this in my hands," Denzelle said to Marsha.

He slid his hand down her thigh to her knee and pulled Marsha's leg up to his hip. His manhood pressed up against the very spot he'd wanted to find all evening.

"Can I?" was all Denzelle said to Marsha, who was holding onto him tightly.

She felt the pressure of him. Her husband was hot.

"Yes," Marsha whispered, and found that she could not resist staring into his eyes.

Denzelle grabbed the back of Marsha's head, kissed her deeply, and slid into his wife. She gasped and pulled back, but Denzelle pulled her closer and held her tighter.

"Don't pull away from me, Baby," he said in a gentle voice. "I promise I won't hurt you."

They held each other for a few minutes. They didn't want to move. This moment felt so wonderfully incredible, neither wanted to spoil it with movement.

Marsha kissed Denzelle and whispered, "I want you so bad, Baby."

That was all he needed to hear. Denzelle rolled Marsha on her back and slid both hands down to grab her butt. He began to move slowly, hardly able to contain himself. Who knew his wife would feel this good? Who knew Marsha had it going on like that?

Marsha moved with her husband. It was like a synchronized series of separate dips and dives that felt like one sinuous flow of good loving. She moaned, "Denzelle" in his ear, and he whispered, "Girl, slow your roll if you want this to last."

Marsha laughed softly and kissed the corner of Denzelle's mouth. He smiled at her and kissed her lips. They smiled at each other and moved with a rhythm that didn't even exist until they came together as husband and wife.

That last set of rifts in their love song sent both of them over the edge. It was one of those true together moments that people in love cherish. There was nothing like making the Song of Songs come to life in the arms of your beloved.

Denzelle clung to Marsha. His heart was so full, he felt tears well up. He wanted to say something hot and sexy, something that would make her blush. But the only thing that fell in Denzelle's heart, and found its way to his tongue was verse 12 from chapter 4 of the Song of Songs: " 'You are like a private garden, my treasure, my bride! You are like a spring that no one else can drink from, a fountain of my own.' "

Marsha smiled into his eyes and whispered, " 'Kiss me again and again, for your love is sweeter than wine. How fragrant your cologne, and how pleasing your name!' " from chapter 1, verses 2 and 3 of that same book of the Bible.

Chapter Thirty-seven

Todd Townsend paced around in the game room of his six-thousand-square-foot house in Governor's Club in Chapel Hill. It was a beautiful yet very overdecorated home. Todd didn't know what made him think he needed a $2.2 million home in the Triangle. He and Tatiana didn't even need all of this space. It was just the two of them, and they didn't have friends, because people didn't like Tatiana. And their families stayed away, because neither side could stand Tatiana.

So there really wasn't any practical reason for them to have this house. The only reason Todd purchased it was to pacify Tatiana, who had cried and gone on a hunger strike until he conceded and bought it. He wished he had had the gumption to stand up to his wife—he could have saved a whole lot of money buying a smaller and cheaper home.

It was six a.m. and his wife had not come home. Tatiana left the church right after the winners were announced. Todd wasn't even sure who Tatiana left with. Xavier had come back to get Camille. So, who gave his wife a ride to wherever she was now? And if that were not bad enough, Tatiana had the gall to call him and lie about needing to be at a long and special meeting for the sake of their church.

Todd didn't appreciate that mess. Tatiana didn't even like going to that church, or any church for that matter. The garage door went up, and Tatiana pulled her Cadillac right beside Todd's brand-new silver Acura RL. She checked her makeup in the mirror and let the garage door down.

The door leading into the house was open, and Todd was standing there, pissed. Tatiana had not expected him to be here. She'd checked his hospital schedule before they even left the house and thought he would be at work when she came home.

"I thought you had to be at work early, Baby," Tatiana said in the sweetest voice she could muster up at this time in the morning. She was exhausted from all of that scheming and plotting, and then polishing off the evening with Luther Howard, who had only recently added her to his booty call list. Xavier had pissed Luther off enough to make him want to dole out some payback by sleeping with his other woman.

"Nope. I have the morning off," he told her.

"I see," Tatiana said. She was relieved when Todd moved out of the doorway so she could enter without having to brush up against him.

"Where in the hell have you been, Tatiana?"

"I told you, I was working on something for the church. So what is your problem?"

"You, Tatiana," he answered. "You are my problem."

Tatiana walked into their state-of-the-art kitchen and got a bottle of water out of the refrigerator. She opened it and began to sip on the cold water. It was clear Todd was not going to let her get off without a confrontation. But she was awfully tired and needed to go to bed and get some rest. She said, "I'm tired, Todd. I spent the evening with important people doing important things. They are working on making things better for preachers like Reverend Franklin, who is running for bishop. And if it were not for Denzelle, Xavier would win hands down. But Denzelle is all in the way, and we were strategizing about how to get him out of the race. So, now I need to go to sleep."

Todd was staring at Tatiana like this was the first time he'd ever laid eyes on her. He had always convinced himself the reason no one liked her was because they were jealous of Tatiana.

At least, that is what she always said when he questioned her about not being able to get along with other people.

But standing here listening to Tatiana lie in his face about where she was, who she was with, and what she'd been doing was too much.

Todd walked out of the kitchen, leaving Tatiana standing in the middle of the floor clueless and nervous. He'd never acted like this with her. He came back with a thick folder in his hand and threw it on the floor at her feet. Papers were everywhere.

"Strategize on this, ho," he said and walked off. He decided to go in to work after all. Todd knew that if he stayed in the house with Tatiana he would slice her up with one of his scalpels.

Tatiana bent down to examine the pictures and papers that were now strewn across the kitchen floor. They were all about her and Xavier. She gasped when she saw pictures of the two of them in bed at the Umstead Hotel in Cary.

"What? You really didn't think I would sit back and let you do all of that with Xavier and not have proof. I knew you'd lie," Todd said.

"But, Baby . . . ," Tatiana began.

She made Todd think of the song "Contagious," by R. Kelly, Ron Isley, and Chante Mooré.

"Tatiana, I have kept a portfolio on you since the day we got married. Did you honestly believe I wouldn't have some kind of protection, seeing that I'm with you because you two-timed Denzelle?"

"But what about forgiveness, Todd?" Tatiana whined. "We've been married too long to let something like this get in the way of our love."

"You mean, get in the way of you and my money," he told her in a hard and bitter voice.

"But forgiveness, Todd. Can you ever forgive me?"

"Oh, I forgive you. I just don't want you anymore," he answered, in a voice that was so calm and quiet, it frightened Tatiana.

"See," Todd went on, "this isn't your first affair in this

marriage. It's only the first time you fell for the guy. I'm tired, and I'm done. Get your mess and leave."

Tatiana was stunned. Of all of the things she would have expected to hear from Todd, this wasn't it. All of these years of thinking she was so cool and so slick and so good and undercover, and Todd knew about her lovers and affairs anyway.

"I don't have anywhere to go, Todd."

"Go over to Xavier's house. Oh, you can't go there, because it's not even Xavier's house. It's Camille's house."

He pulled out his wallet, peeled off a handful of hundred-dollar bills, and threw them at Tatiana's feet.

"This should pay for a couple of days at the hotel off of Holloway Street in Durham. You know, the one that looks like it's closed but everybody is always staying there. It's trashy, just like you."

"I can't stay there."

Todd shrugged and said, "Then your friend, Yolanda. Oh, I forgot, Yolanda isn't speaking to you because she found out you were sleeping with her man."

Todd started laughing.

"So, I guess you'll have to stay at that hotel then."

Tears started streaming down Tatiana's cheeks. She never thought her gravy train called Dr. Todd Townsend would ever come to an end. She never believed Todd would find out about her affairs. Tatiana didn't even believe he'd ever get mad enough to put her out, even if he did find out about the affairs. And she certainly never believed he would not want her in his life.

Tatiana had believed she could treat this man any kind of way and he'd take it until she got tired of doing it. In fact, Tatiana had never really wanted a divorce from Todd. She wanted him dead. But she didn't want to go through a divorce. She had learned that divorces were troublesome and way too messy.

"Please, Todd," Tatiana pleaded. She was not going to accept this from him. As far as Tatiana was concerned, she'd done Todd a favor by agreeing to marry him.

"Get out," he said.

"I have nowhere to go."

"Yes, you do," He said.

"Where?"

"To hell. Tatiana, you can go straight to hell."

Tatiana made a move toward him. She was now crying so hard she could hardly breathe.

"You have the rest of this day to get your clothes and personal belongings out of my house. After that, you stuff goes in the trash."

"What will I get in the divorce?" Tatiana asked.

"Whatever the hell I got in this farce of a marriage," Todd answered.

Tatiana was having a hard time digesting this. If she left Todd now, all she'd have was a life insurance policy.

She dried her tears and patted her face dry. All Tatiana could think about was how much money she'd have to work with at the end of the divorce. It was zilch. The only way she could get her hands on some real money was through the life insurance policy Todd had taken out on himself to make sure she'd always be okay.

Her cell buzzed.

"Your new man is calling," Todd said calmly. He couldn't believe how at peace he was feeling. All of these years of dreading going through a nasty divorce with Tatiana, and now that his fear was a reality, all he felt peace.

Tatiana acted like she didn't hear her husband and tried to ignore the phone buzzing. Finally, it stopped. Then it started up all over again. Tatiana reached into her jacket pocket and pulled it out. She could not believe Todd had called that one so well. It was Luther Howard.

"Hello," Tatiana said.

"Why did you leave and not tell me good-bye?" Luther admonished.

"You were sleeping so peacefully, I hated to wake you."

Todd shook his head. He couldn't believe this mess. Tatiana didn't have any respect for anything.

"I need you to go to the address I'm about to text you and get that stuff I had made up for you. And don't let anybody know where you're going, Tatiana. You think you can pull this off for me without a hitch?"

"Yes," Tatiana said carefully. "But . . ."

"But what?" Luther demanded.

"Todd knows everything about us."

Luther was quiet, and then he laughed into the phone. He said, "He thinks I'm Xavier.

"No."

"He knows this is me?" Luther asked with some concern.

"No."

"Then what?"

Tatiana was not going to answer that question with Todd staring down in her mouth so intently he could probably see her lungs. She just kept being quiet.

"He thinks I'm a new man but not me."

"Yes."

"Good. Keep it that way. So, is he mad? Hurt? Begging? What?"

"He is putting me out and is planning on divorcing me. I have to get out ASAP."

"I see," was all Luther said. He had to think about this for a second. He said, "Your divorce settlement. What will you have to work with?"

"Nothing"

"No-what?" Luther demanded

"No-Nothing," Tatiana said through a new set of tears.

"Absolutely nothing?"

"Nothing," she repeated, hardly able to believe it herself.

"How did you come up with nothing, Tatiana? I always thought you were smarter than that."

"I signed the papers because I wanted to hurry up and marry Todd and I thought . . ."

". . . you thought he would change them once you were married and he started to believe he couldn't live without you."

"Yes."

"Do you have a life insurance policy on the man?"

"Yes."

"For how much?"

"Eight million."

"All yours?"

"Yes."

"I see," Luther said in a very quiet and deadly voice. "You
need to handle your business, and you better be at that meeting."

Tatiana stared at her phone. She couldn't believe that Luther
would be so cold after last night. Right now, she felt like a trash-
bin. Luther Howard had just discarded her like she was a piece of
cold, stale, and day-old pizza.

She looked up from the phone, expecting to see Todd staring or, more like, sneering at her. Todd wasn't even in the room.
Tatiana didn't even know that he'd left. She heard the toilet flush,
and seconds later Todd came back looking pale.

Listening to his wife talking to her new man in his own house
had made Todd sick to his stomach. In fact, Todd's stomach was
so torn up, he had barely been able to get off the toilet to come
back in this room to get upset all over again when he looked at
Tatiana holding the phone in her hand. She was staring at it like
she wanted the man to call her back.

Todd felt like the bottom of his stomach was about to fall
out again. He was sweating and having some trouble breathing.
Todd was upset over Tatiana, but he didn't think his wife's craziness was the sole cause for how he was feeling.

The last time Todd was with Shanna Webster she had talked
him into taking some more of that WP21 Todd bought from the
so-called herbalist brother who sold "natural" aphrodisiacs out
of his home in Bahama, North Carolina. He didn't know why he
listened to Shanna and that herbalist brother about this stuff.
Todd should have known better when an underweight brother

named Zachary Walsh met him at the door of his house speaking with a fake part-African, part-Caribbean accent saying.

"Doktor Townsend, I am Ochi, the African name for laughter."

Todd didn't know what to say to Ochi the laughter man, especially since Ochi frowned and looked real mean and hateful the entire time Todd was at his house. It didn't help that Ochi's front yard was just as unappealing as he was, with the dirt that couldn't grow grass and a batch of wild-acting chickens running around in it. Ochi's chickens were so mean and crazy-acting that they chased Todd when he got out of the car. Todd had run up on Ochi's porch and banged on the door. It had taken everything Todd had in him, not to wimp out and holler, "HELP!"

Those crazy chickens should have been Todd Townsend's clue to move on. But no—he had to prove himself to Shanna, and to Ochi, who kept asking if Todd was man enough to handle his products. So Todd took all of that WP21, even though he had been having some heart health issues for a while. Anyone who knew anything about this drug knew it was bad for the heart. Now Todd was mad, upset, feeling crappier and crappier by the minute, and scared he was experiencing some bad side effects from the WP21.

"Todd, will you forgive me and reconsider your decision?" Tatiana asked him.

Todd ignored his wife, closed his eyes, and prayed, "Lord, forgive me for all of my sins."

He didn't know what made him pray that but he couldn't help it. Right now, Todd Townsend knew he needed something bigger than himself. Todd thought about how tired he was of the daily grind and feeling like a failure in spite of all that others kept telling him he had accomplished. He thought about his wife, who he now knew had never loved him. He thought about how he wished he had listened to somebody with some sense, and left this evil woman alone.

Todd Townsend thought about the heavy ache in his chest,

the nausea, the pain in his arm and shoulders, the urge to run off
to the bathroom again, the need to sit down, and the inability to
stop himself from collapsing on the floor. He had dallied with
the very dangerous WP21, worked himself down to the bone,
and now he was in the middle of a full-blown heart attack. This
was absolutely unbelievable.

How in the world could one of the most renowned trauma
surgeons in the country collapse with a deadly heart attack? Todd
knew this was a deadly attack because he'd lectured on how to
treat patients coming into emergency rooms with this kind of
massive cardiac arrest. Something in Todd urged him to stick his
hand down into his pocket where his cell was.

He looked up at Tatiana, pleading with his eyes for her to do
what she needed to do to save his life. Tears streamed down
Todd's cheeks as he realized that Tatiana was going to stand there
and watch him die.

Eight million dollars. That's all he was worth to this
woman—a measly eight million dollars. Pity. Tatiana didn't know
he had just signed a contract that would make his earnings leap to
eight and a half million dollars a year.

Tatiana could not believe her good fortune. Todd was dying,
and she didn't have to do a thing. Eight million dollars. All she
had to do was play the grieving widow and wait to collect her
money. Then she could do whatever she wanted to do—hopefully
with Luther Howard by her side.

Todd knew Tatiana wanted him dead. But as weary as he was,
Todd wasn't ready to leave this earth today. He prayed in his
heart—lips not moving, eyes closed, and body still—praying only
what the Lord could hear.

"Father, I want to live. Don't take me home just yet. If it is in
accordance to Your will for my life, let me survive this heart attack. Let me live, Lord, Amen."

At that moment, Todd felt a peace he'd never felt in his life.
He felt like he was light enough to float on a fluffy white cloud.
There was no pain—physical or otherwise. He was overtaken by

a strong urge to take in a deep breath, breathe it out, and then go into that peaceful place that surpassed anything his brilliant mind was capable of understanding.

Tatiana watched her husband go through the phases of relinquishing life that she'd seen several times while working in a few hospice settings. She was so happy Todd was dead that it took everything in her to refrain from dancing around the man's body. Two stingy tears rolled down each cheek—more from relief than anything else.

Tatiana dabbed at her face, kicked Todd's foot, and left. She would come back later and "discover" her dead husband. It was a good thing their house was secluded. That way a nosey neighbor couldn't come forth and start talking about "seeing Mrs. Townsend at such and such a time."

Todd waited until he heard the car start, the garage door go up and then back down, and then another minute to make sure Tatiana didn't return and kill him for real. He was very weak but managed to get that phone out of his pocket. He dialed Denzelle Flowers's number. Because at this point, it was the only number he could remember, and Denzelle was the only person he knew he could call. Then Todd prayed that God would keep him alive and get him to the hospital.

Chapter Thirty-eight

"I will turn this in to the register of deeds," Obadiah told Denzelle, as soon as he and Lena finished signing the witness spots on the official marriage license. He folded the license, put it in an envelope, and stuck it in his breast pocket.

"Happy?" Denzelle said to his new bride and wife.

"Yes," Marsha said, trying not to let the small sigh of relief escape. She knew Denzelle was going to do all of the proper legal stuff—it just felt better to have it all behind her.

Marsha smoothed the skirt of her dress. It wasn't what she would have selected when planning a wedding in her mind. But it worked for this morning. She wore her favorite sky blue, silk shirtwaist dress that had a wide skirt, a matching belt, short sleeves, and pearl buttons all the way down the front. She had a doubled-up rope of pearls around her neck and teardrop pearl earrings in her ears.

She was wearing a pair of crimson red pumps with a built-in platform. It was one of those pairs of shoes her good friend Ramon at Sebastian-Fleur continued to hide away for her until the price dropped down to barely nothing. Everybody had commented on those shoes this morning. And Denzelle had made a point of asking her to let him see the shoes on her feet when she walked out of the shower. They almost didn't make it to their own official wedding ceremony after Marsha put on those shoes.

Keisha had done her hair, and laced a strand of pearls around her head, like a very fancy headband. She carried crimson roses, which were her favorite. The roses took care of the something new for her bridal attire. The something borrowed was a pearl bracelet Veronica had loaned her.

"Mom," Marcus said. "You are beautiful."

"Thank you, Baby," Marsha told him, and stood on tiptoe to kiss her son. He had been so wonderful with the way things worked out. She was a blessed woman—two handsome men in her life who loved her with all of their hearts.

"Yes, you are very beautiful," Denzelle said, hardly able to contain his joy. Marsha gazed in Denzelle's eyes, both of them blushing at the memories of this morning.

"You're not so bad yourself," she told her husband.

Denzelle was sharp in his favorite black three-piece suit that had crimson chalk stripes in it. He was wearing a white shirt and a deep red silk tie with black stripes, a deep red silk pocket handkerchief, and his favorite black gators, with the dark red leather piping around the front of the shoe.

Marsha smiled. Her man was a good-looking brother and sexy as can be. All she could think was, "God is good all the time, and all the time, God is good." That phrase was never so applicable as it was right now.

"Now that all of the real business is over," Lena said, "don't you have something you want and need to say to your new hubby, Marsha?"

Marsha turned to Lena and tried to shake her head without drawing attention to them. Lena tilted her head at Marsha as if to say, "Do it!" Marsha mouthed, "No." Lena said, "If you don't tell him, I will."

Denzelle looked down at Marsha, eyebrow raised. Marsha stared up at Denzelle, and then, without warning, popped him on the back of his head. She said, "What in the hell took you so long?"

"Huh?" Denzelle asked, rubbing his head.

"You heard me," she pressed. "What took you so long to

come into my life? Do you know what all I had to go through, waiting on you to show up? What took you so long?"

Denzelle would never fully understand women. He thought the matter with Marsha was "going through" over waiting for the right man had been settled. He looked to Obie for some help. All Obie did was shrug, as if to say, "The hell if I know what this is about."

Lena said, "Let me help you with this, Denzelle. Marsha always said that whenever her true husband showed up, she was going to slap him and ask, 'What took you so long?'"

Then Denzelle laughed. He got it. He absolutely got it. Waiting on him to get it and then do right by Marsha had taken a long time—too long perhaps. He would have slapped himself, too, if he had to endure what Marsha experienced before they came together and married. It was a wonder she didn't get one of his guns and pistol-whip his behind.

Denzelle took Marsha's tiny hand in his, kissed it, and said, "Honey, there is no excuse for what took me so long to use the sense God gave me. But I am so glad I didn't waste another minute being stupid. And I'm sorry it took this long for me to get from there to here, to you."

Marsha smiled.

"I only have one question, though," Denzelle asked.

"And that is?" Marsha queried.

"No matter how long it took me, was it worth the wait?"

She blushed and said, "Without a doubt."

Obadiah's cell buzzed. He looked at it and read the text message quickly.

"That is Bishop Simmons. He needs us at the Board of Bishops meeting after all. So we need to hop on over to the Raleigh Hilton. The meeting to decide on new policies for who can run for bishop starts in an hour."

"Marcus," Denzelle said, and grabbed his car keys off his desk.

"Yep, Pops," Marcus said.

"Get my car."

"Right away," Marcus answered, barely able to contain his pleasure over driving Denzelle's smooth-riding car.

"They are really putting forth a policy that if a pastor is divorced, and his or her ex-spouse is still living, they cannot run for bishop if they remarry?" Veronica asked.

"Yeah," Denzelle said. "And it gets worse. Let's say a pastor is divorced, runs for bishop, wins, and then remarries while holding office. He or she will have to relinquish that Episcopal seat immediately."

"I thought Bishops Simmons and Tate had dealt with that, Obie," Lena said.

"They did, Baby. But our enemies made sure Bishop Jefferson would be at this meeting."

"That man who is married to the Patra lady?" Marsha asked.

"Yep," Obadiah said. "She is Bishop Jefferson's fourth, fifth, or sixth wife. Bishop Sonny Washington and Reverend Marcel Brown have dropped some serious cash on old boy to testify about the perils of divorced pastors and bishops."

"You know that mess is about them trying to stop Denzelle from running for bishop," Marsha said.

"That is exactly what it is about," Obadiah told her. "You are on your way to becoming a first-rate first lady, First Lady Flowers."

Denzelle beamed at the thought of Marsha Metcalf Flowers being the first lady of New Jerusalem Gospel United Church. New Jerusalem had not had a first lady in all of the years he'd served as the senior pastor, and they were long overdue for one.

Marcus pulled up in Denzelle's black Audi. He hopped out and said, "You want me to drive you all over there?"

"Yeah, Son, we do," Denzelle answered. "This is going to be a rough meeting, and Obie and I need to talk and get prepared."

"Then I'll drive Marsha and me to the meeting," Lena said.

Marsha suddenly felt a heavy weight on her heart. What if the policy passed, and Denzelle couldn't run for bishop because of her?

"Don't go there, Honey," Denzelle said, almost as if he'd heard her thoughts. "This is in God's hands. If He wants me to become a bishop, I will. If He doesn't, I won't. I don't need to be a bishop. I was only called to run the race.

"Marsha. My desire is to serve like God has called me to serve. And since you have been in my life, Honey—my heart has been restored once again. Because more than anything, Beautiful, this pastor needed himself a boo."

Marsha bit her lip to hold back the tears. Denzelle had just quoted from her favorite song, written by one of her favorite gospel artists, Jonathan Nelson. "My Heart Has Been Restored" was beautiful. Maurette Brown Clark put a hurting on it when she sang it on her CD, *The Dream*.

Lena grabbed Marsha's arm and said, "Let's go. This meeting is going to be so full of dirt and grime we are going to need a shower when it's all over."

"Then we need to pray, Lena. Denzelle is a bad boy. But he needs more protection than that gun he doesn't think I know is stuck down in his back, up under that fancy suit coat jacket. My husband told me that he never goes to a big church meeting without at least one piece of heat on him. Said it was some crazy folk at those meetings. And sometimes, the only thing that stops them is a modern-day version of Jesus using that whip in the Temple."

Lena started laughing. "Girl, your man ain't lying about that. He better roll up in there packing Jesus and just plain packin'."

Marsha said, "We'll pray on the way to the car. I'm sure the Lord will understand if we are doing a 'pray by.'"

She put her hand on Lena's shoulder and said, "Father, in the Name of Jesus, we come before You and ask You to go before us into that conference room and make a way for our husbands. Put a Blood Covering of Protection over Denzelle and Obadiah, Lord. Put a lamplight to their feet and give them the words You want them to speak. Anoint them with the Holy Ghost, and give them the wisdom and discernment that can only come from

Heaven. Bless them with Your peace. And give them the victory that You ordained for this meeting. Thank You, Father. In Jesus Name we pray, Amen."

"Amen," Lena said, while opening her car door and hopping in. She started up the engine, and they peeled off.

"I need to get myself one of these," Marsha said, admiring the smooth power of Lena's Lexus.

"Nahh, you like smaller cars, Girl. I was looking at that new Cadillac SRX Crossover and thought about you when I saw one in royal Zeta Blue."

Marsha smiled. A royal blue Cadillac SRX was the kind of car she'd love to have.

They hit Highway 40 heading east to Raleigh. Lena was rolling, edging the car over the eighty miles per hour line, right in the high traffic area near Southpoint Mall. She looked around to make sure no cops were around. Last thing she needed was a speeding ticket. Obadiah was always getting on Lena about driving fast.

They hit the Wade Ave exit in record time. Lena raced down that stretch, hopped on the beltway, and rolled right through the yellow light at the Wake Forest Road exit in Raleigh. She turned into the hotel entrance and searched for the closest parking space. The lot was full of cars and church vans.

"Are they planning on having a service with this meeting?" Marsha asked, pointing in the direction of the choir walking toward the hotel entrance with their robes hanging over their arms.

"Obie hadn't said anything about it. But this meeting was called by Sonny Washington and Bishop O. Ray Caruthers Jr. So you know they were not trying to get Obie's or Denzelle's input when they planned it. That would be too much like right, since they are the highest-ranking pastors in the Triangle."

"Well, that is the choir from Sonny Washington's home church. They are the only ones in our conference with those Glodean Benson–pink choir robes," Marsha said.

Lena found a space right next to Denzelle's car. They hopped

out and raced inside. The meeting was to start in twenty minutes, and they wanted to be there before mess starting flying off
the fan. They found the marquee with information about the meeting's location and rushed down a corridor. This room was big and
pretentious even for big and pretentious preachers.

Lena saw Obadiah talking to Bishop Theophilus Simmons.
He was standing with his oldest daughter, Reverend Dr. Sharon
Simmons-Harris, who was a full professor at Duke University's
divinity school. She waved at Sharon, who could almost out-
preach her father—and that was saying something, because
Bishop could preach.

Sharon waved back and hurried over to where Lena and
Marsha were standing. She was a beautiful woman—tall, chocolate, shapely, and with the loveliest smile. She looked just like
her father.

"Hey, girl," Sharon said to Lena, and gave her a hug. She
looked down at Marsha and started grinning.

"See, I told you that boy would come to his senses the last
time I was at your church, and you were walking around wondering if he 'liked' you. I was like, 'like you?' That Denzelle liked
you so much, Marsha, he had to pray to keep from jumping your
bones."

"You are wrong, Pastor," Marsha said, remembering how
well Sharon had called that one.

"Nahh, I'm right. That boy always looked like he wanted to
snatch you up and run off to the hotel. 'Cause Denzelle look like
he got some freak in him," Sharon said, cracking up with laughter.

"I cannot believe you just went there, Reverend," Marsha
told her.

"Well, I did," Sharon said. "Nothing wrong with a good
man with a lil' bit of freak in 'em. Makes for a good marriage.
Don't 'nam nobody wanna be stuck with a boring stick-in-the-
mud like that Reverend Larry Pristeen."

Sharon shook her head, rolled her eyes, and then sucked on
her teeth. She snapped her neck around and said, "Y'all, I can't

stand Larry Pristeen. He is always flirting, but he doesn't want any woman who will require him to date her openly. You do know he has women all over the country in all of those places he preaches."

"Sharon, you are lying," Lena said. "Pristeen is so stiff and prim. How is that joker pulling women?"

"Like that," was all Sharon said, and pointed to a corner where Larry was grinning all over some cute woman who was acting like she'd won the lottery because Reverend Larry Pristeen had "chosen" her.

"Watch him work it."

"We can't see enough from here," Marsha said, and signaled for them to follow her over to where Larry was standing with the woman.

They got close enough to hear Larry's business but not close enough to be detected. Larry Pristeen was in his element. He was surrounded by preachers and a bunch of women who had crushes on him.

"Watch him work it," Sharon said.

Larry smiled down at the woman, who was one of the newly ordained preachers in Chapel Hill. He said, "You have a gift, my dear. The way you roll your tongue around words during a sermon has the potential to make a man feel good."

"See," Sharon whispered. "He just hit on her."

"How?" Marsha asked, clueless.

Lena rolled her eyes and popped Marsha on the back of her head. She said, "Girl, listen to what he just said. 'The way you roll your tongue around.' He is not talking about words in a sermon. He is talking about her rolling her tongue around something she doesn't need to be rolling her tongue around—at least, not on his trifling butt."

"And get this. That girl can't preach her way through a puddle of water," Sharon added. "She is actually okay and decent. But she can't preach. She put Dad to sleep. He was snoring, and I had to act like he had asthma or something.

"Uncle Eddie was playing a game on his iPad during her sermon. Okay? So, she didn't say anything that would make a man feel anything—unless he is Larry Pristeen trying to sneak and get some action."

"Shhh," Lena admonished. "He's going in for the kill."

Larry smiled into the young preacher's eyes and said, "Girl, I want to hug you. You have fire in you, and I want that fire to rub off on me."

He reached out and hugged her. But the preacher gave Larry a chaste, side-church hug.

Sharon was cracking up. She knew Larry Pristeen was not going to let the naive, starstruck preacher get off so easily. He said, "That is not the kind of hug I want from you, my dear. Here, let me position you correctly, so I can get a more desirable hug. Now, stand here like this, and let's see how this works."

To her credit, the new preacher looked uncomfortable and was about to pull back. But she changed her mind when she noticed a few other women with crushes on Reverend Pristeen standing around. So she let him maneuver her and set her up for that hug. Larry said, "Now, I am going to walk up to you and grab your shoulders, and I want you to lean in close to me, so I can feel this hug correctly. Are you ready?"

Lena looked at Sharon and said, "Is he really going to get away with that jacked-up game? I'm insulted for her."

"Keep watching," Sharon told her.

Larry Pristeen got all up on the woman, hugged her, and then drew back quickly like he wanted to make sure he remained chaste and appropriate in his behavior.

The preacher looked confused, and then disappointed, and then kind of mad. She had been hoping for more than this. She was about to walk off when Larry, who knew exactly what he was doing, grabbed her arm gently and pulled her back closer to him.

"How am I to get another and better hug from you if you walk away, my dear? Stand there, so I can give this second hug a better try."

The preacher stood there, hoping it was not in vain. And it wasn't. This time, Larry leaned in closer and whispered, "I need you," in her ear.

"Did he just whisper in that girl's ear," Marsha said, trying to read his lips. "Ooooo, she just put a key card in his hand. What is he going to do with that room card?"

"Ask her to roll her tongue around a 'word,'" Sharon said, laughing.

"I wish Dad would put Larry in his place. But all Dad does is tell me to behave and stay out of it. He said that Pristeen will have his day in court."

Sharon's father looked over at her with her girls, clearly in Reverend Pristeen's business. He pulled out his phone and texted, *Behave. And I need you back over here. Ask Lena where Denzelle is. I see Obadiah. But no Denzelle.*

Sharon said, "Gotta go. Duty and my daddy calling. Oh, Marsha, didn't Denzelle come over here with Obadiah? Dad is looking for him."

"He did come with Obie," she said, concerned. She pulled out her phone to call her husband. Denzelle answered on the first ring.

"Baby, Bishop Simmons is looking for you. This meeting is about to start and they need you."

"Can't, Honey. At the hospital with Todd."

"As in Todd Townsend, Todd?"

"Yeah. He almost died. Massive heart attack. Only reason he is alive is because he prayed and trusted the Lord. The doctors said Todd is a walking miracle."

"How did you find this out, Denzelle? You were on your way here, and now you're at Duke Hospital?"

"Todd was able to call my number. Where was Tatiana when this happened?"

"I don't know where she was then," Marsha said, looking across the room. "But where she is now is walking around the Raleigh Hilton hanging on to Luther Howard's arm."

"That's not a good sign," Denzelle said in disgust. He could not believe Tatiana was now with Luther Howard. A woman could get killed messing around with a man like Luther Howard.

"Is Todd going to be alright?" Marsha asked.

"Yes. And Honey, don't tell Tatiana anything about Todd. She doesn't need to know he survived that heart attack. I have a bad feeling about her and what happened to him. Don't want to tip her off."

"Okay," Marsha said. She was going to follow her husband's directives—especially since he was talking in his FBI voice.

"Everything okay?" Lena asked.

"Todd Townsend had a massive heart attack. He managed to call Denzelle. They are at Duke, and he'll be okay. But Denzelle doesn't want me to tell Tatiana anything about her husband."

Lena pulled out her phone. "I'll text Obie and tell him to give Bishops Simmons and Tate the 411."

"Thanks, Lena," Marsha told her. Todd Townsend having a massive heart attack. Strange. But then, Todd was married to Tatiana. That was enough to drive a man crazy and send him into cardiac arrest. She was so glad her baby got divorced from that she-devil when he did.

Lena looked across the room to where Tatiana was standing, her arm looped through Luther Howard's and holding court with Xavier Franklin and a few younger preachers who wanted to get in Xavier's good graces. Xavier's wife, Camille, was standing off to the side eyeballing Tatiana like she wanted to kill her.

The bishops took their seats at the large podium up on the platform that had been constructed for this meeting. They were an interesting bunch. Some were good bishops and helped keep the denomination on track. Some were mediocre—didn't do too much wrong but never did enough right to make a real difference. And some were just bad news—would do whatever they wanted to do to get money and power. Some of the Gospel United Church's worst problems and biggest scandals had come about as a result of those bishops, or bishops like them.

The senior bishop, Theophilus Simmons, stood up at the main podium and said, "This meeting has come to order. Let us bow our heads and honor the Lord with an opening prayer."

He waited until the room was quiet and he had the attention of most of the folk in it before praying: "Lord, we are gathered here to discuss and make key decisions about who should run for bishop, and be able to run this great denomination. We know You know what is best for us. And we seek Your guidance, so that we will do what is right in Your sight. Thank You, Lord, for being in our midst. Holy Spirit, You are welcome in this place. In Jesus Name we pray, Amen.

"Now," Theophilus began in a quiet voice. He was not happy about this meeting, and hoped he'd be able to keep his cool once this thing was off and poppin'. What was being proposed was not going to do anything but create a big mess. And even worse, this meeting had been called to make it possible to create the mess. When would his church learn that mess like this was always doomed to fail?

"Bishops Washington, Caruthers, and Jefferson, along with Reverend Marcel Brown and Reverend Xavier Franklin, have asked that we come together to discuss policies and criteria for those running or seeking to run for an Episcopal office at the next Triennial Conference. There have been concerns that the reason we have had problems in the ranks is because we do not have the right kind of policies in place to govern properly. They have proposed we make changes concerning who can run for bishop and hold an Episcopal office so that the office of bishop remains sacred and the wrong kind of people cannot get voted in."

Theophilus stopped and frowned. He hated it when folks got all up in some wrong in the church, and then tried to run and hide behind rules and policies. The only reason they had come up with this foolishness was to find a way to get rid of the competition for this bishop's race, in an attempt to make it free and clear for Xavier Franklin to roll up in that spot by a landslide. But he was determined that it wouldn't happen on his watch.

One would think they'd get tired of always coming up with some mammy-made mess, creating all kinds of mayhem, and then always losing—sometimes losing badly. But nothing deterred them—not arrests, losing money, losing churches—nothing. Every time it was time to get ready for the next Triennial Conference, Marcel Brown, Sonny Washington, and a duly appointed crony were right there to make it hard for them to be about the business of the church of the living God.

Chapter Thirty-nine

Theophilus signaled for Obadiah Quincey to come up front and join him and Bishop Eddie Tate at the podium. He kept searching the conference room for Denzelle Flowers but the brother had yet to arrive. He leaned down and whispered to Obadiah.

"Where is Flowers? I can't fight this battle without him being here to speak against this petition."

Obadiah showed Theophilus one of the texts from Lena about Denzelle. He then texted, *D, how fast can you get here? We're about to start the meeting, and Bishop needs you.*

Denzelle called Obadiah. He didn't have the time or desire to send a text. Sometimes texts were good. But then there were times when the only thing that worked was a phone call and a voice on the other end of the phone.

Obadiah answered his phone and told Denzelle, "Hold on a minute," and said, "I need to take this, Bishop," to Theophilus, and walked to a quiet spot to get the 411. Both Lena and Denzelle had been sending him multiple text messages about what had happened to Todd, giving him frequent updates about the good doctor's status.

"Obie," Denzelle said. "I need some more time with Todd. Tell Bishop to let the opposition talk and run their mouths."

"But D, what if they rush through the vote and vote against your interests for running for bishop?"

"Obie, I'm telling you. God is pulling on me to handle business this way. I am willing to go in whatever direction the Lord takes me in, even if it means that I am disqualified from running for bishop. I have perfect peace about this thing. You feelin' me, man?"

"Yeah. And I got your back, D. You have some information about what happened to Todd?"

"Obie, I have the full-blown 411. Todd is awake. They tried to keep him sedated, but he said that he needed to talk to me first. The brother said he couldn't rest until he told me as much as he could.

"Tatiana is having a hot affair with Xavier Franklin. Todd has had a private detective watching her for a long time. He put her out. But get this. We both just found out Tatiana is also sleeping with Luther Howard."

"As in 'the mafia defense kang' Luther Howard, Luther Howard?"

"Yeah," Denzelle said. "Todd's private detective followed Tatiana last night, thinking he was going to get more dirt on Tatiana's affair with Xavier. Poor man got an eyeful. Tatiana was with Xavier, and then polished off the evening with Luther."

"Daaaannnngggg! Baby girl be getting around, D."

"Obie, I didn't know Miss Thang had it going on like that. But get this. Todd told me that when he fell out with his heart attack, Tatiana was watching him to make sure he was dying. He played dead, and then managed to call me. Right now, I could get the police to put out a warrant for her arrest for negligent homicide."

Obadiah glanced across the room. Tatiana was standing next to Luther Howard, grinning, hanging on his arm, and practically lapping up every word coming out of his mouth.

"Do you know Tatiana is here acting like she has just won the lottery?"

"That's because she doesn't know Todd is alive," Denzelle said. "Tatiana wanted Todd dead for that insurance money."

"That is just messed up," Obie said. "Should I call your brother?"

"Nope. I just talked to my old boss, Greg Williams, who is way up in the bureau now. He said they have been after Luther Howard for years. And he also said there is something else about to go down that is connected to the denomination and a few bishops.

"Greg asked me to help him with this case. I'll be undercover—not deep undercover—just laying low enough to find out what's going on. I really believe I'll be able to do more if I drop out of the race and stay in my pulpit.

"And Greg said that he wants Tatiana out on the streets for a while. She is the only link to Luther and this hidden cartel. So play dumb with that ho."

"D, please let me tell her that Todd is alive. Please, Dawg," Obadiah pleaded.

"Okay. Let me make sure he has some undercover cops watching him while he's at Duke Hospital. Wouldn't want that skank rolling up in here trying to finish the job."

"What do I tell her?"

"Play with her head, Obie. Then, tell Tatiana that Todd had a heart attack, but is alive, and will be fine."

"D, I sure hope he is divorcing that skank after all of this."

"My lawyer is on the way to the hospital with the papers already drawn up. The last thing Todd will do before being completely sedated is sign his divorce papers with me as his witness. He will have the sheriff's office deliver them to Tatiana when she is back on the job."

"You know, I'm beginning to like this Todd more and more."

"Me too, Obie. Gotta go."

Both Theophilus Simmons and Eddie Tate were staring at Obadiah, wondering what in the world was going on with him and his boy, Denzelle. This was one time they were glad it took these black church folk too much time to come together, get in their seats, shut up, and sit down. On any other conference day, they would have sent ushers throughout the room with strict instructions to ask anyone who was standing around talking and laughing to leave. Today they needed this time.

Obadiah looked at Theophilus Simmons, who nodded for him to finish what he was doing. Obadiah texted the bishop, *Thank you*, and walked over to where Tatiana was standing with Luther. She was glaring at Xavier Franklin, who was holding on to Camille like she was a piece of Jolly Rancher candy. This was the first time Obadiah had ever witnessed Xavier acting like he wanted to be with Camille.

Obadiah nodded to the Franklins and walked up to Tatiana. He said, "Can I talk to you for a moment?"

Tatiana stared at Obadiah Quincey like he was a crackhead asking her for money for a hit.

"This is about your husband. I just got a call from Denzelle, who asked me to tell you what happened. Can we talk where it's more private?"

Tatiana had been waiting for this news all day. She had even practiced displaying her grief with Luther several times, and made sure her story was airtight. She was so excited about hearing the official pronouncement of Todd's death that she could barely contain her glee.

"Todd? What about Todd?"

Obadiah took one of Tatiana's hands in his, like he would do with someone he had to give news of a death. He closed his eyes for a second to compose himself. Obadiah knew he was wrong. This would have been hilarious if it were not so serious and wicked.

He had to give Tatiana her due. The girl had the perfect expression of "what's wrong" on her face. The only thing that dampened her performance was the twinkle she could not keep out of her eyes.

"Tatiana, Todd is at Duke Hospital in the Intensive Care Unit."

Obie let those words linger in the air, so he could watch Tatiana pull herself together at learning Todd was alive. She looked like she was about to throw up.

"Are you sure about this, Obadiah?" Tatiana asked carefully.

"Yes," Obadiah said in his best pastor voice. He knew Tatiana was trying to find a way to ask how bad off Todd was, if he were on life support, and how long he had left to live.

"It is a miracle Todd is even alive. But what is so miraculous is that he is awake, aware, lucid, and in his right mind. He could have died, but God is so good. Can you believe how the Lord worked this out? It makes me feel like shouting right here on this conference room floor."

"I don't know what to say," Tatiana said.

She couldn't believe Todd survived that heart attack. She was a nurse. She knew what a fatal, massive cardiac arrest looked like. And she knew that that is exactly what happened to her husband. Todd not only survived the heart attack, he was doing well.

"Me neither," Obadiah told her. "This is a Miracle. And all I can say is, Wow—God is amazing."

"Yes, He is," Tatiana answered, thinking that this God was more amazing and frightening than folks realized. Todd should have been dead. He must have gotten to praying and believed enough to turn things around. She hated folks who prayed like that, and never pegged Todd Townsend for being one of those people. This was not good.

"Did he ask for me?" she asked, hoping not to sound too nervous. "Did he want me to come to the hospital?"

"I doubt it," Obadiah said in his kind voice. "Perhaps you should stay exactly where you are and handle your business. I'm sure Todd would not want his heart troubles to interfere with what it is you are trying to do."

"I see," Tatiana said very carefully. She glanced around to make sure there weren't any plainsclothed cops lurking around to arrest her. "Well, I will abide by my husband's wishes. Do you think he will want me to come to the hospital later?"

"I doubt it," Obadiah answered, again in the soothing voice he used when going in for the kill with someone.

"See this is what I think, Tatiana. Todd probably doesn't want you at the hospital or his home or anywhere near him. But there is one thing I'm sure he will want you to know."

"What?" Tatiana asked, clearly hoping it was something that would keep her in good standing with Todd and protect her from him coming after her.

"I'm sure Todd would want you to go to YouTube and look up the song, 'The Rain' by Oran 'Juice' Jones. I may be wrong. But something tells me it is the perfect song for you to watch."

Luther Howard, who had eased over to listen in on the conversation, had to turn away from them, he was so tickled. He had to hand it Obadiah Quincey. That was one smooth-player move. Sounded like something he would have said to a woman who tried to play him. "The Rain" was the ultimate "you've been caught, B, and I hate yo' butt" song.

Obadiah patted Tatiana on the shoulder and said, "My work right here is done."

He walked off, trying not to pat himself on the back. He had to admit, the "Oran 'Juice' Jones" suggestion was the perfect way to end the conversation, and then set it all off where Tatiana Townsend was concerned.

"Can we please get this meeting started?" Bishop Sonny Washington snapped. He was tired of waiting on Theophilus Simmons and Eddie Tate.

Theophilus didn't blink or raise an eyebrow. He moved away from the podium and said, "It's all yours."

Sonny hurried to the front of the room and signaled for Marcel Brown, Ray Caruthers, and Bishop Thomas Lyle Jefferson to come up to the podium and join him. They had been planning on presenting this to the Board of Bishops for weeks, and were not about to waste any more time with their enemies. He figured Theophilus and Eddie were stalling hoping to give Denzelle Flowers a chance to get to the meeting. But that wasn't going to work.

Bishop Jefferson's wife, Violetta, hurried to catch up with her husband. She had been deep in conversation with Glodean

Benson and wasn't paying attention when they finally moved to the front of the conference room. Violetta didn't like being made the poster girl for this scheme. She and Thomas had the worst argument in their entire marriage over what was about to go down.

She tried to get to the podium before her uncle Raphael saw where she was going and hurried to get up front and be seen. Uncle Raphael wanted to be wherever he thought would make him seem important.

"If she slings that fake braid around her head one more time, I'm snatching it right off," Lena leaned over and whispered to Marsha. "Where are Miss Essie and Miss Johnnie Tate when you need them? One of them would have snatched that braid and twirled her around with it."

Marsha had Lena's iPad. She pulled up Violetta's hit song, "Burn de House Down," on YouTube. She whispered, "Check this out."

Lena watched Violetta gyrating and dancing all down on the ground to the hot and sultry song in a pair of "coochie-cutter" shorts, high-heeled sandals that laced all the way up her legs, and tassels on her bare boobs.

"She is working it, Lena," Marsha whispered, and then sneaked and shared the video with another minister's wife, who had just said, "Girl, let me see that."

Soon several other folk were watching the video on their phones and iPads, snickering. So many people began playing the video on YouTube, you could hear the muffled chords of the music around the room. A few people closer to the platform made the mistake of playing the song too loudly.

Violetta recognized the song immediately and could not hide the horrified expression on her face. She thought only the younger members would know about that song. She'd even dressed down for this occasion, hoping to make people stop thinking about her and "Burn de House Down." But her outfit only egged them on. It was kind of hard for folk to forget you were second only to Patra in the outfit she was wearing.

Episcopal Supervisor Jefferson's outfit was anything but cheap in price. It was also anything but modest in style. She had on a tight long-sleeved black sheath dress that hugged her butt like it had been sprayed on. She was wearing large, gold-hoop earrings and a thick gold chain around her neck.

But it was the shoes that sealed the deal with this outfit. Violetta Jefferson was wearing a pair of shiny gold booties that had a black heel that was trimmed in gold. Those shoes looked so good on her feet, several ministers' wives started looking for them online to order a pair for themselves.

Violetta's uncle was also dressed in black and gold. He was wearing a gold, three-piece suit, a black satin shirt and matching tie, a gold lamé fedora, gold jewelry, and a pair of gold gators with the toes cut out. Only today, he also had on a pair of black-and-gold silk socks.

"Her uncle is not all there, is he?" Marsha asked Lena, who was about to say, "I don't think he is," when that suspicion was confirmed by the uncle's response to the song.

As soon as the uncle heard the song well enough to know it was his niece's, he started dancing on the stage like he was the reason for this show. The good news was that the uncle could really dance. The not so good news was that he didn't know the proper dance for this gathering. What he was doing was a far cry from the more acceptable holy dance.

And it didn't take long to figure out that a skinny brother on the "Burn de House Down" video was Episcopal Supervisor Violetta's uncle. He didn't really resemble the video man all that much now. But the moves were such a perfect duplicate of what had been performed on the video, there was no mistaking who it was.

At this point the uncle grabbed the microphone out of Bishop Washington's hand and started singing "Burn de House Down." If he had been singing a church song, folk would have been up dancing and getting into the song with him. But that song was as far from church as moonshine was from bottled water.

Violetta looked like she was torn between dancing with Uncle Raphael and being mortified to the point of having an old-fashioned case of "the vapors." She knew her uncle wasn't all there. But she had underestimated his need to be seen in a large gathering. Her husband pulled out a handkerchief and mopped the sweat off of his head. He had been telling Violetta and telling Violetta her uncle needed treatment and medication. He hoped this performance was evidence he was right.

Denzelle walked in the room just in time to see the uncle do a split that would have put the late, great King of Soul, James Brown, to shame. He popped back up, grabbed a tambourine he'd found on a chair, and started beating it on his behind to the beat of the song—which had been turned all the way up by now.

"You know, that fool can really dance," Marsha said to Lena, who was laughing so hard, tears were streaming down her cheeks. They had seen some wild and crazy mess at gatherings of Gospel United Church preachers and bishops. But they had never witnessed anything like this.

Theophilus and Eddie wanted to laugh, and they also wanted to pimp slap that fool up there dancing like he was on a Beyoncé video. Only Sonny and Marcel could be caught up in something that turned out like this. They didn't even know if the phrase "hot boiling ghetto mess" could truly describe what was going on right now.

Sonny Washington knew Uncle Raphael was going to be trouble when he insisted on coming with them in that outfit. He had tried everything to stop him from being at this meeting. In fact, Sonny had tried to get Marcel to sweet-talk Violetta into telling her uncle to stay in the hotel.

Luther Howard had never liked going to church. But if church was this entertaining, he was up for joining. Never in his life had he seen anything like this at a church gathering, or at any gathering for that matter. He looked over at Tatiana, who was still very nervous about her conversation with that Reverend Quincey. He leaned over and whispered, "Get it together."

"But what about my money?" Tatiana whined.

"What about it?" Luther asked her coldly. "You should be thanking God that you are not behind bars wearing an orange jumpsuit and trying to keep some woman named Big Mama Moo or Luckey Yee Yee from trying to make you give her a lap dance 'cause she just made you her Big House Honey.

"You can kiss that eight mil good-bye. Todd is going to hold what you did over your head so he can be free of you. Count your blessings and name them one by one. What just happened to you was a very close call in my book."

Tatiana nodded and sniffed up her tears. It was going to be devastating trying to live off of her six-figure nurse's salary. She was going to have to move into a three-bedroom town home, and probably clean her own house. Just the thought made her cry to the point of sobbing.

"*SUCK IT UP*, Tatiana," was all Luther said. He didn't even give her his handkerchief—just got a painful grip on her arm to get his message across.

Sonny Washington snatched the microphone out of Raphael's hand and did something he had not had a desire to do in years—pray. He said, "Father God, forgive us our trespasses against You and this meeting. You are welcome, Lord. Put order to this meeting and clear it out of the mess that just transpired, Amen."

Theophilus and Eddie looked at each other, and then looked up at the ceiling to make sure it wasn't popping open and Jesus was cracking across the sky. Several other folk did the exact same thing. And a few texted some family members, *You betta hurry up and get saved.*

Sonny stared out into the audience at Reverend Denzelle Flowers, standing next to a very pretty lady. It was clear he was in love with this woman. And it was clear he wanted this woman by his side. That was just enough to give him the courage to press forward with his agenda.

"Gospel United Church, we called this special session to vote in a new policy whereby a pastor cannot run for bishop if he is divorced and remarries while the ex-spouse is still alive. This policy would also include a clause that prohibited an elected bishop from staying in office if he or she were to divorce or were divorced and remarried while the spouse was alive.

"As you can see, we would not have witnessed that profane display of physical craftsmanship if this law were in place during Bishop Thomas Lyle Jefferson's tenure as an active bishop. He has several ex-spouses who are still alive, and his newest spouse has brought some controversy to the office of Episcopal Supervisor. I'd bet good money that Episcopal Supervisor Violetta Jefferson's family member wouldn't have been an embarrassment to the office of the Episcopacy if this new law were in place when Bishop Jefferson met his most recent wife."

Violetta was pissed. Sonny and Marcel hadn't paid them enough for this level of humiliation. She glared at her husband. But Bishop Jefferson wasn't the least bit concerned about what Violetta thought and felt. He texted, *You should have thought about that when you insisted that your crazy uncle come with us to the States. Get it together and don't ever look at me like that again.*

Violetta bowed her head down to hide her tears. Sometimes Thomas was so mean. She understood why he couldn't keep a wife. If it weren't for his money and secret supply of that WP21 stuff he got from Marcel and Sonny, she'd leave his butt. Thomas had all of that original WP21, and he didn't even know how to use it right. Pitiful.

"We don't need the office of bishop sullied like this again," Sonny Washington was saying. "Join me, fellow bishops, and cast your votes. We need to bring decency and honor and moral standards back to the office of bishop, and to the role of the Episcopal Supervisor."

Sonny knew he'd won this battle by the look on Theophilus's and Eddie's faces. They knew they would not be able to get Denzelle Flowers elected bishop if he remarried. And judging from the way Denzelle was gazing down at that woman, he was going to be hardpressed to avoid matrimony.

Sonny couldn't believe it. Finally, they had won. And the feeling was oh so sweet.

Denzelle watched his mentors digest this moment, and then walked up to the front. He wanted Sonny Washington to have a few seconds to savor his short-lived victory. It was going to be supersweet when he delivered this blow to the enemy camp.

"Bishops Washington, Jefferson, Simmons, and Tate. If I may, I'd like to speak to my brethren in the ministry about my position as a candidate for the office of bishop."

Sonny was feeling good. He handed Denzelle the microphone, anxious to hear how he was going to step down.

Denzelle stared at Marsha, who was looking troubled, and winked. He said, "I am stepping down from my candidacy for the office of bishop because I am already married to my heart and new first lady, Mrs. Marsha Metcalf Flowers. As much as I thought I wanted to run for bishop, nothing compares to finding a woman worthy of the title Proverbs 31 Woman. I don't want anything so badly that I would subjugate my heart as a pastor to sorrow, loneliness, and misery. Plus, I really like being a pastor more than I'd ever enjoy serving as a bishop.

"But there is someone out there who really needs to serve as bishop alongside her father. Reverend Dr. Sharon Simmons-Harris would you, and your husband, the Honorable North Carolina Supreme Court Justice, come forth."

Judge Harris grabbed his wife's hand and pulled her up front. He'd always believed she would make an excellent bishop and be able to handle being the denomination's first woman elected to an Episcopal seat in the Gospel United Church. They reached the stage, and he kissed Sharon and said, "Let them know who you are, Baby."

Sharon took the microphone from Denzelle and said, "I accept the challenge." She turned to her dad and said, "Daddy, it's time for you and Uncle Eddie to get with the program and get a woman on the Board of Bishops."

Theophilus smiled at his baby. She was so much like him,

with just enough of her mother in her to do this job, and to do it right. He walked over to Sharon, grabbed her hand, and said, "We've got work to do. I'm ready to retire, and I want a good bishop in office!"

Folk got up and started cheering "Bishop Sharon! Bishop Sharon! Bishop Sharon!"

Sonny, Marcel, Ray Caruthers, and Xavier Franklin all walked out. They had their work cut out for them. The women in the denomination had been begging for a female bishop for decades. And it would be hard to beat the daughter of the famous Theophilus Simmons.

"That's messed up," was all Marcel Brown could say.

Tatiana stared at Xavier and Camille, and then back at Luther, who was scoping out a new woman. She didn't know how she and Xavier were going to work out being together if he ran for bishop. Camille was not going to stand aside this time. She liked being in the spotlight with the frontrunner for that coveted Episcopal seat, and was not sharing anything with another woman—especially if the other woman was Tatiana Townsend.

Tatiana looked over at Marsha Flowers, beaming and happy and the sole object of Denzelle's attention. If she weren't so mean and hateful, Tatiana would have thrown herself in front of a car. These next months were going to need all of her attention. She didn't have time to get smashed up by a moving car.

Denzelle came down and grabbed his wife. He was so happy and loved her so much. His heart was filled to the brim with joy. So this is what a pastor's heart was supposed to be like. Who knew he needed a boo this much?

Epilogue

Marsha was looking good on her very first Sunday as New Jerusalem's new first lady. Theresa Hopson Green, owner of Miss Thang's Holy Ghost Corner and Church Woman's Boutique, had hooked her up with the sharpest outfit in the Triangle. She was wearing a robin's egg blue, two-piece silk suit. The peplum top had a shawl collar, dainty puffed sleeves, and crimson, blue, and cream–colored crystal buttons down the front. The skirt was full and swirled whenever Marsha moved.

She had on the same crimson-colored, patent-leather pumps with four-inch heels and built-in platforms she wore on her "official" wedding day. As soon as Denzelle saw Marsha pull that particular shoebox out of the closet, he asked her to wear the shoes only, and only the shoes alone. And once again, that request almost made them late for church.

Marsha's jewelry was perfectly matched to the blue-and-crimson theme of her outfit. She had on a pair of gold-hoop earrings with garnet, blue topaz, and mother-of-pearl chips sprinkled all over them, a matching bracelet, and a gold chain with the same stones embedded in the links. Marsha Metcalf Flowers was looking good. The only thing that put a tiny cloud over what was otherwise a perfect morning was that she couldn't drive her brand-new Cadillac SUV—a gift from her new husband—to church.

This was a special morning, because they were installing

Sharon Simmons-Harris as the new lead associate pastor. Sharon had a wealth of experience but not in the capacity of a pastor. She had spent most of her time as a biblical scholar and leading theologian. But she needed to be in the pastor's seat as much as possible to rule out any qualms about her ability to serve as a strong bishop in the Gospel United Church.

The church was packed with members and guests. They wanted to celebrate the kickoff of Sharon's campaign. They wanted folk superexcited about this ground-breaking campaign. The Gospel United Church would be one of the last of the traditional black denominations to elect a woman bishop. The AMEs had several, and the AME Zions needed to elect some more.

The women in the church were so pumped. Sharon, who was also a member of Zeta Phi Beta Sorority like Denzelle's wife, had gotten the Sorors, as well as the Sigmas, involved at the local and national levels. It hadn't been difficult to get Phi Beta Sigma involved with a campaign for a Zeta. Plus, her husband, a high-ranking Sigma, made sure his fraternity brothers were onboard in full force to help his wife win her Episcopal seat.

This morning, the guest section was full of who's who in the ranks of preachers—Bishop Emeritus Murcheson James; Reverend George Wilson from St. Louis, along with his wife, Sheba, and their children; Dr. Saphronia McComb James and her husband, who was one of the most prominent retired pastors in Atlanta; Apostle Grady Gray and his assistant pastor, Dotsy Hamilton, along with a host of members from their church; and Obadiah, Lena, and many of their members from Fayetteville Street Gospel United Church in Durham.

And sitting in the pulpit with Denzelle and Sharon were Bishops Theophilus Simmons and Eddie Tate, along with their wives, Episcopal Supervisors Essie Lane Simmons and Johnnie Tate. They thought it only fitting to have the women behind these two men's extraordinary ministries in the pulpit there to celebrate the candidacy of a woman for bishop—especially since that woman had learned from the best, her father and godfather.

Sharon's siblings, Linda and T.J., along with their spouses and kids, had also made it to Raleigh to celebrate their sister's run for bishop. Linda was a prominent first lady in Atlanta, and T.J. owned a string of parking lots all over the St. Louis downtown area.

Denzelle didn't want to preach this morning. Sharon didn't want to preach this morning. Obadiah didn't want to preach this morning. And Theophilus and Eddie didn't want to preach, either. They needed a really good preacher to deliver the sermon—one who truly understood the structure of their church and what they would be up against when this campaign was up and running at full force.

Everybody voted for Reverend Philip R. Cousin Jr., Senior Pastor at Bethel AME Church in San Francisco, to deliver the Word this morning. And to their credit, Bethel AME had come across the country in full force to support their pastor and the good folk at New Jerusalem.

There were also members, along with the Inspirational Singers Choir, from St. Joseph's AME Church in Durham. St. Joseph's was Reverend Cousin's former church. Reverend Cousin told them that he and the first lady, Angela, couldn't come to a church in North Carolina without the Inspirational Singers, because this was his travel choir when he served as the pastor at that church.

The Inspirational Singers of St. Joseph's AME Church took their places in the choir loft behind the pulpit. Their royal blue and gold–trimmed robes made a pretty striking contrast with the decor of New Jerusalem. The soloist walked up to the microphone, and the musicians opened with the first chords of the song, "Secret Place" by Kevin Davidson & The Voices out of Memphis, Tennessee.

The lead, a known jazz singer named Adia Ledbetter, started singing, and folk started dabbing their eyes with tissues. This song was so perfect for what they had been through, what they were facing, and what they were trusting God to do for them with this campaign to get Sharon Simmons-Harris elected bishop. Ms. Ledbetter's voice rang out, making folk think they were hearing a blend of Sarah Vaughn, Ledisi, and of course Adia's unique vocal style all wrapped up together.

The choir came in with their harmonious section, "Have a little talk with Jesus,/tell Him all about your troubles,/He will hear you cry,/He'll answer by and by."

When they transitioned up to a new key, there wasn't a dry eye left in the church. Folk were standing up with their hands raised, crying and calling on the Name of the Lord. Folk were thanking Him and praising Him and petitioning Him all over the church.

Reverend Cousin was ready to preach but held off when the choir ended the song and started up again. He usually came down to the altar during prayer, or at the end of a service. But this morning he went down to the foot of the altar, because Todd Townsend had come down to the altar while the choir was singing. Denzelle and Obadiah hurried down to stand with Reverend Cousin.

Todd fell on his knees and said, "I want to thank You, Lord, for saving me. You saved my soul, and You saved my life. You are amazing, Lord. And I want to tell You Thank You in front of everybody at this church."

Todd wiped his eyes, stood up, and pulled out three certified checks. He gave one to Denzelle. It was a tithe check from his first month's pay in the new job—$142,000.

Denzelle looked at the check and said, "Todd, I don't mean to be rude, but honestly, dawg, how much money do you make a month?"

"That's about twenty percent of $708,000," Todd told him calmly. "I'm joining your church, Reverend Flowers. I'm turning my life over to Christ. And I'm starting off right with my first tithe check to my new church home."

Reverend Cousin's eyes went upwards and he looked at his wife, as if to say, "Did you just witness that?" Mrs. Cousin just nodded. She was too stunned to say anything.

"Denzelle, use this money to help members who really need

help. I don't care how much you give them, as long as you help with whatever they need."

Todd then put a check for $60,000 in Reverend Cousin's hand. He said, "I know all about your benevolence ministry at the churches you pastor. Never hesitate to call me when you need more, or if somebody at your church is in great need."

Reverend Cousin thanked him and went and gave the check to Mrs. Cousin, who was now in tears all over again.

"This last check is for Reverend Sharon Simmons-Harris's campaign. Reverend Quincey, take it and put it to good use. You'll get one of these from me each and every month."

Obadiah opened the check and whispered, "Thank you, Todd," through tears. It was a check for $75,000, and exactly what they needed to get everything up and running for Sharon's campaign.

Todd started walking back to his seat. His heart was so full of joy he thought he wouldn't be able to contain it. Todd Townsend, who this morning was sharp in a black, three-piece suit with gray chalk stripes in it, suddenly started running all around the church shouting and praising God to the soothing song The Inspirational Singers had started singing again.

Denzelle and his fellow preachers were still at the foot of the altar. He turned around and got down on his knees. Obadiah dropped down on his knees. Reverend Cousin dropped on his knees. Marsha, Lena, and Angela joined their husbands at the altar. They were joined by the pulpit guests. And after that, the whole church went down on their knees to join in for a moment of silent prayer in the middle of the choir's singing.

The pastors were so blessed. Their hearts were rejuvenated. They were encouraged. There was nothing like a pastor's heart, especially when it was healed. They looked up and knew this race for bishop was not for the swift but for those that were willing to endure it to the end.